Everyone l [barcode] W9-BSS-545
Jonnie Jacobs and her mysteries!

EVIDENCE OF GUILT

"A well-written mixing of a who-done-it with a legal thriller . . . Jacobs has shown that she can write a terrific and intriguing on-going series that will keep readers coming back for more."

THE MIDWEST BOOK REVIEW

"Jacobs delivers another breathtakingly intricate, ingenious mystery."

GENE'S MYSTERY BOOKS

"Kali O'Brien will become a staple on your 'must read list.' "

THE QUAIL'S QUILL

SHADOW OF DOUBT

"Kali is a delight . . ."

TOWER BOOKS MYSTERY NEWSLETTER

"Charming, witty and stylish."

GROUNDS FOR MURDER

MURDER AMONG FRIENDS

"Great fun. Kate Austen is savvy, funny and tough. I look forward to many more Kate Austen adventures."

JON KATZ, author of THE FATHERS' CLUB

"An appealing choice for many readers."

LIBRARY JOURNAL

MURDER AMONG NEIGHBORS

"A West Coast COMPROMISING POSITIONS."

KIRKUS REVIEWS

"A charming and appealing first mystery . . . I like Kate Austen a lot."

CAROLYN G. HART

"Neatly plotted and well written . . . Kate Austen is a welcome addition to the cozy world of carpools, babysitters and ever-so-tacky murder."

JOAN HESS

Books by Jonnie Jacobs

The Kali O'Brien Mysteries

Shadow of Doubt
Evidence of Guilt

The Kate Austen Mysteries

Murder Among Neighbors
Murder Among Friends
Murder Among Us

Published by Kensington Books

Evidence
of
Guilt

A Kali O'Brien Mystery

JONNIE JACOBS

KENSINGTON BOOKS
http://www.kensingtonbooks.com

KENSINGTON BOOKS are published by

Kensington Publishing Corp.
850 Third Avenue
New York, NY 10022

First Kensington Hardcover Printing: March, 1997
First Kensington Paperback Printing: April, 1998

Printed in the United States of America
10 9 8 7 6 5 4 3 2

For my husband, Rod

Acknowledgments

I would like to thank Margaret Lucke, Lynn Mac-Donald, and Penny Warner for their help with the manuscript. Thanks also to my editor, John Scognamiglio, for his continued enthusiasm and support. And as always, a special thanks to my husband and sons.

I

In eight years of practicing law, I'd never had a client who gave me the creeps. I'd had clients I didn't particularly like, of course, ranging from the overly brash to the downright sleazy, but never one who caused goosebumps to rise along the back of my neck. And I saw no reason to start now with the likes of Wes Harding.

"Sorry," I told Sam Morrison, shaking my head in apology. We were having lunch together, something we did a couple of times a month. He'd waited until we'd finished our burgers and fries before raising the matter. "I appreciate the offer, but I don't think I'm interested."

"And why the hell not?" Sam leaned forward with both elbows on the table, oblivious of the catsup spill his shirtsleeves mopped up in the process. "Wasn't it only a couple of weeks ago you were complaining about how slow things were? Slow and 'megamonotonous' was, I believe, the way you put it."

He had me there. Solo practice is attractive as a concept, but the reality falls somewhat short. In the year since I'd gone out on my own, my cases had been few in number and all rather pedestrian. Divorces, wills, a couple of DUIs and an occasional commercial dispute. Hardly life on the cutting edge of the law. Besides which, I was barely making a living.

"I'm offering you a piece of something big, Kali. Something that will jump-start those atrophied brain cells of yours and make you feel like you're practicing law again."

Sam can talk like that and get away with it—the prerogatives of age and experience. He's semi-retired now, slowed by the death of his wife three years ago and a more recent string of minor heart attacks. But Sam is still the best lawyer in Silver Creek, and one of the big names in California legal circles.

You wouldn't know it to look at him, though. He's overweight, ruddy in the face, and habitually, if charmingly, disheveled in appearance. His white hair stands in tufts over his temples, and the clean, freshly starched shirt he takes from the hanger each morning is rumpled and stained under the arms half an hour after he's put it on. Today, one of the lower buttons was missing, causing the shirt to gap around his middle.

"It's a high-profile case," he said, "a once-in-a-lifetime opportunity."

I nodded, although I wasn't sure I viewed high-profile cases in quite the same light Sam did.

"There's a tidy sum of money in it for you," he added. "I'm not asking you to work for nothing, you know."

Handing him a napkin, I gestured to the spot of catsup on his sleeve. "Money's not the issue."

"What is it then? Are you like these folks in town who forget that *accused* and *guilty* aren't one in the same?"

I knew they weren't; still I couldn't help asking, "Do you think he's innocent?"

"He says he is."

"And you believe him?"

"I'm inclined to." Sam ran a thumb around his bottle of Bud, then looked up and caught my eye. "In any event, what I think doesn't really matter. Neither, I might add, do your own thoughts on the subject. The law says a man is innocent until proven guilty. And that means in a court of law, not over backyard fences and mugs of beer at the local tavern."

I couldn't have agreed with Sam more—in theory. But I'd known Lisa Cornell, at least well enough to say hello to. And I knew Wes. What's more, I'd seen pictures of Lisa and her daughter. Not the ones published in the paper, but the photos taken at the scene. It wasn't a case I could easily relegate to theory. Even here in the café, amid the lively bustle of the lunch crowd and the clatter of dishes, the memory of those pictures sent a shiver down my spine.

Sam raised the bottle to his lips, took a swig, then wiped his mouth with the back of his hand. "A murder trial is an enormous undertaking. I could use your help, Kali. I can't do it alone." He paused. "Not anymore."

He didn't add, "You owe me," but I knew it was there, in my mind if not in his. Sam's daughter and I had been high school friends. We'd gone our separate ways after graduation, but we'd stayed in touch—until her death from a drug overdose three years later. Although I hadn't seen Sam in the interim, when I moved back home to Silver Creek last year, he took me under his wing as though I were his long-lost daughter herself. He'd introduced me around the local legal circuit, making sure I met everyone from judges to clerks. He'd sent me clients, allowed me to use his law library at all hours of the day and night, acted as counsel and, above all, friend. It's not easy to refuse a friend.

I suspected that Sam's involvement in the case was of a similar nature. Jake Harding, Wes's father, was a fishing buddy of Sam's, as well as the doctor who'd treated his wife during her long, downhill battle with cancer. Jake needed Sam's help; Sam needed mine. I wasn't so sure Wes wanted any of us, but maybe that didn't matter.

Sam lowered his voice. "The cops never looked at anyone but Wes. They saw only what they wanted to see."

"There was plenty there for them to see."

"They never even let on that he was a suspect," Sam continued. "Never read him his rights. Not until after they had what they wanted."

I raised a brow. "That ought to make your job easy, then."

"Well, maybe they didn't cross the line, but they pushed it." Sam started to say something more, then closed his mouth and looked at me glumly. "I guess you don't need to hear the Defense Bar lecture on fair representation."

I shook my head. "I think I know it."

"But you're not convinced."

"Let me think about it, okay?"

He nodded, was silent a moment, then finished off what was left of his beer. "You and Wes were in school together, weren't you?" he asked finally.

"For a while."

Wes was with us through junior high and part of high school. I can't remember when he was sent away exactly, because we continued to talk about him long after. I don't even know *why* he was sent away, really. There were stories that he'd molested a ten-year-old girl, that he'd gotten an-other girl pregnant, that he'd broken into the school at night and left a headless and disemboweled cat on Mrs. Heafy's desk. There were so many stories they've run to-gether in my mind. And, of course, I never did know how many were true. Parents and teachers may have talked among themselves, but they never shared any of it with us.

What I do remember clearly is the way Wes would stare at you. Not mean, like the Armstrong boys, and not loony like old Mr. Wilks, but with eyes that would get under your skin and seek out the dark, uncomfortable places you tried to ignore. He was bad news; we knew that. And in case we didn't, our parents never failed to point it out.

But there was an undeniable fascination there as well. Wes was good-looking—dark hair, dark eyes, a full mouth that curled at the edges in an almost feminine manner. More than that, though, Wes had a way about him, some-thing that pulled at you even when you tried to ignore it.

Can a fifteen-year-old feel lust and loathing at the same time? Because that's the closest I can come to describing the effect Wes Harding had on me. At night he would work his way into my dreams and leave me breathless with an-ticipation. By day I couldn't bear to look at him.

"The boy's had a rough time of it," Sam said, inter-rupting my thoughts as though he'd been listening in.

"He's hardly a boy," I corrected, knowing Sam un-doubtedly referred to me, when I wasn't around, as "the girl." Language that might have earned him a severe tongue-lashing in politically correct San Francisco went largely unnoticed a couple hundred miles away in Silver Creek.

"Jake was sure he'd straightened out, though."

"*Was?*" I asked.

Sam smiled. "Is. He's standing behind his son one hundred percent."

I hadn't spoken to Wes since I'd been back in Silver Creek, hadn't even seen him much, and then only at a distance. His name had come up, however, on a number of occasions. Once in connection with a drunk-driving arrest, once over a fistfight, and several times in the context of "those hooligans out there in the woods," which was the way a lot of the folks in town referred to Wes and his particular group of friends. Myself, I wasn't so sure he'd straightened out much.

"Of course Wes isn't really his son," Sam said. "Jake married Grace when the boy was about ten or eleven. At that age there's only so much you can do."

I nodded. It couldn't have been easy taking someone like Wes into your life. "There are a couple of girls in the family, too, aren't there?" I asked.

He nodded. "Andrea is headed for UC San Diego this fall, and Pammy's a sophomore at the high school. They're nothing like Wes, either of them. But then, they've had the benefit of two parents from the start. It makes a big difference."

I finished off my iced tea, then sucked on a cube of ice. I knew plenty of people who'd grown up without that particular benefit and not a one of them ended up accused of murder.

"I used to see Lisa Cornell at the diner sometimes," I said. "When she worked the lunch shift there. She was a pretty girl. Always friendly and upbeat. Just about every week she'd come in with a new picture of Amy and show it off to anyone who'd take a look. It's hard to believe they're both dead."

Sam regarded me for a moment, his bushy gray brows

pulled tight with a frown. He set his beer on the table and folded his arms in front of him. "I'm not going to twist your arm, Kali. It's up to you. I'll work something out, one way or another."

I watched the waitress deliver ice cream sundaes to a mother and her young daughter. With wide-eyed delight, the girl scooped the cherry and a spoonful of whipped cream into her mouth. She grinned at her mother. I turned back to Sam. "I'll let you know in a day or two," I said.

After lunch I headed back to my office, two upstairs rooms in a converted Victorian. A chiropractor and an accountant occupied the remaining second-floor offices, while the downstairs housed one of the town's two beauty salons. My rooms were airy and light, but spartan. An old oak desk—the kind teachers used when I was in grade school—a couple of chairs, a file cabinet and a wobbly bookcase left by the previous tenant. It was a long way from my plushly carpeted, twenty-seventh floor office at Goldman & Latham in San Francisco. Most days I couldn't decide whether I'd taken a step up or down. I could wax poetic about both places and all that was implied by the differences between them, yet I knew that either way I was bending the truth more than a little.

I dropped my purse into the bottom desk drawer, reached for the stack of mail and kicked off my shoes, letting my bare toes slide across the worn spots in the carpet. Except for the days I was required to appear in court, I skipped the panty hose and heels routine—a decided plus to small-town practice.

I'd come home to Silver Creek to attend my father's funeral, and then, when my life in the Bay Area fell apart, I'd stayed on. An interim measure initially, now augmented by the force of inertia and a blinding confusion about the direction of my life.

Although Silver Creek is no longer the small, sleepy town it was when I was growing up, it's definitely not the place to come if you're looking for a hot time. Or refined culture, sourdough bread or good coffee. A fine place to raise a family, or so I've been told, but of questionable merit to a single woman in her thirties who has yet to give up hope of making her mark on the world.

On the other hand, I was my own boss. And while the majority of my cases might be, as Sam had so aptly quoted, *megamonotonous,* they were all mine. I could come and go without having to walk through a minefield of prying eyes or account for my time. No jockeying for position with other associates, no running interference between client and senior partner, no taking on cases just because they were assigned to you.

Which brought me back to Wes Harding. I set the mail aside and rolled Sam's proposition around in my mind.

Lisa Cornell and her five-year-old daughter, Amy, had been stabbed to death two weeks earlier. Their bloodied and partially clothed bodies had been found in the barn at the back of Lisa's property, along with a family of rats who'd had several days to indulge their appetites.

Wes was first questioned several days later, after the police discovered an unusual, leather-thonged rabbit's foot near the body of the little girl. Apparently a number of people were able to attest to the fact that Wes carried an identical rabbit's foot, one he was unable to produce for the police. His arrest came shortly thereafter, well supported by corroborating evidence.

From what I knew it was all circumstantial, but it was enough to convince the police they had a case. I was willing to bet it was a pretty strong case, too. You don't arrest the son of a prominent physician, even a son who's a reputed troublemaker, unless you're sure you're right. Not in Silver Creek, anyway.

Of course, that didn't mean they *were* right.

Rocking back in my chair, I tucked a foot up under me. The muted sounds of a summer afternoon drifted up from the street below. The murders had shaken this small town, which had felt itself largely immune from the ugliness and brutality that seemed to go hand in hand with urban living. People were frightened, and they were angry.

The murders had shaken me, too. But so had the realization that I'd so easily fallen into the camp of those who presumed Wes guilty. Sam's comment earlier this afternoon had rankled because it came so close to the truth.

But did that mean I wanted to be part of Wes's defense?

The phone rang. I rocked forward and picked up the receiver.

"You're not busy, are you?" My sister, Sabrina, had a way of layering the words with an innuendo that made me bristle. When I'd been on the verge of partnership at Goldman & Latham she'd opened her calls hesitantly, usually with a variation of *I know how busy you are and I hate to bother you.* Now she assumed I had nothing but time.

"Never too busy for you, Sabrina."

"Knock it off," she said lightly. "If you're going to be like that, I'll just stop calling." She paused, and I could hear the clink of ice cubes. Diet Coke? Or a vodka tonic? At three o'clock in the afternoon, it could have been either, depending on her mood. My sister sometimes found it difficult to deal with the demands of a privileged lifestyle.

"Really, I'm glad you called," I told her. "I always like talking to you." That was the truth. Well, maybe I didn't always enjoy the conversations themselves, but I liked the fact that we were comfortable enough with one another to attempt them. That hadn't always been the case.

"Peter ran into an old college buddy the other day," she continued, "on the golf course. The guy's the senior attorney at Golden Gate Savings in San Francisco, and he just happens to be looking for another staff attorney." Her voice rose and became breathless. "Peter told him all about you and he said to have you call."

"He'll have no shortage of qualified applicants. And I know next to nothing about banking."

"You could learn."

"Maybe, if I wanted to."

She gave an exasperated sigh. "It's got to be better than rotting away up there in the boonies."

"I'm not rotting away, and Silver Creek is no longer the boonies."

"Honestly, Kali, I don't understand you."

"Besides, if I wanted to take on something more, I could." I told her about the impending trial and Sam's request for help.

"You want to get involved with murder?" There was heavy emphasis on the last word.

"What I'd be involved in is a trial."

"And you'd be playing some abstract game, trying to find the loophole that would allow a killer to go free." The ice clinked again. From the slow way she sipped I was betting on the vodka tonic. "Why'd he kill them anyway?"

"It hasn't been established that he did."

"I'll tell you one thing: I never believed half those rumors we heard about Wes back in high school." She paused. "Are you going to do it?"

"I don't know. A case like this could help me make a name for myself. Help me get established."

"Established in the middle of nowhere."

"More than anything, I feel I owe Sam. He's put himself out for me this last year."

"He wouldn't have done it if he didn't want to." Sabrina hesitated. Her voice dropped half an octave. "Does Wes still have that gypsy magic?"

"That what?"

"That aura. Mysterious, provocative, unnerving. Don't tell me you never noticed."

What surprised me was that Sabrina had. "I wouldn't know," I told her. "I've only seen him from a distance."

"I bet he doesn't," she said almost wistfully. "He couldn't, not after all these years."

When we hung up I put the matter of Wes's defense out of my mind. I returned a few phone calls, wrote a letter on behalf of Mrs. Gillis, whose neighbor's dog was killing her chickens, then revised Mr. Crawford's will for probably the fourth or fifth time in as many months. Whenever he got mad at one of his four daughters he'd write her out of his will. Then he'd reinstate her when his ire turned to a different daughter, as it invariably did. I didn't know any of the women personally—two lived in Los Angeles, one in New York, and one abroad—but from what he'd told me I couldn't imagine any of them fighting over a run-down cottage, two acres of dry grassland, a 1984 Chevy and a pitifully small bank account.

I did the typing myself, although I had a secretary. Or half of one, at any rate. Myra split her time between my office and the accountant's next door. Since neither office was overwhelmed with clients, it worked fine.

Myra wasn't a great typist anyway. She was okay at the keyboard, despite the long nails, but she was forever transposing words, and sometimes whole phrases, so that nothing made sense. Or if it made sense, it wasn't the sense you intended. She did the same thing with messages. But she was terrific at watering plants and making sure the magazines by the front entrance were current and neatly arranged in alphabetical order.

She was also a genuinely nice person.

Myra's divorce had been my first case after moving to Silver Creek. Although we got a decent property settlement, given the circumstances, it wasn't much. As a single mother with three small children and an ex who seemed disinclined toward steady employment, Myra needed every cent she could earn. It was unfortunate that her skills fell short of her needs.

With the paperwork in order, I made a quick trip downstairs to the rest room. When the building was remodeled sometime back in the late '70s, the great minds in charge removed the upstairs bathroom to make room for a storage closet, leaving only the facilities at the rear of the beauty salon. This was sometimes hell on male clients, who would invariably opt to bounce uncomfortably from foot to foot rather than walk through a roomful of women in curlers.

The smell of permanent wave lotion filled my nostrils the minute I stepped inside. I held my breath and started toward the back of the salon, picking up snatches of the collective conversation en route.

"She wasn't but a child herself," said a blond woman with foils in her hair. "And as sweet as they come. I hope they give him the death penalty."

The woman next to her nodded. "Too bad they can't

make it slow and painful, like what he did to that poor woman and her daughter. Her little girl was the same age as my granddaughter. I tell you, I'd like to pull the trigger on that Wes Harding myself."

" 'Course by the time the lawyers get finished he'll probably get off with a slap on the wrist."

"If that."

"Loopholes and technicalities," chimed in Cherise, who owns the place. "Seems to me the law's pretty clear. You murder someone, you don't deserve any special breaks."

"Criminals get all the advantages these days."

The blonde swiveled her chair to face the others. "It's the lawyers. All they're interested in is the money. Right and wrong don't matter."

Cherise mumbled agreement, snapped the rod on a curler, then looked up. "Oh hi, Kali. Didn't see you come in. Nothing personal in this, understand. You're about as decent as they come."

I let out the breath I was holding. "There's a chance Wes Harding didn't do it, you know."

"Nah." The older woman addressed our reflection in the mirror. "They wouldn't have arrested him if they didn't have proof."

"He ought to be taken out and hung right now," the blonde said with the vehemence of those who know they're right. "Save us all a lot of time and money."

"Hanged," I said.

All three looked at me.

"The word is 'hanged' not 'hung.' "

"Doesn't really matter what you call it as long as Wes Harding gets what he's got coming. Everyone in town knows he's nothing but trouble."

After using the rest room I went back upstairs and phoned Sam.

Somewhere deep inside I'd known I would agree to take the case, although I'd expected to agonize over the decision a bit more first. It struck me, with a certain appreciation for the irony involved, that I was beset with the same lust and loathing I'd experienced as a teen. Only this time it was for the case, not Wes himself.

2

Myra was already at work when I arrived the next morning. On the desk in front of her, an open bottle of nail polish perched precariously atop a stack of case files.

"You're here bright and early," I said.

She nodded, brushing at a wispy curl hanging over her eyes. Myra wore her thick, dark hair pinned at the crown with a tortoise-shell clip, and strands were forever springing free.

"I have to take an extra hour for lunch today. Hope you don't mind."

I didn't, although I suspected it wouldn't have mattered if I did. "One of the kids sick again?"

"No, it's about Marc's school. They're thinking of expanding this *'good-touch, bad-touch'* program to the lower grades. Some psychologist is going to talk to the parents this afternoon. I wouldn't take time off except that a friend of mine is kinda twisting my arm."

" 'Good-touch, bad-touch'? What's that?"

Myra was concentrating on applying color to the nails of her right hand and didn't bother to look up. "It's like a sex-ed, don't-talk-to-strangers thing. You know, good touching is a hug from your mommy. Bad touching is anything that makes you uncomfortable. I guess it's important stuff, but sometimes I think they go overboard. Here I am trying to teach my kids to be comfortable with their bodies, and then some stern-sounding stranger at school lectures them about private parts and abuse. Somehow it doesn't quite fit."

"It's probably important though."

"I guess, but they're just little kids. Do we have to fill their heads with this stuff so early?"

"It's a sad commentary on society, isn't it?"

"Sure is." She held out a hand tipped in deep fuchsia and blew on the nails to dry them. "I guess it's nothing new, though. The friend who's dragging me to the meeting this afternoon says she was abused for years by an uncle. I think that's why she's pushing so hard for this program. She's almost a fanatic." Myra examined her handiwork, then capped the bottle of polish. "I made copies of that letter you asked me to. I set out the original for your signature and stamped the file copy."

"Thanks."

"What do you want me to do with the others?"

"What others?"

She nodded toward the small pile of papers next to the bottle of nail polish. "You asked for two dozen copies."

"I asked for *two* copies. Geez, Myra, why in the world would I want twenty-four copies of a simple letter?"

"How should I know, you're the lawyer." She tightened the cap on the bottle. "But I coulda sworn you said two dozen."

Suddenly it hit me. "How many donuts did you order?"

It hit her too. "Oh gosh, Kali. You're right. How did I manage to do that?" Her expression was stricken. She wrung her hands, heedless of the wet polish. "I'm so sorry. Stupid, stupid me. I don't know how I got them confused."

Myra's not stupid at all, but she does have trouble with some of the finer points of daily living. "It's not the end of the world," I told her. "We'll use the extra copies for scratch paper. And you just saved the gals downstairs a whole hunk of calories." Though I figured I was going to have to come up with the rest of the donuts, and an explanation, before they took it in their minds that I wasn't such a decent sort after all.

I'd hoped to be able to meet with Sam about the Harding case right away, but he was going to be tied up most of the day. He had promised to have the file ready for me by late afternoon, though. "It's probably better if you look over the file before we talk," he said. "Saves time. And that way you can form your own impressions before they get tainted by mine."

His logic was sound, but my workload was light and I was anxious to get started. I was fairly certain of the approach Sam would want me to take anyway. Although he would doubtless argue otherwise, I had no illusions about why he was bringing me in. It wasn't my mind he was after, or my brilliant mastery of the law; it was my legs.

When a case goes to trial, particularly a big case, extensive legwork is inevitable. And invaluable. There is background information to be gathered, leads to be followed and checked, witnesses to be interviewed. Given his age and poor health, Sam needed someone with a sturdy pair of legs to do most of the scouting.

I put in a call to police headquarters and left a message for the chief, who is an old family friend. Next I asked Myra, who was through with the self-flagellation and back to repairing the damage to her nails, to get me copies of the news reports of Lisa Cornell's death. Finally, after tidying up a few things, I left for the diner where Lisa had worked. I wanted to get there around eleven, before the lunch crowd began to build.

Despite the hokey name, the Lazy Q Diner is one of Silver Creek's more upscale establishments. Its offerings are a long way from the braised endive and goat cheese cuisine you find in the San Francisco area, but it's definitely a step up from the hamburger joints and fast-food outlets in town. The couple who run the place are in their mid-fifties, transplants from somewhere back East. I'd never spoken to the husband, who spent most of his time in the kitchen, but the wife, Velma, worked as hostess and cashier, and often helped out with the tables during the lunch-hour rush.

She was there when I walked in and took my order herself. No place in Silver Creek makes decent coffee, at least not to the taste of someone who's been spoiled by the richesse of coffee houses in the Bay Area. I ordered a Coke instead. Although I wasn't hungry, I had a chicken salad sandwich as well, figuring that would give me a double shot at striking up a conversation.

"You must be shorthanded without Lisa," I volunteered when Velma set the soda on the table in front of me.

"Shorthanded and down in the dumps. It's such a tragedy, such a terrible waste."

I murmured agreement.

"We hired a new girl last week, but I'm not sure she's going to work out. Of course, all of us here are still pretty shaken by the whole thing, so maybe we haven't given her a fair shot at it."

"Had Lisa worked here long?"

"Seven or eight months is all. She moved to town after her aunt's death, when she inherited the house. But Lisa had a way about her. Kind of made you feel like you'd known her forever." Velma brushed a crumb from the table. "You come here quite a bit, so you must know what I mean."

I did. Lisa was as sunny and open as a summer's morning. Honey-blond hair, which she wore in a long braid down her back, fresh face, dimples and a smile that never quit. She was the kind of person you take an instant liking to, even before you've exchanged a word.

"She was a good worker, too," Velma continued. "Never short-tempered or frazzled. The only time I saw her without a smile on her face was when she was coming down with one of those headaches."

"Migraines?"

"I guess it was something like that. She seemed to be getting an awful lot of them lately. I didn't want to scare her or anything, but I thought they might be a sign of something serious. She'd been seeing a doctor, though, so I guess he was on top of it."

A group of four women came into the restaurant just then and Velma left to seat them. She stopped back, briefly, with my sandwich before hurrying off to attend to the next cluster of patrons.

I sipped my Coke, devoured more of the sandwich than I'd intended to and mentally ticked off what I knew about Lisa Cornell, which wasn't a lot. She was in her early twenties, a single parent who appeared to structure much of her life around her five-year-old daughter. From the snippets of conversation I'd picked up, I knew she'd swum competitively until reaching high school, was teaching herself to play the guitar and drove an old blue Honda.

The list of things I didn't know was considerably longer. I hadn't known, for starters, that she'd moved to Silver Creek so recently. I'd sort of assumed she'd grown up here. I knew where she lived, but only because that was where the bodies had been found. I hadn't known she'd inherited the house from her aunt.

And what about her husband, assuming there'd ever been one? I didn't know whether he was absent because of death or divorce. And if the latter, whether the breakup had been Lisa's idea or his. I knew nothing about her friends, her background, her interests or hobbies. Nothing about what her life had been before coming to Silver Creek. I tried a few of these questions out on Velma when she was free again, but she didn't know a whole lot more than I did.

"Sorry I can't help. Only thing I know is about the house. That's because I knew the aunt, though not well. Anne Drummond was her name. No children of her own. She died about a year ago and left the house to Lisa. It's a nice piece of property. There was quite a bit of interest in it, but Anne wouldn't sell, even when she knew she was dying and could have used the money to hire a private nurse or something."

"How'd she die?"

"Breast cancer. It got my mother, too."

"I'm sorry."

"Yeah, it's a beastly way to go."

"Did Lisa have other family?"

Velma gave a head shake that was the equivalent of a shrug. "Lisa was as sweet and pleasant as they come, but she kept her distance, at least around me. Never talked much about herself. She was pretty friendly with Caroline, though, one of the other girls who works here. She might be able to tell you more."

I took down Caroline's name and number.

"You with the police?" Velma asked. "I called them right after I heard the news, you know, to see if there was anything I could do to help. They never sent anyone out."

"I'm a lawyer," I explained.

She tilted her head. "Which side?"

"Defense."

She let out a whistle. "Funny, I never took you for one of them."

" 'Them'?"

Ignoring my question, she volleyed one of her own. "You really believe there's a chance Wes Harding didn't do it?"

"There's always that chance."

She took a moment to consider it. "You know, the one thing that's never made sense to me is 'why.' Why would anyone do a thing like that?"

I nodded, acknowledging the senselessness of it. What I didn't bother to tell her was that it didn't have to make sense. Motive wasn't an element of murder. In some instances confessed killers themselves couldn't tell you why they'd done it.

When I got back to the office Myra was just leaving.

"I put your messages on your desk," she said.

"Anything urgent?"

"Not really. Sheri Pearl wants to talk to you about the conservatorship on her mother. She has a few questions about, and I quote, 'the legal ramifications.' "

I suspected that meant Sheri wanted to get rid of at least a portion of her mother's possessions. Her rush to tidy things up irritated me. It didn't help that the conservatorship had been the right thing to do, and that ninety percent of the time the senior Mrs. Pearl couldn't have told you what year it was or what she'd last had for dinner. Bottom line was, I didn't especially like Sheri Pearl, and I did like her mother, Irma. Particularly on those rare occasions when Irma was fully lucid.

"And you missed Tom's call," Myra continued. "He said to tell you 'hi.' "

"Tom?" The mere sound of his name caused my heart to quicken. "He's supposed to be on a Boy Scout camping trip."

"He is, but under the pretext of needing more toilet paper or something, he managed to sneak off to some outpost of civilization where there's a telephone."

"Did he say anything besides 'hi'?"

"Just that the food's lousy, the ground's hard, the fish aren't biting and the mosquitoes are."

"That's it? Nothing about missing me?"

Myra laughed. "Oh, yeah, that, too." She headed for the door. "Don't forget to call Ms. Pearl."

I slumped into my chair, disappointed at missing Tom's call. Tom is part of the reason I'm still in Silver Creek. A big part.

We're neighbors. We're also dating. Or, more accurately, sort of dating, sort of screwing around, which is how I'd explained it to Sabrina. "Well, I hope you're being careful," was all she'd said. I hadn't been sure if she meant that literally or more generally, but I assured her I was. On both counts. I was a veteran of too many soured relationships to let myself be otherwise.

Still, after Myra had gone I pulled out the picture of Tom I keep in the zipper pocket of my purse. It was taken late last summer, the one and only time we'd gone camping together. We'd hiked into Desolation Wilderness, which isn't desolate at all, camped in a meadow by a mountain lake and spent the night under a diamond-studded sky of black velvet. All in all, I prefer the comforts of home, but when I pictured Tom out there now, with a bunch of rowdy ten-year-olds, I felt a pang of jealousy. It seemed an awful waste of a fine body to have him sacked out under the stars alone.

3

Later that afternoon I dropped by Sam's office and picked up the Harding file. Then I headed out to have a look at the barn where Lisa and Amy had been killed. Not that I expected to uncover any new evidence; the police are usually fairly thorough about a crime scene investigation. What I wanted was to have a look at the site for myself. There are lawyers who can work solely from paper, but I find that reports and photos are poor substitutes for the real thing.

Lisa Cornell's house was a couple of miles outside town on a narrow road that wound and dipped, then unexpectedly opened onto an expanse of gently rolling grassland. It was a two-story white clapboard house with a wide porch in front and a good deal of land to either side. I guessed that it had been built sometime around the turn of the century, certainly long before the other houses that dotted the roadside. Once it had probably been the main residence on a ranch of considerable acreage. Over the years parcels had been subdivided and sold off at odd intervals, making for the kind of uneven architectural mix you so often find in rural neighborhoods.

Despite its age, the Cornell place looked to be in good repair. It was clear no one had tended to it since Lisa's death, however. Throwaway papers had collected on the front steps, the roses and petunias along the walk were brown from lack of water and the front screen door was sprung so that it flapped open with the passing breeze.

I made a mental note to ask Sam who would inherit the house now that Lisa was dead. It was a long shot, but people have been known to kill for less.

I pulled into the driveway and parked, then made my way through the orchard to the barn at the back of the property. The building was a weathered gray, and listed slightly to the left. The roof was bare in spots, the siding warped. I suspected that the wide double door at the end hadn't budged since the last horse trotted out many years earlier. I walked the perimeter once, then stopped at a side door, which was slightly ajar.

Never a fan of dark spaces and the creatures that inhabit them, I hesitated, then took a deep breath, scrunched my face up tight and opened the door wider. I entered sideways, leading with an extended hand.

The interior had a musty, sickly-sweet smell that caught in my throat, but it wasn't as gloomy as I'd expected. Sunlight filtered through cracks in the siding and several larger gaps in the roof, revealing nothing more ominous than neglect and grime. Floating in the hot, dry air, particles of dust caught the light like microscopic June bugs, infusing the stillness with an otherworldly quality. From outside I heard the far-off, hollow tapping of a woodpecker. I stepped away from the doorway and inspected the area more closely.

A sagging hayloft stood at one end of the barn, wooden storage shelves at the other. The shelves looked to be hand-made, by someone as inexperienced with hammer and saw as I am. They were filled with old paint cans, rolls of wire mesh, plastic irrigation pipe and the like—scraps from a long line of maintenance projects. A lawn mower, a rusty wheelbarrow, a stenciled headboard and a couple of old kitchen chairs stood in the far corner opposite me. Other than that, the place was empty—a large open space of hard-packed dirt strewn with bits of straw.

To my left, the dirt was darker in stretches, as though discolored by traces of oil. Only I was fairly certain it wasn't oil, but blood. I shifted my eyes and swallowed hard to keep my throat from closing.

How had it happened? I wondered. Had their assailant accosted Lisa and Amy elsewhere and forced them into the barn? Or had mother and daughter come out on some simple, domestic errand and found him waiting, perhaps secreted in the loft or hidden by the clutter at the other side? Or maybe they'd come upon someone in the barn by accident. A thief perhaps—although it didn't look as though there would have been much worth stealing.

They were very different scenarios, pointing to very different sorts of crime. The problem was, of course, I had no way of knowing what had actually happened. Or why. No way of knowing whether the killer was someone other than Wes Harding.

Although it was impossible to tell from looking at the stains exactly where and how the bodies had lain, I forced myself to move closer. The police had searched the area for clues, raking and sifting the debris and bagging everything that might eventually prove useful. No doubt they'd measured and sketched and carefully noted—and in the process distilled a moment of stark terror to cold, flat data.

The data was important. I knew at some time in the future I'd spend hours studying it, but right then, crouching on the bloodstained ground, what I found myself dwelling on was the moment itself. Lisa and her child lying there in the dirt, helpless and alone, while the life drained from them like water into sand.

I was so caught up with imagining what they might have been thinking and feeling, I wasn't at first aware of rustling sounds behind me. As they slowly surfaced in my consciousness, I stopped to listen. Nothing but silence, drifting in and settling like the dust. Then, suddenly, the afternoon quiet was broken by a quick sound near the doorway. I pulled myself to my feet and turned.

Again nothing.

That's when I recalled mention of the rats that inhabited the barn. I cleared my throat loudly and shuffled my feet in the soil to send them scurrying. There was a moment's silence, followed by another rustling sound; then the side door squeaked open and a shaft of light blinded me.

Rats didn't open doors.

Heart racing, I moved back into the shadow and waited for my eyes to adjust. Finally I saw a boy of eight or nine standing in the doorway. A scrawny little guy with hair the color of hay and a mouth like a jack-o-lantern. We both let out a yelp at the same time.

"Jesus, you scared me," I said, before I remembered it was considered poor form to swear in front of children.

"You didn't scare me," he responded with clearly feigned bravado.

"Then why'd you scream?"

"It wasn't a scream." The boy snapped his chewing gum. "And I was startled, not scared."

Seemed like pretty much the same thing to me, but I wasn't about to argue.

He dug his hands into his pockets and scowled at me over a freckled nose, then blew a bubble until it popped. "There was a lady and a little girl died here a couple of weeks ago," he announced. "Murdered."

I nodded. "Did you know them?"

He ignored my question. "My brother's the one who found them."

"Really?" I'd remembered reading that the bodies had been discovered by a boy who lived in the neighborhood. I knew I'd want to talk to him eventually. "Does your brother have a name?"

The boy gave me a disgusted look. "Of course he does." The gum-chewing accelerated.

"What is it?" I asked when it became clear he wasn't about to volunteer the information.

"Emmett. But everyone calls him Bongo. He's thirteen. I'm eight and three-quarters. My name's Kevin."

"Hi. I'm Kali. You live around here?"

Kevin gestured with his head. "Over on Ferndale, but it's close if you come by way of the creek. My brother and his friends like to hang out over here, even though they're not supposed to. My mom gets real mad about things like that."

Good for her, I thought.

"They do it so they can smoke and stuff. You know, and not get caught. My mom would really get mad about that."

"What do you mean, 'and stuff'?" I asked, remembering certain less-than-sterling moments of my own youth. "Drinking? Drugs?"

"Magazines mostly," Kevin said.

"Magazines?"

He drew his shoulders up to his ears, blew a bubble of pink gum, and looked at the ground. "You know, with pictures."

I shook my head.

"Naked women."

"Ah, those. What about you—do you hang out here, too?"

"Nah, not usually. It's kinda boring."

"But you're here today."

He twisted his shoulders in a sort of elliptical shrug. "Bongo says the place is haunted, but I don't believe it. I came to see for myself. Bongo swore to it on Mom's Bible. Says he's heard that woman and her little girl crying and shrieking like they was being torn apart."

"Sounds like Bongo's got an active imagination."

"He says the ghosts will come after you, even if you didn't do anything wrong." Kevin lifted his chin. "I don't believe in ghosts," he said, sounding as though he meant just the opposite.

"I don't either," I told him.

He looked relieved.

"Was there anyone else who hung out around here, besides your brother and his friends?"

Kevin shook his head. "No one except Granger."

"Who's Granger?"

"You know, Granger. He plays the harmonica."

I did not know Granger, or anyone in Silver Creek for that matter, who played the harmonica.

Kevin must have figured that much from my expression because he crossed his arms and explained further. "Granger lives in the woods. At least during the summer.

Some nights he slept in the barn, but that was okay by Mrs. Cornell. She hired him to do work sometimes, and she didn't mind about the barn. She hardly ever used it herself. I think she was afraid of the spiders."

"Sounds like you knew Mrs. Cornell pretty well."

Kevin shrugged. "It's just some days she was out working in the yard or something when I'd ride by on my bike. She usually had some cookies for her little girl and she'd give me some."

"And this Granger would help her?"

"Just sometimes, like when he dug those holes for the rose bushes. She gave him cookies too."

"Any idea where I can find him?"

Kevin raised his shoulders in a small shrug. "He just kind of shows up on his own." Another pink bubble, then a pop. "If I see him, you want me to tell him you're looking for him?"

"No, that's okay." I didn't know Granger, but I thought I knew the type. Nothing would make him disappear faster than finding out someone wanted to talk to him.

"Are you a cop?" Kevin asked after a moment.

I shook my head.

"Another real estate lady?"

"Another?"

"There was one up here the other day."

"How'd you know she was in real estate?"

He shrugged again. "She drove a fancy car. A Cadillac. There was a real estate man too; he had a black Mercedes." Kevin looked toward the driveway at my battered and dirt-streaked Subaru. He turned back to me with an apologetic face. "Guess you're not one of them after all."

Cars were a sore spot with me. My brand-new, silver

BMW had not fared well with my return to Silver Creek. I'd driven home for my father's funeral. In the weeks that followed, while I was trying to help a friend accused of murder, the car's windows had been smashed, the tires slashed, the finish defaced and, finally, the entire vehicle wrecked beyond repair. The Subaru was second-hand, and a very poor substitute. Unfortunately, it was all I could afford.

"I'm a lawyer," I told him, with my own variant of bravado. "And I'm going to want to talk to your brother about the time he found Mrs. Cornell and Amy."

Kevin's mouth worked the gum for a moment. Then he blew a large bubble and removed the wad from his mouth to admire it. "My mom doesn't like him to talk about it," Kevin said, returning the gum to his mouth. "He gets upset, acts real crazy. He even wet his bed once. He paid me five dollars not to tell."

I gave him a sympathetic nod. I knew what kind of shape I'd be in after stumbling across a couple of dead, decaying bodies. And I was well past thirteen. "I won't ask him to go into detail."

"You want my opinion, I think he's just trying to get attention. He got to be famous for finding them, and now nobody cares about that anymore. All they want to talk about is that guy who killed them." Abruptly, and in one smooth motion, Kevin slid past me and darted for the door. "I gotta go. My mom gets mad if I'm late."

With Kevin gone, the enfolding silence was like an echo. I spent another couple of minutes taking in the barn's layout, fixing a mental picture in my head. Then I left as well, heading through the yard this time instead of the orchard. Near the house I passed a tire swing hanging from the branch of an old oak. A purple pail and shovel and a collection of plastic ponies lay in the dirt below. I felt a knot form in my stomach.

The taking of any human life was hard enough to comprehend; I couldn't begin to imagine the sort of sicko it took to kill a child.

4

I drove home with the windows down, the hot air whipping through my hair and pounding in my ears. White noise, drowning out my thoughts.

Loretta and Barney met me at the door, barking their greeting even before I'd slipped the key into the lock. Once I was inside the racket quieted to whines and whimpers, but they made up for it with lively body language. Loretta rubbed her torso hard against my legs, while Barney leaped at me from all directions like a coiled spring gone berserk. Dropping my purse and Wes Harding's file onto the Parsons table by the door, I reached down and gave them each a vigorous scratching behind the ears.

This was further evidence of how much my life had changed. Until a year ago I wouldn't have attempted to raise an African violet without a secretary to water and care for it. Now I found myself responsible for a dog and a half.

Loretta had been my father's dog. I inherited her by default when he died. I also inherited Barney, and Barney's four brothers and sisters, although I hadn't known that at the time.

Officially, Barney is Tom's dog, or rather Tom's children's dog, at least on the days they stay at his place. Hence the name Barney, which they had chosen over a sizable list of suggestions from Tom and myself. Chosen for some reason known only to them, despite the fact that they'd long since outgrown childhood TV shows. Barney is half springer spaniel, half something that I guarantee isn't dinosaur. And his fur is a cocoa brown, not purple.

When Tom was out of town I took care of Barney. Even when Tom wasn't, Barney wound up at my place as often as not. But then, so did Tom. Or he had until recently. In the last few months our relationship had seemed to stall. It was nothing you could put your finger on, and although I was sure we both felt it, we'd done our best to pretend we didn't.

Freeing myself from the canine welcoming committee, I kicked off my clothes and took a long, hot shower, scrubbing away the fine layer of dust and cobwebs from my visit to the barn. The mental picture of Lisa and Amy was not so easily washed away.

I slipped into old jeans and a T-shirt, then made myself a cup of coffee and sat down at the dining room table with Wes Harding's case file.

What it was, actually, was a thick accordion envelope containing several folders, all a bit dog-eared, and a sizable number of loose papers in an equally poor state. Only one of the folders was labeled, and it was empty.

The first thing Sam and I were going to have to settle on was a filing system that made sense. I'm no neatness freak, believe me. My underpants and bras get tossed together in the drawer with my running shorts; my makeup bin looks like it ought to go out with the trash; and the stack of clean laundry in the corner doesn't look much different from the stack of dirty stuff. But I like my paperwork organized. My brain requires all the assistance it can get.

I started with the police report, which was not labeled as such, but appeared to be largely intact. The basic story wasn't much different than what I'd gleaned from news accounts at the time of the crime. Lisa's and Amy's bodies had been discovered on a Sunday afternoon by thirteen-year-old Emmett Langley. What with the rats and the natural process of decomposition, it had been difficult to gauge the time of death with precision. Based on extrinsic evidence, however, the police were able to estimate that the deaths occurred somewhere between seven o'clock and midnight Friday evening.

Apparently a neighbor had seen Lisa watering her yard at about six. The condition of the kitchen indicated that Lisa and Amy had eaten dinner, although Lisa had not yet done the dishes. Her answering machine logged two calls during the evening, one at eight-thirty, the other around ten. Both were apparently hang-ups since the machine had recorded static but no message. In the background of the first call there'd been muffled music and conversation reminiscent of a social gathering.

Lisa never retrieved Saturday morning's newspaper or mail, and she hadn't shown up for her Saturday afternoon shift at the restaurant. Velma had assumed Lisa was suffering from one of her headaches and had decided not to bother her by calling.

Lisa and Amy had both died of wounds to the throat, although in Lisa's case there were multiple stab wounds in the chest area as well. There was a full paragraph describing the length and depth of the cuts, and the muscles and tendons severed, but I skipped over it, knowing that if those details became important to the case, I'd go back and wade through it. There was also a gash on Lisa's left hand that was relatively fresh but appeared to have been sustained sometime before her attack.

Both bodies were found face up, and both were partially disrobed. Lisa's blouse had been ripped open, her denim skirt pushed up around her middle. Amy's shorts were lying in the dirt near her head. There was no sign that either of them had been raped, but both were naked from the waist down. Neither pair of undergarments had been found in the barn or on the surrounding property.

I put the report aside for a moment and took a couple of deep breaths. The images were vivid and unsettling, as was the picture taking shape in my mind. This was an assailant who not only killed in cold blood but seemed to take a certain perverse pleasure in demeaning his victims.

After a moment I shoved emotion aside and thought about the implications for our case. If the attack was an act of deviant behavior rather than clear-cut motive, did that help or hurt our position? It was hard to say at that point, but I thought it probably cut against us. Wes was, after all, a man with a less than upstanding reputation. Whether or not the reputation was deserved, it would be there in the minds of the jurors. I made some notes for myself, then went back to the file.

I read about the rabbit's foot that had been found near Amy's body, the motorcycle tire tracks in the drive, the dirt samples from Wes's cycle that were consistent with the soil on Lisa's property. Again, I skipped the technical analysis. There'd be time for that later.

Wes had been arrested on Tuesday, pursuant to a warrant that allowed the police to search his house. They hadn't found the murder weapon, but they had found an extensive collection of knives. They'd also found a long, blond hair on one of Wes's shirts, and a pair of blood-spotted jeans in the clothes hamper.

Witness accounts of Wes's activities Friday evening were fairly consistent. He'd spent the early part of the evening with some buddies at a local bar, drinking, dancing and carousing with the other Friday night regulars. He was apparently in a foul mood, however, and left about nine o'clock after a nasty exchange with one of the women on the dance floor. Wes claimed to have driven home and gone to bed, but a neighbor heard what he thought was a motorcycle sometime about midnight.

I sipped my coffee, scribbled more notes, and with a growing sense of misgiving, wondered what I'd gotten myself into.

The photos didn't help.

Because of my association with Tom, who is the publisher and editor-in-chief of *The Mountain Journal,* I'd seen photos of the crime scene, including those judged too gruesome to print. But they'd been journalist's photos. The police photographs were far worse. Large, full-color glossies shot under the cold, harsh light of a strobe. Some were taken from a distance, showing the position of bodies relative to the barn's layout, but most were close-ups. Swollen, greenish-red flesh, gaping wounds, exposed torsos. Human life violated.

Sickened, I shoved them back into the folder. At this point they weren't going to tell me anything useful. I switched from coffee to wine and pulled out Sam's case notes. Other than copies of motions filed, some correspondence with the prosecutor and a few pages of what looked to be hieroglyphics, there wasn't much. I'd just begun trying to make sense of Sam's cryptic scrawlings when my efforts were cut short by the peal of the doorbell.

Daryl Benson greeted me with his usual hesitant smile. "Got the message you called," he said, jingling the spare change in his pocket. "You were gone by the time I tried your office, so I thought I'd stop by in person."

Daryl Benson had been a family friend when I was growing up. He'd been a uniformed officer then; he was chief of police now. And counting the months to retirement.

Before my mother's suicide when I was fourteen, Benson had been a regular fixture at our holiday meals and summer barbecues, a sort of honorary uncle whose visits were always eagerly anticipated. I'd seen very little of him after my mother died and my father started drinking heavily, and nothing at all of him in the years I was away at college and then attempting to make my mark on the legal world of San Francisco. But since my return to Silver Creek we'd forged a new bond of sorts. What we shared was not friendship exactly, but a camaraderie born of having once loved the same people and having shared a piece of the past. Sometimes I wasn't even sure I liked Daryl Benson all that much, but he was my only link to parents I'd recently come closer to understanding.

"You want a glass of wine?" I asked, leading the way to the kitchen.

"You got any cold beer?"

I opened the refrigerator, handed him a bottle of Anchor Steam, and poured myself more wine. "Let's go into the other room where it's comfortable."

Benson followed me to the living room, where he eased his bulky frame into the forest green armchair that had been my father's favorite. "Looks like you're making progress," he said with an approving glance at the fresh coat of paint on the walls. "It's a big job. You're smart to tackle it a room at a time."

Smart had nothing to do with it. I was tackling it the only way I could. Renovation didn't come cheaply.

The house had suffered from neglect since my mother's death. At first my father had wanted to leave everything just the way it was, although he had, begrudgingly, agreed to a new roof when the old one leaked so badly the upstairs rooms became unusable. Then, as he lost himself increasingly in his drinking, he'd ceased to care.

I'd intended originally to sell the place, as is. Sabrina concurred, and our brother John, who'd been living in Italy for the past five years, didn't care what we did so long as it didn't involve him. But when my one-week trip home to settle the estate had grown to a month, and then two months, I had reconsidered.

My coveted, on-the-brink-of-partnership position in San Francisco had turned to dust, as had my relationship with the firm's star litigator. There wasn't a lot to go back to but a mortgage I could no longer afford. I'd leased my house in Berkeley, furnished, and taken refuge in the family home I'd been so eager to leave fourteen years earlier.

"The white was a good choice," Benson observed. "It lightens the room considerably. Sticking to something basic like that probably makes things less complicated as well."

I smiled. The color was royal ivory, not white, and it had taken me ten tries to get it right.

"I wanted to talk to you about Lisa Cornell's death," I said, getting back to the purpose of my earlier call.

Benson raised his beer and took a swallow. His bald

head shone like polished stone. "I thought it might be something like that." He wiped his mouth with the back of his hand. "What's your interest in this anyway?"

"Co-counsel with Sam Morrison. That is, assuming it's okay with our client."

"Hell, Wes won't care. He seems to have taken the ostrich approach to this whole business, like it doesn't really concern him. You'd think a man facing a possible death sentence would show a little interest in the outcome."

"How strong is the case against him?"

Benson gave a hollow laugh. "That's a question better put to the prosecutor. But you want my opinion, it's strong enough that I wouldn't want to be standing in your shoes."

Not a heartening appraisal, but then Daryl Benson wasn't a neutral party.

"I was looking through the case file before you arrived," I said, trying to keep my tone friendly rather than lawyerlike. "From what I've been able to gather the evidence is all circumstantial. And there's no motive, no murder weapon, no witnesses."

He brushed the air with his hand. "Don't need them."

"Did your investigation turn up other possible suspects?"

His eyes met mine, kindly. "The evidence may be circumstantial, Kali, but it all points to Wes Harding."

I opened my mouth to argue, but Benson held up his hand. "First off, we've got that rabbit's foot. A guy at the auto shop where Wes works remembers seeing him with it Thursday afternoon. When we questioned Wes on Tuesday he couldn't produce it. 'Might have lost it,' he says. You ask me, it's mighty peculiar he happened to lose it right when he did."

"A rabbit's foot is hardly a one-of-a-kind item."

"This one's pretty close. It's black rather than the standard white, and it's attached to a braided leather strand. But that's not the only thing that points to Wes. Tread marks in the dirt at the end of Lisa Cornell's driveway match Harding's motorcycle, at least as far as we can tell. It's not a perfect print, but the soil was damp so it's more than we might have gotten otherwise. And we found a long blond hair on clothing in Harding's hamper."

"With enough root structure for DNA testing?"

He shook his head. "But the color, length and texture are the same as Lisa's. She used some kind of dye that also showed up on the strand we found with Harding's clothes. May not be exact science, but I'm willing to bet a jury would find it pretty convincing."

I began mentally ticking off the points we'd raise on cross-examination. In a case like this, you try to cast doubt on the state's contention that the evidence points conclusively to the defendant. It's almost always possible to introduce a degree of uncertainty, but it wasn't clear we'd be able to cast enough doubt to sway the jury.

"There were also the blood spots on Wes's jeans," I said. "The police apparently seized them as evidence, but the lab results weren't in the file."

Benson gave a half-shrug. "That's in the DA's hands now. Bottom line is, he thinks there's enough evidence against Harding that he's willing to take it to trial."

"That doesn't mean he'll get a conviction."

A sigh. "You defense lawyers are all alike. You try to muddy the waters with a lot of 'what ifs' and far-fetched speculation. In theory, it's possible to shoot holes in any case, even if you've got a goddamn video of the crime in progress. But I'm telling you, ninety-nine percent of the time, your most obvious suspect is the guilty party."

"In that case, maybe we should just streamline the whole

process," I observed dryly. "You know, have the cops pow-wow over coffee and donuts, and once they've come up with an obvious suspect, simply cart the guy off to prison. It's bound to save time and money."

Benson laughed. "There are times I think that's not such a bad idea." He drained his beer.

"You want another?"

"I could be persuaded."

I got him a second bottle and refilled my own wineglass. "Tell me about Lisa Cornell," I said.

"There's not a lot to tell. Twenty-two years old, worked as a waitress. Didn't seem to have many close friends, but then, between her work, her daughter and her fiancé, she probably didn't have a lot of time for socializing."

"Fiancé?"

"Philip Stockman. Owns the Big Bob Hardware chain, or rather his family does. Phil's kind of the chief honcho, though. I'm not even sure the old man is involved at all at this point."

"Had they been engaged long?"

Benson gave a shrug.

"Funny that she never mentioned him." It was dawning on me that I hadn't really known Lisa at all. "What about her family?" I asked.

"Her parents live in southern California. I've talked to them by phone but never met them. They had the bodies flown down there when we'd finished with them. Stockman was kind of p.o'd about that, as I understand it. Wanted Lisa and Amy buried here in his family's plot."

"Her parents didn't come to Silver Creek themselves?"

"Once, to go through her things and all. But I didn't meet them while they were here."

"What about brothers and sisters?"

"None."

"Was there a husband in her past?"

Benson nodded. "Apparently they split up not too long ago. Lisa's parents couldn't tell us much about the guy."

"Close family."

"Yeah, that was my take on it too. You might try Ed Cole, over in Hadley. He's handling the probate, so he's probably followed up on some of this."

My inner antenna picked up. "Lisa had him draw up a will?"

"No, but Cole handled her aunt's estate. When the parents asked for a recommendation I gave them his name." He looked at me, embarrassed. "I would have given them yours except that Cole knew the property and such."

"Not a problem," I assured him. And I meant it. A little probate work goes a long way. It's tedious and deadly dull stuff.

Benson finished off his beer, stood and stretched. "Guess I'd best be going. I appreciate the beer." He gave me an avuncular smile. "And the company."

"Any time."

The smile lingered. I could tell by his expression that he was seeing my mother's face in my own. "You take care, Kali. I don't like to see you involved in such nasty business."

I gave him the assurances he wanted, then walked him to the door. After he'd left I went back to sorting through Harding's file, making notes to myself and trying to superimpose a sense of order on Sam's chaos. When I finished, I drew up a list of people I wanted to talk to, then checked my watch. Too late to do any real business, but I called Caroline Anderson, Lisa's friend from the Lazy Q Diner, to see if we couldn't arrange a meeting for the next day.

"I already talked to the police," she said.

"I know, but I'd like to talk with you too."

"Is that legal? I mean, my talking to both sides. There's not a problem with that?"

"It's perfectly legal and not at all unusual. If it would make you feel better, you can check with the DA's office first."

She still seemed hesitant.

"It won't take long," I said.

"Okay, I guess. Around one o'clock?"

I took down her address, then fixed myself a quickie dinner of noodles and cheese, opened the novel I'd bought in anticipation of Tom's absence and tried to shake my thoughts free of Lisa and Amy and Wes.

It worked fine until I got into bed. Then I lay there in the dark, besieged by images that took on a life of their own. I found myself trying to imagine what it felt like to have your throat slashed.

5

I awoke the next morning with a sore throat. Whether it was induced by the glinty, razorlike knife that had haunted my dreams, or was simply the precursor to a cold, I couldn't tell. I swallowed a couple of vitamin C tablets just to be on the safe side, gargled with some heavy-duty antiseptic that smelled like tar paper and tasted worse, then drove into town for my appointment with Sam.

He was just sitting down at his desk with a mug of coffee and something that looked like a large, sugar-encrusted donut with a glob of purple jelly where the hole should have been.

"You want some coffee?" he offered by way of greeting.

Sam's coffee is pretty terrible unless you cut it heavily with cream and sugar the way he does. "Thanks, I think I'll pass." I took a chair across from him. "Your doctor know you eat that stuff?"

He licked a finger. "Doctors don't know everything."

"One thing they do know, though, is heart disease."

Ignoring me, Sam bit into the pastry.

"I thought you were supposed to be watching your fat and cholesterol."

"I do. It's chicken or fish and fresh vegetables for dinner almost every night."

"And anything you want during the day?"

His eyes settled on mine for a moment. "You reach an age, Kali, where you start to see that longevity isn't all it's cracked up to be. I'd rather enjoy the years I have than live forever on some damned bean sprout diet." He broke off a sizable hunk of pastry, dunked it in his heavily creamed coffee, then plopped it into his mouth with a self-satisfied smile. "That reminds me, Jake Harding and his wife have invited us for dinner on Saturday."

"Us?"

"Jake would like to meet you. It'll be a good opportunity to bring everyone up to speed on the case. I hope you're free, about seven?"

"Don't you think I should meet with Wes first? Make sure *he* wants me working in his defense?"

"Sure. Why don't you go there this afternoon? I'll call over to the jail and have your name added to the list. I'd like your take on Wes anyway."

"You've told him that I'll be working with you?"

Sam nodded. "Not you specifically, but he knows I'm going to be calling in someone to help. I don't expect there to be a problem."

Sam's secretary popped in for a minute with some letters for him to sign. When she left, he brushed away the crumbs and cleared a spot on his desk, which he then used for a foot rest.

"Now the way I see it," he said, "we'll need to take a two-pronged approach with this thing. We'll chip away at every piece of state's evidence we can—you know the game there—but we'd also be wise to come up with another suspect to toss to the jury. We've got to make our theory of what happened at least as plausible as theirs."

"From what I read in the reports, that's not going to be easy."

"No, it isn't. I have a feeling we haven't seen the worst of it either."

"Any chance of pleading to a lesser offense?"

"I doubt Willis would go for it."

"Curt Willis is handling this for the prosecution?"

Sam nodded.

He was right; we'd never plead it out. Curt loved trials the way young boys love fresh dirt.

"Not that it matters in any case," Sam continued. "Wes won't hear of it. Claims he's been singled out on account of his reputation and previous brushes with the law."

"How does he explain the evidence against him?"

"He doesn't. He told the police he didn't know Lisa Cornell, and that's what he tells me too. Says he must have dropped the rabbit's foot somewhere and stained his pant leg when he got a bloody nose."

"What about the blond hair?"

Sam shrugged. "He says he's partial to blondes."

"Does he realize he could be facing the death penalty?"

California law allows the prosecutor to seek the death penalty when a homicide involves any of a number of special circumstances, one of which is multiple victims. Not only did we have two victims, we had real heartbreakers— a loving mother and her young child. Added to that, we had a defendant with a reputation for stirring up trouble and a crime that had apparently been committed in cold blood. I had to believe Willis would seek the maximum penalty.

"I've tried getting through to him," Sam said. "Maybe you'll have better luck. In the meantime, we're stuck with the story he gave the police."

"A story that's so lame, it's laughable."

Sam removed his feet from the desk and leaned forward. "A story that's so lame, it just might be the truth. If he were guilty, don't you think he'd have come up with something better?"

It was a thought that had crossed my mind too. But it wasn't really an approach you could argue to the jury.

"The trouble is," I said, "the jurors' sympathies are going to be with Lisa and Amy. That's going to make it hard for them to find reasonable doubt."

"It's all in how you package it. What we need to do is portray Lisa Cornell in a way the jury will find a little less sympathetic." He sipped his coffee. "I'll start working on the necessary motions. Why don't you find out what you can about Lisa? Let's see if we can't come up with another way for this to have happened."

"It won't be easy. Lisa was about as likable as a new kitten."

Sam looked at me over the rim of his cup. "Nobody's life is spotless, Kali, and nobody is without enemies. If you look hard enough, you'll find dirt."

Trash the victim: It was a common enough defense strategy, but it left an unpleasant taste in my mouth. I thought about arguing the point but knew I'd lose. Instead, I told Sam about my appointment with Lisa's friend from work, Caroline Anderson, and about my meeting with Kevin in the barn.

"Do you know anything about a man called Granger?" I asked after a moment. "He supposedly lives in the woods and sometimes slept in Lisa Cornell's barn."

Sam shook his head. "Never heard of him. You think he knows something?"

I shrugged. "Probably not, but I think it's worth following up. I'm willing to bet he wasn't interviewed by the police."

"Do what you need to, money's not a problem. Jake has given us a green light on this."

"It's a good thing, since we're starting with nothing."

"Worse than that, I'm afraid. We're starting with a client who's painted himself into a corner and doesn't seem to care."

After leaving Sam's I stopped by my office to make a few phone calls on other cases and to down a cup of honest-to-goodness coffee. Then I drove over to talk with Caroline Anderson.

Silver Creek has more than doubled in size since the time I was growing up. The open pastures I remember from my youth have given way to strip malls and seemingly endless stretches of tract housing.

The Andersons lived in one of the newer developments near the highway, where the houses were packed in so tight you could practically hold hands with your neighbor by leaning out your bedroom window. The houses were small and pretty much identical, except that some had the garage on the left and some on the right. Most of the yards were landscaped, though barely, and without inspiration.

The Andersons' was not. Instead of the rectangular patch of green and lone, staked sapling, their yard was fashioned from raw earth and weeds. A child's tricycle was parked near the front door.

I rang the bell and waited. Inside a baby cried and a television audience found something uproariously funny. I was just about to ring a second time when the door opened.

"Caroline?" I asked.

She nodded wordlessly, a baby on her hip, a toddler at her feet. She was about Lisa's age, but without Lisa's sparkle. Thin, almost bony, with pale lashes, washed-out coloring and hair that went several directions at once. The only distinctive thing about her was a bruised and swollen lip.

"I'm Kali O'Brien. We talked yesterday. I wanted to ask you about Lisa Cornell."

Caroline pulled the baby closer, as though I might have designs on snatching it away. "I've been thinking about that," she said. "There's really not much I can tell you."

"Whatever you know, it's more than I do at this point."

"I don't see why you want to know about Lisa anyway. She's not the one who did anything wrong."

"Look, I know you probably think I'm the enemy here, but I'm not. I knew Lisa too, and I'm sickened by what happened to her."

Caroline's expression remained skeptical.

"The thing is," I continued, "if Wes Harding is convicted and he didn't do it, then the real killer gets off scot-free."

Of course if Wes Harding *did* do it and *wasn't* convicted, the outcome was the same. And as much as I professed to believe in the American judicial system, I knew it was far from perfect. I pushed that thought aside for the moment.

"I could use your help," I said.

"It's just that . . ."

"I won't take up much of your time," I assured her.

Caroline's eyes flickered to the street, then back to me.

The baby drooled onto the front of Caroline's blouse. She wiped its chin with her hand. "Oh, all right. But only for a few minutes. I've got to put this guy down for his nap."

With the toddler clinging to her leg, Caroline ushered me inside. The place was tight and boxlike. A kitchen to the right, living room straight ahead, stairs to the left. I'd seen mobile homes more spacious. We moved into the living room, which was furnished with a green and brown plaid couch, an orange recliner, a large-screen television, and an assortment of toys.

"Watch your step," she said, kicking aside a plastic fire engine. "Kids' toys can be lethal."

I stepped carefully. "Is that how you hurt your lip?"

She turned. Her eyes met mine briefly, then shifted away. "Yeah, I tripped." But there was a telling pause before she spoke, a skipped beat that made me think the toys were getting a bum rap.

"I'm sorry," I said. "I wasn't trying to pry; it's just that it looks painful."

"It's not so bad." Her voice was defensive.

We sat on opposite ends of the couch, the toddler burrowing under the seat cushion between us. The baby began to wail.

"What is it you want to know?" Caroline asked, bouncing the infant on her knee.

"I understand you and Lisa were pretty good friends."

"Not really."

I heard a car slow down on the street out front. Caroline stiffened. The car passed and she relaxed.

"Velma seemed to think you two were friends."

"I mean we were friends, but not like best friends or anything." The baby kept howling. Caroline tried draping him over her shoulder and patting his back. "I don't think

Lisa had any really good friends. She was kind of a private person."

"Standoffish?"

Caroline shook her head, offering the baby her little finger to suck on. "No, not like that. She was friendly, and people liked her. It's just that she kept her distance. We'd talk about kids or customers or about Carl, but not much that was personal."

"Carl?"

"The cook. Or rather the *chef,* as he wants to be called. Velma's husband." With a sigh, Caroline unbuttoned her blouse. "Oh, all right," she said to the yowling infant. "I give up." She brought him to her breast and he quieted instantly. "This kid's as stubborn as a mule. Takes after his father."

There was an interval of silence.

"You were telling me about Velma's husband," I prompted.

"Yeah. The guy's a lech. And crazy besides. You go to pick up your order and he makes you lean way over to get it so he can look down your blouse. You don't give him a peek, he makes sure your next meal is either raw or overcooked. The way he's always making suggestive remarks, you'd think he was eighteen instead of almost sixty."

"Why do you put up with it?"

She shrugged. "It's not a bad place to work. Even with Carl. And I make decent money."

"Is that why Lisa put up with it too, because of the money?"

"Lisa never got too upset about Carl. She'd threaten him with everything from bringing a sexual harassment suit to telling Velma, but it was all talk. It was almost like she enjoyed the attention. Jeremy, stop it!"

Caroline turned to rein in the toddler, who was now using the cushion between us as a trampoline. In the process she detached herself from the baby's mouth. He let out an angry, ear-splitting wail. Caroline sighed again, rehooked the baby, then turned back to me as if it were all my fault.

Which in a way maybe it was. "Look, I'm sorry," I said. "I can come back another time if that would be better."

"It won't be any different." Her tone was resigned. Jeremy tried crawling into her lap, whimpering that he was hungry. "You just ate," she protested as she endeavored to nudge him to the side.

The kid was not easily dissuaded. He butted the baby with his head and continued to whimper. "I wanna cookie. And juice."

"Wait until I'm finished here, would you?"

It was clear that waiting was not Jeremy's strong suit. And putting up with whiny kids was not mine.

"I'll get it for him," I offered. "If you'll tell me what and where."

"No, he can wait for . . ."

Jeremy had been tugging at the baby's bootie. Suddenly it came loose and Jeremy toppled back against the coffee table. Although he didn't appear to be hurt, he wailed loudly.

Caroline sighed. "Okay, you win. Cookies and juice." She turned to me apologetically. "Is it okay if we move into the kitchen?"

"Sure."

Still holding the baby to her chest, she tried to open the refrigerator with her elbow. When I repeated my offer of help she smiled gratefully. "Thanks. The apple juice is in a pitcher. You can use the Snoopy cup by the sink. The cookies are in the drawer next to the stove." From the look on her face you'd have thought I was offering to scrub the kitchen floor, which I'd noticed needed it badly. The soles of my shoes stuck with every step.

I poured Jeremy's juice and dug out the bag of frosted animal cookies. We settled at the Formica table, which had been squeezed into one end of the narrow kitchen. The windows were bare, and the blue and white wallpaper had already begun to peel at the edges, but I noticed she'd hung an embroidered sampler on the wall near the door. *Home, Sweet Home.*

When she saw me looking, she laughed. "My mother-in-law made it," she said, in a voice that spoke volumes. "Now, where were we?"

"You were saying that Lisa was friendly, but distant."

"Right. Sometimes it was more than distant. There was a restlessness about her that was hard to pin down. It was like she was there, but she wasn't."

"Do you think she was involved with drugs?"

"I couldn't say for sure, but I'd guess not. I don't know how she'd afford them, for one thing. And she was pretty careful about her body because of the headaches. Besides, she was into being responsible. I got the feeling she'd knocked around quite a bit before, but now she wanted to get her life back on track for Amy's sake."

"How about recent conflicts? Was there anyone who was angry with her?"

Caroline's tone had lightened considerably after we'd shared the quip about her mother-in-law. But now her expression grew subdued again. She hesitated, then shook her head. "Nothing that I recall."

"Do you know where Lisa was living before she moved to Silver Creek?"

"The Bay Area somewhere. Maybe Berkeley. But I don't think she was there long."

"Did she ever talk about her husband?"

"She didn't go on about him, if that's what you mean, the way some people do after a marriage has gone south. But she'd mention him now and then, in passing. His name was Jerry. Jerk-head Jerry was how she referred to him. To tell the truth, I don't think she had a lot of respect for men, period."

"I understand she was engaged, though, to Philip Stockman."

Caroline gave a derisive laugh. "Some days she was, some days she wasn't. You could say she had mixed feelings about it."

"Any idea why?"

She shrugged. "I guess one bad marriage is enough to make you gun-shy."

I nodded. I'd had the bad part without the marriage and it had certainly made me gun-shy. "Did she ever mention Wes Harding?"

"No. Why?"

"I was wondering if they'd crossed paths."

Caroline shook her head. "I don't recall her mentioning him. Like I said, though, we didn't get into a lot of personal stuff."

Despite the disclaimer, it seemed to me that Caroline knew a fair amount about Lisa.

"The only time we talked was at work. Duane didn't like me hanging around with . . ." Caroline looked embarrassed. "With 'her type,' was how he put it."

I raised a brow. "Her type?"

"You know, because she was divorced. Duane was afraid it might rub off or something." The baby had fallen asleep.

Caroline adjusted her blouse, then leaned back against the chair. She seemed uncertain what she wanted to say next. "Lisa talked about taking a class over at the community college. She wanted me to go too so we could commute together. It was only one evening a week, but Duane about had a hemorrhage."

"So you didn't." My response was blunter than I'd intended, but Caroline didn't pick up on it.

Her voice was flat. "By that time Lisa and I weren't such good friends anyway. We both had our own lives, you know. Our own interests." She let her gaze grow distant.

Jeremy had finished his cookies. He climbed off the stool and put his head in his mother's lap. She ran her fingers through his honey-brown hair.

"I've got to put the kids down for their naps now."

I carried Jeremy's juice cup back to the sink. "Thanks for talking to me."

"I hope it helped."

6

It was close to four o'clock when I pulled into a parking space in front of the county jail. I'd stopped at the grocery along the way to buy dog food and toothpaste, then driven the four-lane highway to Hadley at well under the speed limit, which said something about my level of enthusiasm for meeting with Wes.

True to his word, Sam had taken care of the necessary approvals. I showed my ID to the sergeant at the desk, signed my name, paraded through a metal detector and found myself upstairs in the spartan, windowless attorney's room before I'd had a chance to catch my breath. I was standing, silently practicing my introductory remarks, when the guard brought Wes to the door.

"Handcuffs off or on?" the guard asked, addressing me.

In truth I'd have been more comfortable with them on. That was not the way to gain a client's confidence, however. "Off," I said, without meeting either man's eyes.

The guard grunted. "I'll be outside if you need me." He closed the door and snapped the lock.

Wes eased himself into the nearest chair. He was shorter than I expected, maybe 5´10˝, broad-shouldered and solidly built. His hair was dark and glossy, the way I remembered it, but now dusted lightly across the crown with silver. His skin was smooth and unwrinkled, and seemed swarthier than it had in his youth. Noting the broad cheekbones and deep-set eyes, it struck me for the first time that Wes might have a trace of Hispanic blood in his ancestry.

He tilted his head and gave me a long look. "Well, well, Ms. Attorney. I take it you're the newest hired gun on my defense team."

I took a seat opposite him, the narrow table between us. "I'm Kali O'Brien," I said, opening my notepad. "I'll be working on your defense with Sam Morrison. But only if that's the way you want it."

" 'The way I want it,' " he mimicked. "Jesus, that's a good one. I can't remember the last time I had *anything* the way I wanted it."

Wes rubbed his wrists where the handcuffs had been. His hands were large and muscular, his fingers thick. His arms were thick too, and covered with curly, dark hair. A thin, satiny white scar ran diagonally across his left forearm, almost as if it had been brushed on with acrylic.

"So which is it?" I asked. "You want me on the case or not?"

"Sure, the more the merrier."

I clicked my pen, cleared my throat and wondered what in the hell I was doing there.

Wes leaned back in the chair, arms behind his head. "Kali O'Brien," he said, giving the words rhythm. "Kali-o, calico. I remember you. We went to school together."

"For a while."

"Until I got kicked out. That's what you mean, isn't it?"

His eyes locked on mine. They were dark, like the rest of him, and suddenly without expression. Sorcerer's eyes was the way I'd thought of them in high school. *Gypsy magic,* in Sabrina's words.

I ignored the look, and the question. "I want to go over a few things with you," I said. "I know you've covered this before with Sam, but we need to do it again. Let's start with the Friday night in question. I believe you left work about five, is that right?"

"Yeah, more or less."

"More or less?"

"I don't punch a time clock."

I tapped my pen against the table. The noise resonated off the bare walls and floor. "After you left work, what did you do?"

He shrugged. "The usual."

"I need to know the particulars, everything you did that evening from the time you left work until you went to bed."

"Everything? You mean like when I took a leak and that kind of stuff?"

I ignored the smirk. "If it's relevant."

A fly buzzed overhead. Wes stood, slapped it between his palms, wiped his hands on his pant legs, then looked at me with a flicker of something close to amusement. The guy had good reflexes; I miss half the time even with a fly swatter.

He sat down again, folded his arms across his chest. "You were part of that high school crowd that hung out near the quad during lunch period, weren't you? Always joking around with one another in Latin or some damn language no one even speaks anymore."

"You were telling me about Friday night."

"*Veritas.* That means truth, doesn't it?"

I didn't answer.

"How about *stercus accidit;* you know what that means? Shit happens. I saw it on a bumper sticker, in Latin. Which one should we choose for the motto of our case?"

"About Friday."

He looked at me for a moment, then shrugged. "There's not much to tell."

"Why don't you give it a try anyway."

Wes leaned forward, elbows on the table. "I left work, went home, took a shower, had a beer. I watched a little of the A's game on television before meeting some friends down at the Oasis."

"And then?"

"And then I drank some more beer, ate a burger— excuse me, two burgers, with cheese—shot the breeze for a while, played a little pool. Pretty much what I do every Friday night."

"Except usually you're there to close the place down, and this particular night you left early."

He shrugged. "I was tired. I went home and went to bed."

"Is there anyone who can verify that? Anyone who saw you go into your house or called you at home that evening?"

"No calls. I think the police talked to the neighbors."

And one of them had heard a motorcycle on the street long after the time Wes claimed to be in bed. I decided to leave that for later. "Did you place any calls yourself? Maybe you called out for a late-night pizza, or left a message on a friend's machine."

Wes rubbed the back of a finger along his jaw, his brows furrowed. Finally he shook his head. "Not that I recall."

"You apparently got into an argument with a woman down at the Oasis," I said. "Can you tell me what it was about?"

"No."

"No?"

"No." His eyes met mine; then he sighed. "If I knew, I'd tell you. She just pissed me off, is all. I can't even remember why. It was nothing."

"You remember her name?"

"Doreen, Darnelle. Something like that. She's there most Friday nights."

"Your friends say you were in a foul mood all evening. Was Doreen the cause of it?"

"I told you, the thing with her was nothing. It was just one of those days, you know?" His voice dropped and grew thick with sarcasm. "Or maybe you don't. Maybe for you everything goes the way it's supposed to, like clockwork."

Oh boy, did he have that wrong.

Wes watched me, his gaze unwavering.

"How did you know Lisa Cornell?" I asked.

The muscle in his jaw twitched. "I didn't."

"You sure?"

"I said I didn't."

"Then how do you suppose your rabbit's foot got in her little girl's pocket?"

"How the hell should I know?"

"Take a guess."

Wes shrugged. "I lost it a couple of days earlier. Maybe the kid found it."

"A guy you work with says he saw you with it on Thursday."

"So maybe it was only one day earlier that I lost it. Or maybe the one the police found isn't mine."

"And the dirt on your motorcycle?"

"Dirt's dirt. The stuff at the Cornell place isn't monogrammed, is it?"

"Dirt's *not* all the same. Besides, we're talking about more than dirt here. There's vegetation, road oil, that sort of thing."

Another shrug. "I ride through those hills all the time. It must be a coincidence."

"There's an awful lot of coincidence about this."

"You got a better explanation?"

I rolled the pen in my hands, exasperated. The room was hot and stuffy, layered with the odors of unwashed bodies and disinfectant. I wondered if the holding cells were as bad.

Suddenly Wes rocked forward. The skin around his eyes and mouth was tight. "You don't believe me, do you? You think I killed Lisa Cornell and her kid."

"What I think isn't the issue."

His laugh was bitter. "Right, you've got to defend me either way."

"I don't *got* to do anything."

"You get paid either way too. Buy yourself a fancy new car, go out to dinner. Maybe when this is all over you'll take a little breather at some resort in the south of France. Win or lose, it's all in a day's work to you."

"To a certain extent that's true," I said, with growing irritation. "But I work hard. And win or lose, I'll have earned my fee."

"That's reassuring."

"And I'll have done my best for you."

This time the laugh was more of a snort. "Right, I forgot. You're one of those super-achiever types. Wouldn't dream of doing less than your personal best. I know you went to a big-name college, and I bet you went to some equally big-name law school. Me, I'm such a fuck-up. It's a good thing I've got you on my team."

I swallowed my anger, which I realized was really more frustration than genuine outrage. And it was directed as much at myself as at Wes. Why had I let him get under my skin?

"Believe it or not," I said carefully, "lawyers are more effective when they don't take a personal interest in their cases. I'm a good lawyer and I'm going to do the best job I can for you. So will Sam. But it will be much easier, and much more effective, if you cooperate instead of fighting us at every step."

Wes's expression was one of clamped-down anger. He looked at me and said nothing.

"Okay," I began again, recapping, "let's see what we've got. Someone killed Lisa Cornell and her daughter. It wasn't you. Unfortunately, you have no alibi and the police happen to have quite a bit of evidence against you."

"Truth is often stranger than fiction."

"We're going to have a hard time selling that to the jury."

His expression was derisive. "The courtroom angle's a bitch, isn't it?" He turned so that he was no longer facing me.

"You know, there's a chance you might be able to plead to a lesser offense. You were drinking that night, and angry about something. Maybe you took a ride through the hills on your way home, got lost or sidetracked and wound up at Lisa Cornell's place. She might have startled you or maybe threatened to call the police, and you panicked. We could make a case for something less than murder one."

Wes slammed his fist against the table and flew to his

feet. "Jesus, don't you listen? I didn't do it." He banged on the door for the guard. "Enough of this crap. I'm out of here."

"Think about it," I told him.

"Hey, guard!" He beat on the door with his open palms.

"Please, Wes. At least *think* about your defense." My voice had an urgency that surprised me.

It must have surprised Wes too. He turned to look at me.

"Sam and I know the law," I told him. "But you're the one who knows where you were that night, what you did or didn't do. It would help the case if we had a coherent scenario that would explain away the evidence against you." I paused. "And we certainly don't want to be surprised in court."

The guard opened the door and nodded in my direction, ignoring Wes as though he were invisible. "You finished here?"

I nodded. "I guess so."

The guard thrust Wes against the wall face first, then reached into his pocket for the handcuffs. I turned away, embarrassed to watch.

"Remember Mr. Alridge's history class?" Wes asked over his shoulder. "You sat two rows in from the front, on the left by the windows."

The handcuffs snapped shut with a sharp click. Glancing back, I could see the hard metal edge dig into the flesh of Wes's wrist.

"Bet you don't remember where I sat," he said.

The guard turned him around and propelled him toward the door. Wes stopped and twisted back to face me. "In fact, what I remember most about that class was watching you. It was a whole lot more interesting than history. You'd sit there with that look of rapture on your face, like you were interested as hell in all that stuff about George Washington and the Continental Congress. But you used to spend an awful lot of time tugging at the crotch of your jeans." He grinned. "I always wondered if you had your mind on history at all."

After the guard ushered Wes out I stuffed my papers into my briefcase and stomped down the hall to the elevator. The only thing worse than an uncooperative client was one who was also hostile. As far as I could tell, I'd just grabbed the brass ring.

He was also wrong. I *had* liked history. Alridge was one of those teachers who made the subject come alive. Could I help it if tight jeans had been the fashion?

Angrily, I poked the elevator button. Wes had been wrong about something else too. I'd known exactly where he sat. In history and every other class we had together. It was always in the last row, at the back of the room. And it was always the first spot my eyes were drawn to each day. Gypsy magic.

I shifted my briefcase to the other arm and took a deep breath to calm myself. Most of what I needed to do in preparing the case didn't directly involve Wes anyway. With luck, I could do my part without having to interview him further.

Still, I thought it would be helpful if he'd give us something more to work with than "I didn't do it."

Unless, of course, there was nothing more to give because he really hadn't.

The elevator arrived and I got on. Two floors down, I was joined by Curt Willis, deputy DA and prosecuting attorney in the Harding case.

"Hey, Kali," he said by way of greeting. "It's been awhile."

I couldn't honestly say whether it had been or not, but I nodded anyway. Curt's a master of small talk and doesn't much care what you say in return. He's about my age, honey-blond hair with matching brows and lashes. Good-looking without actually being attractive. At least not in my book. I find him a bit too polished to be considered sexy, although we'd dated a couple of times when I first got to town.

"I visited your old stomping grounds last week," he said. "San Francisco's quite a place."

I nodded again.

Curt smiled, looked at his watch. "Say, it's just about quitting time; you want to have a drink? It would be nice to talk to a thinking human being for a change. I don't believe I've had a conversation all day with anyone brighter than a toadstool."

"Surely it's not that bad."

"Close."

Although I hadn't actually accepted Curt's offer, we struck out in the direction of Ollie's as though I had. Curt seemed to assume I would join him, and the appeal of a drink won out over any reservations I might have had.

Friday nights are usually pretty busy, but we were early enough to get a table away from the noisiest part of the room.

"I hear you're working on the Wes Harding case," he remarked after we'd settled in.

"Along with Sam Morrison."

Curt gave me a Cheshire cat grin. "You're going to lose this one, sweetheart. Take it from me."

I wasn't bothered by the *sweetheart* bit; that's the way Curt talked. But I was caught somewhat off guard by the conviction in his tone.

"I wouldn't be so sure about winning," I told him. The words were pure bravado on my part, and I hoped they didn't sound as phony as they felt.

He grinned again. "This case is going to be my ticket out of here. It's already made the Sacramento papers, and there's a woman at a television station in San Francisco who wants to follow the whole trial. People are going to be watching this, Kali, important people. It's the opportunity I've been waiting for."

Like most lawyers, Curt liked winning. More than that, though, he wanted to make a name for himself in a bigger pond than the likes of Silver Creek. The scuttlebutt was that he was a hard worker and fairly bright, but he'd had the misfortune of being a mediocre student at a mediocre law school. From there, it's a tough road to the top.

Our drinks arrived. I licked at the salt on my margarita. "You want to be careful what you wish for, you know."

"You mean about getting out of this town?"

I nodded.

Curt curled his fingers around his glass. "I don't understand how you could have traded a prestigious San Francisco practice for this." He gestured with his arm. I assumed he was referring to the town rather than the bar.

"As I've explained before, it wasn't exactly a trade. Not a voluntary one, anyway."

"With your credentials and experience, you must have a wealth of options. What does Silver Creek have to offer?"

"Free parking?"

He laughed. "Given the wages in this two-bit town, you need free parking."

In truth, my options had not been as wide-open as Curt imagined. With a growing glut of lawyers, particularly at my mid-career level, and firms everywhere cutting back, the market was tight. I could have beat the bushes for a job in another big firm, gone through the whole prove-yourself-worthy-of-partnership contest, and then found myself once again bounced out the door for reasons over which I had no control.

My other option was to go it on my own, which is what I'd chosen to do. Why I'd chosen to do it in Silver Creek was less clear to me.

Curt downed half his vodka martini in one swallow. "You think I ought to set my sights on San Francisco or Los Angeles?"

"Depends on whether you prefer fog or smog."

Nary a chuckle. Curt took his career options seriously. "It's a long shot, I know, but someday I might even wind up being appointed to the bench." Finally, he allowed himself a smile. "Wouldn't that be something."

"You'd better concentrate on winning this case first."

"Oh, I'm going to win it." He reached into his briefcase, pulled out a file and slapped it on the table in front of me.

"What's this?"

"The lab report on clothing items taken from Wes Harding's place. The blood on the jeans was definitely not Wes's." He paused for effect. "Not only does the blood group match Lisa Cornell's, it's type B, which is found in only seven percent of the entire Caucasian population."

"That's still a lot of people."

He nodded. "Yeah, including me. But the jury's not going to be looking at the rest of that seven-percent pool. They're going to know the blood was Lisa's."

"Did they do a DNA analysis?"

Curt shook his head. "The sample wasn't fresh enough for that."

"Then there's no way to prove it's Lisa's blood. You're talking probabilities, not certainty."

"Sweetheart, there ain't nothing in life that's certain, but this is about as close as you get."

7

I suppose on one level it was good news. If the prosecution had a slam-dunk case against Wes Harding, who could blame us for losing?

"You won't hate me for trouncing you in court, will you?" Curt asked with a self-satisfied smile.

While Curt's certainty about the case made me uneasy, it also made me more determined than ever to fight back. I gave his hand a gentle pat. "You're not going to be the one doing the trouncing, *sweetheart.*"

It surprised me to discover I meant it. I don't like to lose, but more than that, I found myself feeling oddly supportive of Wes.

Curt's smile broadened. Lack of confidence was not one of his shortcomings.

He signaled the waitress and ordered us each a second drink. By unspoken accord, we left further discussion of the Wes Harding issue for another day and venue. Instead, we swapped lawyer jokes and told war stories about cases and clients from hell. I declined his invitation for dinner largely because I felt we'd about run out of things to say to one another.

Not that it wasn't pleasant while it lasted. Despite his smug and sometimes pompous posturing, Curt Willis was an easy companion. There'd been a time, once, when I'd been angry with Tom and full of enough wine that I'd actually considered the possibility of romantic involvement. Luckily, Curt had had as much to drink as I had, and he'd passed out on the living room sofa before I had a chance to consider further.

We parted ways at the door to Ollie's. I stopped back by the office, picked up my messages and the file of clippings Myra had set out for me, then headed home by way of Taco Bell. My take-out meal was cold by the time I got back, but at least I didn't have to cook. Or clean up afterwards.

What with Curt's announcement about the blood-type results and the two margaritas I'd put away at Ollie's, I wasn't in much of a mood for work. Nonetheless, in the interests of keeping my clients happy, and thus in a mood to pay their bills, I made myself a cup of coffee and set about returning the most urgent messages.

This was the downside of small-town practice. While I'd been at Goldman & Latham, I'd often worked late nights and weekends, but rarely had I been called upon to deal with flesh-and-blood clients other than during regular office hours. Since a round or two of telephone tag was more or less expected, few people sat around awaiting your call. Small-town clients, on the other hand, expected more personalized service.

There were only five messages, and I took care of the first three quickly. The remaining two were from Ms. Sheri Pearl, daughter and conservator of the more affable Mrs.

Irma Pearl. On the bottom of the second message Myra had penciled in her own communication—*Would you PLEASE call this woman before she has a blowout in her bloomers!*

I placed the call, giving a silent prayer of thanks when the answering machine clicked on. I would leave a quick message and be off the hook, at least temporarily. But no sooner had I started to leave my name than the phone picked up.

"Goodness, Kali, I've been trying to reach you for days."

Sheri was apparently home after all. "I've been swamped," I told her.

"I made an appointment for next week, but I wanted to talk to you first so you'd have a chance to think things through before our meeting."

And therefore bill her for a short conference rather than a lengthy one. Clients seem to think they ought to get your thinking time for free.

"I've been going over Mother's finances—and between the money she poured into sweepstakes and the bogus investments she got herself involved in—well, there's not a lot left. Certainly nothing liquid. I need to raise some cash and I thought I'd start by selling the house. There's no sense keeping it."

"Except that your mother gets such pleasure from visiting for the afternoon."

"She's never going to be able to actually move back. You know that as well as I do. And the place is an effort to keep up."

"I thought your cousin was staying there."

"She is, but that's certainly not a permanent solution."

I was sure none of us imagined it was. But Irma Pearl hadn't wanted to sell the place, and it had only been five weeks since she'd moved into the nursing home, on what she undoubtedly assumed was a temporary basis. Not that Irma's wishes mattered anymore. Not legally anyway. That's what conservatorship is all about.

"Besides," Sheri added, "the market for houses in that price range is quite strong at the moment. And summer's a good time to sell. We could probably move it fairly quickly."

The picture was becoming clearer. Sheri was, among other things, a real estate agent.

"I thought I'd sell the duplex as well," she continued in an off-hand manner, as though we were playing Monopoly.

"That's steady income."

"And a steady headache."

Double commission time, I thought, rather nastily. "We'll have to get court approval," I told her. "They oversee sales of real property."

"The court oversees everything," she said, exasperated. "I'm the one who does all the work while they sit there and create new hoops for me to jump through."

She had a point. Being a conservator was, for the most part, a royal pain in the behind. You took it on out of love or a sense of duty, and not because of any inherent rewards. "Have you talked to your mother about this?"

"Mother doesn't know day from night half the time." Sheri sighed. "I'm going to have to sell the house; there's no way around it. But I don't see the point in upsetting Mother by bringing it up just yet."

Much as I hated to admit it, Sheri was probably right. Besides, I reminded myself begrudgingly, it was Sheri, not Irma, who was my client. "I'll get going with the preliminaries. We can talk about the details next week when we meet."

"That's fine." She paused for a moment. "I hear you're involved with the Lisa Cornell case."

"Right."

"You don't happen to know what's going on with the house, do you? I've got a client who might be interested."

"That's not my area of involvement, I'm afraid."

"Well, if you hear anything, let me know. It's an unusual piece of property. Runs all the way past the creek, then fans out so there's access from the old highway where Foster's Freeze used to be. There's a lot of potential there."

When someone, particularly a real estate someone, starts talking about potential, it's a sure sign there's an unspoken agenda. But I figured Sheri wasn't going to tell me anything more on her own, and I didn't have the energy to push it. My only hope was that whatever potential finally won out, it didn't involve subdividing the property into postage-stamp lots. There was enough of that going on around town already.

I made one last phone call, to Sam, to tell him about the lab results on Wes's bloodstained jeans. He wasn't in and I decided against leaving a message, although I was certain I found the news more troublesome than he would. Sam's a great believer in keeping the world on an even keel. "It's not a good development," he'd say when I told him about the blood-typing, "but it's not the end of the world either."

Maybe not, but I thought it pointed the way pretty clearly.

I was pulling out my notes on Irma Pearl's conservatorship when Sabrina called.

"I've got a new lawyer joke for you," she said. In the background I could hear the clink of ice against glass. Vodka tonic. After five o'clock there was never any doubt.

"I don't like lawyer jokes," I told her.

"You'll like this one. See, this man breaks into a bunker in Iraq and finds Saddam Hussein, Muamar Gaddafi and a lawyer. The guy has only two bullets in his gun. What does he do?" She waited.

"I give up."

"He shoots the lawyer twice."

"This is supposed to make me laugh?"

Sabrina sighed. "I thought it might. What's the matter, you didn't used to be so testy."

"Sorry. Bad day."

"Did you call the attorney I told you about at Golden Gate Savings?"

I hadn't even written down his number. "I'm not interested in working for a bank, Sabrina."

"It's this Wes Harding thing, isn't it? That's what's got you so riled up."

"I'm not riled up, I'm tired." But she was right, Wes Harding was on my mind.

By the time I'd finished talking with Sabrina I was in no mood for work. I took Loretta and Barney out for their evening romp, then poured myself a hefty shot of brandy and settled in with a "Star Trek" rerun. If Tom had been there with me it would have been a nearly perfect Friday night.

Summer mornings in Silver Creek are magical niches in time that make me happy to be alive. In the Bay Area I'd grown accustomed to waking under habitually gray skies and rarely seeing the sun until noon. But here in the foothills the sun slides easily over the horizon, spreading fingers of pink and purple across the vast expanse of open sky. The morning breeze is cool enough that it prickles the skin, but the air underneath is awash with the promise of warmth. I made myself a cup of coffee and took it out back with the file of news clippings on Lisa Cornell's death.

I moved my chair to a spot in the sun, propped my feet on a section of fallen pine and started going through the articles chronologically. Early pieces focused on the grisly nature of the crime scene itself and expressions of disbelief from neighbors. There was some speculation about the deaths being the work of a serial killer, but this was discounted almost immediately by a police spokesperson, who noted there was nothing about the crime to support the premise. Also squelched at the outset was one man's theory about a federally sanctioned invasion of alien body snatchers.

The press had been thorough, talking to friends and neighbors in addition to official police sources. One article made note of a taxi cab that had been seen that Friday night stopped beside an empty lot near the Cornell place. Another alluded to sightings of a van and a pickup truck, both of which had struck their respective viewers as "suspicious." There was, interestingly enough, no mention of a motorcycle by any of Lisa's neighbors.

After Wes was arrested, the stories shifted focus. One account, based on interviews with his buddies, covered his activities on the evening in question. It added nothing to the information I'd gleaned from the police report. A second piece delivered a spattering of background information on Wes. He had dropped out of school during his senior year, then earned a high school diploma by taking the GED exam. He'd spent two years in the army, a month in detox, and a couple of weekends in jail. His employment record was spotty, but he'd earned good marks from his boss at the auto shop where he'd been working since his return to Silver Creek three years ago.

In addition, there was the son-of-the-prominent-physician angle, which appeared in one form or another in every article. Jake Harding's capsule bio was given almost as much attention as Wes's, although the papers were careful to note that the relationship was that of stepfather and son rather than a biological one.

There'd been little coverage in the papers recently, but I knew all that would change once we got closer to trial. Too bad I didn't share Curt's enthusiasm for finding myself front-page news.

I slipped the last of the clippings back into the file, then shut my eyes for a moment to enjoy the caress of golden warmth on my back. Eventually I took my empty coffee cup and dragged myself into the house. I wasn't eager to tilt at windmills, especially on what was shaping up to be a spectacular Saturday. But in the interest of thoroughness I thought I should talk to Lisa's neighbors myself. And while I was at it, with Wes Harding's. There was a small chance one of them had seen something that never made it into the official report—or the newspapers.

Wes lived in a narrow, two-story house that reminded me of those San Francisco Victorians that had yet to be gentrified. The neighborhood was in the older section of town, a pleasant if somewhat time-worn stretch up the hill from the public square. I tried the houses to either side of him and across the street. No one had seen Wes come or go the Friday night of the murders. The gentleman who'd reported hearing a motorcycle around midnight was Vic Lorrey. He lived four houses to the south of Wes, near the intersection.

"That damn thing drives me crazy," Lorrey said, tapping his cane on the ground for emphasis. "Roars past at all hours of the day and night, loud as a jet engine. Half the time I think that young punk guns it just to annoy me."

Lorrey had been a big man; you could see it in his features. His body had shriveled with age, but his voice was still deep and strong. "It's been a whole lot quieter since they locked him up," he added tersely.

"What time was it you heard the motorcycle?"

"Late. It woke me from my sleep."

"And you're sure it was Friday night you heard it?"

"Of course I'm sure. That's what I told the police."

Lorrey hadn't opened the screen door. I felt like I was talking through a wall. "What time do you normally go to bed?" I asked.

"It varies."

"What time did you go to bed Friday night?"

He hesitated. "I'm not sure."

"So you don't really have any idea what time you heard the motorcycle?"

"It was late, like I told you."

"Midnight?"

"Maybe."

"What makes you sure it was Wes Harding you heard?"

"Who else would it be?" Lorrey snapped. "He's back and forth all day long, all night long. A goddamn neighborhood nuisance."

"Wes works during the day," I pointed out.

Lorrey's mouth puckered. "Don't think you can dissuade me, young lady. The racket goes on day and night. I know what I hear. It's that damn motorcycle."

Score one for our side, I thought. As a witness Vic Lorrey would not stand up well under cross-examination. It brought me up short to realize I felt a little like a gunslinger looking to add another notch to her pistol.

I didn't fare as well in Lisa's neighborhood. I trudged from house to house like an encyclopedia salesman, while the sun got higher and brighter and hotter. No one had seen anything unusual that night. No one could speculate on any reason why Lisa and Amy had been killed. I talked to the woman who'd seen the suspicious truck, but she couldn't tell me any more about it than that.

"It was a truck," she said.

Old? New? Color? Insignia?

"A truck," she repeated. And no, it hadn't been parked at the Cornell place; it had mercly driven up the road slowly.

I was about ready to give up when I chanced onto Mrs. Arabagucci. She was a substantially built older woman, with broad shoulders, wide hips, and heavy legs. Her hair was thick, more gray than black, and pulled into a knot at the back of her head. She looked about as friendly as a bulldog, but looks can be deceiving. As it turned out, Mrs. Arabagucci was not only willing to talk to me, she'd clearly been talking to just about everyone in the neighborhood. Moreover, it was Mrs. Arabagucci who'd told the police about the taxi.

"Turns out it was nothing," she said, leaning on the hoe she'd been wielding when I interrupted. "That new couple about half a mile up the road called a cab to take them to the airport. The police verified it, though it's still about the stupidest thing I've come across. Can you imagine the expense of taking a cab to the airport?"

I'd come across things a whole lot stupider, but I murmured something that sounded sympathetic anyway. "I understand there were other neighbors who spotted suspicious vehicles that night."

"That's right. The woman up the road a piece saw a pickup truck drive past, and Sally Baund saw a light-colored van. Neither one amounted to anything."

"Where's Sally Baund live?" None of the neighbors I'd talked to so far had mentioned the van.

She gave me the address and pointed up the hill. "You won't be able to talk to her, though. She's in Boston visiting her daughter. This murder business upset her something terrible. Her doctor thought it would be best if she got away for a bit."

The Baund house was one of several I'd tried where no one was home. I made a note of the name and address for follow-up at a later date.

"Did you happen to see a motorcycle that night?" I asked.

"Didn't see one; didn't hear one. I usually hear them when they go by. This is the first straight stretch in quite a while and the bikers use it to full advantage. There seem to be a number of folks who have nothing better to do than charge through the hills at high speed. Though not so often at night."

Interesting. Not one neighbor had heard a motorcycle that night. We'd be sure to make a point of it at trial. Of course, it was unlikely that anyone approaching the property with criminal intent would have roared up the road with tires squealing and engines gunned.

"Did you know Lisa Cornell?" I asked.

"Of course I knew her. We're all pretty friendly up here. Not close, mind you, but friendly."

"Can you think of any reason she might have been killed?"

Mrs. Arabagucci shook her head. "She was as nice as they come. A quiet thing, just like her aunt, but without the same standoffish air. A couple of months ago I took up babysitting for her on Wednesday evenings. Told Lisa I didn't want to be paid, that Amy was a joy to be around, but she wouldn't hear of it. Not only paid me, but fixed me something special to eat every time."

"What was Lisa doing Wednesday evenings?"

"I didn't ask her," Mrs. Arabagucci said pointedly. "It was only for a couple of hours. I'd get there at 5:30 and Lisa was usually home by 7:30 or 8:00."

"Maybe dinner with her fiancé," I mused, thinking out loud.

Mrs. Arabagucci frowned. "Possibly."

"You sound doubtful."

She hesitated. "I raised four daughters, and I learned early on to recognize the signs of a young woman off to meet her beau. Lisa wasn't like that. It wasn't really my business where she went, you understand, but she never seemed particularly eager to go."

Of course, a woman who was feeling ambivalent about her impending marriage might not glow at the prosect of seeing her intended.

"Besides," Mrs. Arabagucci continued, "I got the distinct impression this was a short-term arrangement. Lisa thought she was imposing on me and made a point of letting me know it wouldn't be much longer. She didn't say it like a woman about to be married either."

I left my card in case Mrs. Arabagucci thought of anything further, then made a note to myself to look into

Lisa's Wednesday evenings. Sam wanted dirt. I doubted that an unpleasant evening's activity qualified, but it was likely to be the closest we came.

I spent another half hour talking with the remaining neighbors. All to no avail.

8

When I finished, it was a little after one. I didn't have to meet Sam at the Hardings until six. Since the day was about shot in terms of anything but work, I decided I might as well go for broke and pay a visit to Emmett Langley, known to his friends as Bongo. I was tempted to see if I could make my way through the woods, the way the boys did, but my last case of poison oak had been unpleasant enough to convince me the car was a wiser choice.

I'd checked the address before leaving home that morning. 57 Ferndale. I couldn't identify the house, but I knew the road well. My junior year in high school I'd had a crush on a boy who lived on the same street. I blushed to think how many times I'd driven that route in the hopes of catching a glimpse of him.

It turned out that Bongo's family lived a couple of miles from the stretch of road where I'd wasted so many hours. Theirs was a small house in need of a large amount of work. Much the same could be said for the woman who opened the door.

"Mrs. Langley?"

She nodded.

I introduced myself and explained why I was there.

She scowled at me through a screen door with enough gaping holes to make you wonder what she thought having a screen door accomplished. "I don't want him talkin' about it anymore," she said. "Poor boy's been through it all 'nough times as is. He's a delicate child. This thing's about tore him up."

I nodded sympathetically. "I understand how difficult it must be, for both of you. I won't need to get into the graphic details, and I promise not to ask anything more than is necessary."

"Doesn't matter. Whatever you ask, it'll set his mind to it again. I won't have it." She started to shut the door in my face.

"I can get a subpoena," I said. "Or I can have him come down to my office and answer my questions there. I just thought it might be more comfortable for him if we talked here."

She crossed her arms. "What is it you want to know?"

"I just want to hear his account of what happened."

Mrs. Langley glared at me for another minute, then thrust the screen door open with her elbow. No wonder it had so many holes. "Just remember, he's only thirteen."

She led me through the house, past the flickering light of the television, to the backyard. A boy was sitting on an old wooden bench, his back to the house.

"Emmett, honey," Mrs. Langley called to the boy from the porch steps. "This lady needs to ask you some more questions about those murders."

I'd thought she might stick around for a little metaphorical hand-holding if nothing else. But once she'd delivered her meager introduction and given me another stern look, she darted back inside, letting the door thump shut behind her.

The boy was listening to some dissonant rap song and whittling a piece of wood. He didn't bother to look up until I stood directly in front of him.

I reintroduced myself and sat down on the other end of the bench. I don't know much about children, but the kid didn't strike me as delicate. If anything, he was overweight, with a shadow of dark fuzz on his upper lip and the blight of adolescent acne around his nose and chin. But I suppose frailty is as much a state of mind as body.

"Do you prefer Emmett or Bongo?" I asked.

He ignored me.

"I just need to ask you a few questions," I said. "Mostly it will be a repeat of what you've already told the police."

"Why don't you just get it from them?"

"I've read their report. That's why we don't have to go into a lot of detail. But I'd like to hear what happened for myself."

He continued whittling, his expression flat.

"What are you making?" I asked.

"Don't know yet."

"It takes effort to work a piece of wood into the proper shape, doesn't it?"

"Depends."

From the pile of shavings at Bongo's feet, it was obvious he'd been at it awhile. Maybe the important thing was the process rather than the product.

"Why don't you tell me about finding the bodies," I said finally.

"What's to tell? I opened the door and they were there. Hard to miss 'em."

"This was Sunday morning, about ten?"

"Yeah."

"What were you doing at the Cornell place?"

"Looking for my brother."

"Your brother?"

"My brother Kevin." Bongo shaved the wood with short, quick strokes. "Turns out he was home, but I didn't know that then. I thought he might be over talking to Mrs. Cornell."

"And you just happened to look inside the barn?"

"I heard a noise, like a cat. I thought maybe it was trapped or something." Bongo didn't miss a beat, but something about his manner rang false.

"Let's get something straight. I know you and your friends used the barn as a place to hang out. That's not what I'm concerned about right now. But I do want the truth."

Bongo glanced over at the house.

"She can't hear us," I said. "And I'm certainly not going to tell her. Now, were you really looking for your brother?"

"Just leave me alone. I already told the police everything I know."

"Were you meeting a friend?"

He shook his head, eyes on his whittling.

"Is the noise part true?"

Silence.

"You went in there to have a cigarette, didn't you?"

More silence.

"Or maybe to look at magazines. The kind you don't want your mother to see."

The knife scraped against the wood furiously.

"Was anyone else there?"

"Not that I saw. But I didn't stick around to find out. As soon as I saw 'em, I was out of there."

"As soon as you saw the bodies?"

He nodded.

"How long are we talking about here? Five minutes? Ten minutes?"

"Probably less than a minute. One look at them was enough."

I stood and rubbed my butt. The bench was not only hard and rough, but uneven. "Besides the two bodies, was there anything else that caught your eye that morning? Gum wrapper, matchbook, loose button? Anything at all."

"I tol' you, as soon as I saw 'em, I tore out fast."

"And then what?"

He looked perplexed.

"What did you do after you left the barn?"

"I came home and told my mom."

"And she called the police?"

He nodded. "I didn't touch anything."

"Did the police think you might have?"

A shrug. "They asked." He peeled off another long piece of wood with the knife.

I watched him work for a moment. "What do you know about a man called Granger?"

The knife stopped in midair. Bongo looked up. "I know who he is. Why?"

"I understand he hung out around the barn too. I was thinking maybe he saw something."

"Granger's a fool. You can't believe anything he says."

"I'd still like to talk to him. Any idea how I'd go about finding him?"

"No." Bongo's vehemence surprised me. "You'd be wasting your time anyway," he added, turning his attention back to his whittling.

I picked up one of the smooth wood shavings from the ground. It had a sharp piney smell I remembered from my youth. "When you saw the bodies in the barn did you know right away who they were?"

"I just assumed it was Mrs. Cornell and her little girl. I didn't get too close." Bongo stopped whittling and looked up at me, briefly, then turned his gaze away. "It was gross. Totally. So much worse than the . . ." His voice faltered. "It was the most disgusting thing I've seen in my whole life. Makes me want to puke just thinking about it."

I could imagine how the memory might haunt him. "I'm sorry you had to be the one to find them," I said gently.

His eyes grew teary and his bottom lip quivered. He kicked at the dirt and pine shavings with his toe. "Yeah, me too."

Maybe there was some truth to this "delicate" business after all.

"Almost every night I dream about them. Still. They come out of nowhere, grinning at me, teasing me. Their touch is cold and clammy, like the trail of a slug. Some nights my whole body feels that way, and I have trouble breathing."

Indeed, talking about the event seemed to have the same effect. Bongo's words were short, shallow stabs of sound. "They chase after me," he said, wiping the corner of his eye with a dirty sleeve. "I try hiding from them, I try screaming. But they won't leave me alone. No matter what I do, they're there."

"Is there someone you can talk to about your dreams? A minister maybe, or a doctor?"

"It wouldn't make any difference."

"It might."

He went back to his whittling. His skin was drained of color. "I don't think so," he said flatly. "I really don't."

9

By the time I made it to the Hardings for dinner that evening, I was feeling more than a little burned out on the whole business of murder and its many repercussions. The last thing I wanted was to spend another three hours or so in the shadow of Wes Harding.

But I'd promised Sam I'd be there, and I knew Jake and Grace were expecting me—although I suspected they weren't any more excited at the prospect of the evening than I was. Having a child charged with murder had to be painful, and sharing that pain with a stranger, even an attorney, couldn't be easy.

My knock was answered by a young woman I took to be one of Wes's sisters, probably the eighteen-year-old, although these days it's hard to tell. She held a portable phone to her ear, punctuating the conversation on the other end with a strategically timed "Really?" and "What did he say?" She used the intervening stretch to motion me inside.

The front foyer was large, with a high ceiling and a light oak floor. Off to the side, an ornately carved table held an arrangement of yellow roses and a large crystal bowl with three artistically placed ceramic pears. On the wall above was a portrait of three young women. I recognized my friend with the phone, and assumed the other two were her sisters. They all had fair complexions, pert noses and straight white teeth. Their features had nothing in common with Wes's.

"Mother's in the kitchen," the young woman mouthed, pointing me down the wide hallway. "The door straight ahead."

The young woman herself turned off into the den, leaving me to navigate my way to the kitchen on my own.

It was one of those gourmet kitchens you see in the Sunday supplements, with a center island, professional-quality stove, brass hood, and counter tops of polished marble. Even though I hate to cook, I'd give anything to have a kitchen like that.

"Mrs. Harding?" I said, pausing at the doorway. "I'm Kali O'Brien."

The woman looked up from the cake she was frosting, finishing the job with one smooth stroke, then removing her apron. She wore slacks and a silk blouse. Both looked to be expensive in that understated way that meant they probably carried a designer label as well as a hefty price tag. Her diamond jewelry had a similar simple elegance.

"It's nice to meet you." She offered me her hand and a smile, but both seemed rather tentative. "Sorry I had to send Andrea to the door. This frosting sets up too quickly to leave it, even for a moment."

"No problem."

"And call me Grace. Under the circumstances, we can hardly stand on formality." This last was said with a measure of embarrassment.

At first impression, Grace Harding had appeared to be only a few years older than her daughter. Her hair was a frosted blond, cut to chin length and styled with an experienced hand. On closer inspection, I noticed the slightly uneven coloring of her skin and the network of fine lines around her mouth and eyes. She was an attractive woman nonetheless, and considerably younger than I'd expected. Maybe fifty at most. Which meant she had to have been fairly young when Wes was born.

"Can I get you something to drink?" Grace asked. "The men are out back. I was just about to join them."

I accepted a glass of white wine and she poured another for herself.

Her hands gripped the stemmed glass tightly. "This is a bit awkward, having your son's attorney in for dinner." She laughed nervously. "I don't imagine Emily Post ever laid out the proper etiquette for a situation like this."

"Probably not." As one who gave more weight to common sense than etiquette, however, I was hardly the last word on the matter. "This whole thing must be hard on you."

"My husband thought it was important that we all get to know one another." Grace studied me silently for a moment, then sighed. "Well, I suppose we should join the others."

Holding my drink steady, I followed her out the French doors and onto a wide redwood deck where Sam and Jake were guffawing over some tale of political stupidity.

"I've been looking forward to meeting you," Jake said when we'd been introduced.

Jake Harding appeared to be in his late fifties, with a finely chiseled face, crinkly eyes and a full head of hair, silvered at the temples. His manner was relaxed and easy, like someone central casting would pick to play the compassionate doctor in a commercial for health coverage. "Sam's been singing your praises for quite awhile now."

"I hope he put in a good word for himself as well."

"No need for that. Sam and I go back a long way. Did he ever tell you how we met?" Jake chuckled, pumping more levity into the situation than it seemed to warrant. "Our fishing lines got tangled. There wasn't another soul for miles around, and we ended up not ten feet from each other without knowing it."

Sam smiled as he passed me a platter of chips and dip. "Let's not bore her with the details."

"You're just worried word will get out that you couldn't cast a straight line."

"It wasn't me and you know it."

Grace smiled, a strained tweaking of the mouth that never reached her eyes.

I scooped up a handful of chips, settled into one of the comfortably upholstered deck chairs, and gazed at the canyon beyond. The Hardings' house was set on the ridge, one of a number of houses that had raised the ire of environmentalists and oldtime townsfolk over the past dozen or so years.

Generally, I tended to side with the slow-growth people. I liked my hills dotted with trees rather than houses, and I'd take a pasture of cows over a strip mall any day. Nonetheless, if you were one of the lucky ones who could afford to live up here, I could understand how you might see things differently. The setting was hard to beat. And from what I'd seen of the house, it was nothing to sniff at either.

"This is beautiful," I said, genuinely impressed.

Jake nodded. "We spent a lot of time designing the house to reap the full benefit of the site."

"We put the pool on the other side of the house," Grace added. "When the girls were younger their play area was over there too."

I reflected, briefly, on the many ways Wes's childhood had differed from that of his half-sisters'. Even, I imagined, after his mother had married Jake.

"What was Wes like as a boy?" I asked, finding myself genuinely curious.

Grace laughed self-consciously. "Goodness, that was quite awhile ago."

"I'm just looking for a general impression."

"Well, he wasn't an easy child, even as a baby. It seemed like he was always wound up as tight as a top. He kept it inside, though, so it was hard to know what he was thinking. Wes was shy too." She took a sip of wine and frowned. "Maybe that's not the right word, but he was never comfortable with new situations or with people he didn't know well. He didn't make friends easily."

Jake reached for a corn chip. "Wes was ten when I married Grace, fourteen when Andrea was born. He never had half the advantages the girls have had."

"You tried," Grace said with emotion. "You gave him a home and loved him like your own son."

"He had a way of finding trouble in spite of it. Maybe if we'd—"

"We did the best we could." Grace's voice was sharp. "And he's never seemed to appreciate any of it."

Jake's jaw tightened.

Grace touched her husband's hand, offering an apology for her snappishness. She turned to me. "As you can tell, this is something of a sore point between us."

"I imagine raising children is never easy."

"No, it isn't," Jake said with a laugh. "Let me get more wine." He went inside and returned with the bottle.

"I take it Wes didn't grow up in this house," I said as Jake refilled my glass.

"We moved in the year he left home," Grace explained.

The year Wes was sent away, I amended silently.

Jake finished refilling the other glasses. "When I started my practice here I lived in that little place on Elm that Wes has now. Used to make house calls in those days. A terribly inefficient way to practice medicine, but you do get to know your patients."

"How did Wes end up in the house on Elm?"

"We moved to Pine Hills right after we were married, but we kept the old house as a rental property. It came vacant again just when Wes moved back to town. The place needed work and he agreed to fix it up in lieu of rent. He's done a good job too."

"As far as it's gone," Grace amended.

From Jake's expression it was clear they'd been over this ground before. "Grace thought we should hire a professional," he explained. "Get the whole thing fixed up quickly and sell it."

"With Andrea headed off to college, we could use the extra money."

"We're doing fine without it. Anyway, Wes has been taking his time with the renovation—sanding the wood, stripping the old wallpaper off before painting, replumbing the fixtures, that sort of thing. No question it's slow going, but he was doing it the right way."

"I suppose I should be glad he found *something* to do right. Lord knows there hasn't been much of that." Grace raised her glass to her lips, then set it down abruptly. "I think I'll check the roast. It should be about ready by now."

"Wes's arrest has been hard on her," Jake said, when she left. "She's worried about what will happen to him, worried about what it will do to the girls. She's even afraid that it might affect my medical practice. Although I must say that so far people have been very understanding."

"I should hope so," Sam humphed. "Anyone who's raised a kid knows you don't have a damn bit of a say in how they turn out."

Just then a lanky, barefoot and bare-legged girl appeared in the doorway.

"Speak of the devil," Jake called out good-naturedly. "Pammy, come meet Ms. O'Brien."

"Kali," I amended, hoping he wasn't one of those parents who insisted their children address every adult by surname.

Pammy wasn't particularly interested either way. She murmured a "Hi," stole a quick sip of her father's wine, gave him an impish grin when he started to protest, then grabbed a handful of chips and headed back inside. "Mom says dinner's about ready," she called over her shoulder.

Jake laughed. "Case in point. The girl has a mind of her own. You can be sure that whatever I say to her goes in one ear and out the other." He stood. "I'll go see if I can give Grace a hand."

I started to follow, but Sam cornered me and we hung back for a moment.

"How'd it go yesterday with Wes?" he asked.

I shrugged. "The man has an attitude."

"Wouldn't you, if you were looking at murder one?"

"I guess it would depend on whether or not I was guilty. In either case, the last person I'd want to piss off is my attorney."

"Got to you, did he?" Sam's bushy white brows pulled tight above his eyes. "If you're going to survive in this business, Kali, you've got to develop a thick skin. Concentrate on building your case and don't let Wes, or anyone else, get to you."

"How are we going to build any kind of decent case when all the evidence lines up on the other side?" I told him about the lab report Curt had shown me the evening before.

"I got a call about that myself, yesterday afternoon."

"So, what do you think?"

He sighed. As I had predicted, his response was philosophical. "I think we're going to have to find a way to deal with it."

Inside, Grace was busy with the salad, Jake with the wine. Andrea was no longer clutching the phone to her ear, but she held it in her hand as she put the finishing touches on the table. I seized the opportunity to slide down the hall to the bathroom. Only I suppose in this instance, powder room would be a more apt description. Marble floor and vanity, polished brass fixtures, large mirrored walls and a display of fancy soaps and lotions. It was the sort of place where you end up wiping your hands on your slacks because you don't want to dirty the towels.

By the time I rejoined the others we were ready to sit down for dinner. Andrea had detached herself from the telephone but looked as though she'd rather be clutching it than her dinner fork. When Grace introduced us, she forced a smile, then looked away.

Except for the expression of utter boredom, Andrea was a pretty girl, with shoulder-length hair, blond like her mother's, and a clear, pale complexion. She wore the black leggings she'd worn earlier, but she'd changed the oversized tee for a silk shirt. She lifted a brow at her sister's loose-fitting cutoff overalls.

"You're coming to dinner like that? You look like you should be milking cows."

Pammy mooed in her face.

"Girls, please. We have company."

"Which is exactly," Andrea huffed, "why she should make an effort to look presentable."

Pammy gave us a silent but dramatic version of "who? me?" Not as pretty as her sister, Pammy had a mouth full of braces and hair that was neither blond nor brown. Though it had been permed at some point in the past, it was now more unruly than curly, and would probably have obscured half her face without the barrettes that held it in place. But there was an appealing perkiness about her that Andrea was lacking.

Jake cleared his throat. "I understand you grew up in Silver Creek," he said, nodding in my direction.

"Yes; in fact, Wes and I were in school together for a while."

Grace looked up from her roast beef, confused. "You were a friend of his?"

"Not a friend, really. We had a couple of classes together."

She nodded, apparently relieved. "It would surprise me if anyone in that group of his amounted to much."

"It certainly was rough there for a while," Jake said evenly, "but Wes has turned out just fine. Not everyone has to go to college or be a superstar."

Andrea snickered. "Auto mechanic, my life's ambition."

Grace gave her a stern look, then turned back to Jake. "That's not what I meant," she said pointedly.

"Have you done much criminal work in the past?" Jake asked, directing his question my way.

"Some, not a lot."

"Kali knows her stuff," Sam said.

Jake made some more inquiries, mostly about my education and training, then hit me with the big question I'd known was coming.

"What's your assessment of the case? Are the odds as bad as they appear?"

"It's kind of early to tell."

"I'm not asking for promises, just your gut-level feeling."

I shook my head. "Feelings don't bear on much of anything at this point."

Grace cut a string bean in half, then set her fork down next to her plate. "Don't the police have quite a bit of evidence against Wes?"

"There's no shortage of evidence the DA can use, but none of it's conclusive. We're hoping to chip away at most of it. We're also exploring other angles."

Jake was refilling the wineglasses. He looked up. "What other angles?"

"Nothing specific just yet. We thought we'd look into Lisa Cornell's background. She's relatively new to town. Also, there's a homeless man who lives in the woods near the Cornell place. It's possible he saw or heard something that could help us."

Sam's head nodded in agreement. "Apparently there's been quite a bit of interest in the property Lisa Cornell inherited from her aunt. That's an avenue we'll pursue as well."

Grace pushed the string bean around on her plate. "Don't you think the police have done that already?"

"Not necessarily," Sam said. "The police see what they want to see. Once they identify a suspect, they focus on that person to the exclusion of all others. They build a case against him based on their interpretation of the evidence."

He paused to tear off a piece of roll, then held it in his hand while he continued. "But there are a lot of twists you can put on the facts. That's one of the approaches we take in trying to counter the prosecution's position. But the police also reach the wrong conclusion sometimes simply because of a missing piece they've overlooked. That's why we want to explore every possible angle."

Jake appeared thoughtful. "I understand that Lisa Cornell was engaged. Don't statistics show that women are killed most often by a spouse or lover?"

"What the statistics show," I explained, "is that most people are killed by someone they know. With women it's often someone they've been involved with romantically, but there can be other connections as well."

"Don't you think it's worth exploring?" Jake's tone was patronizing, and I bit back the urge to tell him so.

"I'm sure the police talked to the boyfriend," I said, "but I intend to also. If nothing else, he's likely to know about Lisa's recent activities. His name is Philip Stockman. His family owns the Big Bob Hardware stores."

Pammy bobbed to attention. "You're kidding. His son goes to our school." She looked at Andrea. "Danny Stockman. He's a year behind you, I think. Do you know him?"

"Great," Andrea huffed, her voice thick with sarcasm. "This gets better and better. As if it's not bad enough having a murderer in the family, now it turns out his victim is practically related to someone I went to school with. Thank God I graduated so I don't have to face all that when school starts."

"Your brother has been charged," Jake said, emphasizing the last word, "not convicted. You watch what you say, understand?"

Andrea lifted her chin and met his gaze. "Half-brother," she corrected.

"Danny's mother was killed in a boating accident when he was a baby," Pammy said. "He wrote a story about it for the school literary magazine."

"Are you sure it's the same family?" I asked. "If this guy has a sixteen-year-old son, he must be quite a bit older than Lisa."

Andrea arched her perfectly tweezed brow and looked at me as though I were unbelievably out-of-it. "So?"

I shrugged. Maybe I was.

Jake drummed the table lightly with his fork. "I'd like to be kept apprised of these other leads you're following. I've got my own network of connections, and I may be able to help out. I'm always amazed at the volume of information that travels via the grapevine."

Throughout the discussion Grace had remained quiet, pushing the food around on her plate without ever taking a taste. Now she folded her hands and looked up. "What about trying to work out some sort of deal with the DA's office?"

Jake's eyes met hers. "Grace, we've . . ."

She turned to me. "Do you think there's a chance they'd let him plead to a lesser charge?"

"Wes doesn't want that, I'm afraid."

"Maybe you could talk to him, change his mind."

Jake placed a hand over hers. "We've been over this, Grace. You don't want him to spend the rest of his life in prison if he's innocent."

She pulled her hand away. "It's better than being dead, isn't it?"

Jake's expression was pained. I wondered if, like me, he wasn't so sure.

10

After dinner Grace retreated to the kitchen, steadfastly refusing my offer to help. Sam and Jake moved to the living room with glasses of brandy. I passed up the brandy and instead stepped outside to drink in the freshness of the night air. The sun had set and a few stars glimmered above, but the sky was still cast in gradations of blue and gray. I took a seat, leaned back and gazed out at the hills, lulled by the pleasant drone of crickets and the faint rustle of the breeze in the grass. I wondered, fleetingly, what sounds greeted Wes's ears right then.

"Do you mind if I join you?" Pammy slid into the seat next to mine, tucking her feet up under her. She rested her chin in her hand. "So, what do you think? Is my brother guilty or not?"

Before I could decide how to answer she jumped ahead.

"That's okay, I know you can't tell me. I'm not sure I want to know anyway." She shifted position and sighed. "Unless you're certain he's innocent, that is." She paused and looked over at me. When I didn't respond right away she sighed again. "Yeah, that's what I was afraid of."

"Just because I'm uncertain doesn't mean he's guilty." The fact of the matter was that as his attorney, I didn't want to know the truth.

"Andrea is sure he did it." Her voice was thin, like a puff of dust. "That's what my mom thinks too, though she'd never admit it. I don't know about my dad. Sometimes I think his standing solidly behind Wes is all for show, and other times I think he really believes Wes is innocent. Maybe he just wants to believe it so bad he's convinced himself it's so."

"And what about you—what do you think?"

She pulled a loose thread from the bottom of her cut-offs and rolled it into a ball. "I don't know what to think. Wes has been really nice to me. I know he's got a reputation as a rowdy, but I've never seen that side of him. In fact, I've only seen him lose his temper once, and that was when he'd had a lot to drink."

Pammy played with the ball of thread for a moment, rolling it between her palms. "There's no way I can imagine him doing what was done to that woman and her little girl, but there's an awful lot of people who think he did it. I keep wondering if maybe they know something I don't."

"Or maybe it's the other way around. Maybe you know Wes better than they do."

"I get along better with Wes than I do with anyone else in the family. Better than I get along with my mother and sisters anyway."

I nodded. I knew about sisters. Sabrina and I had been like oil and water the whole time we were growing up.

"Sometimes I'd drop by his place after school or on weekends, help him strip wallpaper, work on his car, stuff like that. It wasn't so much real conversation as just hanging out." She paused. "Wes and I are a lot alike actually."

"Alike how?" Myself, I didn't see much similarity.

A shrug. "We like the same movies and we're not real social." She laughed unevenly. "We're both big disappointments to our parents."

Wes, maybe, but I couldn't understand how the Hardings would be disappointed in Pammy. I started to tell her so. "Everybody feels that to some extent, but—"

She cut me off. "Spare me the lecture; I've heard it. And I'm not saying my parents don't care about me. It's just that my mother wants me to be more like my sisters—you know, pretty and popular. And my dad . . . well, what he really wanted was a son. Someone he could take fishing and hunting, do the male bonding trip with. It didn't work out with Wes, and then he ended up with three daughters. I was his last hope."

"Daughters can hunt and fish."

She responded with a disgusted laugh. "Not these particular daughters. Andrea wouldn't do anything that might muss her hair or cause her to break a nail, and I don't have the patience for that stuff. Or the stomach. That's another way I'm like my brother." This last was said with a hint of adolescent pride.

"I thought the group of guys Wes hung out with saw guns as the answer to everything."

"Some of his friends are like that, but not all of them. If you ask me, it's mostly for show anyway. Besides, Wes is squeamish about blood."

Recalling the headless cat that Wes had supposedly left

in the chemistry lab in high school, I wasn't so sure. But I found Pammy's fondness for him touching. "His arrest must be hard on you."

A quick nod, and then a scowl. "What really bugs me is that my parents won't talk to me about it. My dad says there's nothing to discuss, and my mother finds it an embarrassment. Her biggest worry, I think, is what her friends will say."

"She's probably more worried than she lets on."

"Don't bet on it. She wasn't any too happy when Wes moved back to Silver Creek in the first place. I think she'd tried to forget all about him. But having him right here in town, getting in hot water all the time—she could hardly ignore that."

"Wes does seem to have a way of attracting trouble."

A flock of birds flew overhead and Pammy was quiet for a moment. "I think he does that on purpose. He likes the image of being bad. I've heard him tell people his name is John Wesley Harding, like the outlaw, even though it's really plain old Wes."

"The outlaw was named Hardin; Harding came from a Dylan song."

"You're kidding. I wonder if Wes knows that. Of course, Harding isn't his real name anyway."

"It isn't?"

She shook her head. "The way I understand it, my dad wanted to adopt Wes, but they couldn't track down my mom's first husband to get his consent. Wes started calling himself a Harding anyway. He never knew his real dad, who was apparently a total loser. Andrea says that's the reason Mom has a problem with Wes; because he reminds her of his father."

She wouldn't have been the first woman in history

to think that way. But it seemed unfair. Who wanted a mother who associated you with some of the worst years of her life?

"Wes was lucky to get a second chance with someone like your dad," I said.

"Yeah, although they sent him away to some militaristic boarding school when he was sixteen, so it must not have been as cozy as they'd hoped."

Having known Wes during that period, I was fairly certain things weren't cozy at all. But what had been at the heart of all that anger and acting out? It struck me that I'd never once wondered what the world looked like through Wes's eyes.

"Tell me about Wes," I said. "What's he like?"

"When he's here at the house he's kind of quiet. But he's different when my parents aren't around."

"Different how?"

"Looser, funnier. He has a way of imitating people that cracks me up. He can do Mom perfectly."

"Have you met any of his friends?"

"A few. I usually leave if they come over."

"How about girlfriends?"

"He's got a bedroom drawer full of condoms, so I guess he must, uh . . ." she gave an embarrassed shrug, ". . . date, but I've never heard him mention any girlfriend in particular. When he's had a lot to drink he sometimes talks about a girl named Kathy. She was big-time rich, or her family was, anyway. They had houses everywhere—Palm Springs, Maui, Aspen, even a flat in London. She had horses, so there must have been a ranch in there too. If you believe Wes, anyway. I don't know how much of it's true because he gets really mad and talks in circles."

"Has he mentioned anyone else?"

She shook her head. "He's a private person, even with his friends."

"He never mentioned Lisa Cornell?"

"The dead woman? No. Why would he?"

I shrugged. "I'm trying to figure out the connection between them."

"You think there is one? He told the police he'd never heard of her."

That's what he'd said, but to me the evidence indicated otherwise.

It was only nine o'clock when I got home that evening, but I couldn't settle in. I tried television. I tried the book I'd picked up at the library earlier in the week. Even vacuuming. Everything chafed, as though I were suspended in skin that wasn't my own.

I called Sabrina, who wasn't in or wasn't answering. Ours may not have been the easiest relationship, but the very fact that she saw things so differently than I did was sometimes a tonic.

Finally I took Loretta and Barney for a walk, thinking the night air might clear my mental palate.

We headed down the road past Tom's house, which stood in darkness save for the single interior light that was supposed to fool burglars. When we walked at night I kept the dogs on a leash, which they considered an unnecessary hindrance and I considered a measure of precaution. We moved more slowly that way, having to coordinate ten legs and three strong wills, but at least I could think my thoughts without constant worry about their safety.

My thoughts this evening were largely of Wes Harding. And they came unevenly, in bits and pieces. The past mixed with the present, Pammy with the girl I'd been when Wes and I were in school together.

I wanted to understand Wes. Yet he was a puzzle, just as he had been when we were growing up. Then he'd been a "bad boy," but not a person you actually feared. And the bad, being draped in mystique, caught your imagination the way innocence and purity never would. The Wes Harding of my girlhood had been an untethered force, like the handsome villain in a tale of gothic suspense. An entity unto himself.

I realized I'd never envisioned the young Wes with a mother and father and baby sister. Probably two baby sisters by then. I'd never considered that he might have fears or worries or sorrows of his own.

Wes was still attractive. Still something of a mystery. I wondered what fears and sorrows he lived with today. And I wondered what he was hiding.

Sunday morning I put thoughts of Wes Harding aside and went to visit Irma Pearl. Although she was not, technically speaking, my client, I felt a responsibility toward her. Maybe I was subconsciously trying to make up for the visits I hadn't paid my father in the last years of his life. Or maybe it was the fact that I didn't entirely trust her daughter, who *was* my client.

The Twin Pines Rest Home was named for two spindly pines that stood on either side of the front entrance. Like the residents inside, they'd seen better days.

Irma Pearl had chosen the Twin Pines herself, back when she'd first been diagnosed with Alzheimer's. She was adamant about not wanting to be any more of a burden on her daughter than was necessary. By the time Sheri approached me about handling the conservatorship proceedings, however, Irma had trouble remembering that decision. It wasn't that the Twin Pines was so bad—in the scheme of things, it was fairly decent. But it wasn't home, and that was where Irma wanted to be.

To her credit, Sheri had tried that, bringing in private-care nurses to help her mother with the myriad of daily tasks that were now beyond her. But it was an expensive and imperfect solution. On the other hand, cutting all ties with home and spending the remainder of your days in a convalescent center didn't strike me as so perfect either.

I checked in at the nurses' station, then went to find Irma. On her good days she was often outside, with friends, or in the lounge watching television. The bad days she usually spent in her room, which was where I found her this morning.

I knocked on the already open door. "Good morning," I said, crossing to the far side of the room. Irma sat in a straight-backed chair, near the window. She was still in her nightgown, though she'd thrown a shawl over her shoulders. The thin white hair she usually twisted into a bun now hung limply around her face. She wasn't a frail woman, but at that moment she looked as fragile as crystal. I handed her the box of chocolates I'd brought with me.

"A present for me? How lovely." Her face lit up for a moment, then went blank. She blinked at me. "You're not Sheri, are you?"

I shook my head. "I'm a friend of Sheri's."

"Do I know you?"

"We've met a couple of times. I'm an attorney. My name's Kali O'Brien."

Irma smiled, smoothing the collar of her gown. "Of course, Kali. How could I have forgotten? I'm so sorry, dear, it's just that . . ." She made a meaningless gesture with her hands. "Just that things get mixed up in my mind sometimes."

"That's understandable. It's hard to keep track of everyone you know."

She nodded. "Sometimes I can't even remember which ones are dead and which ones aren't." The hands fluttered in her lap. "Can I have a piece of candy? It's still morning, I think, but I ate a good breakfast."

I peeled off the wrapper and opened the box. After much deliberation Irma chose a piece with white chocolate glaze. She plopped the whole piece in her mouth at once.

When she finished the candy she peered into the box and surveyed the remaining choices. "I was hoping maybe Sheri would come today and take me home."

"You enjoy those visits, don't you?"

There was a girlish laugh. "You don't *visit* your own *home,* silly."

"Isn't this your home now?"

"Goodness, no." She reached for another chocolate. "We're just here today to see my grandma. She's very old." Irma leaned forward conspiratorially. "She's so old, she can't even go to the bathroom by herself." A thin line of chocolate drool dribbled down the side of Irma's chin. "She's so old, even, that she *smells,* but we can't say anything because it might hurt her feelings." She held the box of chocolates out to me. "You want a piece?"

I shook my head. Whatever my ill-defined objective in visiting Irma Pearl, the answer was fairly clear to me. There wasn't anything to be gained by involving her in the difficult and emotionally laden decision of selling the house that was once her home.

I spent another few minutes talking with her, then headed out to pay a visit to Philip Stockman. A visit that was bound to be as uncomfortable as my visit with Irma, although for entirely different reasons.

I considered calling ahead and then discarded the idea. It might have been the mannerly thing to do, but it wasn't likely to help. By showing up at Stockman's door unannounced, on the other hand, I might be able to get in a word or two before he slammed the thing in my face. At the very least I'd be able to get a firsthand impression of the guy.

The Stockman home, set a good quarter mile up a winding private drive, was large, though not nearly as large as I'd expected. Nor as grand. It was an older house, immaculately maintained, but with none of the showy extravagance that often seems to follow money.

I rang the bell and braced myself for a quick rebuff.

The door was answered not by a man, or even a teenaged boy, but by a tall, stern-faced woman who appeared to be in her late forties. I might have taken her for a housekeeper but for the fact that she was dressed in an expensive-looking silk shirtwaist and clutched a section of the morning newspaper in her hand.

"I'm here to see Philip Stockman," I said. "Is he in?"

"Do you have an appointment? He didn't mention it."

I shook my head, taken aback by the question. "No appointment. Do I need one?"

"You should have called first. However, since you're here . . ." She looked at her watch. "Mr. Stockman is still at church, but he should be back any minute. Why don't you come inside and wait."

She didn't ask for my name, which was too bad, because I was dying to know hers. And her connection to Philip Stockman.

The door opened wider and she stepped back, motioning me into the hallway. I caught a whiff of furniture polish—the real beeswax stuff, not the aerosol imitation you buy in the grocery.

The house was furnished in a style befitting its vintage— lots of brocade and velvet and spindly furniture of dark mahogany. Undeniably elegant, but too stiff and formal for my tastes.

The woman led me to a small sitting room, offered me tea, which I declined, then announced she'd let Stockman know I was here as soon as he arrived. At the doorway she hesitated, started to say something, then apparently decided against it. With a nod in my direction, she was gone.

Left to my own devices, I explored the room. The bookcase on the far wall held a collection of works in what looked to be German, several volumes on California history and two rows of *Reader's Digest* Condensed Books dating back to the 1950s. Prominently displayed on a separate, angled shelf was a leather-bound Bible, which from the inscription at the front I gathered had belonged to Philip's grandfather. There was a sepia-toned globe of the world at one end of the sofa and a lace-covered table dotted with ceramic knickknacks at the other. The magazines on the low table in front were a mix of Christian-living and business-related publications, although a copy of *Popular Mechanics* had somehow found its way there as well. A crystal candy dish, filled with sugar drops, rested atop the piano. I took a cinnamon ball and sucked on it while I listened to the grandfather clock tick away the minutes.

I was about ready to give up and come back another day when I heard a car pull to a stop in front of the house. Moments later a fair-haired man, thick around the middle, strode into the room and offered me his hand. "I'm Philip Stockman," he said, settling himself on the edge of the chair across from me. "Thank you for waiting."

I murmured something unintelligible. This was not the reception I'd expected.

Philip Stockman looked to be in his early fifties, with a broad, flat face, determined mouth and pale eyes that were magnified by silver-framed glasses. His hairline had receded to a wide U, leaving him with a high, polished forehead surrounded by closely cropped gray. He wasn't unattractive, but he was certainly not the sort of man I'd have pictured with Lisa Cornell.

"Let me tell you a bit about the job first," he said, "and then if you're interested, we can get into the details."

So that was it. I started to explain. "I'm—"

Stockman cut me off. "Please, let me finish." He cleared his throat. "The job is ostensibly one of housekeeper, but in truth what I need is a babysitter. Or more accurately, a chaperone." He offered a weak smile. "You can't tell a sixteen-year-old boy you're leaving him with a babysitter."

"I imagine not, but why I'm—"

He continued as though I hadn't interrupted. "I know

there are people who leave children that age alone, but I don't approve. It's just asking for trouble. There are far too many temptations, even for the best of them."

His eyes narrowed ever so slightly. "Not that Daniel would cause any problems himself. He's a good boy, and he's been raised properly. But you never know when friends will show up uninvited. You get a bunch of kids together and . . . and things happen." He pressed the fingers of his two hands together and frowned. "My sister, Helene, lives here with us. You met her earlier."

I nodded, even though it wasn't a question.

"She and I run a family business," Stockman continued, "a chain of hardware stores. We're going to be traveling quite a bit in the next few months and I need someone to hold down the fort while we're gone. We wouldn't expect any heavy cleaning; just a little cooking and picking up around the place."

When he paused I seized the opportunity to set things straight. "Mr. Stockman, I'm not here about a job. I'm here about Lisa Cornell."

Stockman's face froze, as though he'd been unexpectedly doused with ice water.

"I'm an attorney looking into her death."

"I thought they already had the guy."

"They have *a* guy. I represent him."

There was a moment's silence while the words sank in. "You're working for the guy who killed Lisa?" His voice was tight and rose with each word. The muscle under his eye twitched.

"I'm working for the man who's accused of killing her."

The twitch grew more pronounced. "That must be quite a burden," he said with thinly veiled hostility.

"Not nearly so heavy as the burden of putting away an innocent man."

Stockman took off his glasses and wiped them on his sleeve. "That's pure poppycock, you know. The man's as guilty as they come. If he burns in hell for all eternity, it won't be punishment enough as far as I'm concerned."

"Why do you think he's guilty?"

"He was arrested, wasn't he? The evidence they have against him is more than ample. I guarantee you that rabbit's foot didn't walk there on its own. I know his kind. Believe me, they have no respect for anything." He gave me a hard look. "What's your name?"

"Kali O'Brien." I handed him a business card.

"You have one hell of a lot of nerve, Ms. O'Brien."

Helene entered just then, with tea. A pudgy teenage boy trailed behind her.

"This woman's not here about the job," Stockman said brusquely. "She's an attorney. She wants to talk about Lisa."

"Lisa? Why would . . ." A look bounced between them and she stopped midway across the room. "Philip, I'm sorry. I just assumed . . . I mean the other . . ."

He sighed, long and loudly. "It's okay, Helene. You might as well set out the tea since it's made."

Helene gave me a dirty look, as though my sole purpose in visiting had been to trip her up. She set the tea tray on the table between us, handed me a cup and sat down without saying a word. The boy, who I assumed was Daniel, grabbed a handful of cookies from the tray and sat near her.

Stockman sipped his tea, his expression stern. "Ms. O'Brien, I'm a Christian and a gentleman, and a proud

American. And I have faith in our judicial system, so I'm not going to throw you out of here on your ear. I'll talk to you, but I don't want to hear any nonsense about innocent defendants or tainted evidence." He set the cup down. "Now, what is it you want to know? I don't have all morning."

"I'm trying to find out more about Lisa. Her friends, her hobbies, her activities the night she was killed. I understand the two of you were seeing each other."

"We were engaged," he replied, with emphasis on the last word.

"Had you known her long?"

"Long enough. We met in church. Lisa sang in the choir."

Daniel added three spoonsful of sugar to his tea, then proceeded to slurp it noisily.

"Her voice was lovely," Stockman continued, "like everything else about her. If you'd known her, you'd appreciate what a terrible loss her death is."

"I did know her, though only slightly."

"Lisa hadn't had an easy life, but she didn't let that stop her. She talked about going back to school after we were married, maybe getting her degree."

"How did you feel about that?"

"It was all right by me. We have a housekeeper who comes in to clean twice a week, so Lisa would have had plenty of free time."

"You were going to continue living here after you were married?"

He looked surprised at my question. "Yes, of course. I've lived here since I was a child. There's not another house of this quality in the whole county. And the furnishings are pieces my parents collected during their travels, selected by them especially for this house."

I wondered how Lisa felt about the arrangement. I know what my own reaction would have been. Something of my skepticism must have shown. "There's plenty of room," Philip said. "And Helene would be lost without us."

"I've practically raised Daniel," Helene added. "I couldn't bear to lose him." She smiled at the boy, who continued to munch on his stack of cookies, oblivious to the expression of affection.

Lisa was getting a package deal, I thought. Along with a husband, she got his house, his sister and his son. And probably a lot of family history. "Had you set a wedding date?" I asked.

"Not a specific date, no."

"It was set," Helene said with a certain huffiness, "until Lisa put it off."

Stockman gave his sister a harsh glance. "She just needed a little more time to adjust to the idea," he explained. "I think her first marriage made her a little gunshy."

"The guy was a total jerk," Daniel said, chomping into yet another cookie.

"Daniel, please." Stockman's voice was sharp.

"What guy?" I asked.

"Her husband."

"You've met him?"

"Only once," Stockman said, taking over for his son. "The man showed up here in town a couple of months ago. Wanted to spend time with Amy. That's the kind of father he was. Hadn't seen the kid for over a year, then suddenly he's got this hankering for a relationship."

"What was Lisa's reaction?"

Distaste colored his face. "Lisa wanted Amy to know her father."

"Do you know where I might reach him?"

"Sorry, I don't." Stockman's tone was brusque.

"How about his name?"

"Sylva. Jerry Sylva. Lisa went back to using her maiden name after they separated."

We were close to finishing our tea and I hadn't even begun with my questions about Lisa's death. "I'm trying to trace Lisa's activities the day she was killed," I said. "I know she got home from work about four. Do you have any idea what she might have done between then and the time she was killed?"

"Not specifically," Stockman said. "She was planning to come for dinner that evening. Nothing fancy; it was our standard Friday night arrangement. A chance for the kids to get to know one another."

Daniel smirked.

"She called that afternoon to say she wouldn't be able to make it. Apparently a woman from her support group needed some help."

I sat forward. "What support group?"

"The chronic pain group. Lisa suffered from headaches. The doctors couldn't come up with a cause. Couldn't do much to help her either. It was one of those mysterious maladies that baffles modern medicine. Anyway, she joined this group—I think they learned stress reduction techniques, shared ideas for coping, that sort of thing. I'm not much on this therapy stuff myself; in fact, I think it's a crock of you-know-what. Lisa thought it was important, though. And it was run by a doctor, so I figured there couldn't be too much voodoo in it."

"Was the group helping her?"

Stockman adjusted his glasses. "Not that I could tell. If anything, the episodes were becoming more frequent. And she'd started getting stomach pains as well as headaches. I wanted her to see a specialist at UC Medical Center in San Francisco. Offered to pay for it myself. But Lisa claimed she was getting a handle on things."

"Can you tell me more about this woman who needed help?"

"I'm afraid not. Lisa said she got a call from the woman. That's all I know."

"What about the woman's name?"

"Lisa never mentioned it."

"I wonder if the police were able to track her down."

Stockman shrugged, looked at his watch.

"You told them about the phone call, didn't you?"

"What's there to tell?" His tone was sharp. "Anyway, they didn't ask. They had their man."

Helene returned her empty cup to the tray. "I don't see what all this has to do with Lisa's death."

"If my client didn't kill her, someone else did."

"Surely you don't think it was her friend?"

"I haven't thought that far yet, but I'd like to talk to the woman. Do you know the name of the doctor who ran this group?"

"Markley," Stockman said with growing impatience. "Or something close to that. He has an office in Sierra Vista. The group met Wednesday evenings."

Mrs. Arabagucci's babysitting time. So much for that mystery. I'd been hoping for something more. Something that might have given us a solid lead.

"When Lisa called that afternoon to bow out of dinner how did she seem?"

Stockman looked at his sister, then back to me. "I didn't actually speak with her. Helene did."

"We didn't talk long," Helene said. "Lisa gave me a short message to give to Philip, which I did. There was nothing in any way noteworthy about the conversation."

Stockman glanced at his watch again. I could tell he was getting antsy, and Daniel had gone through the entire plate of cookies.

"One last question," I said. "Did Lisa ever mention a drifter called Granger?"

Stockman shook his head, but Daniel blinked to attention.

"Isn't he that crazy guy who's missing half his teeth?"

"You know him?"

"Yuk, get real. But I've seen him around—eating out of garbage cans." Daniel wrinkled his nose in disgust. "He hangs out in the woods behind the school sometimes. The guy's a total loser."

Stockman gave his son a stern look.

"I know," the boy said, raising the pitch of his voice, "people like that need our prayers not our censure, and you shouldn't open your trap until you've walked a mile in the dude's shoes. Well, let me tell you, you'd have to fumigate them first."

"Daniel, that's quite enough." Stockman offered me a thin, apologetic smile. He stood, signaling the end of the interview.

I thanked him for seeing me, which was an honest expression of gratitude. I'm not sure I'd have been as cordial had our roles been reversed.

The wooded area behind the high school was not my idea of an exciting place to spend a Sunday afternoon. There'd been a time, many years earlier, when I'd considered the place a safe haven, and infinitely preferable to Mr. Dodge's math class. But even then I'd have drawn the line at squandering a fine summer's day on the place.

I brushed away loose debris from a log and sat, feeling more foolish by the minute. Daniel had said Granger *sometimes* hung out in the woods. And the boy didn't strike me as the most reliable source, in any event.

Overhead, a blue jay mocked me.

"Go pick on someone your own size," I told him.

The bag from McDonald's lay at my feet. I'd brought it along in the hope of luring Granger with the scent of grease and fried fat, but I knew that once I unwrapped it, the jay wouldn't leave me alone.

It was a warm day, even here in the shade. I wished I'd thought to pick up a drink for myself when I'd stopped for the burger and fries. A drink and something to read.

I reached for a stone and tossed it against the tree to my left. Bull's eye. I tried the one a little farther away and missed by a mile.

Was this what small-town practice had brought me? Was it what I wanted? To be sitting on a dusty, bug-infested log in an area of woods littered with candy wrappers, crumpled cigarette packs and used condoms? Maybe Curt Willis was right about wanting to get out.

Of course, I'd had the other. Would have had it still if things had gone the way I'd planned.

I picked up another stone and tossed it hard at nothing in particular. It landed without a sound. But would I be happier if I were still at Goldman & Latham? I wouldn't be wasting my Sunday hanging around the woods, that was for sure, but more likely than not I'd be working. Sitting at my desk in an office with sealed windows and poor ventilation, wearing panty hose instead of jeans. And I'd be billing my time in ten-minute increments.

I started humming to let Granger know I was here. I also opened the bag and spread the contents on the log. The blue jay moved in closer, to the branch just above me.

At least my clients at Goldman & Latham had been guilty of nothing worse than unfair business practices or reneging on a contract. At the end of trial the judge would bang her gavel, a sum of money would change hands and that was that. Occasionally a client would wind up in jail, but never for very long, and certainly not on death row.

I stopped humming and started whistling, thinking that maybe higher-pitched sound waves traveled farther. It was either that or call for the man by name, as though he were a dog, and I refused to stoop to that.

The jay squawked impatiently, drowning out my loudest whistle. Disgusted, I broke the burger and fries into pieces and laid them out on the log.

"Bon appetit," I called to the bird, and left.

Two things surprised me when I looked up Dr. Markley in the phone book. The first was that the doctor was a she, not a he. The second was that she was a psychiatrist.

Had Lisa intentionally misled Stockman, or was he simply oblivious to the details in Lisa's life? Having heard his views on therapy, I could understand the former. But having once dated a supreme egotist myself, I wouldn't rule out the latter either.

Calling on a Sunday afternoon, I expected either an answering service or a machine. Instead, I got the doctor herself.

"My conversations with Lisa are confidential," she told

me after I'd explained why I was calling. "Even though she's dead, I have to respect her privacy."

"Yes, I know that. But you might still be able to help me."

I heard the shuffle of papers on the other end of the line. Dr. Markley mumbled something to herself, then said, "How about tomorrow at one? The patient I usually see at that time is on vacation this week."

Monday was the preliminary hearing. Although Sam would handle most the of arguments and cross, I hated to miss any of it.

"If Monday's not good for you," she said, "I'm afraid we'll have to wait until the following week. I've just returned from a conference and my schedule is backed up through Friday."

"Monday will be fine," I said. The judge would call a noon recess anyway. I wouldn't miss much.

"I doubt I'll be able to help," she said, "but I'm happy to do what I can."

12

The preliminary hearing is essentially the prosecution's show. They're required to demonstrate that they have enough evidence to try the defendant for the crime in question. Period. The proceeding is pro forma in all but a handful of situations, and ours, unfortunately, was not one of them. There wasn't a chance in hell the judge would dismiss the case at this stage, no matter how persuasively Sam and I argued.

Although our presence at the hearing was required, Curt Willis was clearly the man of the moment. And from the looks of things, not at all reticent about embracing the role.

Curt was holding an impromptu press conference on the courthouse steps when I arrived. Dressed in a new, well-tailored suit, with his hair stylishly trimmed and his briefcase in hand, he faced the bank of lights and microphones as though he were an old hand at stardom. His expression was earnest but relaxed. When he spoke to reporters off the record he was probably even jovial. A man among men.

I couldn't hear what he was saying, but I could tell from his manner that he was playing to a simpatico crowd.

I tried to slip past unnoticed, but just as I made it to the top step, I felt the sudden, intrusive glare of a strobe light in my face. "Can you tell us something about Wes Harding's defense?" The voice was female, and not one I recognized. I turned and was blinded by a second flash.

Several women with placards jostled the reporter aside. "How can you defend a man who kills innocent children?" one of them shouted.

"Their blood will be on your hands," cried another, shoving her sign in my face.

The reporter tried again. "Is it true that you're only on this case as a token woman, to win jury support?"

Around me, a small crowd had begun gathering. A man with a television camera stepped to the front, following my every move like a bug-eyed cyclops. Another man bumped me from the left, almost deliberately. The women with placards began waving their signs and humming something that sounded like a funeral dirge. I caught sight of Helene Stockman behind them and wondered if she was part of their contingent.

As I moved toward the door, they closed in, faces tight with animosity. My stomach clenched and I worried that the scene might turn ugly.

"Did you know that your client is a Satanist?" one of the women shouted. "That he belongs to a cult that drinks the blood of the innocent?"

The reporter pushed her way toward me. "Ms. O'Brien, do you think—"

"No comment," I said, cutting her off.

With pen poised, she turned to the woman who'd spoken about Satan. Disgusted, I elbowed my way past them and into the building.

After the din out front the courtroom seemed unusually quiet. People packed the visitor's section in the rear, but they talked in hushed tones, as though they were in church. My footsteps on the old oak floor echoed loudly enough that I broke stride and tried to step more softly. The last thing I wanted was to call attention to myself by breaking the stillness.

I saw Grace Harding sitting ramrod straight in the front row with Pammy. Sam and Jake were standing off to one side, talking. Andrea was nowhere to be seen.

Grace nodded at me as I passed by, but she didn't smile.

"I see you made it safely past the alligators in the alley," Sam said.

"Barely." I was still seeing spots from the flash. "At least Curt's happy. I think he must have sent personal invitations."

Sam nodded. "I wouldn't be surprised to see him handing out cigars when it's all over."

"You'd think those bloodhounds could find something more newsworthy to cover," Jake muttered.

"It's the nature of the business," I explained. "Importance is measured by sales figures and ratings. Murder is always a big draw." Particularly the murder of a woman and a child, I added to myself.

Jake pulled a handkerchief out of his pocket and wiped his brow, then began tapping his foot with nervous energy. His suit was pressed, his shirt starched, his shoes polished, yet he looked like a man who was worn and frayed around the edges.

"Shouldn't you talk to them too?" he asked. "Listening to Willis, they're bound to get the wrong picture. I think they need to hear our side as well."

What side? I thought glumly. That wasn't the thing to say to the defendant's father, though; not at this point. Not with him seeming half-undone himself.

"We'll present our case at trial, where it counts," Sam said. "There's no point tipping our hand ahead of time. That would only give the prosecutor a preview of our defense strategy."

Jake made another swipe at his brow, then scanned the packed gallery of the courtroom. "This is disgusting," he said. "Voyeurism of the worst kind. Don't they realize a man's life is at stake here?"

Sam clasped Jake's shoulder. "Concentrate on giving Wes your support. Forget about the rest of it." He nodded toward the door, where a guard was bringing in Wes. "You'd better take a seat now."

The jailhouse overalls had been replaced by a well-tailored dark gray suit. The shirt was crisp, the tie an urbane diagonal stripe. With his face freshly shaven, his hair clipped and neatly combed, his tattoos well-concealed, Wes Harding looked like a different man. One who could almost have been standing in Curt Willis's place. Almost. Wes had the same self-contained air, but his expression was more sullen than cocky.

He took a seat at the far end of the counsel table, folded his arms across his chest and stared dead ahead. When Sam leaned over and whispered something in his ear Wes didn't bother to acknowledge the words.

The room quieted as Curt strode down the aisle and took his place at the prosecutor's table. He shuffled a few papers, passed a file to his assistant, glanced my way and smiled. The smile of a wily fox. But in his eyes I saw a hint of anxiety, like a young boy with his heart set on making the team.

Judge Seaton entered, called court to session, then scowled over the tops of his glasses at the gathered crowd. Many judges—most judges, I'd venture to say—enjoy being in the limelight. Seaton did not. Fiftyish, with stooped shoulders and a face like weathered stone, Seaton conducted his courtroom with as little intervention on his part as possible. Not because of any fine-tuned philosophy of judicial restraint, but because he was about as timid as they come. The fact that he had a courtroom full of spectators and journalists watching his every move no doubt displeased him beyond measure.

Curt Willis, on the other hand, chose his poses carefully for full audience effect. This despite the fact that the only person he had to convince was Seaton. His opening remarks were eloquent and dramatic, although orchestrated more with an eye to the personality game than the law. Nonetheless, he was good. It was all I could do to keep myself from nodding in agreement.

Finally he called his first witness, the police officer who'd responded to the initial call. In the wake of Curt's questions, the officer verbally reenacted the scene, step by step. The medical examiner was next, followed by the county criminalist.

Curt had dropped the theatrics and was now building his case in a sound and straightforward manner. Occasionally Sam would stand and object to the phrasing of a question, which Curt would simply restate in another form. There was no new evidence introduced, no surprise eyewitness or shocking revelation. Not that I expected any. The prosecution only has to introduce enough evidence to show probable cause. Curt was no more inclined to lay out his whole case at this stage than we were.

As the hearing progressed, I jotted notes to myself, looking for inconsistencies we might exploit at trial. Nothing, not even a toe hold. I might as well have been writing out my grocery list.

I'd instructed Wes along similar lines. If any of the testimony rang false with him or suggested a possible defense, he was to make note of it. He hadn't picked up the pencil once all morning. When Seaton called the noon recess I looked over at Wes.

"Well?" I asked.

"Well what?"

"You heard the evidence. This afternoon the prosecutor is going to argue that it all points to you."

"Yeah? Well, he's going to be wrong."

"Then how about you give us another explanation to throw to the judge."

A puff of breath, scornful and exasperated.

"We need our own version of events, Wes."

"I'm working on it, okay?" He pushed himself back from the table and stood. The guard was at his side in an instant. "If I come up with something," Wes muttered, "I promise you'll be the first to know."

I took a deep breath and held it for a minute. Attorneys who screamed in court were not regarded with favor.

Sam slipped his notepad into the scruffy brown briefcase he carried. "Willis is doing a decent job," he said.

"You sound surprised."

"Do I? I guess maybe I am. He has a reputation as something of a lightweight."

"This case is important to him. He sees it as his ticket to something bigger and better."

Sam smiled, but his eyes remained solemn. "This case is important to all of us." He turned. "Are you going over to Dr. Markley's now?"

I nodded. "I won't be long. I can't imagine the good doctor is going to give me much of her time."

Dr. Markley's office was located in a room at the back of her house. I entered through the side gate, as she'd instructed, and followed the flagstone path past the plum tree to the unmarked green door and rang the bell.

Dr. Markley was younger than I expected, probably in her late thirties. She had thick chestnut hair that hung in waves about her face. Her skirt was denim, topped with a loose-fitting jersey and applique vest. She looked like someone who'd be more at home canning the summer's harvest than probing people's psyches.

After directing me to a seat by the window Dr. Markley took the one opposite for herself. Her office was light and airy, definitely more comfortable than chic. There was a desk at one end, an overflowing bookshelf near the door and an assortment of large pillows along the wall. Something resembling an upholstered dentist's chair, sans instruments, stood in the far corner. A fat gray cat was curled in the chair's hollow. He lifted his head and yawned as I sat down.

"You wanted to ask me about Lisa Cornell?" Dr. Markley said. Her voice was soft and low, as unhurried as a feather floating in a still room.

I nodded. "I was hoping she might have told you something that would shed light on her death."

The doctor's gaze drifted to the garden outside before shifting back to me. "It's hard to lose a patient. Particularly one as young and full of life as Lisa."

"I understand she was seeing you in connection with re-curring headaches."

"That was an issue, yes."

"*An* issue? There were others?"

Dr. Markley sighed. "The whole area of confidentiality becomes murky when we're dealing with a patient who's been murdered. There are no ethical canons that cover a situation like this." She paused to smile. "Even if there were, I don't think I'd follow them if it meant letting a killer go unpunished."

I smiled back.

"On the other hand," Dr. Markley continued, "I can't simply go around repeating what Lisa told me in confi-dence. I have a responsibility to my profession, as well as to Lisa's memory. So if I sound vague, it's because I'm try-ing to walk a tight line. I hope you understand."

I did, and told her so.

"Lisa came to see me about her headaches. But the rea-son she ended up here in the first place is that medical sci-ence couldn't find a cause or cure. Emotional pain often manifests itself as physical pain. That's the avenue we were exploring."

"Get in touch with your feelings, that kind of stuff?"

A gentle laugh. "I hope there was a little more to it than that."

"But it wasn't simply a stress management class, then?"

Her expression was puzzled. "Not at all."

"Or a forum for handling chronic pain. It sounds more like group therapy of some kind."

"Well, yes, I suppose." She offered a wry smile. "Except it wasn't much of a group, just me and Lisa."

I sat forward. "Just the two of you?"

"That's not unusual. Most therapists prefer to work one-on-one."

"But what about Wednesday nights? I'd understood you ran a support group for people who suffered from chronic headaches. One of the women from the group called Lisa the night she was killed. Lisa ended up canceling a date with her fiancé because the woman needed help."

Dr. Markley looked perplexed. "There were just the two of us. Lisa's standing appointment was Wednesday at six. Now and then we'd meet another time during the week in addition, but she always came on Wednesday evenings. How did you get the idea it was some sort of group?"

"From Philip Stockman, her fiancé."

"I see." A frown creased her brow, then gave way to another smile, so faint it was barely visible. "Lisa must have presented it to him that way to keep the peace. He's apparently a . . ." She paused, looking for the right word. ". . . a man of strong opinions. He doesn't approve of therapy or, I might add, of therapists. Lisa's style was to avoid confrontation whenever possible."

"But what about this woman who phoned her?"

"I have no idea. Are you sure Lisa said it was someone from the group?"

"That's what Stockman says."

She held out her hands, palms up. "I'm afraid I can't help you there."

"From what you've said, it sounds like Lisa was willing to bend the truth to avoid confrontation. Do you think she might have invented the phone call the same way she did the group? Because it was easier than going into her real reasons for canceling the date."

"Perhaps."

"The white lie approach to carefree living."

There was that faint smile again. "You've never done something similar?"

"Sure." More times than I liked to admit. "But I can't imagine marrying someone I couldn't be honest with. Talk about setting yourself up for a dysfunctional marriage."

Dr. Markley pressed the fingers of her hands together. "People have different ways of handling conflict, different ways of working out the inevitable kinks in a relationship."

"And Lisa's was to avoid conflict."

"I shouldn't have told you that."

"Was that what you and Lisa were working on—her lack of assertiveness in relationships?"

Another faint smile. "Sorry, I'm not about to let you trip me up twice."

The cat stretched, jumped to the floor and meandered to the door, where it began meowing loudly. Dr. Markley rose and went to let him out.

"You sound as though you might have been there yourself," she said.

"In therapy?"

"I was thinking more in terms of assertiveness in relationships."

"Ah, that." The doctor was perceptive.

"It's not an uncommon problem. For women anyway."

Too bad I couldn't afford a professional visit. Given my history of failed relationships, I could probably have used some help. "You mentioned that Lisa's headaches were a manifestation of emotional pain. What sort of emotional pain might—"

"That was a possibility we were exploring," Dr. Markley said evenly, "not a certainty."

I backed up and tried again. "Were you making progress?"

She sighed. "With the headaches, no. If anything, they'd become worse the last few weeks."

"But there was progress of another sort?"

"Lisa had a high level of unexplained anxiety. I had her keep a diary of thoughts and feelings associated with the headaches. I thought that might help unlock the source of her anxiety. The fact that the headaches were becoming more frequent might have indicated that we were close to finding the underlying cause."

"What kind of underlying cause are we talking about?"

"I'm not sure."

"Do you have any theories?"

There was the barest beat of hesitancy; then she shook her head. "Sorry, I don't."

"What about the diary? Was there anything there that might shed light on her death?"

"Lisa never showed me what she wrote. It was purely to trigger her own thinking."

"So she might have written about something that was bothering her? Something that ultimately led to trouble?"

"She might have."

"Did Lisa ever talk about Philip Stockman?" I asked.

"Of course."

"I understand she had some reservations about going ahead with the wedding. Was that part of what you were exploring?"

Dr. Markley smiled. "I told you," she said, "I can't reveal a patient's confidences." Her tone was firm but not brusque.

"Not even if they point to a motive for murder?"

"Philip Stockman adored Lisa."

"How do you know?"

She pressed her fingertips to her temples. "I guess I

don't know for sure. Only what Lisa told me. But she gave him no reason to be angry. I doubt he was even aware of her ambivalence."

"She called off the wedding," I said.

"She postponed it. That's different than calling it off."

Dr. Markley was the expert, but it seemed to me that the distinction wasn't so clear. "Do you have any idea why she would have canceled her Friday evening date with Stockman?"

She shook her head. "Lisa may have simply preferred an evening alone."

"What about Wes Harding—did she ever mention him?"

There was a moment's hesitation during which Dr. Markley's gaze once again settled on the garden. "I'm sorry," she said, biting her lower lip. "I've already said more than I should."

"Lisa's dead, Doctor. I understand your desire to protect her privacy, but don't you think finding her killer takes precedence?"

"I do, absolutely. But there's nothing I can tell you that will help." She folded her hands in her lap, thumbs pressed together. Her eyes met mine. "I'm as disturbed by Lisa's death as anyone. Maybe more so. I know therapists aren't supposed to have favorites, but we do. I imagine lawyers feel the same, so maybe you know what I'm talking about. Lisa and I clicked from the start. Believe me, if I had knowledge that would help find her killer, I'd use it."

It wasn't until I was back in the car, playing the conversation through in my mind, that I thought to wonder if Dr. Markley had revealed more than she'd intended. I remembered her brief hesitation at the mention of Wes's name. Her assurance that she had no information that would help *find* the killer. Did that mean she had faith the killer had already been found?

But if she had information that implicated Wes, why would she withhold it?

13

I got back to the courtroom just as the clerk was finishing the swearing-in of a new witness.

"Who's that?" I whispered to Sam, sliding into the chair
to his right.

"Harlan Bailey. He works at the auto shop with Wes."

I glanced to the end of the table where Wes sat, arms
again folded across his chest, his mouth and jaw tight. It
was the look he'd worn all morning, but I sensed an un-
dercurrent of uneasiness that hadn't been there earlier.

"Why's he testifying?"

Sam shook his head. "Beats me. I don't like the feel of
it. His name was added at the last minute."

"What does Wes say about it?"

"That the guy's an asshole and a twit."

"Helpful. Anything else?"

"Nothing worth repeating. How'd you make out with Dr.
Markley?"

I started to whisper a response but stopped when I felt
Judge Seaton's eyes on us. He glared in our direction for

a few seconds longer, cleared his throat and, point made, turned his attention back to Harlan Bailey, who was explaining his association with Wes.

I scribbled a note for Sam. *There's no chronic pain group. Lisa was in therapy. Phone call remains a mystery. Let's talk later.*

Sam groaned and Seaton glared again.

Curt addressed the witness. "Now then, Mr. Bailey, I'd like to draw your attention to Wednesday, August sixth. Were you working at the auto shop that day?"

"Yeah, I work Monday through Friday every week. Sometimes on Saturdays too. It depends."

"And was Wes Harding also at work that day?"

"Yeah, he was."

"This was the Wednesday before Lisa Harding was killed, is that correct?"

Sam stood to object.

Curt held up a hand. "Sorry; let me rephrase that. How can you be certain of the day in question?"

"I know it was the sixth because my mother called that morning before I left for work."

There was a titter from the back of the room. Seaton ignored it.

"And how does this phone call make you certain of the date?"

"It's her birthday. She calls me every year, before I get a chance to call her. Then complains that I never remember."

This time the chortling was more widespread. Seaton, himself, worked to keep a straight face.

"So, on Wednesday, August sixth, you and Wes Harding were both at work. Did Lisa Cornell come to the shop that day?"

He nodded.

"You'll have to answer 'yes' or 'no,' " Seaton instructed, "so the court reporter can record your response."

Bailey nodded again, then amended it to a "yes."

I glanced down at Wes, who hadn't moved. His face was turned away from me, but I could see the muscles in his neck tighten.

"Was Lisa Cornell a regular customer at the shop?" Curt asked Bailey.

"I don't think so. I'd never seen her anyway."

"How can you be certain then that the woman at the shop was Lisa Cornell?"

"I took her MasterCard at the register. I noticed the name because Lisa is my mother's name too, and it being her birthday and all, it seemed kind of funny. Then I saw Ms. Cornell's picture in the paper after she was killed. I recognized her even before I checked the name."

"Did you have occasion to talk with Lisa Cornell the day in question?"

"Not really. I told her about the name coincidence, gave the little girl a lollipop. We keep them there at the register for anybody who wants one, but that was about it."

"Was there any interaction that you're aware of between the defendant and Lisa Cornell?"

"I don't know that you'd call it interaction, exactly. Wes had been out in the shop. He walked into the office to pick up a work order. Lisa kind of smiled at him and made this shrugging gesture with her shoulders."

"And what did you understand that to mean?"

Sam stood. "Objection, calls for an interpretation."

"Overruled."

"Your Honor, Mr. Bailey is not an expert in reading body language."

Seaton glowered. "Overruled," he said again, more forcefully.

Bailey looked to Curt, who nodded. "It didn't mean anything," Bailey said. "She was just being friendly. Seemed like a real nice lady, not all caught up in herself like some."

"After Lisa Cornell smiled at Wes, what did he do then?"

"Right then, nothing. He just walked past her like she wasn't there. But later, as she was leaving, he called her a bitch."

Curt feigned shock. "But all she'd done was smile at him."

"Objection."

"Sustained."

Curt's brow furrowed. If he'd been playing to a jury he'd have scored big. He wasn't, but with the press there in full force he'd accomplished almost as much.

"Did the defendant make this comment to Ms. Cornell's face?"

"No, we were standing at the register. He'd come back to pick up part of the work order he'd missed, and I was finishing with the MasterCard authorization."

"Can you remember his exact words?"

"Well, he kicked the wastebasket with his foot and said . . ." Bailey looked at the judge. "This involves some strong language."

"That's allowed, if it's an accurate quote."

"Well, after Wes kicked the wastebasket real hard, he called her a fucking bitch. He said it kind of under his breath, but the words were clear. So was his tone."

"You're sure he was talking about Lisa Cornell?"

Bailey nodded, then glanced at the court reporter and changed it to an "absolutely."

"Wes's reaction surprised me," he explained, "because the woman seemed so nice. I asked him if she'd caused trouble before. Some customers do, you know, and we like to keep track of them."

"What did Wes say then?"

"That it was personal."

"Did he elaborate?"

"No, and I didn't ask. You could tell he was in one of those moods where you didn't want to mess with him."

"Objection," Sam said. "Your Honor, the witness needs only to answer the question. I ask that the last part of his response be stricken."

"There's no jury here," Seaton said, sounding annoyed at the interruption. Then, addressing Curt, he asked, "You want to ask the witness *why* he didn't inquire further of the defendant?"

Curt posed the question; Bailey repeated what he'd said about Wes's mood.

Seaton's message had come through loud and clear—let's not get caught up in technicalities.

Curt finished up with a few additional points, then turned the witness over to the defense. Sam stood, hesitated, then passed. "No questions at this time," he said.

"This was not a stellar day for us," Sam grumbled later, over beer. We'd gone straight from the courthouse to Ollie's.

"You didn't expect Seaton to dismiss, did you?"

"No, but I didn't expect to get slammed in the face, either. Not only does the prosecution have physical evidence linking Wes to the crime, now they've managed to connect

Wes to Lisa Cornell. You realize they've set the stage for establishing motive. They're going to deliver the jury a tidy package."

"I imagine we'll be able to pick at the ribbons a bit."

Sam ignored my attempt to be reassuring. "And then, as if that weren't enough, this woman from Lisa's group turns out to be a phantom lead."

"The group part anyway."

"Dr. Markley had no idea who might have called Lisa?"

"None. She doesn't do group therapy at all, and she hadn't put Lisa in touch with any of her other patients. Dr. Markley was reluctant to reveal details from her sessions with Lisa, but I got the feeling she really had no clue about the call."

"It's gotta be important. Maybe someone wanted to make sure Lisa would be home that night."

"If there really was a call."

Sam squinted at me, perplexed.

"She might have used the phone call as an excuse to get out of her dinner date."

"Just made it up out of thin air, you mean?"

I nodded. "Of course, to a certain extent that only begs the question. We don't know whether Lisa simply felt like spending a Friday night away from Stockman, or whether there was something she intended to do instead."

"Something that ultimately led to her death." Sam stared glumly into his beer. "We're on a backward roll here, Kali."

"Still, if she was going to invent an excuse, why not say she had a headache or something? Why come up with a phony call from someone in a support group that doesn't exist? It makes me think there might be something there yet."

Sam signaled the waitress. "You want another?" he asked me.

"I'll switch to Coke." I like beer, but a little goes a long way. And the house wine at Ollie's comes out of a gallon jug that's usually been open for months.

"I think Lisa might have mentioned Wes's name to Dr. Markley," I said after the waitress took our order. "When I asked the doctor about it she hesitated, then sidestepped the question by saying she couldn't discuss details."

"After listening to that Bailey fellow today, it wouldn't surprise me."

"What did Wes say? Did you ask him?"

"I asked; he didn't say diddly. Claims he was speaking about women in general, not Lisa specifically."

The waitress brought our drinks. Sam raised the bottle to his lips. "What we've got here, Kali, is kind of a mishmash. One of those cases where there's no clear defense strategy. We'll cross-examine prosecution witnesses, question reliability of evidence, chip away at their case and harp on the fact that the police failed to pursue other avenues, but it would sure be a heck of a lot better if we had some ammo of our own."

"You mean like an airtight alibi and another suspect with motive, means and opportunity?"

"I'm not greedy. I'd settle for one of the above."

"Well, unless there was someone hiding under Wes's bed that night, we aren't going to get an alibi."

"You'd think that a neighbor, a passing car, *someone* would have seen or heard something at the Cornell place." Sam pressed the beer bottle to his temples. "You've talked to all the neighbors?"

"Most. A couple of them I haven't been able to reach. I'll give you the list of names."

"And what about this homeless fellow; you've checked with him?"

"I'm trying."

"Good. It's just wacky enough, it may lead us some-where." He frowned. "The other-guy defense is always a good one. You're working on that too, right?"

"Right, but we haven't exactly struck gold."

"I've got experts going over the lab reports, crime scene photographs, that sort of thing. I'm hoping we'll be able to show that the prosecution is making some mighty big leaps."

I nodded. It was standard defense strategy. Sometimes it worked, sometimes not.

"I'll follow up on this Bailey fellow. I'd like you to keep looking into Lisa's background. I know she was a real sweetheart and all, but no one's so squeaky clean you can't find something of interest. Look for anything—drug use, gambling, sex habits, relationship with the ex. Hell, maybe she had ties to some devil worship sect that practiced rit-ual child abuse."

I thought of the women on the courthouse steps who'd said the same thing about Wes. "That's not funny, Sam."

He lowered his beer bottle and regarded me with un-expected seriousness. "I'm not trying to be funny," he said. "I'm trying to save a man's neck. A man who happens to be the son of a very good friend."

I returned his gaze. "I'll look into it," I told him.

But I wouldn't necessarily like it. Trash the victim was not my favorite game.

14

Tuesday morning I decided to pay a visit to Ed Cole, the attorney handling the probate of Lisa Cornell's estate.

The phone book listed his office as being on the main road through Hadley. After several passes through the center of town I found Cole's office, finally, in a strip mall at the outer edge of the business district. It was conveniently sandwiched between the Nu U Aerobics Studio and a Baskin-Robbins ice cream store. Cole's name was stenciled on the glass door in gold lettering, directly above a sign that read PUSH.

I pushed, and found myself stepping into a field of green and blue shag. The walls were paneled in dark wood—the kind that's sold by the sheet at Home Depot. A vinyl couch of faded orange stood by the door, and across the room was a heavily cluttered desk. Behind the desk, typing away laboriously with two fingers, sat a man. At least I assumed it was a man. The only part I could actually see was the top of his head—a ring of curls crowned with a shiny bald spot.

"Let me guess," he said, without raising his head. "You're pregnant."

My breath caught halfway to my lungs. My clothes were feeling snug, but I hadn't considered *that* possibility. I glanced at my midsection, afraid of what I might find there. "I think it's more what I've been eating," I told him.

Finally he looked up, and then blushed right to the circle of smooth flesh at the top of his head.

"Oh, gosh," he stammered, "I thought you were Tina, my secretary. She's been feeling, uh, indisposed these last couple of days. She had a doctor's appointment this morning and I just, uh, assumed that you were her."

He looked stricken. I hastened to reassure him, but sucked my stomach in all the same.

"Are you Ed Cole?" I asked.

"I'm afraid I am." Cole was about my height, with a slight build. Rising, he offered his hand and an apologetic smile. "This is really very embarrassing."

"I just hope you aren't clairvoyant."

He blushed. "No, I'm simply an oaf with a big mouth."

"If it makes you feel any better, you haven't offended a paying client. I'm here about Lisa Cornell." I introduced myself and explained my involvement in the case.

"I heard the courtroom was packed yesterday," he said, gesturing to the chair on my side of the desk. "And that popular sentiment against your client is running high." Despite the words, his tone was matter-of-fact rather than offensive. In any event, he was right.

"Since we're looking at a trial rather than a popularity contest," I said, "sentiment doesn't matter much."

Cole shook his head. "It would matter to me. In fact, I

wouldn't touch a case like that unless I was damn sure I was on the winning side."

"Winning side or right side?" I realized, too late, how self-righteous the words sounded.

Cole shrugged them off and gave me a good-natured smile. "Both, I guess. A stable client base isn't easy to come by; I wouldn't want to see mine disappear overnight."

This was something that had begun to worry me, as well. Part of the reason I'd taken the case was to build a name for myself. But I hadn't counted on the swell of animosity against my client. "Do you think that would happen?" I asked.

"Let's just say, I don't want to be in a position to find out." He smiled again and folded his hands on the desk. "All that's beside the point, though. How can I help you?"

"I understand there's been quite a bit of interest in the Cornell property."

He nodded. "It's a nice piece of real estate, almost ten acres with a stream and a pond. You don't find property like that very often. Usually when you get a good-sized parcel, the bulk of it's a ravine or otherwise unusable. Plus, here you've got access from two sides. There have been people interested in the place for years, but Anne never wanted to sell."

"Anne?"

"Anne Drummond, Lisa's aunt. She left the property to Lisa when she died, with the understanding that Lisa would come live here. Anne had a bee in her bonnet about keeping the place from being developed."

"She had no children of her own?"

He shook his head.

"Is there anyone in particular interested in the property?"

"No one that comes to mind. For a number of years Larry Cox was after Anne to sell to him. He had the place just east of hers. Wanted to combine the properties and turn them into a dude ranch. You know, for tourists."

"Has he inquired about the property since her death?"

"No. He sold his place a couple of years back and moved to Wyoming."

"How about more recent interest?" I asked. "Maybe from a corporation or development company?" That seemed to be the growth wave of the moment.

Cole tugged on an earlobe. "I had an inquiry not long ago from a gentleman named Simmons in the Bay Area. He was rather vague about who he was representing. I had the feeling it was either a corporation or some well-known individual who wanted anonymity."

"Do you have his number?"

"I'm sure I do, somewhere. There have been several other calls since Lisa's death. I've been telling people to call back in a couple of months. We can't sell until we get the estate sorted out."

"Who inherits now that Lisa is dead?"

He frowned. "That's an interesting question. Lisa's mother claims she does. As far as I know, Lisa died without a will, so the woman may be right, except for the question of Lisa's husband. I haven't found a record of the divorce, and when I tried to track the guy down I got one dead end after another."

"You never reached him?"

"The last address I have is in Santa Cruz. I talked to the woman he was living with there. She says they broke up in June and she hasn't seen or heard from him since. Only she didn't put it quite so politely."

"He was apparently here in town not too long ago to see Amy."

Cole nodded. "So I heard."

The phone rang and Cole picked it up. "No, she's not," he said, and then a moment later, "Hold on while I find a pen."

He opened a drawer, closed it, tried another, then began shuffling through the heaps of paper that covered the desk. Finally he stood up and began patting his own pockets.

I reached into my purse and handed him a pen.

He mouthed a silent "thanks," then took a message of considerable length. "That was the veterinarian," Cole said when he hung up. "Tina's veterinarian, that is."

I was happy to see I wasn't the only person who found myself acting as secretary for my secretary. I asked, "Do you know anything about a diary Lisa kept?"

"What kind of diary?"

"I'm not sure what it looked like, but it was a recording of thoughts and feelings associated with her headaches."

Cole shook his head. "I don't recall seeing anything like that among her things at the house. I'm fairly certain it wasn't among the items seized by the police."

"Do you think there's a chance I could get into the house and take a look around?"

His forehead creased. "I don't . . ."

"It's not just the diary. Lisa may have received a phone call the night she was killed. It was apparently a friend who needed help. Lisa canceled her date with her fiancé because of it."

"And you think this call is somehow relevant to her death?"

"That's what I'd like to find out."

Cole seemed to retreat into himself for a moment as he mulled this over. "You really think Lisa Cornell was killed by someone other than your client?"

"If she was, Wes Harding shouldn't have to pay for it."

"The police have been through everything at least once, and her parents took some personal items."

"I'd still like to look around."

Cole thought for a moment longer. "Okay," he said finally. "I have to go out there today anyway. I guess it wouldn't hurt if you came along. But it will have to be quick. I've got a meeting back here later this afternoon."

"I won't slow you down, I promise."

"How about an hour from now? We can ride out together."

"Great."

I checked my watch and then took off for a stroll around Hadley, a town that has been recently discovered by tourists and those who feed off them. The town is quainter than Silver Creek; quainter now than it was a few years ago, in fact. I'm thankful that for all its changes, Silver Creek has been spared that kind of pseudo-Disney renovation.

I passed up a gourmet cookie franchise, a T–shirt outlet and several antique shops, but succumbed to the temptation of a double latte at the town's newest sidewalk café.

When I returned to Cole's office a woman with dark, unruly hair was sitting at the desk where he had been earlier. I gave her my name, which she managed to forget by the time she buzzed Cole.

"There's a Ms. . . . uh, a woman here to see you," she told him, then hung up quickly.

"Well," I said to Cole on the way to the car, "was she or wasn't she?"

He went through the blushing routine again. "Almost four months."

"And she didn't know?" I tried not to sound too incredulous.

"Tina has trouble with details."

It sounded as though our secretaries had a lot in common.

"She'd been told she could never have children. She and her husband took up raising dogs instead." Cole opened the car door for me and tossed the fast-food wrappers from the front seat to the back. "They have seven wolfhounds and a very small house."

"Sounds like fun."

Cole sighed. "I hope they manage to find room for the baby." He started the car and pulled onto the highway.

"How well did you know Lisa Cornell?" I asked.

"Not well at all. I knew her aunt, but I never met Lisa until after Anne died. I'd never even heard mention of Lisa until Anne revised her will."

"She revised her will? When was this?"

"About six months before her death." Cole grew silent for a moment. "By the time they discovered the cancer it had spread pretty far. The doctors gave her a year, and she only got half of it."

"When she learned of the cancer, that's when she revised her will?"

He nodded. "She'd originally left the property to Lisa's mother. My father drew up that will more than twenty years ago." Cole slowed as we passed a bicyclist. "A lot of people do that, you know; forget about updating their will as times change. When you know your time's about up, though, I guess you want to get your affairs in order. At least Anne did."

"Did she say why she was making the change?"

"Not specifically, but I know she wanted the house to go to someone who would live here. I think she was worried Lisa's mother would sell the place."

"Were Lisa and her aunt close?"

"I got the feeling it had been several years since they'd seen each other. I doubt they'd even been in touch until Anne learned she was sick. But Lisa lived with Anne for a while when she was a child. I imagine there's a pretty strong bond that develops in a situation like that."

"What made Mrs. Drummond think Lisa wouldn't sell?"

"She worried about that," Cole said, "but the two of them apparently talked it over."

"Anne Drummond must have cared deeply about the property."

"She did. But she was also a funny lady; you couldn't always follow her logic."

"She lived alone?"

He nodded. "She was married, but her husband ran off years ago. They'd only been married a short while when he left her. He was a handsome fellow, although I never did like him much. He was one of those types who smiles too often and walks with a swagger. Thought he was better than everyone else."

Sounded a lot like one of my old boyfriends, only he'd had the decency to run off before we made it official. "She never remarried?" I asked.

"Nope. Never got a formal divorce either. Some people thought that was because she was still pining for him, but you want my opinion, I think she just forgot about him."

We pulled into the long gravel drive and parked. "Did Anne Drummond leave everything she owned to Lisa?"

"Just the property and furnishings." Cole searched

through his pockets for the key. " 'Course there wasn't much else except for a small savings account. Left that to charity."

He opened the door and we stepped inside. "Things are pretty much as they were when Anne lived here," he said, flipping on a light. "I don't think Lisa had much stuff of her own, or maybe she just preferred what was here."

The house had a heavy, closed-up smell and a visible layer of dust, but it was otherwise clean. The decor was simple but inviting. Lots of pine and oak and nubby fabrics in solid, strong colors. An oil landscape hung above the stone fireplace, a braided rug lay in front of the hearth. Otherwise the walls and floor were bare.

Although it was clearly a house that had been lived in, most of the personal touches were Amy's. There was a stuffed tiger on the sofa, a glazed clay impression of a child's hand on the mantel, a copy of *Ranger Rick* on the coffee table. Games and children's books filled the bookshelf near the door.

Comfortable and homey. I tried not to dwell on the two people whose abbreviated lives were reflected in the surroundings.

"What are you looking for?" Cole asked. "Maybe I can lend a hand."

"I don't know exactly. A desk calendar, address book, bills—anything that might help me piece together what happened the night Lisa died. I'm also looking for a small notebook she might have used as her diary."

Cole jangled the keys and change in his pocket. "Her parents took a lot of her papers, but you're welcome to look around. I think there's a calendar by the phone in the kitchen. She had some letters and manila envelopes in the bedroom, though they were probably among the things her parents packed up. I need to verify a few items for probate; then I'll come back and help you look."

I found the calendar by the phone—a week-at-a-glance publication from UNICEF. It was still open to the first week of August. Nothing was penciled in for the night she died, not even her date with Stockman. There was a ten o'clock dentist appointment for Amy written in for Wednesday, a notation about two dozen cookies on Tuesday, and a cryptic "GD" listed for Sunday. Granger? I'd have to check to see if anyone knew his last name.

I flipped through earlier weeks and found nothing illuminating.

I didn't find an address book, but I did find a short list of numbers at the front of the phone book. I copied them onto the back of an envelope I pulled from my purse. I recognized Caroline's name and Mrs. Arabagucci's, and surmised the others would prove to be of a similar nature.

From the kitchen I moved on to Lisa's bedroom—a large, sunny, second-floor room at the back of the house. There was a four-poster bed to the left of the door, a tall chest at one end of the opposite wall, a rocking chair and low table at the other. As was true with the rest of the house, the room had little in the way of Lisa's personal touch. No photographs, books, mementos. But maybe they'd already been packed up by her mother and stepfather.

I started with the bottom drawer of the chest, which was empty, worked my way up past the jeans and T-shirts to the underwear in the topmost drawer. Amid the simple white cotton briefs and bras I found a pair of lace G-string pants that suggested "gift." I wondered if they had come from Philip or a previous admirer, and whether Lisa had found skimpy lingerie as impractical and uncomfortable as I did.

Cole appeared in the doorway just as I finished my search. "Any luck?" he asked.

I shook my head.

"I've got an inventory for the stuff her parents took back at the office. It wasn't much. They tagged the furniture they wanted to keep and asked me to ship it when the legalities were straightened out."

On our way downstairs we passed what was clearly Amy's room. Pink-and-white-striped wallpaper, a ruffled bedspread, and an abundance of stuffed animals.

"Mind if I look here too?" I asked.

"Go ahead, as long as it won't take too long."

I gave the closets and cupboards a cursory inspection. Nothing but toys and children's books. The drawers held clothing, both child-size and doll-size. On the wall shelf, next to a wooden puzzle which spelled "Amy," I found crayons and a spiral sketchbook.

Opening the book, I flipped through the pages. They were filled largely with colorful, childlike scribblings. At the back there were pages of adult-quality sketches followed by a child's attempt to imitate them. Several depicted dilapidated barns and gnarly trees. Another was a page of tiny flowers that reminded me of the wallpaper from my grandmother's house when I was young. In addition, there were three pages of eyes and brows, as if the artist had been perfecting her technique, and a couple more of complete faces. The corresponding child's sketches would have been indecipherable on their own, but with the adult drawings as a guide, I found it relatively easy to make sense of the younger artist's efforts.

Cole peered over my shoulder. "Like mother, like daughter."

"Lisa drew these? They're quite good." This was another

side of Lisa I wasn't familiar with. I knew the wide smile and friendly manner, the proud and devoted mother, the waitress with boundless energy. But her artistic talent, like her upcoming marriage and her problem with the headaches, was an area we'd never touched on. I wondered what other facets of her character I'd find if I looked.

"I assume they're hers," Cole said. "There were a couple of sketchbooks among the things her parents packed up and took with them."

He turned to the last page—stick figures of a mother and daughter holding hands. The body lines were too sure to have been drawn by a child, but the red crayon smiles, which extended well beyond the confines of the face, bore the clear stamp of a five-year-old hand.

I had a sudden vision of Lisa and Amy, curled side by side on the sofa, heads bent, maybe giggling in conspiratorial fashion as they crafted the picture together.

My chest grew tight and my throat burned. Mother and daughter, both now dead.

15

When I got back to the office I found the door locked. Taped to the front was a note from Myra: *Be back soon.* Since she hadn't bothered to indicate the hour, or the date, I had no idea when "soon" might be. Not that Myra's notion of time and my own had much commonality anyway.

Once I opened the door it was clear she'd at least been there that morning. The day's mail was stacked on the left side of my desk, phone messages on the right. There was nothing of note in either pile except for a white business-size envelope marked "personal and confidential."

That always gets my attention, even though nine times out of ten it's a gimmick. The last such missive had offered me a record-breaking low price on hand-tailored suits from Hong Kong.

I took the letter into my office and opened it. This time it wasn't a sales pitch.

The envelope contained a single sheet of standard typing paper, erratically folded over on itself. The note, typed on what looked to be a manual machine, consisted of two lines: *Who the hell do you think you are, anyway? I wait for the day you suffer like they did.*

I read the note a second time, and then a third. My heart, which had stalled for a beat or two, began thumping noisily, like a dog's tail against hard ground.

I knew I shouldn't take it personally. Criminal cases tend to push people's buttons. And a case like ours, which involved a particularly disturbing crime, was bound to tap the public's frustrations and fears.

Nonetheless, the words had the intended effect: first shock, and then alarm. I felt goosebumps run across my shoulders and up my neck. For a moment I had trouble breathing.

Finally I wadded the letter up tight, tossed it into the trash and tried my best to forget I'd ever seen it. Out of sight, out of mind.

I reached for the stack of phone messages but ended up dialing Sam instead.

"Have you received any hate mail?" I asked.

"For which particular sin?"

I told him about the letter, tried to make light of it and failed miserably.

"No, nothing like that," Sam said. "Not recently anyway. I've had my fair share of hate mail on previous cases, though, and I'm sure I haven't seen the end of it." His tone, like his message, was reassuring.

"It's more upsetting than I thought it would be."

He mumbled concurrence. "It always is, but I don't think you should worry about it unless you get others. Judging from what went on in court yesterday, people's feelings are running pretty high. That's not unusual in a case like this."

With the phone tucked under my chin, I sorted through the stack of mail a second time, just to be safe. The tension across my shoulders eased when I found nothing the least bit suspicious.

"What did you learn about the Cornell property?" Sam asked.

"Nothing useful. There's interest, but there's been interest for years. Cole gave me a couple of names. Most are people he knows, but one, a guy by the name of Robert Simmons in the 415 area code, might lead to something. I'll call this afternoon."

I removed a flyer for a free blueberry muffin from the stack of otherwise mundane mail. "When all's said and done it's really not much of a lead. Even if you wanted the property enough to kill for it, there's no guarantee you'd be the one to end up with it once Lisa was dead."

"Unless you inherited directly."

"Yeah, I had thought of that." I read the fine print on the flyer and discovered the muffin was free only with the purchase of a full dozen. I dropped it into the trash. Then I bent over a second time and retrieved the note I'd wadded up earlier.

"Any idea who that would be?" Sam asked.

"Probably Lisa's mother, but maybe her husband." I repeated what Cole had told me. "If the divorce wasn't final, the property might arguably go to him."

"How about the Friday night phone call? Any luck there?"

"Nothing. I wasn't able to find Lisa's diary either. I have a feeling it could prove to be important. Her parents packed up a couple of boxes of stuff. I thought I'd check with them, see if they have it."

"Good thinking," Sam said. "You ought to be able to get

a feel for the mother's interest in the property as well. Where do they live?"

"Los Angeles."

"That's good. You can get down and back in a day. You think you could do it tomorrow?"

I rocked forward. "Who said anything about a personal visit?"

"If they've got the diary, you're going to want to look at it, right? So you'll end up going there anyway. Jake Harding wants us to leave no stone unturned. An expense this minor, it's nothing. We don't even need to clear it with him."

"It wasn't the expense I was thinking of."

Sam made a sound of disgust. "Planes are safer than cars, Kali. But if you'd rather take a couple of days and drive down . . ."

The thought of spending seven hours on the road, each way, did not have a lot of appeal either. Especially since the drive down I-5 involved long, tedious stretches of arid flatland. It had to be the most boring route in the world.

I sighed. "At least I'll be flying in clear weather."

"Take along a good book and you won't even know you've left the ground."

"Ha." I always knew. And it amazed me every time that we not only left the ground but returned to it without mishap.

Sam must have leaned back in his chair. I heard a creak and then a shuffling sound as he got comfortable again. "I went out to the auto shop this morning, talked with Harlan Bailey. The guy told the same story he did yesterday in court, but I found out that he and Wes are not on the best of terms. Office politics in the service bay, I guess. We ought to be able to use that to impeach his credibility as a witness."

"Did he elaborate on yesterday's testimony?"

"I got the feeling there wasn't much to elaborate on. The guy's taken one little incident and made it into a whole miniseries. Probably with coaching from Willis."

"Maybe we can use that too."

"With luck maybe we can find someone who's heard Wes use the same language on other occasions, with respect to other women. If so, we can show there was nothing personal about the remark."

"Great defense," I said glumly. *"People of the jury, our client didn't have anything against Lisa Cornell personally; he thinks all women are bitches.* That's not going to win us many points, Sam."

"Hopefully," he said after a short pause, "we'll be able to do better than that."

When I got off the phone with Sam I tried the number Cole had given me for Robert Simmons and got a recording. It was one of those that did nothing but repeat the number you'd reached and advised you to wait for the beep. I left my name and number, then tried Caroline. I hadn't known about the diary when I'd talked to her last. I was hoping she'd be able to help me locate it.

Caroline's line was busy, so I returned phone calls from the stack of messages Myra had left me. I tried Caroline again about fifteen minutes later.

Still busy.

Finally I decided to drive over and talk to her in person.

There was a pickup truck in the driveway, a stroller on the porch. Music, heavy on the bass, was pounding away inside the house. When I got to the door I could hear a baby crying as well. I rang the bell, then knocked loudly.

Footsteps from inside. After what seemed to be a long time the door opened.

The figure in the doorway was male. And big. Over six feet, with broad shoulders and the kind of well-developed muscles that come only through diligent effort. His hair was long on top but cropped close on the sides. He was wearing a sleeveless T-shirt and elastic-waist shorts. Rubber-thonged sandals on his feet. One hand held a can of beer, the other gripped the handle of a plastic infant seat. The infant in the seat was howling.

"Yeah?" he said.

"Is Caroline around?"

"No, she isn't." He eyed me suspiciously. "Who are you?"

I decided on the friendly approach. "Kali O'Brien," I said. "You must by Duane."

That suspicious look again.

"I wanted to talk to her about Lisa Cornell."

The look grew wary. "My wife's got nothing to do with that."

I explained my involvement. "Your wife and Lisa were friends. I was hoping she might be able to clear up a few things for me."

He bounced the baby, shifted his weight to the other foot. The muscle in his cheek twitched. "I doubt it," he said brusquely. "They worked together is all. Aside from that, they didn't have much in common."

Jeremy rode down the hallway on a plastic tricycle and rammed against Duane's leg. "Watch it," Duane warned.

Jeremy giggled and rammed him again, harder.

Duane hooked the infant seat over his arm, switched the beer to his other hand, and rapped his knuckles once lightly against the boy's head. "You're cruisin' for a bruisin', tiger."

Remembering Caroline's bruised and swollen lip, I cringed inwardly. But Jeremy seemed unperturbed. Still giggling, he rammed Duane's leg once more, then pedaled back up the hallway.

Duane took a swallow of beer.

"How well did you know Lisa Cornell?" I asked, raising my voice to make myself heard over the baby's wailing.

"What makes you think I knew her at all?"

I shrugged. "Maybe I'm reading between the lines." Easy to do given his expression when I'd first mentioned Lisa's name. Plus the fact that Caroline had told me Duane didn't like Lisa's "type."

Duane pulled a pacifier out of his pocket, dribbled beer on it and stuck it in the baby's mouth. "Who did you say you were again?"

I explained a second time.

His thumb traced the seam of the can.

"I get the feeling you weren't any too fond of Lisa," I said after a moment.

"Where'd you get that?"

"Reading between the lines again."

He sighed. "I never wished the lady harm, but you're right, I didn't particularly like her. And I didn't like my wife palling around with her either."

"Why's that?"

A shrug. His eyes slid away from mine. "I didn't like her energy."

"Her energy?"

"Vibes. You know, her aura." He brushed the hair off his forehead with the hand that held the beer. "I just didn't like her much, okay?"

"What did she—"

"I got to finish feeding the kids," Duane said, cutting me off. "I'll tell Caroline you came by. But like I said, she won't be able to help."

The door closed before I could hand him my card.

I didn't have a whole lot of faith in Duane's passing on the message. I stopped at the corner gas station and used a pay phone to call the diner.

Caroline's voice held an edge of alarm until I identified myself.

She let out a long breath. "I was afraid something had happened to one of the kids. Hardly anyone calls me here unless it's an emergency."

"They're both fine," I said. "I was just out there."

The note of alarm surfaced again. "You were? Why?"

"I wanted to ask you a couple more things about Lisa Cornell."

"Geez, you went out to the house?"

"I thought you'd be there. Don't you usually work the evening shift?"

"I had to switch today."

"What I need to talk to you about won't take long. I could come by the diner right now if it's convenient."

"Did you see Duane?" Her tone was guarded.

"Briefly."

"What did he say?"

"That you and Lisa didn't have much in common besides working at the diner." When she didn't say anything I continued. "He also seemed to think she might have been a bad influence."

Caroline snorted. A voice from the background hollered her name. "I gotta go," she said.

"What time do you get off? I'll meet you then."

"Don't bother. I've already told you everything I know."

"What about her diary. Did Lisa happen to mention where she kept it?"

"She never mentioned it at all."

I made one last attempt. "Lisa got a phone call the Friday night she was killed. From a friend who needed her help. She canceled her dinner date with Philip Stockman on account of it. Was the call from you?"

Caroline made a sound, a kind of choking laugh. "Lisa would hardly have canceled a date on my account."

"Why, did you have a falling out?"

"Look, I've got to go. Like I told you before, Lisa and I had our own lives."

There was something about her tone that gave me pause, but Caroline hung up before I had a chance to inquire further.

Myra was back at her desk when I returned to the office.

"Sorry I had to run out like that," she said, running a hand through the tangle of dark curls. "Marc fell off the jungle gym."

"Is he okay?"

"Yeah. He hit his head. They wanted me to take him to the doctor for an evaluation, but he seems to be fine. Kids are pretty resilient."

If they're lucky, I amended silently, thinking of Amy.

"That new client called," she said. "The one who owns the apartment complex. He wants you to send him a bill for the work to date." She hesitated. "Apparently, he won't be needing your services in the future."

"Did he say why?"

"No, just that he felt it wasn't going to work out."

I felt my stomach clench. As far as I could tell it was

working out just fine—until I'd taken on a controversial case. A case I'd hoped would help me make a name for myself. Instead, it was going to cost me one of the precious few clients I had.

"Mr. Sturgis called too. He wanted you to know that the Harding case made the *San Francisco Chronicle*. His daughter faxed him a copy this morning."

"Great. Don't tell me he's going to pull out too."

"Not at all. In fact, he wanted you to autograph the article when he gets it. His daughter is sending the actual clipping by mail."

"Autograph it?" I said, incredulous. "I hope you told him 'no.' "

"I told him I'd ask." She raised her chin. "Though I don't see the harm in it."

"This isn't some Hollywood soap opera, Myra. Two people are dead and a man's life is at stake."

The chin jutted forward. "You don't have to get all preachy. I'm not saying you should book yourself on 'Rinaldo,' but I don't see the harm in pleasing a client."

"I'll think about it," I grumbled. And then I laughed. "Besides, it's not 'Rinaldo'; it's 'Geraldo.' "

She gave me a smarmy, cheek-sucking look and began rolling a pencil between her palms. "How's the case coming along?"

"About as expected. The judge found sufficient cause to hold Wes for trial. Now we've got sixty days to put together a winning defense."

"Only sixty days?"

"That's my feeling too, but Wes insists on exercising his right to a speedy trial."

"So what's the winning strategy going to be?"

"At this stage we're still probing, hoping something major will turn up."

"Like what?"

I shrugged. "A witness who saw or heard something inconsistent with Wes's guilt. A bungled investigation, evidence that's been compromised. Maybe something in Lisa's life that points to a different killer. If none of that pans out, we'll take every opportunity to cast doubt on the prosecution's case."

Myra thought for a moment, frowning. "Lisa might not have been the intended victim, you know."

"Mistaken identity, you mean? Like maybe the killer went to the wrong house?" Except in the movies, that sort of blunder was generally limited to cases involving organized crime or drugs.

"No, that's not what I meant." Myra took a breath. "What if it was Amy the killer wanted? What if she was the target and Lisa was just incidental?"

"Why would anyone want to kill a five-year-old child?" I asked.

But I knew the question was foolish even before it left my lips.

16

"It happens," Myra said, her tone defensive.

I nodded. Children were killed by their parents some-times, out of despondency, or anger, or some twisted act of revenge against a spouse. But generally the murder of a child was tied to kidnapping or sexual assault. Death was the ultimate guarantee of silence. Was that the reason Amy had been killed?

Myra crossed her arms on her desk and leaned forward. "The psychologist who talked to the parents' group the other day said people who abuse children often threaten them with physical harm or death. A person like that is so terrified of being discovered, he'll find a way to justify the killing."

"You're suggesting someone might have been molesting Amy?"

She got defensive again. "It's just a thought. It came to me because of what the psychologist said."

"It's an interesting possibility."

"Maybe Amy was killed to keep her from telling what

had happened. Lisa might have come into the barn while the killer was still there, so he had to kill her too."

It didn't make sense that Amy would have been wandering around the barn alone at night. "Or maybe," I added, "Lisa discovered what was going on and tried to stop it. Assuming there's any truth to this abuse business to begin with."

Myra slumped down in her chair. "I wish my friend had never suggested having this program at the school. She thinks it's important, but like I told you before, she has her own agenda. I guess if you've been abused yourself, you become something of a zealot when it comes to sparing others. Myself, I just get depressed by these stories."

"What did you think of the psychologist who spoke to the group?"

"I liked her, and I trust her. She's very down to earth. Doesn't use a lot of fancy jargon, and she isn't afraid to laugh." Myra sighed. "Maybe it'll be okay because of her. I don't think she'll push the kids beyond what they can handle."

Myra's theory about the murders played through my mind during the flight to Los Angeles. It was enough, almost, to make me forget I was flying.

A five-year-old child as the primary victim. Her death as the catalyst for both killings. It certainly put a different spin on things. Although, to be honest, it didn't do much in the way of clearing Wes Harding.

Wes's rabbit's foot near Amy's body.

The torn clothing and exposed bodies.

A little girl and a grown man in a dimly lit barn.

They weren't images I wanted to dwell on, but once

they appeared I had trouble ignoring them. By the time the plane touched down at the Burbank airport my anxiety about flying wasn't the only thing scrambling my stomach.

Lisa's mother and stepfather lived in San Marino, an enclave of wealth and exclusivity at the foot of the San Gabriel Mountains. The streets were wide and serene. The lawns a lush green, and as manicured as a putting green. There was an air of tranquillity that hovered over the community, a stillness that set it apart from the hectic energy of the surrounding areas.

I found the address with ease. The house was a sprawling white stucco with a red tile roof and recessed windows. A low wall lined the front and sides of the property, but I could see a bed of roses through the gate. The neighboring houses were all of a similar style and construction, probably built around the same time. By most standards they would have been impressive homes, but in the context of San Marino they were undoubtedly modest.

Before heading for the door I sat in my rental car for a few moments, gathering my thoughts. What did you say to the mother of a murder victim, especially when you'd aligned yourself with the man accused of the crime? What *could* you say, besides "I'm sorry for your loss"? And even that, no matter how heartfelt, seemed almost a mockery.

Finally I willed myself from the car, took a deep breath and rang the bell. An Hispanic woman opened the door a moment later, then nodded with recognition when I told her my name.

"I tell Mrs. Reena you coming here," the woman said, and started off. When I didn't follow immediately she turned and gestured me forward.

I followed her to a glass-walled room at the end of the hall, where she mumbled a rudimentary introduction and then quickly departed.

The woman sitting on the sofa glanced up and frowned. She looked to be in her early fifties, although she was clearly doing everything in her power to keep the signs of aging at bay. Her hair was a solid shade of honey blond, feathered around her face and fuller in back. Her makeup was artfully applied, and her dress, though snug, was well-tailored. She held a drink in one hand, a cigarette in the other.

The man standing behind her, kneading her shoulders, was probably ten years her junior, although it was hard to tell because he had the kind of smooth, urbane features that merely mellowed with age. A second drink rested on the table to his left.

"Maria said you were a friend of Lisa's." Reena Swanson's voice had the raspy quality of a longtime smoker. And the crisp intonation of someone who didn't wish to be bothered.

"I knew her," I said, "but not well enough to be called a friend."

Reena studied me a moment, her gaze level, the eyes cool. "I'm not interested in semantics," she said, crinking her neck so that her shoulders molded to her husband's fingers. "A little deeper, Ron, especially on the right side."

"Lisa was a lovely person," I said. "Always upbeat and friendly."

"Really." Reena dipped her head further forward. Her expression was hard to read, but it made me uncomfortable.

"I'm very sorry for your loss," I said, rather stiffly.

She looked up, frowned heavily, then stubbed out her

cigarette. "What was it you wanted? You certainly didn't come all the way to L.A. to tell me what a wonderful daughter I had."

I felt both taken aback and chastised. "I understand you packed up some of your daughter's belongings. Had them shipped back here."

Husband and wife exchanged glances.

"Did Cole put you up to this?" Ron asked.

"Put me up to what?"

Reena waved her hand in disgust. "It doesn't matter," she said to her husband. "None of it's worth much. Besides, he made an inventory of everything we took."

"What is it he wants back?" Ron asked with a sigh.

There was only time for a quick round of soul-searching, not one of my fortes. Honesty won out. Although it probably had as much to do with not wanting to involve Cole as with any clear aversion on my part to stretching the truth.

"Ed Cole has nothing to do with my being here," I explained. "I'm an attorney representing Wes Harding."

"Harding?" As recognition struck, Reena Swanson's features clouded. "The man who killed Lisa and Amy?"

"The man accused of killing them."

There was a moment's silence.

"Are you telling us he didn't?" Ron asked, incredulous.

"I'm simply trying to get some information."

Silence again filled the room.

Reena's face was tight, with all the warmth of marble. She reached for a cigarette and lit it, hands shaking. Then she folded one arm across her chest and glared at me. "You've got a fat lot of nerve, showing up at our door like this."

"It's not a comfortable position, believe me. I may not

have known Lisa well, but I did know her. And I liked her."

Ron eyed me warily. "So what is it you want?"

"It doesn't matter what she wants," Reena said, standing abruptly. Her voice was raspy, her features squeezed tight with anger. "Whatever it is, it has nothing to do with us."

I looked toward Ron, then back at Reena. "I know the loss of your daughter and grandchild must be terribly painful—"

Her gaze turned to steel. "You don't know squat, my dear." She reached for her drink, lost her balance and had to steady herself by catching hold of the table.

"Reena. Please." Ron Swanson came around the edge of the sofa and tried to calm his wife.

She wrenched away. "My daughter was lost to me a long time ago. Isn't that right, *honey?*" She turned to Ron with an ugly expression.

He looked at her sharply.

"And I never met my granddaughter. Never so much as talked to her on the phone."

"Reena, you're letting yourself get worked up."

"Damn right I am." She spat the words at her husband, then turned back to me. "I never even knew I *had* a grandchild until last year. So don't talk to me about loss. And don't try to involve me in this . . . this problem of yours. It doesn't affect me in any way."

I shifted my weight, discomfited at what I'd unleashed. "Still, you can't pretend it never happened," I insisted. "If nothing else, there's the property, and whatever else is part of your daughter's estate."

"Ain't that a hoot?" Reena finished off her drink and stared hard into the bottom of the glass. "Looks like little

Lisa's managed to thumb her nose at me all the way from the grave."

Ron Swanson had been hovering off to the side, looking about as comfortable as a man with a toothache. "Nothing's settled," he told his wife. "Cole was talking worst-case scenarios."

"Worst case," she repeated, stepping back unsteadily. She held the glass at eye level, regarding her husband through the bubbled surface. "I guess all the best-case scenarios have been taken."

He moved toward her, his voice full of concern. "You've got to put the past behind you, Reena."

"Easy words for someone like you." With a violent shudder, she turned, raised her arm and hurled the glass in her husband's direction. Fortunately she had a weak arm and a poor aim. The glass missed Swanson by a wide margin and shattered against the tile floor.

For a moment no one moved. Then, with a cry of anguish, Reena flung herself onto the sofa and began pounding the cushion with her fists.

Ron sat beside her and reached out to touch her arm. The flailing continued for a few seconds longer. Then, abruptly, she turned and crumpled into his embrace, where she began sobbing in great waves against his chest.

I let myself out and headed for the car, feeling guilty and vaguely voyeuristic at the same time.

As I reached the front sidewalk, I heard Maria call after me. "Mr. Ron," she explained, "he want to talk to you."

"Back inside?"

She shook her head. "The Crossing. In about half an hour."

"The Crossing?"

"A bar, not far from here. I tell him yes?"

I had a moment's hesitation about meeting a man I didn't know in a strange bar. But I figured if it was close to San Marino it had to be fairly safe. And I hadn't yet found what I'd come for. "I'll be there."

She gave me the address and directions, then retreated back up the walkway and into the house, muttering to herself.

17

The Crossing wasn't the dark, back-alley beer joint I'd half expected. In fact, it was so trendy I felt out of place, like a country cousin at a yachting party. The decor was glass and brass, garnished with enough greenery that the place could have passed for an indoor botanical garden.

I had planned to sit at the bar while I waited for Swanson, sip a glass of wine and maybe pick up a bite to eat. But the bar was packed three and four people deep, a wall of racket and commotion that showed no sign of thinning. I opted instead for one of the few available tables and had to peer through a tangle of schefflera in order to keep my eye on the front door.

I ordered a glass of chardonnay and a plate of fried zucchini sticks. My glass was almost empty by the time Ron Swanson arrived.

I stood and waved to catch his attention. Three men at the end of the bar waved back, and one of them blew a kiss. They seemed to find the exchange hilarious.

"Thank you for agreeing to meet me," he said. The waitress arrived, and he ordered a double martini. "I apologize for the scene back at the house. Reena's not usually so high-strung. This whole thing's been very hard on her. Hard on us both."

"There's no need to apologize, Mr. Swanson."

"Ron, please." He pressed his palms together, elbows on the table in front of him. "It's just that I didn't want you to think that, well . . . to get the wrong idea."

"The wrong idea about what?"

"About Reena. About me too, I guess."

I wasn't sure I followed his meaning. "It's understandable that you'd be upset. Your wife especially."

He ran a hand across his forehead. "It's the anger I'm talking about . . . I mean, she *is* angry, but it's because she loved Lisa, despite everything. I wouldn't want it coming out at trial that her own mother didn't care about . . . about what happened to her."

"Or that she blamed you in some way," I added.

He nodded, looked around to see if his drink was on its way. "Yeah, that too."

"Does she?"

"Does she what?"

"Blame you? I got the feeling maybe she did."

He shrugged. "It's a complicated situation."

I waited.

After a moment he cleared his throat. "Do you have children?" he asked.

"No, I don't."

"They're their own people, you know. No matter what you do, no matter how hard you try, they ultimately follow their own mind."

"Is that what Lisa did?"

"I don't know what she was following. From everything Reena's told me Lisa was a happy, easygoing child. Then, when she reached her teens, things changed dramatically."

They usually did when hormones kicked in. "How old was Lisa when you and your wife married?"

His eyes again scanned the room, looking for the waitress. As she approached with his drink, his scowl eased. He sipped first, then reached into his pocket to pay the bill.

When the waitress left he took another sip before nodding in my direction. "Lisa was almost fifteen. I'm sure Lisa's age, the fact that Reena and I married rather quickly, the move to San Marino, they were all part of the problem. Reena had been married twice before. Neither marriage lasted long. I'd guess that was a contributing factor as well."

He paused, took another couple sips of his drink.

"Knowing Reena, I'm sure there were men in and out of the picture during the intervening years, but in terms of family it was just the two of them, Reena and Lisa, for most of Lisa's life."

I nodded, encouraging him to continue.

"Then I show up. There she is on the verge of womanhood herself, and suddenly Lisa has to share her mother with a stranger. A male." He sounded embarrassed. "A man's presence in a situation like that . . . it alters things, recasts them in ways that aren't always entirely obvious."

"You sound like a shrink."

He smiled. "A radiologist, actually. But I have a psych background, and a buddy who's an analyst."

I shifted in my seat. "Are you saying that Lisa was jealous of her mother?"

"There was a certain degree of rivalry, I think."

"Kind of a modern-day slant on Freud?"

Ron smiled again. The martini seemed to have relaxed him. His features were looser, his gestures less sharp. Or maybe it was my own glass of wine that softened the edges.

"Nothing quite so deep," he said. "Nothing you could really put a finger on either. It was always just beneath the surface."

"How did Lisa act when you were around her?"

"At times she was standoffish or sassy. Other times it was almost like she was flirting. Again nothing overt." He rubbed his chin. "I guess maybe coquettish is a better word. More subtle and childlike."

"How did you react?"

"For the most part I ignored it."

"For the *most* part?"

He sighed, sipped his gin. "I wanted Lisa to like me. The wicked stepmother persona is just as uncomfortable for stepfathers, you know. It's not an easy role."

"I imagine not." My dealings with Tom's children had been an eye-opener in that regard.

"Besides, I knew it was unlikely I'd have a child of my own. Lisa was my one shot at family."

"By fifteen, most of us want to forget we're part of *any* family."

Ron acknowledged the remark with a smile. "The funny part is, things seemed fairly smooth at first. Lisa didn't react badly to the news that we were going to be married. We included her in the wedding, took her on all but four days of our honeymoon. I thought we were off to a great start. I don't know . . . Maybe it was just that the novelty wore off, or maybe I tried to be too chummy too fast."

As the waitress circled by our table, Ron caught her eye. "Would you like another?" he asked me.

"Sure."

The waitress cleared our empty glasses and left.

"In retrospect," Ron said, "I can see that things started to change almost immediately. But at the time it took me a while to notice. Of course Lisa was sick a lot during that time too."

"Sick how?"

"Stomachaches. Odd, unexplained pains. I'm sure it was psychosomatic, but it put a strain on all of us."

"How about headaches; were they part of it?"

He thought for a moment. "They might have been, but I don't recall that specifically. The symptoms seemed to change from week to week."

"But they eventually disappeared?"

He nodded. "Although to tell you the truth, I can't remember when that was, exactly."

Our drinks arrived, and Ron took a moment to refortify himself.

"They must have cleared up by her junior year, though. That's when she began hanging out with a tough crowd, thumbing her nose at our rules. The classic symptoms of self-destructive behavior."

"Drugs?"

He nodded. "Drugs, sex, letting her appearance go, her grades slide. It seemed like our hands were tied. The more we clamped down, the more she rebelled. She moved out of the house altogether in the middle of her senior year."

I was intrigued. The Lisa I'd known was so unlike the young woman Ron Swanson was describing. "Where did she go when she left home?"

"Not that far. She moved in with some guy who had an apartment in Alhambra. But she finished high school; I give her credit for that. After she graduated she took off and didn't tell us where she was headed. We've barely seen her in the last six years."

"What about her husband? Do you know anything about him?"

"Not much. We met him for the first time last year when he showed up at our doorstep looking for Lisa. I gathered they'd had a fight or something."

"What was he like?"

"Young, good-looking in that healthy, southern California way. He was a musician, or so he said, though he made his living as a chauffeur for one of those airport limo services."

Ron paused. "That was when we first learned of Amy."

"It must have been a shock."

He nodded. "It was. For Lisa to have kept something like that from us . . . it seems so spiteful."

We sipped our drinks in silence for a moment. Ron seemed lost in some private rumination, and I needed a chance to collect my thoughts. The more I learned about Lisa, the less I understood her. But that wasn't why I'd come to Los Angeles.

"Lisa apparently kept a journal of some sort," I said. "I'm hoping it might tell us something about what led to her death. It's not at her house. Do you think it might be among the things you had shipped here?"

"It doesn't sound familiar, but I can look."

"I'd appreciate it." Then I had another thought. "When was the last time you spoke with Lisa?"

Ron frowned. "I think it was just after Anne died. Anne Drummond, Reena's cousin."

"I thought they were sisters."

"Not technically. Reena lived with Anne's family after

her own parents were killed, so in some sense they felt like sisters."

"Yet Anne left the property to Lisa instead of Reena."

Ron gave a hollow laugh. "Reena was a little surprised about that. It wasn't so much the inheritance as the idea of the thing. Not that we couldn't use the money, what with the HMOs taking control of medicine these days. But I think, mostly, Reena was hurt at being overlooked in favor of Lisa. Especially after the way Lisa had treated us."

And Reena had been listed as beneficiary in the original will. It didn't make a lot of sense. "Were Reena and Anne close?"

"I think they were at one time, but . . . well, you know how things go."

I nodded, waiting for him to continue.

"After Reena's second marriage fell apart she kind of went off the deep end. Was actually hospitalized for a period. Lisa, who was only four at the time, went to live with Anne. I gather that made for some tension between Anne and Reena. And they weren't at all alike. Reena's quite emotional." Ron smiled slightly. "As you can probably tell. Anne was strong-willed and opinionated. Very much her own person."

He paused to take another swallow of his drink. "Anne's husband ran off and left her when they'd only been married a year or so. She never brooded over it, though, or let it color her thinking. I got the feeling she thought Reena lacked a certain . . . inner strength. It's not true. But Reena's a romantic at heart, and Anne was a pragmatist."

"Sounds like you knew her fairly well."

"Reena and I stayed with her for a short while after we were married, and Anne would come to L.A. every couple of years. In fact, we left Lisa with her when we took the four-day honeymoon by ourselves." He laughed without humor. "Lisa and Anne must have really hit it off."

Ron checked his watch. "Anyway, I never meant to bend your ear like this. It's just that I didn't want you to get the wrong impression about Reena." He tried something that looked like it was supposed to be a smile. "I know how you attorneys operate, and I wouldn't want you to do anything that might hurt her further."

I found his concern for Reena touching. I also thought to wonder if it was really the reason behind our meeting.

18

The alarm rang at seven the next morning. I reached over and turned it off, fully expecting to roll out of bed a minute or so later. When I opened my eyes a second time it was past nine, and the jangling was coming from the telephone. Groggy and blurry-eyed, I rolled over to grab the receiver but succeeded only in knocking it onto the floor out of reach. I scrambled out of bed and picked it up just as the answering machine kicked in.

"You weren't still in bed, were you?" Sam asked when the line had cleared.

I grunted.

"Sorry. I thought for certain you'd be up by now."

I sat on the edge of the bed and pushed the hair out of my eyes. "So did I."

"Late night?"

"In part."

What had done me in wasn't so much crawling into bed at 2 A.M. It was the endless stretch of time between then and the hour when my mind finally stopped churning.

"You want to get some coffee and call me back?" Sam asked.

"It's okay; I'm awake. I'll put water on while we're talking. The phone's one of those cordless things." By then I'd made it to the kitchen and was already filling the kettle. Loretta and Barney sat on either side of my feet, patient and hopeful.

"How was the trip to L.A.? Did you find Lisa Cornell's diary?"

"No diary, although her stepfather said he'd look through the boxes of stuff they packed from her house." I checked the dogs' bowls; neither was empty. "Forget it, guys. Coffee's not your thing."

"You got a guy there?" Sam asked.

"I was talking to the dogs."

"Oh."

While the water heated, I filled Sam in on my trip. Once again I found myself caught up in Lisa's story, intrigued by facets of her life I'd never suspected. The more I learned about her, the more of a puzzle she became. Of course, I'd only heard her stepfather's version of things. Having been an errant daughter myself, I knew that family matters were always open to interpretation.

"The drug angle might be worth pursuing," Sam said. "A lady with a coke habit could make enemies pretty easily. Even if she was only hooked on pain killers or tranquilizers, it would give us an opening."

"Lisa's stepfather was talking about her behavior in high school. To my knowledge, there hasn't been a hint of drug involvement recently."

"Maybe that's because nobody's looked." Sam's tone was huffy.

I pulled a mug out of the cupboard. "All right. I'll check into it."

"And see if you can find out anything more about the family. You want my opinion, the dynamics there are rife with possibilities."

"For the soaps maybe." The morning was warm, the air in the kitchen close and stale. I opened the back door and discovered the air outside was fresh but even warmer. The heat hit me like a blast from an open oven. Loretta and Barney wasted no time retreating into the relative cool of the dining room.

"Lisa Cornell's mother must have been plenty irked to discover she'd been cut out of the will," Sam pointed out.

"Assuming she knew she'd been in it in the first place." I decided stale was preferable to sweltering and shut the door. "Myra had an interesting observation." I told him her theory about Amy.

Sam's groan was tortured.

"What's the matter?"

Because I was holding the phone with my shoulder while measuring out the coffee grounds I missed part of his answer. The only words I heard clearly were "skin flicks."

I moved the receiver back to my hand and held it firmly against my ear. "What was that again?"

"What I said was, that among the items seized by the police from Wes Harding's residence were a couple of skin flicks. I just got the updated list yesterday afternoon."

"No one's trying to make a case that he's a Boy Scout, Sam."

"The thing is, one of the films is about a woman and her daughter."

"So?" I started to pour water through the coffee grounds.

"The daughter's a little older than Amy, and the woman's dark rather than fair, but it's kind of interesting, the parallels."

"Sam—"

"The other thing," he said, cutting me off, "is that they both wind up dead."

I set the kettle back on the burner. "That doesn't prove anything."

"No, but the prosecution's going to make it into something, you just wait. This is going to be a jury trial, remember. Folks around here aren't going to think much of a man who watches that sort of filth."

"What's the matter, Sam? Sounds like you're getting spooked."

"Maybe I am. Maybe I got reason to be spooked. Hell, the DA's got what's practically a textbook case, and we've got zip."

"It's not a textbook case, and you know it. There's no murder weapon, no witness, no confession, no motive." This was a reversal in roles, me bolstering Sam, and it made me nervous. "You're not giving up, are you?"

His response was quick and unequivocal. "Not in a million years." Then he sighed. "I'm just frustrated, is all. Everything is ten times harder when you've got a personal interest in the case. Jake calls me every night, wants to talk strategy and evidence. Half the time he drifts into a rambling soliloquy about Wes's childhood and how nothing's ever gone right for him. It gets me wound up in a way I wouldn't be otherwise."

That was understandable. "Just remember your heart condition," I warned. "Stress is one of the things you're supposed to avoid."

"And how's a body supposed to do that?" he groused. "Stress isn't something you can politely decline, like a jelly donut."

"You haven't done so well along those lines, either." I half suspected Sam took his doctor's orders as an invitation to battle. "Try not to fret over it. We'll pull together a case. A good one."

"Question is, will it be good enough." Sam's voice was throaty. He sounded tired. "Why don't you go see Wes today, find out what he has to say about this latest development. And see if he has any bright ideas about where we should go next in terms of a defense strategy."

The new jail, constructed only five years ago, is one of few air-conditioned county buildings. That's no small perk on a sweltering summer's day, but it wasn't enough to put me in a charitable mood. Wes didn't appear to be in any better humor. It was obvious from the outset that my visit wasn't the highlight of his day.

After we'd gone through the handcuff routine with the guard Wes slouched down in his chair, crossed his arms and eyed me suspiciously. "You here with good news or bad?" he growled.

"What makes you think I have either?"

"I'm pretty sure you didn't drop by for a social visit."

I eased my chair back from the table, wishing I'd found a polite way to remain standing. The posture of authority comes easier to me when I'm on my feet. I wished, also, that I'd given more thought to how I was going to conduct the interview. Wes Harding had a way of throwing off my normal rhythm.

"Well," Wes said, pulling on an earlobe, "let's make it snappy. You're eating up my hour in the exercise yard."

"You'll have plenty of opportunity for that in the years ahead."

A faint smirk. "Only if you don't do your job."

I rose and stood behind my chair. It may have looked ridiculous, but I felt better. "I could do my job more effectively if you'd participate in the process a bit."

"That so?" He rocked his chair backwards. "You're forgetting it's my body here behind bars, my neck in the noose. I kind of feel like I *am* participating in this whole experience."

"I think you know what I mean."

He turned away to glare at the wall. "Try getting yourself locked up," he mumbled. "You'll get a fine, hands-on education in participation."

Despite the air-conditioned interior, my skin was warm. I could feel my blouse sticking to my back and shoulders. While Wes's eyes were diverted, I reached around and tugged at the neck.

His gaze slid back and fixed on a spot just over my left shoulder. "So, what is it you want from me?" he asked.

"Why don't you start by telling me about those videos the police seized from your place. The ones that are triple X-rated."

The eyes flicked to my face and held there. His mouth twitched in a deliberate, bad-boy grin. "You want the play-by-play description, or just the plots?"

"How about the one with a mother and daughter? How long have you had it?"

"That make a difference?"

"It might."

"I can't remember how long. A couple of years probably."

"You watch it often?"

"Nope."

"You want to try and be a little more specific?"

Wes shrugged. "What's the big deal here? I've got some films that aren't exactly *Mary Poppins*. I've probably got a copy of *Playboy* and the Marquis de Sade around the house too. None of that makes me a killer. I don't see the connection."

"The DA will find one. And even if it doesn't make a lot of sense in your mind, it just might in the jury's."

He pressed the knuckles of one hand into the palm of the other. "Then it's a fucking, stupid system."

"Maybe, but it's the system we have to work in."

Wes said nothing.

"Couldn't you at least have warned us about the videos? Sam asked you if there were going to be any surprises. You didn't tell us about Harlan Bailey and you didn't tell us about the films. Makes me wonder what else you haven't told us."

"I didn't think they were important. Hell, they aren't even mine."

"They aren't?"

"I'm keeping them for a friend."

"Which friend?"

He shook his head. "Uh-uh. That's the reason I'm keeping them. If the guy's wife finds out, he's in big trouble."

"It can't be bigger than the trouble you're in."

"I told you, the videos have absolutely nothing to do with the case. Or the murders."

"But you've watched them?"

"Some of them."

"How about the one with the mother and daughter?"

"Yeah, once. It's not really my kind of thing."

"You watch it recently?"

Wes looked at the ceiling, tapped his foot, then rocked forward so that his body was halfway across the table. "Listen Ms. Big-Shot Attorney, you may have a fancy degree and all, but you're barking up the wrong tree."

I stepped back. He was probably right. I was less inclined than Sam to see the importance of the tapes. I wasn't so sure Willis would see it either.

"Who's Kathy?" I asked, switching trees.

Wes swallowed. "Where'd you hear about Kathy?"

"From Pammy."

His expression relaxed. "Oh."

"Who is she?"

"A friend. From a long time ago."

"Girlfriend?"

"In a manner of speaking."

"Is she the reason you hold women in contempt?"

A puzzled expression. "Where'd you get that?"

"Your comment to Harlan Bailey at the shop. The way you explained it to Sam, you were talking about women in general when you called Lisa Cornell a bitch."

Wes started to say something, then stopped. Closed his eyes for a moment.

"So," I said, "are you going to tell me about Kathy or not?"

"There's nothing to tell. It's been over for years."

"Tell me anyway."

He shrugged. "We went out for a while, then we didn't." There was a trace of bitterness, then a quick recovery.

"You're really coming out of left field today, you know that? First the damn video and now this. Why don't you quit wasting time and get on with preparing for trial?"

"Whose idea was it to stop going out?"

He hesitated, then said, "Hers."

"Where's Kathy now?"

Wes gave a brittle half-laugh. "You aren't going to like this."

"Try me."

"She's dead."

I folded my arms. "Not stabbed, I hope." It sounded crass, and I regretted it the minute the words were out.

"She died of a drug overdose," Wes said. Although I'm sure he tried, he couldn't keep his voice from faltering.

"Were you with her?"

Wes's face hardened. He stood and leaned across the table. "You listen, and listen good. I may not be a prince in a three-piece suit. You know, a guy with a Rolex watch and a Harvard education. But I'm not the lowlife you think I am either."

"I—"

"And I'm *not* guilty of murder."

I stepped back a bit but held his gaze. "Then quit stonewalling and face facts. The police have physical evidence linking you to the crime. You've got no alibi. You've got a co-worker who will testify that you made hostile remarks about Lisa Cornell. You won't explain any of it to us in a way that will allow us to put a favorable spin on it. And now we discover that you're addicted to pornographic snuff films. You tell me what the jury's supposed to think."

Wes's eyes narrowed but he made no response.

"You'd better hope that Willis doesn't find out there's a dead ex-girlfriend in your past."

Wes straightened, shoved his hands in his pockets. The muscle in his jaw worked furiously. We glowered at each other in silence, until, finally, I turned away and crossed to the wall at the rear of the room. Wes Harding was a most exasperating client.

"It would be nice," he said with tight control, "to think there was someone who believed me, someone who believed *in* me."

"Your family does."

Wes laughed hoarsely. "My dad maybe."

"And Pammy."

"Yeah, and Pammy. But not my own attorneys."

"We weren't hired to believe in you; we were hired to defend you. That's what you should be worrying about."

Wes sat again and stretched his legs out straight. The orange overall pants ended well above his ankles. "Let me tell you the way I see it," he said. "Sam's a straight-ahead kind of guy. He doesn't really care whether I'm guilty or not. He's got a job to do and he's going to do it. But with you, it's a different story. You do care. And you're having trouble convincing yourself you're on the right side."

"You want me off the case?"

"I didn't say that. I'm just telling you what's going on here, why you get in my face the way you do."

"I get in your face," I replied, "because I'm trying to do what I was hired to do. You're the one pushing for a speedy trial. Most defendants want to drag it out, give their lawyers ample time to prepare. Two months is difficult under any circumstances. It's especially hard when we don't get any help from you."

"I've been trying to help," Was said levelly. "You just don't like my answers."

"You've got the last part right." I capped my pen and snapped my notebook shut. Enough was enough. It was almost like he was trying to keep us in the dark.

I was halfway to the door to call the guard when a thought struck me. I turned to face Wes. "Are you protecting someone, is that what's going on? You're taking the blame, risking your freedom and maybe your life, rather than tell the truth and implicate a friend?"

Wes chewed on his cheek for a moment. "You think I'd do that?"

"People have done it before."

"Yeah, but do you think *I'd* do something like that. This is John Wesley Harding we're talking about, remember? The rotten apple, the town bad-ass, the guy who can't do anything right."

I folded my arms and looked him in the eye. "You might."

"This is a real kick," he said, tapping his fingers against his thigh. "Almost worth the price of admission. Ms. Fancy Attorney, one-time Latin scholar and high school valedictorian thinks that bad dude Wes might, just *might*, have a sliver of good hidden somewhere deep inside. The frog prince."

I wasn't going to get sidetracked. "So, are you protecting someone?"

Wes rose, pressed his knuckles against his open palm and regarded me through half-closed eyes. "I hate to rain on your parade, sweetheart, but if I had any idea who the killer was, I'd talk. Loud and fast." He dropped his hands. "Now, if we're finished, I've got only a few minutes left before my time in the yard is up. At the very least I'd like a quick peek at the sky."

On my way back to the office I sifted through my conversation with Wes Harding and found myself as frustrated as I had been initially. But I also found myself glancing frequently, and without meaning to, at the cloudless blue sky above. It stretched across the horizon like taut silk and filled me with an odd, unsettling melancholy.

Myra was sitting cross-legged on the office floor, papers spread out around her. She was singing under her breath, keeping rhythm with the bobbing of her head.

"What are you doing on the floor?" I asked, although I had a pretty good idea. The desk was so cluttered, you'd need a degree in archaeology to make your way through it.

"I'm putting together the pleading on the Johnston case."

"All you had to do was staple it and slip it in an envelope."

A moment's pause. "Somehow I dropped it." She looked up, then reached for the loose sheet of paper near her left knee. "I also forgot to number the pages, so I have to kind of read the last paragraph on each page to see what comes next. Don't worry though; I've got it almost all together."

Knowing Myra, it would read like a Mad Libs party game. "Why didn't you just reprint it?" I asked.

Myra set the sorted pages in her lap and looked up at me. "Gosh, I never thought of that. It would have been quicker, huh?"

"Certainly easier."

She stood and handed me my messages. Then, as if I

couldn't read, she recapped the morning verbally as well. "Ron Swanson called, said he couldn't find anything in Lisa's stuff that looked like a diary. The program chair from the Christian Women's League called; she was awfully sorry, but they've had to cancel your speaking engagement for later this month."

"Did she say why?"

"No. She was kind of vague about it."

I groaned. Another fallout of the Wes Harding case, no doubt.

"Someone named Bud called, but didn't leave a last name. And Dr. Markley called."

"She did?"

"Twice. She wanted you to call her today." There was a moment's hesitation. "Are you, uh, seeing her? Professionally, I mean."

"It's about a case. Why, do you know her?"

Myra nodded. "Sort of. She's the psychiatrist who's going to be doing the program at the school—the good-touch, bad-touch sessions."

"Lisa Cornell was seeing her about headaches," I explained. "Did Dr. Markley say why she was calling? When I talked to her yesterday she didn't seem to think she could be of any help."

Myra shook her head. "It must be important, though. She called twice."

I'd started to move into my office when Myra asked, "What did you think of Dr. Markley?"

"You're still having doubts about the program?"

"I guess I'm worried about stirring up trouble where there isn't any. It's like that friend of mine I told you about. She started seeing Dr. Markley for an eating disorder and then they discovered she'd been abused by her uncle when she was young. Now that it's out in the open nobody in the family's speaking to anyone else, and I can't say my friend is any happier. I mean, if you've got to be hypnotized to remember something, maybe you're better off not remembering it, right?"

"Dr. Markley uses hypnosis?"

"She did with my friend. I got the impression that's a specialty of hers—exploring the subconscious, emotional amnesia, that sort of thing. It's supposed to give you a handle for working through unresolved conflict." Myra gave an embarrassed laugh. "You hang around someone who's seeing a shrink, you pick up the lingo."

"Are you saying that Dr. Markley helped your friend remember things that had happened to her in the past? Memories she'd repressed?"

Myra nodded. "Of course, this program in the schools is aimed at preventing things from happening in the first place."

Unresolved conflict. Emotional amnesia. Repressed memory. I wondered if Lisa's problems followed a similar pattern. I couldn't wait to talk to Dr. Markley.

I called her number and got the service. I left my name, and both work and home phone numbers. Then I tried Bud and got a disconnected number. Because Myra transposed numbers as freely as she did letters and words, I tried a couple of variations but wasn't able to locate a Bud at any of them.

I went back to the front of the office.

"Did Bud say what he was calling about?"

Myra shook her head. "Only that he was calling from San Francisco."

So that was the problem. "I need to know things like that Myra. Different area code."

"Oops. Did I forget to include that?"

She'd finished compiling the pleading, but there was still one piece of paper remaining on the floor. "Rats," she said in disgust.

"Here, give it to me." I stuck the loose page in where it belonged. "Did you ever keep a diary, Myra?"

"In high school; not since."

"Where did you hide it?"

"I didn't; there was a lock on it. I wore the key around my neck."

"Did Dr. Markley ask your friend to keep a diary?"

Myra looked surprised. "As a matter of fact, she did. It wasn't so much of a diary really, as a log of her memories and dreams. It helped guide their sessions together. Why?"

"She asked Lisa Cornell to keep one too, but no one seems to know where it is."

"You think that's why she was calling?"

"Not about the diary per se. But I'm hoping it might relate to Lisa's own unresolved conflict."

19

D r. Markley was so much on my thoughts that when the doorbell rang at nine o'clock that evening I half expected it might be her. Instead it was Tom.

"What are you doing here?" I gasped in surprise.

He grinned. His response was edged with lighthearted sarcasm. "It's good to see you too."

"I thought you weren't going to be back until the weekend."

"Chicken pox," he said, stepping closer.

"You've got the chicken pox?"

"Not me. Two of the boys. We decided to cut the trip short and come home early."

Tom wrapped his arms around my waist and kissed me lightly. Then a second time, not lightly at all. His clothes were clean, his skin scrubbed, his hair still damp from the shower, but I caught the lingering scent of woodsmoke beneath the aftershave. It was a surprisingly erotic aroma.

I nuzzled into the crook of his neck. "I missed you."

"Probably not as much as I missed you."

Barney yipped and pranced at our feet. Loretta tried to inch between our legs. We did our best to ignore them.

"You want to get a bite to eat?" Tom asked somewhere between kisses.

"I already ate, but I wouldn't mind tagging along for the company."

"How about pizza?" he murmured in my ear.

"Sounds fine."

"Raffino's okay?"

I nodded, sliding my cheek against his.

Tom didn't move except to snake his hand under my blouse and unsnap my bra.

"I thought you were hungry," I said.

"I was."

"And now?"

He smiled. "Absolutely ravenous."

We moved into the bedroom and out of our clothes, more or less in one continuous motion. A trail of discarded apparel marked our path.

Tom never did get dinner. Whether it was the rigors of the week or the fervor of the homecoming—which took us well into the night—he was out like a light soon after. I stayed awake long enough to drink in the tracery of moonlight on his back and the easy comfort of his breathing. I was probably the only person in the world grateful for chicken pox.

Tom was up early the next morning, as usual. It's an annoying habit he shows no inclination of rectifying, despite my unflagging efforts to convince him otherwise. I heard him banging around in the kitchen, whistling under his breath and occasionally conversing with the dogs. By the time I'd showered and joined him, the coffee was ready and the table set with a platter of French toast.

"The sun's barely up," I mumbled.

"You just don't like mornings."

"Mornings are fine; it's dawn I have trouble with."

"Best part of the day." He handed me a plate. "Here, have some breakfast while it's hot."

I poured myself a cup of coffee and took a seat at the table, where Tom joined me. His arms were tanned from a week outdoors, well-muscled from a lifetime of activity. He has a slim, athletic body, thick sandy hair and a soft, slow way about him that I find incredibly sexy. Even at daybreak.

Reluctantly, I turned my attention back to my toast. "This is good," I said. "Much better than the stuff I make."

"That's because you leave out the vanilla."

"Until you told me, I never knew I was supposed to put it in."

"You still forget half the time."

"Force of habit," I said.

He laughed. "The only cooking-related habit you have is eating."

I watched him load his plate with another two pieces, his fourth and fifth. "Talk about eating," I said pointedly. "Didn't they feed you on this camping trip?"

Tom cut a large bite and held it on his fork. "You ever watch a bunch of ten-year-old boys eat? It's enough to take away anyone's appetite." His foot found mine under the table. He traced a bare sole up the inside of my leg. "I missed you," he said.

I smiled.

"Although it was nice to have some time with Nick. Father-son bonding and all."

I reined in my smile just a bit. Although I understood, in theory, that divorce was hard on children, it was difficult to work up much compassion for a kid who seemed to go out of his way to be annoying.

"Lynn's apparently having a rough time right now," Tom said, "and the kids are feeling it. Nick especially. He has a tendency to see himself as the great healer of all that's wrong."

Among other misguided notions, I thought. "What's the problem?"

"I'm not sure, since I've only heard about it second-hand. I gather things aren't going as well with Damon as Lynn anticipated."

Tom had grown up in Silver Creek as I had, aligning himself with my older brother John in teasing me and Sabrina throughout our childhood. After college he'd wound up in Los Angeles, working for the *Times*. His return to Silver Creek was prompted by a quest for a better, simpler life for his family. But shortly after moving back Lynn had run off with the contractor they'd hired to remodel the house.

Although I didn't know Damon well, I'd met him on several occasions and heard about him on numerous others. He was younger than Lynn, something of a physical specimen (for those taken with the Mark Harmon type) and apparently a fine contractor. I found him pleasant enough, but I couldn't for the life of me understand what he might have offered Lynn that Tom couldn't. Of course, Tom never talked much about his marriage or its shortcomings, so there might have been an important piece of the puzzle I was missing.

Tom frowned slightly. "According to Nick, they've had some major fights of late."

I tried to read Tom's voice to see how he felt about this. I couldn't pick up on any emotion at all. But I didn't know if that was because there was none there or because he was carefully disguising it. Tom's a master at disguising emotion.

"Fights about what?" I asked.

"I don't know. I'm not sure even Lynn and Damon know." Tom speared the last piece of French toast with his fork. "You want this?"

I shook my head.

"Technically, I still have today off," he said. "Nobody at the paper knows I'm back. You want to play hooky with me? Maybe take in a movie or go on a picnic?"

I hesitated.

"Spend the day in bed?"

I laughed. "Sounds lovely, but I can't." I explained my involvement in the Wes Harding case. "I want to reach Dr. Markley today, if possible. I'm hoping she's got something for me that may help. There are also a slew of loose ends I haven't begun to nail down." I got up to get the coffeepot. "You want a little more?"

Tom held up his cup. "What kind of loose ends?"

I shrugged. "Lisa Cornell's neighbors, the phone call she may have received Friday night . . . There's also a homeless man who sometimes slept in Lisa Cornell's barn. It will probably go nowhere, but I can't write it off until I've talked to him. A fellow by the name of Granger." I took a sip of coffee. "During the school year he hung out in the woods behind the school. Now that summer's here, it's anybody's guess where he is."

"Try the library."

I forced a laugh. "Fiction or nonfiction?"

"I'm serious. Today's Friday. Story hour's at eleven. There's a good chance he'll be there."

"At the children's story hour?" I couldn't tell if he was pulling my leg or not.

Tom nodded. "As I recall, Granger liked listening to the stories. He also picked up discarded food from the kids' lunches."

I set down my cup. "You know him?"

"I interviewed him for the piece I did on the homeless last spring. You do occasionally read what I write, don't you?"

I'd forgotten that piece, but I remembered it now. Moving, and at times humorous, it was a break from the more analytical and often controversial studies Tom usually favored.

"What was your impression of Granger?" I asked.

Tom shrugged. "He's harmless, I'd guess. Smart enough to figure out where his next meal's coming from." Tom leaned across the table and picked up my hand. "Sure I can't talk you into taking the day off?"

"Sorry. We've only got two months to prepare for trial."

"Dinner tonight, then?"

"Didn't we try that last night?"

"You complaining?"

I was most decidedly not.

I had my doubts about story hour, but it was better than sitting in the woods trying to snare Granger with a cheeseburger. Besides, there were a couple of new books I wanted to put on hold and this would give me a chance.

The library was located in the old section of town, in a wing of what used to be the grammar school and is now the community center. Mrs. McKay, the regular librarian, wasn't in, but one of her young assistants was: a moon-faced girl with dark hair tied in a ponytail and a mouth full of braces. She was reading a paperback but looked up when I approached.

"I'm looking for a man who sometimes attends your story hour," I said. "His name is Granger."

She tugged at her ponytail. "Today's session was canceled. Mrs. McKay is ill."

"Do you know the man I'm talking about?"

"I've seen him."

"Was he here today?"

"I couldn't say for sure. I posted a sign on the door, so a lot of people left without coming inside. You can look around if you want."

The place was empty except for a middle-aged woman browsing through the display of new fiction and a mother and son in the children's corner. After placing my holds I wandered through the stacks, looking for anyone who fit Granger's description. On my way out I passed through the children's area and paused.

"Excuse me," I said, addressing the young mother, "were you here for story hour?"

"It was canceled today." She didn't bother to return my smile.

"Do you come every week?"

"Usually." The child pulled a handful of books off the shelf and onto the floor. "No, no," the woman said. "We take books off the shelf one at a time."

"I'm looking for a man who attends fairly regularly, a kind of drifter. Someone without a child. Would you recognize him?"

She nodded, then frowned. "Are you a friend of his?"

"I've never met him, but I need to talk to him. Have you seen him today?"

The woman was busy reshelving the books her son had

hauled to the floor. "No, I haven't," she sniffed. "But I wasn't looking, either. I don't know why Mrs. McKay tolerates him."

Mrs. McKay not only tolerated, but welcomed and encouraged, just about anyone who professed an interest in books. I suspected she viewed Granger as one of hers, regardless of his age or appearance.

"Do you know where I might find him?" I asked the woman.

She regarded me coolly. "No, I don't."

I wandered outside and sat on the bench in front of the library, careful to avoid the soft, sticky wad of pink bubble gum stuck to the seat. I hadn't found Granger, and I hadn't, despite repeated attempts, been able to reach Dr. Markley. I *had* determined that the Bud who'd left a message yesterday was actually Robert Simmons, the man who'd contacted Cole about the Cornell property. But I hadn't spoken with him, only his machine. I was quickly piling up a column of big, fat zeros.

Just as I was about to drag myself to the car, I caught strains of music, very faint, coming from somewhere behind the building. I couldn't tell for sure, but it sounded enough like a harmonica that I scurried to have a look.

It was indeed a harmonica. The man playing it was sitting in the shade on the rear steps. He was skinny, almost gaunt, with a misshapen nose and stringy gray hair that fell past his shoulders. His pants were worn and rumpled, rolled at the cuffs. Despite the heat he wore a baggy army-surplus jacket.

I waited until he finished the song before speaking. "Are you Granger?" I asked.

He ignored me, cupped the instrument in his hand and started playing again. Then stopped abruptly. "Who's asking?"

"Me." I gestured to the steps. "May I join you?"

When he said nothing I took a seat on the step below him, near the railing. On closer examination I saw that the man wasn't as old as he first appeared. Maybe early forties. His skin, though weathered, was largely free of wrinkles.

"*Why* are you asking?" he said.

"I have something for Granger." I opened my purse and pulled out a twenty-dollar bill. "I need to ask him a few questions. Are you Granger?"

"Some days I am."

"And other days?"

He grinned, flashing teeth that overlapped at odd angles. "Other days I ain't so sure." He eyed the twenty dollars. "Are the questions hard? What if I get 'em wrong?"

"There's no right or wrong answer. I just wanted to talk to you about Lisa Cornell."

His eyes, a pale, milky blue, turned a shade darker. He picked up the harmonica and began to play a slow, sad ballad I recognized from my childhood.

"I understand she sometimes let you spend the night in her barn."

Granger continued playing the song through until the end; then he said, "I wasn't like them kids, I always axed first. And I never left things a mess, neither."

"Kids. You mean the boys? The ones who used the barn as a clubhouse?"

"You got a cigarette?"

I shook my head. "Sorry, I don't smoke."

"Them boys do." He started to play another song, then stopped and giggled instead. "That's not all they do, neither. Oooh, la!"

I knew about the beer and the girlie magazines. If it went further, I wasn't interested in hearing about it. "You know Mrs. Cornell and her little girl are dead, don't you?"

Granger nodded, suddenly subdued.

"Were you around the barn the weekend they were killed? Maybe you saw someone, or something. It could help us learn what happened."

"It's awful dark inside the barn. I feel my way around mostly."

"Were you there that night?"

He scratched his cheek and looked over at me. "Have to check my appointment book." He reached into a jacket pocket and pulled out an old Payless Drugstore coupon book. "What night was it you wanted to know about?"

"August eighth. A Friday, about three weeks ago."

Granger scratched his cheek again, flipped through a couple of pages, then back to one that offered savings on cat litter. He scowled and looked up. "August eighth's missing. Musta been my secretary took it."

I drew in a slow breath, for patience. "But you'd remember if you saw something, wouldn't you?"

He giggled again. "Depends on what I saw."

My hopes of learning anything from Granger were dwindling fast. "Lisa Cornell was good to you. Letting you use her barn, giving you work occasionally."

"And food," he added with solemn regard.

"So if you knew something that might help us find her killer, you'd want to help, wouldn't you?"

He nodded gravely.

"Do you remember seeing anyone unusual around the barn?"

"Frogs and snails and puppy dog tails."

"The boys?"

"Boys will be boys."

"Anyone else, besides the boys?"

"You could ax Charlotte."

"Who's Charlotte? Is she a friend of the boys?"

"Spider."

Nervously, I brushed my legs. "Where?"

"In the barn. Charlotte lives in the barn."

This had a familiar ring to it. "Charlotte is a spider in the barn?"

"Ain't you never read *Charlotte's Web?*"

"Not for a while."

"Charlotte sees everything. She's so tiny, people don't know she's there."

"Does Charlotte tell you what she sees?"

He squared his shoulders. "We talk some."

"Did Charlotte mention anything about visitors? Did she say anything about Lisa's and Amy's deaths?"

"Sure you ain't got a cigarette?" Granger asked, angling to get a better look at the contents of my purse.

"Sorry. How about a candy instead?" I pulled out a package of Tic Tacs and handed it to Granger, who poured out a handful and popped them into his mouth.

"Oooh la," he said, biting down. "These buggers are powerful."

"Yeah. I should have warned you to take one at a time." I waited until his mouth was empty, then tried my question again. "Did Charlotte see what happened the night of the murders?"

Granger fanned his mouth and shook his head at the same time. "Only afterwards."

"Afterwards?"

"When they found the bodies."

"Charlotte was there when that boy, Bongo, discovered them?"

Granger's face scrunched together. "Boys will be boys. That's what Charlotte says."

"What else does she say, about the murders?"

Silence.

"Could you do me a favor and ask Charlotte again what she remembers? I could take you there now if it would help. We could stop by the store for cigarettes after we're finished."

Granger thought about that for a moment. His expression grew forlorn. Then he shook his head and said, "I can't do that."

"Why not?"

"Charlotte's dead."

"How could she be dead?" I asked, unable to keep the irritation from my voice.

"You sure you read that book? It says right there at the end that she died."

I wanted to scream. If she was dead, she'd been dead for decades. If she was dead, she couldn't have seen Bongo discover the bodies. Or talked with Granger about what she'd observed. Sorting this out and explaining it to Granger was going to tax my brain beyond measure, and I doubted it would make a difference. Exasperated, I gave up and handed over the twenty dollars.

"You ever been to Paris, France?" Granger asked.

"Once. Why?"

He wadded the money and crammed it into a jacket pocket. "Just wondering if it's like they say it is."

"How's that?"

Another gap-toothed grin. "Oooh, la."

20

I leaned my elbow on the desk and reread the page of notes I'd scrawled—one of my many attempts at organizing a coherent defense. I crossed off a few lines, added another, then crumpled the paper into a ball, took aim and pitched it into the trash. Shooting baskets, office style. It was one of the more useful lessons I'd learned during my tenure at Goldman & Latham.

I could also twirl a pen with my fingers, like a minibaton, and play a halfway decent game of pool. These particular talents had earned me the respect of my fellow attorneys, mostly male, and probably stood me in as good stead as my substantial monthly billings. Of course, none of it mattered one iota when the firm fell apart.

I scribbled a couple of ideas on a clean sheet of paper, and decided I didn't like that direction any better. I squeezed the page tight and shot again, this time a bank shot off the wall behind the basket. Perfect.

I told myself I was thinking, but in truth my mind was

meandering, like a bee in a field of flowers. It drifted from random thought to random thought, now and then settling for a moment before picking up and moving on again. Not that I didn't have plenty to think about. But I was having trouble holding onto whole thoughts, especially when I tried to organize and shape them in any coherent way.

As I was winding up for yet another bank shot, the phone rang. I'd pretty much given up on Dr. Markley, but for a brief instant after I picked up the receiver I held my breath in anticipation.

"Where the hell have you been all morning?" Sam grumbled.

I exhaled, deciding to ignore the baggage and stick to the question. "At the library," I told him.

"Research?"

"Story hour." Then, before he had a chance to explode and maybe strain his heart, I explained that I'd found Granger.

"And?" Sam inquired. His voice held a trace of eagerness it hadn't before.

"The guy's loony. I doubt he knows anything, and even if he did, we'd never get a straight story out of him."

"Damn. Not that I didn't expect it."

I crumpled another sheet of paper, blank this time, and tried shooting over my shoulder. The paper fell a good two feet from the wastebasket. "So why were you trying all morning to reach me?"

"You gotta go see Wes."

"I went yesterday."

"So I heard. But you need to go again, today."

"And why's that?"

"Because he wants to see you, that's why."

"Wes wants to see *me*? You must have got the message wrong. We aren't exactly chummy."

"Cut the wise stuff. Go see him, okay? Then give me a call and let me know what this is all about."

The day was hot, even hotter than it had been on my last visit. It was the kind of white heat that swallows you up in an instant. Although I wasn't thrilled about the idea of spending more time with Wes, the lure of air-conditioning balanced the scales a bit.

The bracing crispness of the jail was nice—for about ten minutes. Then goosebumps formed along my arms, and my fingertips turned white. The powers that be had cranked the fans up quite a bit since yesterday.

"You wanted to see me?" I said to Wes when the guard left us alone.

He sat without looking at me. Wiped his palms against his pant legs. His face showed signs of sleeplessness. "Yeah, I did," he said after a moment.

We sat in silence. A silence that fairly echoed off the bland gray walls of the visitor's room. The overhead fluorescent lighting flickered intermittently. A steady stream of cold from the air-conditioner blew in my face. I tried to keep from shivering.

Wes scowled at a spot somewhere near his right shoe. Finally he raised his eyes. There was none of the cocky belligerence in them that I'd seen earlier.

"What are the chances of beating this thing?" he asked.

"With a jury trial, that's hard to predict."

"The prosecution's got nothing concrete, though." It was half-statement, half-question.

"They wouldn't be bringing it to trial unless they thought there was a good chance they'd win."

Wes turned his attention back to the spot on the floor. "They're going for the death penalty," he said.

I tried to keep my tone gentle. "You knew that."

"Yeah, I guess I did." He paused. "But there's different kinds of knowing."

I nodded.

"What you said yesterday, it got me thinking."

"About what?"

"A lot of things. Like no matter how much the police fucked up, I'm the one's going to pay the price."

"Statistically, we've got the advantage. The burden of proof is with the prosecution."

Wes frowned. "Statistically, you've got the advantage in Russian roulette too." His hands made another pass down his pant legs. "How's the defense shaping up?"

"We haven't settled on an approach yet."

"In other words," he said slowly, "it doesn't look good."

"It could be better." I didn't like the message, but I didn't want to gloss things over either. "They've got evidence tying you to the crime—the rabbit's foot, the dirt from your motorcycle, the blood that matches Lisa's type on your trousers. There's also that comment you made about Lisa being a bitch. Add to it the fact that you were in a bad mood Friday night, drinking heavily, that you left the bar earlier than usual and have no way to verify your whereabouts thereafter. If I was sitting on that jury, I'd be hard-pressed to think there wasn't *something* strange going on."

Wes's eyes were dark. Flat. They seemed to sink into their sockets.

"And that's just the bare bones of it. By the time the prosecutor gets through embroidering things, I'm willing to bet the jury's going to have a pretty vivid picture in their minds."

The eyes closed. He rubbed his hands over his face.

I could see that Wes was hurting and I softened my tone. "In order to win," I said, "we've got to offer them something. Some picture of our own, or at the very least some new twist that will make the jury see the prosecution's picture in a new light. That's where we need your help."

I waited, and when Wes didn't say anything I continued. "The biggest hurdle, I'd say, is the rabbit's foot. It's an unusual one to begin with, and they've got a witness who will testify he saw you with it Thursday afternoon. Now we can argue that the one found at the murder scene isn't yours, but—"

"It's mine," Wes said slowly. "And I didn't lose it. I gave it to Amy myself."

I sucked in my breath and waited. The air no longer seemed chilly, but I shivered anyway.

Wes studied his hands.

"When did you give it to her?" I asked, not sure I really wanted to know the answer.

"Friday evening. I went out there to see Lisa. Amy was kind of hanging around, you know how kids do, bugging her mother. I thought maybe the rabbit's foot would keep her occupied so Lisa and I could talk without being interrupted all the time."

My mind was filled with questions, all of them scrambling to be heard. I grabbed one at random. "What was it you wanted to discuss with Lisa?"

Wes slouched down in his chair, worked the fabric near his knees. "Christ, how can things turn out so wrong? How can things happen that make no sense at all? It's like that guy who woke up one morning and discovered he was a termite."

"Huh?"

"That German writer, what's his name, Khadafi or something."

"Kafka?"

Wes nodded. "That's the guy."

"It was a cockroach, not a termite. And I think he was Czech."

He shrugged, then sat forward, his expression suddenly intense. "The thing is, the world's suddenly upside down. It's out of your hands. Out of anyone's hands, really. Rolling out of control, faster and faster. Gathering speed. Taking on kind of a life of its own." He sat back. "Feels almost like you've got dynamite strapped to your back and the timing device is on autolock."

"You're losing me," I said. And scaring me a little too, because it dawned on me that Wes might be working up to a confession. "Let's back up a couple of steps, okay? Why don't you tell me why you went to see Lisa Cornell in the first place."

Wes stood, popped a knuckle, then began pacing. "This is where it gets kind of complicated," he said.

I waited while he crossed the room, then turned and retraced his steps. Although his gait was smooth, he was clearly agitated.

"I met Lisa a couple of months ago," he said slowly. "Over at this bar in Coopertown called the Last Chance. The Oasis is kind of my regular spot, but sometimes I'm in the mood for something different. A different crowd, a different pace. Something that's a little quieter. There's a guy there who plays the sax. He's good."

Wes paused, made another pass across the room. "Anyway, I was sitting there one night, just listening to the music, when I caught sight of Lisa over at the bar. I didn't know her or anything. I just noticed her because she was good-looking. And unusual. What with that long, honey-colored hair and a kind of a natural, freshly scrubbed look. She wasn't the type you normally see sitting alone at the bar. For a while we played one of those eye games. I'd glance over and catch her watching me. As soon as I did, she'd look away. But the minute I dropped my gaze I knew she was back to staring. A couple of times she'd smile, ever so slightly. I figured she was looking for some company, you know? But just as I was getting ready to go over and buy her a drink, this other guy came in and joined her."

I knew I shouldn't interrupt but did anyway. "What other guy?"

Wes shrugged.

"What did he look like?"

"Tall, tanned, longish hair that kind of hung in his eyes. The sort that thinks the world owes him a living."

Definitely not Philip Stockman.

"A couple of weeks later I saw her again. She went through the same flirty routine with her eyes, but I'd decided she wasn't going to make a fool of me twice, so I didn't play along. Next thing I know, she's sliding into the chair next to mine. It was pretty clear she was coming on to me, but there was something kind of wholesome about it too. We had a couple of drinks, talked about music— turns out she plays the piano and guitar, and we joked about going on the road together. Made a long list of silly names for the group."

Wes paused and chewed on his bottom lip for a moment before continuing. "One thing led to another, and before you know it we ended up back at my place. By then we were going at it pretty hot and heavy, the preliminaries anyway. And she wasn't holding back any. I mean, it wasn't one-sided; she was just as eager as I was. Then boom, out of the blue she turns real cold and distant. Says she's got to leave. Tells me she's worried about leaving her kid. Hell, she had all evening to think about that."

"What did you do?"

"Do? I didn't *do* anything, but I was pissed as hell. The way I figured it, she got her jollies out of leading guys on."

"Did she mention anything about a headache?"

Wes laughed harshly. "No, but that would be classic, wouldn't it? 'Not tonight, dear' on a pick-up date. Anyway, about a week goes by; then she shows up one day at work. All sweet and innocent."

"Is that when you made the comment about her to Harlan?"

"Yeah. I was still pissed. Then she calls me on Thursday and says why don't I come over to her place Friday evening for a drink. Gives me this song and dance about how sorry she is for what happened. How she can't understand what got into her. She told me she was seeing some shrink about these weird fears she has. It sounded kind of lame, but it was certainly a novel approach. She came across as real sincere too."

"So you went to see her Friday evening?"

A weary sigh. "Yeah, jerk that I am. I stopped by after work."

"And?"

"That's it. We had a beer, talked. I asked her if she wanted to go dancing or something later on, and she said she couldn't, but maybe another time. It was weird. I couldn't figure out where she was coming from, why she'd even bothered asking me over if she was just going to put me off again."

"What time did you leave?"

"Six, six-thirty."

Lisa had canceled the dinner with Philip around four. Was Wes's visit the reason? Or was it something else?

"Did she say why she couldn't go out that night?"

He shook his head. "Although she did apologize. Said that something had come up at the last minute. Who knows if it's true? Could have been her way of yanking my chain again."

I sat back a bit and mulled this over. "What you've told me explains the rabbit's foot and the dirt on your motorcycle." I paused. "You did go over there on your bike, didn't you?"

Wes nodded.

"But what about the bloodstains on your pants?"

"Lisa scraped her knuckle when she was getting out the beer. She washed it off, then pressed her thumb against it to stop the bleeding. But she didn't put a Band-Aid on it or anything. Later, when we were sitting on the back porch drinking, she must have brushed her hand against my leg."

" 'Must have'? You don't remember getting blood on your pants?"

Wes's eyes met mine, then slid away. "I remember her hand touching my leg."

It all fit rather nicely. Too nicely? I wondered if Wes was telling the truth or if he'd concocted a story to fit the evidence.

"Why didn't you tell the police all this at the beginning?"

He shrugged. "They asked if I knew her, and I didn't,

really. It just seemed easier than getting into the whole thing. If I'd had any idea they'd try to pin the murders on me, I'd have handled it differently, believe me."

"What about after you were charged? Why not tell the truth then?"

Wes leaned his shoulder against the wall and crossed his arms. "Think about it. First off, how many people are going to believe me? The newspapers made it sound like Lisa Cornell was as wholesome as fresh milk. Turns out she was engaged to some wealthy, well-respected guy. Why in the world would she have the hots for ol' loser Wes? The story sounds like a crock of shit. If anything, it gives me a motive. I end up looking guiltier than before."

Unfortunately, he was right.

"Besides," Wes mumbled, "it's humiliating. You think I want the whole town laughing at me behind my back?"

"I don't see what there is to laugh at."

"No? Well, you and I don't travel in the same circles."

"Why come forward now?"

Wes snorted. "I'm kind of short on options."

I clicked my pen, thinking. "Did anyone see you and Lisa together that night in Coopertown?"

"Lots of people, I imagine. We weren't hiding. But I didn't sit down and gather up people's names and addresses, if that's what you mean. What difference does it make anyway?"

"Not a lot, I guess. But if people saw you together, it would add credibility to your story." It might also provide fuel for Curt Willis to use against us.

Wes started pacing again. "You don't believe me, do you? You think I'm making this whole thing up."

"It's not that I *disbelieve* you."

"But you've got your doubts all the same. Christ, I don't

know why I bothered telling you this. You of all people."
He made a disgruntled gesture with his arm, then stopped
his pacing to face me. "If I was going to make up a story,
don't you think I'd make up one that was a little more believable? One that made me look a little less a fool?"

I didn't think Wes looked like such a fool, myself. In fact,
I found the episode oddly touching. But I've had enough
experience with the masculine ego to know that male and
female logic aren't the same.

The "believing" part was more troublesome. Lisa certainly wouldn't have been the first woman to have walked
both sides of the line, good girl and bad girl at the same
time. And whatever else Wes was, there was an undeniable
magnetism about him. Besides, he was about as different
from Philip Stockman as was possible.

So Wes's explanation was believable enough in the general sense. The difficulty came from the fact that I wasn't
sure *I* believed it. And the last thing I wanted was to commit myself to some story that would leave us out on a limb
in the middle of the trial.

I asked, "Do you have a regular girlfriend?"

"Not at the moment."

"Not since Kathy?"

He moved away from the wall. "Kathy's got nothing to
do with this."

"Except that women you get involved with have a way of
winding up dead."

"You're disgusting, you know that? You're just like
them."

"Who?"

He ignored my question. "You learn this stuff in bitch-
training school? You must have all had the same teacher."

More than the words, it was his tone. I shoved back my chair and went to call the guard.

Wes crossed his arms, glaring at me. But what I saw in his eyes wasn't anger so much as pain and confusion. And a trace of fear.

"Wait," he said when I was halfway across the room. "I'm sorry. I shouldn't have said that."

"No, you shouldn't have."

I hesitated. It wasn't entirely his fault. I'd pushed him. Goaded him, in fact. The dynamics of the present were, I realized, heavily colored by the past. Wes Harding still had a way of getting under my skin.

"You feel like telling me about Kathy?" I asked after a moment. "I don't want any surprises once we're in trial."

Wes returned to his chair. "It was about four years ago. She was a teacher. Her family lived on the East Coast. Very wealthy, very snooty. I never met them until we went back to tell them we were getting married. From the minute we walked off the plane it was clear we were from different worlds. Her parents loathed me. Kathy's mother pretended I wasn't there, wouldn't even talk to me if we were in the same room. Her father was more direct. He took me aside and explained that Kathy was 'slumming' just to get back at her family. He offered me ten thousand dollars to get out of her life for good."

Wes's voice turned husky. "I laughed in his face. Told him there wasn't any amount in the world that would tempt me. A month later Kathy called off the wedding and moved back home. I never did find out how much he offered her."

I felt a strange turbulence inside. It was no wonder Wes had an attitude about women. "When did she die?"

"About eight months later. I only found out because our old landlady tried to forward some mail." He looked down at his fingers. "Her family never even bothered to contact me."

21

My visit with Wes left me feeling wound-up and edgy. I took the long route back to Silver Creek, using the driving time to think through this latest twist to our case.

If Lisa had been in the habit of picking up strange men, there were any number of possible suspects out there. Unfortunately, Wes was as likely a candidate as any of them. And the story he'd just told me, while explaining the evidence, also drew a nice little picture for motive. I hated to think what the prosecution would do to it. A man given to bursts of temper. A woman toying with him, making him appear, in his eyes at any rate, a fool. The only point in the whole account that Willis would need to challenge was the ending—the part where Wes claimed to have left Lisa's place while she was still alive.

And yet, as Wes had pointed out himself, it was hardly the tale he'd hit upon if he was going to make something up.

It fit, and yet it didn't. If Lisa had come on to Wes in the bar, as he claimed, why did she suddenly get cold feet later in the evening? Had Wes turned rough once they were somewhere private? That might have been a point he glossed over in recounting the events to me. But then why did she call him less than a week later and invite him to drop by?

By the time I got back to the office my mind was a fog. And I still had more questions than answers. I called Sam anyway, knowing he would be waiting to hear from me.

"You think this is fact or fiction?" he asked when I'd finished explaining.

"I'm not sure, but I'm leaning toward fact. Of course, that doesn't mean he hasn't embellished it a little here and there. And he refused to say anything more about those videos, so there may be more there than he's admitted."

Sam mulled this over. "Why would a woman like Lisa Cornell go around picking up strange men?"

"Because that's the only kind there are."

"Huh?" Sam was clearly in no mood for my attempts at humor.

"I'm not sure. It might have been the excitement, the thrill of the conquest. Philip Stockman is one extreme; maybe she needed to balance the scales. Or maybe she had a low sense of self-worth. I had a college roommate who did the same kind of thing. It was as if she needed constant reassurance that men found her attractive."

"Sort of a *Looking For Mr. Goodbar* thing?"

"Right. Or maybe she simply found Wes attractive."

"Still sounds odd. Lisa Cornell must have had plenty of men interested in her."

"It doesn't seem so odd to me. Dr. Markley talked about Lisa's unresolved conflict. Maybe this is part of it. The behavior fits with what I know about childhood trauma and repressed memory."

Sam humphed. "I'm too old for this psycho-babble."

"I'm pretty sure Lisa talked to Dr. Markley about Wes. Remember I mentioned that fact after I saw her? At the time it didn't make sense, but it does now. Maybe if I tell Dr. Markley I already know about Lisa's going with Wes back to his place, she'll be more willing to fill in the blanks."

"People really talk about stuff like that in therapy? It's like airing your dirty laundry."

"That's kind of the point, I think."

Sam sighed. "Do you think Stockman suspected what she was up to?"

"That same thought crossed my mind. Lisa had just canceled out on their dinner, after all. And postponed their wedding not too long ago. Maybe he was getting suspicious."

When I got off the phone with Sam I called Tom. "How would you like to take a drive to Coopertown with me tonight?"

"Sorry. I'm afraid I'm going to have to cancel out on dinner as well. I was just getting ready to phone you."

"How come?" I could feel the disappointment settle over me.

"Tonight's Erin's drama production. The class has been working up to it all summer and she's pretty excited. I didn't think I'd be back from the camping trip, but now that I am, I can't skip it."

"No, of course not."

"You could come too, if you'd like." It was a nice gesture, but clearly an afterthought.

"Thanks, but I think your daughter needs you to herself tonight. Maybe it will go toward making up for the week you spent camping with Nick."

"I feel like a heel. First falling asleep on you last night, then standing you up tonight."

"Don't feel bad," I told him. "You may have fallen asleep last night, but you put on a stellar performance beforehand."

"Stellar, huh?" He laughed. "That's good to hear."

The temperature had dropped some by the time I left for Coopertown later that evening, but it was still a warm night. A night better suited for sitting under the open sky and sharing a bottle of wine with a friend than holing oneself up in the dank, stale interior of a bar. But the friend I had in mind was unavailable and the bar in question demanded a visit.

The Last Chance was on the main road through town. By day it was probably drab and cheerless, so nondescript you wouldn't notice it. But at night it was plastered with lights. Above the door, *Last Chance* flashed on and off in bright green letters. The window to the left was a collage of flickering beer ads, and the eaves along the front were draped with strings of colored bulbs that looked as though they'd been left over from Christmas.

What the owners spent on outside electricity they more than recouped by keeping the lighting inside to a minimum. The haze of smoke in the air didn't help matters.

I sat at the bar and ordered a beer. The bartender, a gnarly man who bore a striking resemblance to Popeye, delivered my bottle indifferently, without saying a word and without once making eye contact. It was clear he wasn't given to small talk. When he returned with my change I decided to go for the direct approach.

"How long have you worked here?" I asked.

"Couple of years. Why?"

I pulled a picture of Lisa Cornell out of my purse. "Does this woman look familiar to you?"

He barely glanced at the photo, then shook his head. "I don't have much of a memory for faces."

That's because you never look at them, I thought. "She would have come here alone, maybe met someone."

He shook his head again. "Can't say as I've seen her."

"Does anyone else work behind the bar?"

"Ricky. He ought to be here any minute. He'll probably remember. Recognizes every broad that was ever here."

"Why's that?"

"He plays this game, kind of like taking bets with himself. Tries to figure out which ones are going to score and which aren't."

"Does he do the same with the male customers?" I asked.

The bartender looked at me like I was crazy. "Why would he want to do that?"

I shrugged, and decided I didn't have the energy for male consciousness-raising.

While I waited for Ricky, I sipped my beer and looked around. The place wasn't exactly jumping with activity, but it was a weeknight. Most of the patrons were male, and most were alone. There were only two other women in the whole place. They sat together in the far corner with a dark-haired man who was leaning so far across the table in their direction he was practically horizontal.

I finished my beer, went to the ladies room and checked for peepholes before using the facilities. It was that kind of place. I'd just ordered a second beer when Ricky arrived.

He was younger than the other bartender, probably in his forties, with a tight goatee and a sizable beer belly.

"Hal says you want to talk to me."

I nodded and again pulled out Lisa's picture. "Did you ever see her here?" I asked.

He frowned. "I might have."

"What does that mean?"

He shrugged and started to turn away.

"Wait," I said, reaching for my wallet. I tried to be cool, but I felt like an absolute jerk. It wasn't the money; it was the triteness of the situation.

Ricky didn't appear to have the same aversion to clichés that I did. He took the money and shoved it in a pocket. "Yeah, I seen her. She was here a couple of times. Haven't seen her for a while though."

I decided not to tell him she was dead. That kind of stuff makes some people clam up fast. "Did you ever see her with anyone?"

He nodded.

"Broad-shouldered fellow, dark hair?" I'd intended to bring a picture of Wes too, but I'd realized just as I was leaving that I didn't have one.

"The guy she usually met had light-colored hair, long and kind of shaggy."

It sounded like the man Wes had seen her with the first time. "Did they come here regularly?"

"Couple of times is all that I seen her. The guy used to come more often; then he disappeared for a while. He was back a few weeks ago, though."

"Alone?"

"Was when he came in. I didn't keep track after that."

"Did you ever see her with anyone else?"

Ricky tugged at his whiskers. "One time, I think, she ended up having a drink with a different guy. But she didn't make a habit of it."

"Can you describe this other man?"

"I can't remember much except that I'd seen him here before. Dark coloring, tattoo on one arm."

It appeared the first part of Wes's story checked out. "Did you happen to see if they left together?"

He gave me an oily smirk. "Yeah, they were together. Like they was stuck to each other with glue."

"How about this other man, the one she usually met. Did they leave together?"

"Sometimes, not always."

"And were they, uh, like glue as well?"

Another smirk. "They weren't brother and sister, that's for sure."

I wrote my number on a slip of paper. "If this other man comes back again, would you give me a call? It doesn't matter what time it is."

Ricky fingered the paper, then shrugged and let his eyes drift away. "I might."

I pulled out another bill and handed it over. "You call me when he comes in and I'll make it worth your while, okay? Double what you got tonight."

Sleazy dialogue in a sleazy bar. My twenty-seventh floor office with a view of the San Francisco Bay seemed light years away. I thought of it with longing. And yet, there was something galvanizing, even gratifying, about fitting the pieces to the facts. A kind of symmetry you didn't often find working on the twenty-seventh floor.

Dusk had turned to darkness by the time I started home. It was the kind of inky darkness you get when there's no moon, and no city lights reflecting off the horizon. The road was narrow and unlit, twisting through the rolling foothills with only cattle for company. What had been a leisurely, scenic drive on the way over was going to require more concentration at night. I began to wish I hadn't had the second beer. I began to wish, even more, that I'd made another trip to the rest room before leaving.

Traffic was almost nonexistent, which made the driving a little easier. I rolled down the window for fresh air, flicked on my brights for better vision and punched the tape player. It picked up in the middle of a Bach quartet.

Of its own accord, my mind began to run through what I'd learned from the evening.

Wes's story jibed with what the bartender had told me. Whether or not Lisa made a habit of meeting men in bars, she'd done it at least twice: Wes and the fair-haired man. Was the other man someone she'd once picked up, the way she had Wes? Or was he someone she knew through a different avenue altogether? In either case I wanted to talk with him. And I wanted to know why Lisa was meeting him in a bar half an hour from home.

But the questions that occupied me most involved Wes. I found myself thinking about the story he had told me, thinking that it just might, actually, be true. The entire thing, word for word.

The realization hit me like the shock of a cold shower. If Lisa and Amy had been alive when Wes left them, then the man I was defending was innocent.

The revelation wasn't as liberating as I'd have expected. In fact, it was downright scary.

About ten minutes from town I noticed the glare of headlights in my rear-view mirror. I'd been vaguely aware of a car some distance behind me, but while my mind had been drifting the car had pulled closer and was now right on my tail. The harsh lights from behind made it difficult to concentrate. Made me feel like a trapped animal.

Because the road was too narrow and winding for the other car to pass I sped up a bit, hoping to put more distance between us. It wasn't enough to satisfy the other driver. He stayed close to my bumper, even when I accelerated further.

About a mile on, the road straightened for a stretch. When the car behind me made no effort to pass I slowed to let him by. He slowed also, like a pilot flying in precision formation. Annoyed, I pulled as far to the right as I could without straying onto soft shoulder. But the car still wouldn't pass. Finally I picked up speed again. He did the same.

Suddenly fear rose in my throat. I was alone on an empty road. The nearest house was miles ahead. I hit the button for the window and cranked it up. Then I reached around and hit the door lock. Not that either would deter a serious pursuer. I checked the speedometer, wishing I'd bought the new rear tire Tom had been urging. This was not the time for a flat.

The car's interior held nothing I could use as a weapon. No tire iron, pocket knife or heavy flashlight. And the canister of pepper spray I'd carried so religiously in the city was at home in my bedroom drawer, where I'd stashed it upon my return to Silver Creek.

Again I glanced in the rear-view mirror, trying to make out faces in the car behind me. The glare was too bright. I couldn't even tell the type of car, except that it appeared to be a large American model, riding maybe a little lower to the ground than was standard.

Had I chanced onto some maniac rapist? Or was it something I'd stirred up with my questions about Lisa and Wes? Or was I, maybe, reacting with unwarranted paranoia?

I tried to convince myself of the last option but failed miserably. My heart was racing and my hands had begun to tremble.

Stay calm, said the voice of reason. Drive carefully. Eventually you'll come to a more populated area where you can get help.

Unless he runs you off the road first, I thought.

I gripped the wheel, pulled myself up straight, checked the gas gauge. Almost half full. At least I didn't have to worry about that.

Just then the lights of an oncoming car reflected in the darkened sky. As it approached, I slowed to a crawl and flashed my high beams like crazy to get his attention. When he was almost beside me I tooted the horn.

The car sped past, not even bothering to flash his lights in return.

The car tailing me had pulled back a little, but once the oncoming car was past he inched forward again. Then started flashing his lights in a mockery of my own feeble efforts. From where I was sitting the effect was something like that of a strobe light, and I had to concentrate to keep my eyes focused on the road.

When we finally approached the outer limits of Hadley I began to relax. I planned to pull up in front of the police department and lean on the horn. I thought it unlikely the car behind me would stick around for the finale, but I wasn't taking a chance.

I slowed at the first stop sign but didn't come to a complete stop. The car behind me did the same. At the second sign I was forced to stop by a truck coming from my right. Before I could start up again the car from behind swung alongside of me. I cringed, hit the horn and peeked to my left, into the passenger-side window of the other car.

It took my eyes a moment to focus. The car had pulled ahead and through the intersection by the time it dawned on me that I'd just been mooned.

22

Kenny Rogers was crooning about love gone bad as I pulled out of the driveway the next morning on my way to work. I'd returned home the previous night still giddy with relief at learning I'd been tailed by immature males rather than maniac killers. But this morning I'd woken in a cold sweat, racked with lingering doubts.

If we hadn't reached town when we did, would things have turned out differently? What if I'd panicked and driven into a ditch or the path of an oncoming car? More to the point, what if it hadn't been just a couple of rowdies out having a good time? Was it possible that someone had singled me out for the sole purpose of spooking me?

I tried to remember whether anyone had left the Last Chance when I had, or been nearby when I got into my car. But my mind had been on other things and I hadn't noticed.

It was the top of the hour as I pulled onto the main road. Music gave way to news. The president was spending the week at Camp David. A hot spot of world strife had been doused, temporarily anyway, by renewed peacekeeping efforts. The price of gold was up, silver down. The stock market was even. I listened with half an ear.

"Closer to home," the newscaster continued, "an automobile accident has claimed another life."

My ears pricked up. Could it have been the car following me last night? I didn't want to think about what might have happened if our bumpers had connected.

"The wreckage was discovered late yesterday afternoon by a hiker in the Cottonwood Canyon area. The blue Mazda apparently plunged off an area along Route 12 that is known for its hazardous turns. Authorities estimate that the car had been in the canyon for several days."

I let out the breath I'd been holding. Different part of the county, different time frames. Nothing linking the two incidents but my own skittishness.

"The driver of the vehicle, Dr. Donna Markley of Sierra Vista, appears to have been the only occupant. It is not known how she went off the road or when the accident occurred."

My whole body tensed. I reached over and turned up the volume. What I really wanted was to hit rewind. The newscaster had already moved on to other matters.

That was the problem with radio news: You miss it and it's gone. With the newspaper you can go back and reread a story as many times as you like, dissecting it word by word.

I'd let my attention wander, but I was sure I'd heard the name correctly. And there couldn't be two Dr. Markleys in Sierra Vista. I turned left at the next intersection and headed to the police station to see Daryl Benson.

Most days I have to wheedle my way past Helga, who watches over the inner sanctum of the police department like an armed sentry. But when I got there today she wasn't yet at her desk. I mentally thumbed my nose as I passed.

Benson was hunched over his desk, phone pressed to his ear, when I rapped softly on his open door. He grinned and motioned for me to sit.

A moment later he hung up and said, "What a wonderful surprise. You had breakfast?"

I nodded.

"How about a cup of coffee then?"

"I'll pass, but thanks."

Benson frowned, rocked back in his chair, eyed me warily. "This is shaping up to look an awful lot like a business call. You've got that look about you."

"Well, I—"

"And here I was hoping you had stopped by just to say hello."

I offered an apologetic smile. "Not this morning, I'm afraid."

"So what is it? Something to do with Wes Harding, I bet."

It was my turn to frown. "That's what I'm not sure about. I heard a report on the radio about an auto accident near Cottonwood Canyon. A woman was killed. Dr. Donna Markley. She's a local psychiatrist. What can you tell me about it?"

"Not much. The sheriff's department got that one."

"But you must know something," I said.

He shrugged. "There's not a lot to know. A man was out walking with his dog when he discovered the wreckage. He peered inside, saw a hand, vomited, then hiked out and called the sheriff. The woman was dead. She appears to have been the only occupant of the vehicle. Looks like she missed the turn, swerved right when she should have gone left and wound up on the canyon floor. It's nearly the same spot where those two high school kids were killed a couple of years ago."

"Any idea when it happened?"

"The clock in the car stopped at eight o'clock. That's either A.M. or P.M., but from what they've pieced together, it looks like the accident was Wednesday evening. Apparently she saw her last patient Wednesday around four o'clock. Neighbor doesn't recall seeing the doctor's car in the driveway that evening. She didn't think much of it at the time since the doctor travels quite a bit."

"Nobody reported her missing?"

"Sad, isn't it? She lives alone. Her patients assumed there'd been a change of schedule they'd forgotten. Couple of them called and left a message on her machine, but that was it."

My own messages would have been among them. Three or four calls. And even though it had struck me as odd that Dr. Markley hadn't called back, I'd never thought to check further. I didn't want to think that she might have been alive, desperate for help, while I was growing impatient waiting for her call.

"What's your interest in this?" Benson asked.

I explained Dr. Markley's connection with Lisa Cornell, then hit the highlights of my visit earlier in the week. "When she called me the other day and left a message I assumed it was because she had something more to tell me."

"About Lisa Cornell?"

"It was the only thing that made sense."

He screwed up his face in a look of disapproval. "You're casting around for another killer, right? Some major lead the police overlooked."

"It happens," I said.

"Not very often."

"Your guys were so sure it was Wes, they didn't look for other possibilities."

"It walks like a duck, it quacks like a duck, you're going to assume it *is* a duck. Sure, maybe it's an alligator in disguise, but that's highly unlikely. Shit, Kali, there're always other possibilities. You'd never close a case if you exhausted every avenue of 'might have been.' It would take years."

I flashed him a smug smile. "That's why we have courts and quaint, curious notions like burden of proof."

He laughed. We'd covered this ground before, innumerable times. "You making any headway?"

"It's slow. But this is one time that duck of yours just might turn out to be an alligator."

"I'm sorry, then, that you didn't get to hear what the doctor lady had to say."

"So am I. Were any other cars involved in the accident?" He shook his head.

"Any witnesses?"

"None that have come forward."

"How about skid marks?"

"I don't know for sure. Like I said, this one's the sheriff's." He paused. "Are you getting at what I think you are?"

"It seems suspicious to me that she died when she did, the way she did. It wouldn't even have been fully dark at eight o'clock."

"Those high school kids I was telling you about—they drove off there in broad daylight."

"But they were probably horsing around, maybe drinking beer or popping pills, right?"

"Smoking marijuana." He conceded the point with a

glum nod. "But take a look through the department's traffic reports. What you'll find is that accidents happen day or night. Some of the time drugs or alcohol are involved, but sometimes they're not. You turn your attention elsewhere for a moment, overcompensate when you realize you're in trouble. Maybe you're going faster than you should be. It's usually just simple carelessness."

"Or maybe your brakes don't work," I added, "or someone nudges you from the rear at just the wrong moment. Will you do me a favor and talk to someone in the sheriff's department? Find out if there was anything suspicious about the accident. Also find out what you can about Dr. Markley's activities that evening. Where she was going, where she'd been." I could do it myself, but not without jumping through a lot of hoops. And that kind of jumping took time.

"You and your favors," Benson grumbled. "What do you ever do for me in return?"

"I feed you on occasion."

"Not often enough."

"As soon as you've got something for me, give a call. Then pick your night and your menu."

A sly smile. "This is a whole lot of information you want."

I held up my hands. "Okay, I'll throw in an apple pie too."

"À la mode," he said.

As soon as I got to my office, I called Sam. "Did you listen to the news this morning?" I asked.

"Why would I do that?"

"Keep up with what's going on in the world."

"That's what newspapers are for."

"I share your bias, but print media is under a real handicap when it comes to late-breaking news." I told him about Dr. Markley's death. "Maybe I'm wrong, but I can't help wondering if she knew something that had a bearing on the case."

"Why wouldn't she have told you when you went to see her?"

"I don't know. Maybe she'd forgotten about it, or maybe she needed to think about how much of a patient's confidence she could reveal."

"Any ideas what it was?"

That required a different level of wondering. "It could have been about men," I said, and then told him about my trip to the Last Chance the night before. "For an engaged woman, Lisa showed a surprising interest in other men."

Sam snorted. "That certainly ought to qualify as 'unresolved conflict.' "

"Or maybe it was a specific name. Somebody who'd threatened her or roughed her up a bit. It might have been something Lisa mentioned in passing, something that didn't pertain directly to her therapy."

Sam was silent a moment. "Didn't you tell me that Dr. Markley specialized in childhood abuse?"

"She was heading up the good-touch, bad-touch program at the elementary school. And she was seeing a friend of Myra's who was abused as a child. But I don't know that she necessarily specialized in it."

"That stepfather, what's his name?"

"Ron Swanson."

"Right. You said Lisa's behavior took a turn south soon after he came into the picture?" Sam didn't wait for a reply. "And he admitted to you, as I recall, that he tried to be chummy with her."

I closed my eyes for a moment. "I hope that's not it."

"Why? You got a soft spot for the guy?"

I did, albeit a small one. But that wasn't it. "Do you know how hard it would be to lay that theory out as the main line of our defense? Lisa can't talk. Neither can the therapist she confided in."

"There might be others who knew what went on."

"We'd never find them, not with what little time we've got."

"Too bad Dr. Markley didn't leave a more detailed message."

"With Myra taking it down," I said, "a message wouldn't have been much help." I rolled a pencil between my thumb and forefinger. "I'm thinking that Dr. Markley's death might not have been an accident. Lisa Cornell was her patient, and Lisa was murdered. Now the doctor is dead too."

"Could be coincidence."

"Could be. But if it's not, then Dr. Markley must have known something important."

Sam was quiet for a moment. "If there's a silver lining to all this," he said finally, "it's that Wes couldn't have killed her. Not sitting behind bars the way he is. If the doctor's death is somehow tied in with Lisa's and Amy's, it points away from Wes."

Except that Wes and his buddies were experienced hands when it came to automobile repair—and disrepair. If you were going to mess with a car's brake line or steering mechanism, it helped to know what you were doing.

A conspiracy seemed far-fetched, but I couldn't entirely discount it.

23

I don't often get hunches, but when I do I'm usually right. This time the weight of reason was with me, as well. If Lisa's and Dr. Markley's deaths were related, then the therapy sessions had to be the key. That didn't narrow things down much in terms of suspects, but it did give me a next step.

I checked my notes to see if there was any mention of Lisa Cornell's primary physician. I didn't think there had been, and I was right. Somewhat reluctantly, I called Philip Stockman at work. When the receptionist answered I asked for him by name, as though we were old buddies. The ploy might have worked except that he was out of town on business and wasn't expected back for several days. I asked for Helene next. The receptionist put me through and Helene herself answered on the second ring.

I gave her my name, stumbling a bit in the process of reconfiguring my spiel. "Sorry if I sound surprised," I said. "I expected a secretary, maybe a whole string of them."

"We're a family operation," she explained. "Even

though we've grown considerably, Philip insists we answer our own phones whenever possible. If you allow your top executives to insulate themselves from everyday people and problems, there's no way they can know the business."

"I couldn't agree with you more."

Her tone had softened a bit as she went through the recital of company policy; it was obvious she'd covered that territory before. Now, as she remembered who she was talking with, her voice grew distant. "What can I do for you?" she asked.

"I'm trying to find the name of Lisa's physician."

"Her physician?"

"The one she saw about her headaches. I tried to reach your brother, but he's out of town."

"Why are you interested in Lisa's doctor?"

In light of the half-truths Lisa had told Stockman I crafted my answer carefully. "The doctor who ran Lisa's chronic pain group was killed in an auto accident. I had a few questions I wanted to follow up and I thought her medical doctor might be able to help."

"I'm still not sure I understand."

"Sorry I can't be more specific. I'm not sure what I'm looking to find myself."

"I don't see what any of this has to do with Lisa's death."

"The Friday afternoon call from someone in her group. I think it might be important." I paused, waiting for Helene to jump in. When she didn't, I continued. "Lisa's regular doctor might be able to tell me more about this group and the kind of help they offered one another. Maybe he's even referred other patients there."

Helene sighed. "I suppose it couldn't hurt. The man's name is Dobbs. Dr. Carl Dobbs. Philip checked up on him when it seemed he was making no progress in finding the

cause of her headaches. He's a neurologist, board certi-
fied. Top schools too. Philip wanted to meet him, but Lisa
wouldn't hear of it. She wanted to handle things herself."
This last was said with some distaste.

"When Lisa called to cancel dinner did she say anything
about who the friend was or what kind of help was
needed?"

"No, she didn't."

"But she did say that it was someone from this pain
group?"

Helene hesitated. "I can't remember her exact words,
but that was the impression I got."

It would have been helpful to know what Lisa had said.
If she hadn't actually made reference to the nonexistent
support group, what had led Helene to believe the caller
was part of it?

I put that thought aside for the moment when another
struck me. "How did your brother feel about Lisa's canceling dinner? Was he upset or worried?"

"Philip doesn't allow himself to become upset over little things." Helene's intonation was that of a devoted fol-
lower.

"Did he change his plans for the evening?"

"As I recall, he worked."

"Worked?"

"Yes. After dinner he came back here to the office to finish up a few things."

"Was anyone else there?"

"On a Friday evening? I doubt it."

"Do you happen to remember what time he got home?"

"No," she said frostily, "I was already in bed. Now, if
you'll excuse me, I have work to do." She hung up with an
abrupt click.

I found Dr. Carl Dobbs listed in the phone book and called his office. "All I need is about ten minutes," I explained to the receptionist.

"I can fit you in next Thursday at two-fifteen."

"I really need to talk to him today."

"I'm afraid I can't—"

"Please, it's important. It involves the death of one of his patients." I didn't bother to explain that the death had occurred some time ago and had nothing to do with the physical condition he'd been treating.

"Just a moment, please." She put me on hold, where I listened to several bars of "Rhapsody in Blue" before she came back on the line. "We did have a cancelation at eleven. Can you get here by then?"

I checked my watch. Dr. Dobbs's office was located in the new medical complex just outside of town. Fifteen minutes even with traffic. "I'll be there," I said.

Like most foothill towns, Silver Creek was a mix of old and new. The original town center still bustled with activity, and the older residential neighborhoods, renewed and refurbished, were much in demand. But it was the outskirts of town where you could see the signs of growth most clearly. Shopping centers and fast-food outlets had sprung up in pastures where cows had grazed during my childhood. Showy houses, and not so showy housing tracts, were now carved into the gently rolling hills.

The Highland Medical Center was among the new additions. It was an open, zigzagging structure landscaped with shade trees, low-growing shrubs and beds of brightly colored flowers. There were benches for the weary and waiting and, off to the side, a small courtyard of picnic tables.

Dr. Dobbs's waiting room was empty when I arrived. Nonetheless I sat for more than half an hour, leafing through dog-eared copies of *Good Housekeeping* and *Business Week,* before the nurse called me into his office. And then I waited another ten minutes for the doctor himself to appear. When he did I explained that I was there about Lisa Cornell.

"I'm not asking you to betray patient confidences," I said, "but it would be helpful if you could tell me about her headaches and why you referred her to Dr. Markley."

Dr. Dobbs pressed his fingertips together and scrunched his brows in thought. He was probably in his late thirties, but he had a thin, serious face and owlish glasses that made him appear somber beyond his years. "I read about what happened to Lisa and her daughter. Such a senseless loss of life."

"And now Dr. Markley is dead too. Have you heard?"

He looked surprised. "How?"

I told him what I'd heard on the radio. "Did you know her well?"

"Not personally. But I've referred patients to her, run into her at professional gatherings, that sort of thing." He raked a hand through his closely cropped hair. "In fact, I saw her just last week. My God, and now she's dead. Something like this brings you up short, doesn't it?"

He reached for the intercom and asked the nurse for Lisa Cornell's file. Then he rocked back in his chair and addressed me. "Lisa had recurring headaches most of her life, but they were never debilitating. This last year they increased in both frequency and intensity. We did a blood workup, ran a CAT scan, tested for allergies. All negative."

The nurse brought the chart. Dr. Dobbs opened it and spent a few moments reviewing his notes before looking up again. "We tried changing her diet, her sleeping patterns, the soap she used. None of it had any impact. Once she even had an attack here in the office. We ran some tests right then, traced her activities and the food she'd eaten prior to coming to see me. Nothing showed up with any consistency."

"So you referred her to Dr. Markley."

"Not to Dr. Markley specifically, but I suggested she see a therapist. It's not uncommon for headaches to be brought on by stress or emotional upheaval. I'm not saying that was necessarily true in Lisa's case, but I'd tried everything I could. Unfortunately, there are some conditions that medical science simply cannot treat successfully."

"Do you have any idea what kind of stress she might have been under?"

"That's not my area of expertise, though we did talk about it in general terms." He checked his notes again. "From what I was able to pick up, her life seemed to be going well. She was thrilled to be living in Silver Creek, in a house of her own. She loved to garden—I remember that because we tested for a reaction to plant sprays and so forth. I believe she was engaged, or at least seeing somebody on a regular basis. I gather things had been rough for her in the past, but she'd moved to town hoping to make a new start. She wanted a good life for her little girl."

"Do you know how, or why, Lisa chose Dr. Markley?"

He shook his head. "I imagine Donna's being a woman might have had something to do with it. People often seek out a therapist of the same gender. I gave Lisa a couple of names. I'm sure Donna's was among them."

"Because of Dr. Markley's work with repressed memory of childhood trauma?"

He made a dismissive motion with his hands. "I refer patients to doctors I trust. Their specialties have very little to do with it."

"Did she ever report back to you about her work with Lisa?"

Dr. Dobbs chewed on his lower lip while he thought. "Not formally. About a month ago we had one of those brief conversations in the elevator. As I recall, she said that she was finding Lisa Cornell a most interesting patient. From that I inferred they were working well together. There was nothing specific said."

I'd seen the doctor glance at his watch twice during our last exchange. I took the hint, thanked him for his time and left.

On my way out I ran into Jake Harding in the building lobby. He was walking with another man but waved his companion on when he saw me. "I've been thinking about calling you," he said pleasantly. "But I didn't want to seem pushy."

"I wouldn't consider a call pushy. What was it you wanted?"

"Mostly I just wanted to hear your thoughts on the case. This whole business is so damn frustrating for me. I feel like there's got to be something more I can do."

"You're doing a lot as it is." Support, whether moral or financial, wasn't easy to come by, and Jake was offering Wes both.

Another man exited from an office down the hall and nodded at Jake as he passed.

"Is your office in this building?" I asked.

"Second floor at the end. I moved here when the center was first built, about seven years ago. It's been wonderful having a lab right here on the premises. With so many doctors in one place we're able to pool resources and share equipment. Everybody benefits, including," he added with a smile, "the patients."

As much as I hated to see the rolling hills and giant oaks losing out to urban sprawl, I found the nearby presence of a modern medical facility reassuring.

"I was just heading out to grab a bite to eat," Jake said. "Would you like to join me?"

"Sure."

"It won't be fancy. I thought I'd pick up a sandwich at the deli and sit outside. Sometimes the lunch hour is my only chance for a breath of air." We stepped through the double door and outside into the afternoon sunshine. "Air-conditioning may be a wonderful invention, but it will never replace the lovely feeling of a fresh breeze."

I murmured agreement. I was most appreciative of the fact that my own office windows cranked open. They hadn't at Goldman & Latham.

We made our way across the parking lot to the adjacent deli. Jake ordered a roast beef sandwich on a croissant, a side order of macaroni salad and a bag of barbecue chips. It's funny how so many doctors eat as if they've never read a nutrition article in their lives. I had a turkey on rye. Straight, no mayo.

"Sam tells me you went out to see Wes the other day," Jake said.

We'd found a bench in the shade and unwrapped our sandwiches. I was chewing by then so I could only nod.

"I try to get by there as often as I can. Of course, they're stricter about letting families visit than attorneys." His gaze drifted across the lawn. "Visiting Wes in jail is painful for me. His mother can't handle it at all. She's been out there only once."

"He knows his family's behind him, though. That's important."

"I'm afraid it may not be enough." Jake's tone was gloomy. He offered me a potato chip, then crumbled another and tossed it to the birds. "How did Wes seem?"

That was a tough one. He'd been nasty and arrogant but clearly scared. And for all his bravado I had the feeling that what scared him as much as anything was being seen as vulnerable.

"I think he's ready to cooperate with us," I said finally.

"That's good. I could never understand why he was being so difficult."

"I think it was a front. Wes is big on keeping people at arm's length, isn't he?"

Jake nodded. "Has been ever since he was a kid. He wants to make sure everyone knows how tough he is."

I thought back to the young man I'd known in high school. How much of the image had been mere bluster? And how much pain had it concealed?

"Forgive me if I'm out of line," Jake said, "but were you here for a medical appointment, or was it something to do with the case?"

I told him about my conversation with Dr. Dobbs. I assumed, correctly as it turned out, that Sam had kept Jake informed about our progress. "I was hoping Dr. Dobbs could give me some information about Lisa Cornell's treatment with Dr. Markley. I don't know whether you heard, but she died recently in an auto accident."

Jake nodded and his expression darkened. "It was on the radio this morning."

"You knew her?"

"Not well, but our paths seemed to cross rather frequently."

"I only met her once," I said, "but I liked her. She managed to instill confidence while still coming across as very down to earth."

Jake nodded again. "I didn't always agree with her methods, and I've got mixed feelings about psychiatry in general, but Donna Markley herself was a delightful person."

"I understand she used hypnosis."

"It's an approach that seems to be rather popular these day."

"Does it work?"

"It can. An awful lot depends on the individual situation."

I wanted to know more. "Is it true that under hypnosis a person might remember something she'd repressed? Something from the past she had no present memory of at all?"

His smile was amused. "That also seems to be a popular avenue of exploration."

"Is that what Dr. Markley did?"

"She'd done a bit of work in that area." Jake frowned, clearly uncomfortable talking about another doctor's work. "Of course, that was only a small part of her practice. I'm sure she used a more conventional approach with most of her patients."

I picked up on Jake's uneasiness. "You don't think recovered memory is valid?"

"On the whole, no. There are too many variables. A movie, a book, a childhood dream—even a suggestion by the therapist, however well-intentioned—these things can blend with truth and become fixed as a real memory. Of course, I don't pretend to be an expert on the matter."

He checked his watch and stood. "This has been very pleasant, but I'm afraid I need to get back to work."

I rose and walked with him back toward the parking lot. "Would a repressed memory of a childhood trauma manifest itself in headaches?"

He appeared thoughtful. "It might. But you have to remember, there are literally hundreds of things that can cause headaches."

"I wish I knew whether Lisa's were connected in some way to her death."

Jake touched my shoulder lightly in a fatherly gesture of goodwill. "I know you and Sam are on top of this, and I'm grateful for all you're doing. You'll let me know if there are any new developments?"

"Of course."

As he headed back inside, I thought again about Lisa's sessions with Dr. Markley. Had they ventured into Lisa's subconscious memory? Had they revealed a secret so terrible someone had killed to protect it?

24

I found a pay phone in the cluster of shops near the deli and started to call Caroline Anderson. She probably knew Lisa as well as anyone, and I needed some answers. After dropping in my quarter I reconsidered and hung up. I'd have better luck in person.

Caroline opened the door with a smile that withered when she saw me. "I can't talk to you right now," she said. "I was just getting the kids fed so I could put them down for their naps."

"I only have a couple of questions. I promise to make it quick. Or I can wait until they're in bed, if that would be better."

She ran a hand through her tangled blond hair. "Why do you keep bothering me? I don't know anything about what happened."

"I don't mean to bother you. It's just that there seemed to be a lot of things going on in Lisa's life that don't make sense. One of them might have led to her death."

Caroline looked at me with a mix of sullenness and frustration.

"Please," I said. "I could really use your help."

"Oh, all right." She sighed, opening the door wider. The bruising around her lip had faded to a light teal. "Like I told you before, though, I didn't spend a whole lot of time with Lisa these last couple of months, so I don't see how I'm going to help you."

I followed her into the kitchen where the baby, in his high chair, was busy mashing banana into his hair. Jeremy sat at the table slurping a bowl of Cheerios.

"You're sure Lisa never said anything about keeping a diary?" I asked.

"Not to me."

Maybe I was making more of the issue than I needed to, but the diary was likely to be our only avenue into what went on in Lisa's therapy sessions. And those discussions might well hold the answer to Lisa's death, as well as Dr. Markley's.

"Did Lisa talk much about her headaches?"

Caroline brushed crumbs off a chair and offered me a seat. "She'd complain about them, but who wouldn't? I gather they were pretty awful."

"Did she say what might have caused them?"

"Caused them?"

"Like maybe tension or worry?"

"No, just that she got them. And that they'd gotten worse in the last year. She was seeing a doctor about it."

"Was there any pattern to the headaches?"

"Not that I was aware of." Caroline pried what was left of the banana from her baby's hand. He began to wail immediately. "Jeremy, reach into that box of Cheerios and give a handful for Ty."

Most of the reading I'd done about repressed memory had been in the context of legal proceedings, and I'd tended to focus on that rather than the psychological aspects. I wished now that I'd paid more attention to some of the characteristic behaviors.

"Did she mention nightmares? Or trouble sleeping?"

Caroline shook her head. "Nothing unusual." With the baby newly engrossed in tossing Cheerios, Caroline began the job of wiping banana from his hair.

"How was Lisa's health otherwise?" I asked.

"It seemed okay. The headaches made her sick to her stomach, and some days she was really low on energy, but aren't we all?"

"How about her family? Did she talk much about them?"

"I know that her parents were divorced not long after she was born. And then there was another marriage and divorce as well, while Lisa was still young. She was in high school when her mother married this last guy. It wasn't like Lisa talked about them much, only that she wanted things to be different for Amy."

"Different in what way?"

"The traditional American family and all that." Caroline forced a laugh. "Like me and Duane. Mother, father, two kids and a house with a sandbox. Lisa had this notion that if you had the right players, you'd end up happy."

"Lisa wasn't?"

"It was hard to tell with Lisa. One day she'd be bright as a penny, all talkative and bubbly, then the next thing you know she'd be down in the dumps."

"But she wanted Amy's life to be better than hers had been?"

Caroline nodded. "That's what she kept saying. To listen to her, you'd think she'd had a dreadful childhood.

But it never seemed to me she'd had such an awful time of it." Caroline retrieved Jeremy's bowl. "Go wash your hands and face, now," she told him. "I'll be in to read to you in a minute."

Ron had told me that Lisa's behavior changed after she entered high school. The good student, dutiful daughter had become rebellious. It could have been hormones. It could have been resentment about her mother remarrying again. Or it could have been something more traumatic.

"Was there any common theme to her grumblings about family?"

"Like what?"

I wasn't sure. "Alcoholism, physical violence, family tensions, that sort of thing."

Caroline shook her head. "Not that I recall."

"What was her relationship with her stepfather?"

"Chilly. Although, if you ask me, a lot of it was her own fault."

"In what way?"

"You know, not making an effort at it. She was barely civil to him the time he showed up at the restaurant."

"He came to Silver Creek to see her?" My surprise was evident from my tone. "When was that?"

"A couple of weeks before she was killed. Seemed like a nice enough guy to me. He was at a conference in Sacramento. Took a day to drive up special. Lisa acted completely indifferent."

Ron Swanson hadn't mentioned that visit. I couldn't recall his words well enough to know whether he'd deliberately misled me or simply sidestepped the issue. Either way, it annoyed me that he hadn't been straight.

Caroline pulled the baby out of his chair and washed

his face with a wet towel. "I really need to put this guy down."

I started to rise, then thought of something else. "Did you ever go with Lisa to the Last Chance over in Coopertown?"

"Are you kidding? When would I find time to do that?"

"Did she mention going there herself?"

Caroline balanced the baby on her hip. "No. Why?"

"She apparently met some guy there a couple of times. I thought you might know who he was."

She chewed on her bottom lip. "Philip Stockman?"

"No. From the description it wasn't him."

There was a moment's silence. Caroline's face grew pale. She stared at her feet. "It wasn't Duane, was it?" Her voice was strained, barely more than a whisper.

"What makes you ask that?"

"Was it him?" she repeated, the pitch rising. She lifted her eyes to meet mine. They shone with anger. "Is that what this is all about?"

Caroline's response caught me off guard, but it also confirmed something I'd halfway suspected. "Was there something going on between Lisa and Duane?"

For a moment she didn't move. Then she slumped into the chair and sucked in her breath. The baby bounced in her lap. "I don't know."

I could hear the trepidation in her voice, and my heart went out to her. "But you think there might have been?"

"Duane says there wasn't." Caroline began to cry softly. The baby pulled at the neck of her shirt and gummed the fabric near her chest, but she seemed not to notice.

"What made you suspicious?"

"It seemed strange the way he turned against her so suddenly. Lisa and I used to get together a lot, with the kids and all. Sometimes she'd be here when Duane got home from work, and we'd all have a soda or a beer or something before she left. Then, for no reason, he tells me one day to stay away from her."

"Did he say why?"

"Just that I was spending too much time with friends and I needed to focus more on the family."

There had to have been more to worry Caroline than that. "What else?" I asked gently.

She tightened her hold on the baby, kept her eyes on his chubby feet. "My friend, Paula, she saw them necking at the Lowrys' barbecue earlier this summer. She went inside to use the bathroom and found them in the hallway. Duane and I had a big fight about it that night. I figured he told me to stay away from Lisa so I wouldn't get in the way of his little adventure."

"What did Duane say?"

Her laugh was bitter. "He swears there was nothing to it, got mad at me for doubting him. He tried to pin the whole thing on Lisa. Said she'd been making eyes at him for months, that she threw herself at him before he knew what was happening."

"You didn't believe him?"

She gave another hard laugh. "Duane's had a roving eye as long as I've known him. But I always trusted him. I figured there wasn't much harm in looking. I guess it was too much to expect that eventually his hands wouldn't start to rove too."

"He could be telling the truth, you know."

"I doubt it. Lisa wasn't that kind. She wouldn't even sleep with her fiancé."

"What was *her* explanation for what happened at the barbecue?"

Caroline sighed. "I didn't ask her. I just stopped seeing her, stopped returning her calls. The experience kind of put a damper on our friendship. Even if it was just that one time, she didn't have to go along with it. We were supposed to be friends, after all, and Duane is my *husband*."

Had Lisa simply *gone along with it,* as Caroline suggested, or had she come on to Duane the way she had with Wes? And had it gone any further?

"Does Duane have a temper?" I asked.

Caroline shrugged. "I've seen worse."

"What about your lip? Did he do that?"

Instinctively, her hand rose to touch the bruise.

"Did you have a fight?"

Maybe it wasn't any of my business, but that usually didn't stop me. I leaned forward and briefly touched Caroline's arm. "Was it about Lisa?"

She shook her head.

"There are places you can go for help, you know."

Caroline's hand returned to stroking the baby's fuzzy head. "It wasn't Duane's fault," she said. "He was trying to kiss me and I pulled away. It was after you called the first time."

"When I said I wanted to talk to you about Lisa?"

She nodded. "It started me thinking again about Duane and Lisa. Worrying that he'd been cheating on me. Anyway, I turned away unexpectedly and our heads collided."

"And then?"

A slight smile. "And then we made up. Duane acted so sweet, you wouldn't believe it."

"And he's stayed sweet?"

"It's not what you think. Duane talks tough sometimes, but he's not mean. He would never hurt me on purpose.

Not like that." She took a breath. "What hurts is whenever I think about him and Lisa together. That hurts bad."

"For what it's worth," I said, "Duane doesn't fit the description of the man Lisa met at the Last Chance."

Caroline presssed her lips together. "That's something, I suppose."

"And I know of at least one other man who claims Lisa was a tease."

Caroline looked doubtful.

"Personally, I'd give Duane the benefit of the doubt if I were you."

"Mommy!" Jeremy's shriek reverberated down the hallway from the other room.

"I'm coming, sweetie."

"And I'm leaving," I said, thanking her for her time.

I was rewarded with a tentative smile and a face that was only partially teary.

I headed back to the office feeling disgruntled and testy. I wasn't at all sure I was making progress. Certainly none that was going to exonerate Wes. It was like being in a field of prairie dogs; I'd see what looked to be a promising lead, but by the time I got closer it had disappeared, only to pop up again at a later date elsewhere.

I was glad I was meeting Tom for dinner that evening. I'd try to leave the prairie dogs behind.

Although the menu at Raffino's listed such tempting fare as veal piccata and fettuccine with clams, the food itself was marginal. As far as Tom and I were concerned, the real attraction was the outdoor patio, where the feather-touch of warm evening air and the sweep of black velvet overhead more than made up for inadequacies in the kitchen.

Tom raised his wineglass and tapped it lightly against

mine. "You're not mad at me for standing you up the other night?"

I shook my head. "How was Erin's performance?"

"Quite good. She made a terrific prince."

"Prince?"

"They did a modern adaptation of 'Sleeping Beauty.' "

"And how's Lynn?"

He shrugged. "Damon's moving out."

"Permanently?"

"That's the big question. Seems like instant family was more than he bargained for."

"I thought he and the kids got along."

"They do, but apparently he feels that having them under foot doesn't allow him enough 'personal space.' "

I raised a hand in protest.

"I'm only reporting what I've been told."

"It's Damon's house, though."

Tom's face darkened. "Yeah, that's a problem."

I was feeling a little the way you do when there's been a small earthquake; you sense the imbalance, but everything looks the same. "What's going to happen?" I asked.

A half-shrug. Tom ran his hand through his hair and smiled grimly. "Life is full of surprises."

Wasn't it, though. I tried to read his reaction, but I couldn't decipher the expression on his face or the tone of his words. Tom has a tendency to bury his feelings, the way a dog buries a bone. I'm sure that, like a dog, he pulls them out when he's alone and gnaws on them, but he guards them vigilantly otherwise.

"You heard about Dr. Markley?" he asked, cutting abruptly into my speculation about Lynn.

I nodded.

"The photos looked bad. The car was almost flattened.

It must have rolled a number of times before coming to a stop."

"Who's covering the story for you?"

"Charlie. Why?"

"Just wondering if you'd heard anything that might indicate it wasn't an accident."

"You suspect foul play?"

"The timing seems suspicious. I can't help thinking there might be a connection between her death and the Cornell murders."

"I'll ask around." Tom paused. "Sounds like you're thinking that maybe Wes Harding is telling the truth."

It wasn't a question, but it invited a response. "There was a lot going on in Lisa's life, more than I'd imagined. The headaches and therapy, a family background right out of afternoon television, an ex-husband no one knows much about, a fiancé she felt it necessary to lie to."

"And you think somewhere in all of this there's a motive for murder?"

"I think it's worth exploring. Lisa herself was something of a mystery." I told Tom about the shaggy-haired man she'd been meeting at the Last Chance, and about the incident with Duane Anderson. I left out her flirtation with Wes, which I regarded as confidential. But it was that revelation, and Wes's discomfort in retelling it, that had first persuaded me he might truly be innocent.

The waiter brought our salads and refilled our wineglasses. Tom sipped thoughtfully for a moment.

"Lisa struck me as the girl-next-door type," he said. "Like someone you might find in an ad for Ivory soap or Sunshine laundry detergent."

I looked up. "You knew her?"

"I'd seen her at the diner. Then about a month or so ago she came by the paper to look through old editions."

"What was she after?"

He shrugged. "She spent a couple of hours going through the files, then wanted to see the property records."

"What property?"

"I don't know. That's not the kind of stuff we have. I sent her over to City Hall."

My fork was halfway to my mouth. I set it down and made a mental note to try reaching Robert Simmons again. He had been interested in buying the Cornell place, and Lisa herself had been interested in property records. Maybe there was something to the real estate angle after all.

"What were you doing fielding research inquiries?" I asked Tom. The newspaper was small, but not that small.

"Lisa came to my office. I guess it was because she knew I worked there."

"You don't work there; you own it. Why would Lisa come to you personally to ask about old papers?"

He shook his head. "We'd kid around sometimes at the diner. I gave her a ride home once when her car wouldn't start. I guess mine was the only familiar name on the door."

"So she just walked right in?"

"Apparently so."

The waiter cleared our salad plates. I waited until he left, then turned back to Tom. "You never told me you knew Lisa."

"I didn't."

I sat forward. "But you did." The words had a sharpness I hadn't intended.

"Okay, if you want to mess with semantics, I did. But barely." The lines in his brow deepened. "What's the problem here?"

I didn't know exactly. Tom was right, though; it bothered me that Lisa had come to see him. Most people who wanted old papers went to the front desk.

"Did she flirt with you?"

Tom frowned. "Flirt?"

"Yes. You do know the meaning of the word, don't you?"

"What's with you tonight?"

I smiled weakly over my wineglass. "Humor me."

"No, Lisa did not flirt with me," he said. "And, for the record, I didn't flirt with her, either."

I leaned back. Duane, Wes and the shaggy-haired man, but not Tom. It did indeed take all kinds.

I touched his hand. "Believe it or not, that was an inquiry of a professional nature. It goes to defense strategy."

He gave a clipped laugh. "No wonder lawyers have a bad name."

We drove home with the windows down and the radio volume up. It made me feel like a teenager again.

"Do you think kids still park at that same spot down by the river?" I asked.

"Probably." His fingers traced a lazy *s* on the back of my neck. "You interested in reliving your youth?"

I gave it serious consideration. Tom's truck had a bench seat, fairly wide, and no floor gearshift. I'd certainly managed under worse conditions, but I'd been younger then and my back more forgiving. "I think I'll opt for the comfort of a mattress."

"You're getting old, Red." He shook his head sadly.

"Guess I'm going to have to look elsewhere for excitement."

"You want excitement?" Strategically, I placed my hand on his thigh.

He grinned. "Let's get back in one piece, first."

My message light was blinking when we got home. Sabrina had called, and the bartender from the Last Chance. His message was brief. "That man you were looking for, he's here."

I found Tom stretched out on the bed, hands behind his head. He was still dressed, but his feet were bare. He grinned. "What was that you were saying about excitement?"

I took a moment to admire the view, then told him about the message. "I'm sorry. I've got to talk to him."

"You can't do it another time?"

I wavered. If only I could be certain there would be another time. Finally I shook my head. "This might be my only chance. I think I'd better see him tonight."

Tom groaned and rolled off the bed. "Okay. Let me get my keys."

"I think it would be better if I went alone."

"What? Are you crazy?"

I hoped I wasn't. "I suspect he'll be more willing to talk if it's just me."

"And what if he's somehow tied to the killings?"

"It's not late, and there are bound to be other people at the bar."

Tom shook his head. "I'll drive you and wait outside if you want. But it's—"

His words were interrupted by the chirp of his beeper. He checked the display, then grabbed the phone and punched in a number.

"What is it?"

"I don't know, but it's Lynn's number. Something must have happened to one of the kids."

I held my breath until I'd listened to enough conversation to pick up on the fact that no one was hurt. Then I went into the other room to wait. Tom came in a moment later. His expression was grim, but more angry than frightened.

"Is everything okay?" I asked him.

"Nick got sprayed by a skunk. He's hysterical and, unfortunately, so is Lynn. I've got to go take care of this."

Tom pulled on his shoes. "Hopefully it won't take long. We can head over to the Last Chance as soon as I'm finished."

"I don't know how long the shaggy-haired man will be there. You go take care of Nick; I can handle the Last Chance alone."

Tom started to grumble a protest, then wisely ceased. He knows how much I dislike being lectured to.

"At least take my cell phone," he muttered. "And don't do anything stupid."

I readily agreed to both.

25

The Last Chance was more crowded than it had been on my previous visit, but it still wasn't packed the way some places are. The music was subdued, the noise level almost tolerable. The tables were occupied by singles and couples, rather than large groups, and about half the spots at the bar were empty. Ricky, the bartender, was making change for a big-bellied man in lizard-skin boots and a pair of jeans at least one size too small for his frame.

I slid onto the nearest stool and caught Ricky's eye. "Is the man still here?"

Ricky nodded, then leaned on the counter, bringing his face close to mine.

"Where?" I asked.

He held out a hand, palm open. A snide smile flickered across his lips. "You're forgetting something."

I opened my purse and counted out the bills. He counted them again himself, before folding his wealth and slipping it into his pocket.

"There at the end of the bar," Ricky said. "The guy in the denim shirt."

Although the man was sitting, I could tell that he was long and thin. He was clean shaven, with a narrow, angular face and dusty blond hair that hung unevenly around his face like the dry, wild grasses of summer. When I got closer I saw that his nose was slightly bent, as though it had been broken at some point and never set.

Luckily, the stool next to him was vacant. I slid onto it, ordered a beer and waited for him to glance my way.

He didn't. Instead, he remained hunched over his nearly empty glass, fingering a pack of matches.

Finally I grew tired of the passive approach. "You come here often?" I asked, grimacing inwardly at the clichéd opening.

The man looked over, letting his eyes run down my body and back up again. They were glassy and a bit bloodshot. "Some," he said. "How about you?"

"Just once before. I'm kind of new to the area."

"That makes two of us." He hailed the bartender and ordered another beer. "Where are you from?"

"The Bay Area. How about you?"

"Oh, a little bit of everywhere."

"My name's Kali," I said, with a smile twice as wide as usual. I've never felt comfortable with bar-scene maneuvers, but I reminded myself that I was here on business.

"I'm Jerry." He nodded, but seemed unable to come up with anything close to a smile.

"So, Jerry, how'd you get from everywhere to here?"

"It's a long story." He drained his glass. "Looks like I may be moving on again soon. I got fired today."

"I'm sorry."

"Don't be. It was a shitty job."

"What sort of job?"

"Road construction. Spent the whole day out there on the hot, dusty pavement breathing exhaust fumes, worrying that some half-assed driver was going to plow through the cones and run me over."

I sipped my beer. "Why'd you get fired?"

"Smoking dope on the job." He flashed a grin. "How about you? What do you do?"

"I'm a waitress," I said.

"That's a shitty job too."

I shrugged. "It pays the rent."

"Life of Riley, ain't it? You bust your butt all day so you have a place to rest it at night." He pulled out a pack of Camels and lit up. "You want one?"

I declined with a shake of my head. Then I took a deep, silent breath and mentally crossed my fingers. "It was a woman at work who introduced me to this place."

Jerry offered a polite grunt and tucked the pack of cigarettes back into his shirt pocket. "She come with you tonight?"

"She was killed a couple of weeks ago. You might have seen her here, though. She used to come here pretty often." I had no idea whether that was true or not, but it made a good story. "She had long hair that came halfway down her back. She wore it in a single braid most of the time."

His face remained impassive.

"You might have read about it in the papers too. Lisa Cornell. She and her little girl were murdered."

Jerry blew a long plume of smoke. He cupped the cigarette in his hand and studied the glowing tip. "Yeah, I read about it," he said after a moment.

"Did you ever see her here?"

He stubbed out his cigarette and looked at me. "You worked with Lisa?"

I nodded, hoping I hadn't just painted myself into a corner.

"I was married to her," he said after a moment's pause.

I leaned back and let out a breath. Of all the possible connections between Lisa and the shaggy-haired stranger, I hadn't expected that. "How terrible for you to lose a wife and daughter in such a horrible way."

Jerry nodded, folded his hands and stared at them silently for a moment. "At least they caught the bastard who did it."

I murmured something indecipherable, which he probably took as agreement.

"You work with Lisa long?" he asked after another stretch of silence.

I gave a shrug. "Ever since she started at the Lazy Q."

He cocked his head. "So you probably know all about me, right?"

"We didn't talk much about personal stuff."

"Well, whatever she told you about us, don't believe it."

"The only thing I knew was that she'd been married once."

"Figures." He wrapped his hands around his beer. "She never talked about us getting back together?"

I shook my head.

"Never mentioned seeing me?"

"Like I said, we didn't get into personal stuff."

His expression grew sullen. He folded the matchbook between his fingers, struck a match and blew it out.

"Were you really going to get back together?"

"Who knows? Lisa wasn't exactly sold on the idea." He struck another match and watched it burn down to his fingertips. "We were both young when we met, both of us kind of screwed up. And then the baby came along—"

"Your daughter Amy?"

"Wish to hell I knew." He gave a small, hard laugh. "Lisa never told you that part, did she? I bet it was always what a deadbeat I was, and nothing bad about herself at all. She had this image of herself as a goddamn debutante or something. Honest-to-God truth was, she went after anything in pants." He glanced at my blue jeans over the top of his beer glass, then grinned. "Guess that saying doesn't apply anymore. I think she did draw the line at women."

"Is that why you got divorced?"

"It's why we split up. Lisa didn't hand me the divorce papers until a couple of months ago. Wanted to wrap up all the legalities so she could get remarried." He paused. "You ever meet that guy she was going to head down the aisle with?"

"Philip Stockman?"

"Yeah. What a pitiful specimen. An old fart too, and living with his sister. The whole setup was weird. I tried to convince her it was a mistake, but she said she was doing it for Amy's sake."

"Stability?"

"And money." He spat out the words as though they were distasteful. "I got to take a piss. I'll just be a sec."

I ordered us both another beer. Jerry was gone quite a bit longer than a second, and I began to worry that he'd slipped out a back door, or maybe passed out under a urinal. When he returned the unsteadiness of his gait was more pronounced. When he sat down I realized why. The pungent odor of marijuana hung about him like cheap perfume. He slid back onto the stool and gave me a glassy-eyed grin.

I nodded toward the bottle of beer. "My treat."

"Thanks." He took a sip and picked up where we'd left off. "She wouldn't have been happy with him. No way. I knew that even if she didn't."

"Stockman?"

Jerry nodded.

"Is that why you moved here, to be near Lisa and Amy?"

"Who the fuck knows why I came. It was one of those harebrained ideas that seemed to make sense at the time." He lit another cigarette. "I ran across this picture of Amy she'd sent me not long ago. Kid looked like me, you know? Then when Lisa sent the divorce papers I started thinking about her and us, and about what we'd had going. There was a lot of good mixed in with the bad. And times change. Lisa wants to do the picket fence routine, I figure I could give it a try. Maybe I don't have the money this other guy has, but I know I gotta be better in the sack than him."

"So you tried to convince her to give it another shot?"

"Basically."

"And she wasn't interested?"

"I don't know what she wanted. I don't think she did either. But she was getting cold feet about going through with the wedding."

Remembering my friend-of-Lisa persona, I nodded. "I remember they had set a date and then she postponed it."

"And then she called it off altogether," Jerry said.

"She broke off with Stockman?"

"She was gonna break off with him, anyway. I don't know whether she actually got around to it or not. She was kind of distracted because of those headaches she was getting."

Jerry's eyes had grown more glazed. He rested so unsteadily on one elbow, I was afraid he might keel over. "She ever tell you about that shrink she was seeing?"

"She mentioned her in passing."

"Sounded like a real trip—hypnosis, guided imagery, tapping the unconscious and all that crap."

"What kinds of things were they looking for?" I asked.

"Who knows?" Jerry guzzled what was left of his beer. A thin stream missed his mouth and ran down his chin. He wiped at it with the back of his hand.

"I don't think Lisa bought into most of it, anyway," he continued. "She was supposed to be keeping some sort of journal where she recorded her dreams and fears, that sort of shit. But she hated to write, so she didn't."

"She didn't keep a journal at all?" No wonder I was having trouble tracking it down.

"Not the kind her shrink wanted. Lisa liked to draw. She had notebooks full of sketches. She used to draw some when we were together too, but that was different." He picked up his empty glass and looked at it. "You want another?"

"I think I've had enough."

He hailed the bartender and got himself a fresh beer. "She told me she was waking up in the middle of the night, sweating and confused. She'd try to sketch what she was feeling. I can't see that they'd be much help. They were pretty weird."

"Weird how?"

"Kind of . . . what's that word—abstract. Like that guy who paints people with three eyes and no neck."

"She drew people?"

"People, trees, spooky old barns. All the stuff was kind of dark and grim. And weird. But she drew other things too, when she wasn't half-asleep." He paused. "Seems ironic, her dying in that barn. It was in a lot of her drawings, like maybe she had a premonition or something." He listed in my direction, his elbow sliding across the bartop. "You sure she never talked about me?"

"Not to me."

His expression was gloomy. "You'd think she might have said something. That she'd have cared just a bit."

"Look on the good side," I said sympathetically. "She didn't say anything bad about you either."

Jerry burped. "I got some good grass back at my place. What's say we head over there? We'll pick up a six-pack and some munchies on the way."

"Some other time maybe." I plastered on a big smile, but I think he was too drunk to notice.

"I got to hit the head again. Why don't you order another round, on me. I'll just be a jiffy."

When he had gone I found Ricky and gave him a twenty for cab fare. "If you let your friend drive home tonight," I warned him, "you're leaving yourself open for a lawsuit."

He laughed. "What are you, my guardian angel or something?"

"Pretty close. I'm an attorney. And now that you've been warned, you can't claim you never knew he was drunk. So don't be stupid and pocket the money for yourself."

I pushed open the door and stepped outside, sucking in the fresh air as though I'd been too long underwater.

26

I was still in bed when Daryl Benson called at eight the next morning.

"Did I wake you?" he asked.

"Not really," I lied.

"I checked on Dr. Markley's accident like you asked me to."

I pulled myself to a sitting position. "And?"

"There were no skid marks, you were right about that." Benson's voice spiraled a little at the end, as though he hadn't finished his thought.

"Anything else?"

"Not about the accident per se. There's some question about what the doctor was doing on that stretch of road in the first place. She'd called a friend before leaving her office and was supposedly headed straight home."

"Will the sheriff's department investigate further?" I asked, removing my leg from the vicinity of Loretta's wet nose. She'd padded over to the bed when the telephone rang and was now giving me a doleful look, the canine equivalent of *poor me, I'm so hungry.*

"They don't really have much to go on, Kali. The absence of skid marks doesn't necessarily spell foul play."

"It's suspicious, though."

"Maybe, but not unheard of."

"It seems as if her death has got to be connected in some way to Lisa Cornell's." Loretta had maneuvered her front paws onto the mattress and was trying to ease the rest of her body on as well. "Does the sheriff know she was Dr. Markley's patient?"

"Yeah. For what it's worth, I passed on your concerns." Again there was an odd, unfinished quality to his words.

"Thanks. I appreciate it."

Benson drew in a breath. "There's something else you should know. It's about the Harding case. We've just turned up some female undergarments in the compost bin belonging to Wes's neighbor. One pair was a woman's, the other a child's."

My throat closed down so that I had trouble speaking. "Were they Lisa's and Amy's?"

"That hasn't been determined. The sizes are right."

For a moment I couldn't move. It was as though the wind had been knocked out of me. Finally I swung my legs over the side of the bed, causing Loretta's feet to slip to the floor. "Are you at the station?"

"Yeah."

"Stay there, okay? I'll be by in half an hour. Maybe less."

On the way into town I made a quick stop at The Sugar Plum for two coffees and a dozen of their legendary cinnamon rolls. More than Daryl Benson and I could finish, but I knew the rest would be snatched up in short order by members of the department. It never hurt to have the police think kindly of you.

"How did your detectives happen to be searching the compost bin in the first place?" I asked. We'd settled in Benson's office with our coffee. The box of sweet rolls was between us.

"Curt Willis was interviewing the neighbor, Mrs. Lincoln. In the course of their conversation, it happened to come up that Wes sometimes used the bin to dump his lawn clippings." Benson added sugar and stirred the coffee with the end of his pencil. "Willis asked us to search there for the missing murder weapon."

"Did you find it?"

He took a bite of roll and shook his head. "But we did find the underwear."

I sipped my coffee, but I couldn't eat. My stomach felt as though it had been tied into a knot. I'd been inclined to believe Wes's story. To feel sorry for him, even. What's worse, there was a part of me that wanted to believe him still.

"Is there any way to determine whether the clothing actually belonged to Amy and Lisa?"

Benson frowned. "Probably not. Looks like there may be some bloodstains. We should know that fairly soon. But it's going to be difficult to do much in the way of meaningful testing. You've got decomposing lawn clippings, carrot peels, God knows what all in there. The bin's pretty ripe from what I've heard."

"A compost bin seems like an odd place to discard hard physical evidence." Although fabric would eventually decompose, it would take significantly longer than lawn clippings and carrot peels.

"The criminal mind is not always a logical one," Benson

observed. "Particularly in a situation where a person's trying to get rid of evidence in a hurry."

A neighbor's compost bin still seemed to me an unusual choice. "Are the items here at the station?"

"You want to take a look?"

I did, although I wasn't sure why. "Can I?"

"Just don't touch anything. We've had a criminalist go over them once, but I'm sure he'll want to do further testing."

Benson took a last, long swallow of coffee. He led me down the hall, and then down the elevator to the lab. He mumbled an exchange with the technician in charge and we passed through to an interior room. There, spread out on a mesh pallet for drying, were two pairs of underpants—one pink and decorated with kittens, the other a lacy-style black nylon. The pink pair was small, similar to the ones favored by my niece. I felt my eyes begin to sting.

"We've already dried and tested the outer garments, of course," Benson said. He went to a drawer at the back and pulled out a number of transparent, sealed plastic bags. "You want to take a look at these, you can. Without unsealing them, of course. I'm guessing you and Sam are going to have your own experts run through things a second time anyway." He spread the bags on the table.

One bag held Lisa's jeans; another, her jersey top, which was stained with an inky substance I knew must be dried blood. Amy had been wearing a pair of shorts, pink like her underwear.

"It's the victim's blood," Benson said. "In both cases. The two bodies were far enough apart in the barn that the samples weren't cross-contaminated. There's no trace of the assailant's blood."

The knot in my stomach twisted tighter, and I was glad I hadn't eaten. Seeing the physical evidence, clothing worn by a woman I'd known, now grossly discolored by her own blood—it made the crime real in a way even the most graphic photographs had not.

Benson lifted the plastic packet containing Amy's striped T-shirt and held it in his hand, as though testing its weight. "It takes a real sicko to cut the throat of a child," he said at last.

I nodded numbly and turned away. There would come a time, as we got closer to trial, when I would have to immerse myself in the evidence, maybe even stand by while one of our own defense experts examined the bloody clothing. But at the moment I wanted to banish the images from my mind forever.

"I'm no fan of your client's," Benson said as we wound our way back to his office, "but for your sake I'm sorry to see all the chips lining up with the prosecution."

I shook my head to clear it. "I'll let you in on a secret," I told him. "They aren't lining up as neatly as you think." My tone suggested a conviction I didn't feel, but I was reasonably sure the gist of our conversation would make its way back to Curt Willis. And the last thing I wanted was for him to know how desperate we were.

Benson held the elevator door, then smiled at me fondly. "It's a funny position, being chief of police and finding myself rooting for the defense attorney."

"Is that what you're doing?"

Instead of answering he let his eyes linger on my face. "You remind me more of your mother every day," he said at last.

There was a moment of awkward silence. My mother's

suicide was one of the shared memories on which our current friendship had been forged. It was a powerful bond, but an uncomfortable one for both of us.

The elevator came to a stop and we exited.

"What kind of lab work are you doing on the underwear?"

"The usual. We want to see if we can tie it conclusively to the victims. And, of course, to the defendant. We'll look for trace evidence, run blood and semen tests . . . but the truth is, I don't think we'll find much."

I turned. "There was nothing in the file to indicate that either victim had been sexually molested."

"They weren't," Benson said. "But it takes a certain kind of depraved individual to rip the underwear off a woman he's murdered. The way I figure it, he's a guy with a fetish." Benson scratched his chin. "There was a man in town years ago who used to go around stealing ladies' underwear off the clothes line. By the time we caught up with him he had suitcases full of the stuff. 'Course he was harmless."

I couldn't imagine Wes Harding fueling his desire with a pair of nylon briefs, even if they were black and lacy. Not that I had much to go on but instinct.

On the other hand, Wes saw himself as a man whose advances had been spurned. A guy like that just might be thinking in terms of power rather than passion. Strip your victim of her dignity as well as her life.

So I supposed it might have fit—except for the fact that I didn't want it to. Maybe it was the gypsy magic Sabrina had talked about, or maybe it was simply seeing Wes as the man he really was, without the posturing. Whatever the reason, I found I didn't want to believe he was a killer.

27

I'd spoken to Mrs. Lincoln earlier, when I'd canvassed Wes's neighborhood in the hopes of establishing an alibi. But I couldn't recall the woman specifically until I pulled up in front of the address Benson had given me, a small, white frame house immediately to the south of Wes's. Then I was able to recollect a woman in her late fifties, bone thin, with almost lashless eyes. She hadn't been home the Friday night of the murders, but she'd told me she had no complaints about Wes as a neighbor.

As I was getting out of my car, she came down the front path from the house, her purse over her arm. I met her halfway.

"I remember you," she said when I introduced myself. "We talked a week or so ago."

"I'd like to ask a couple more questions, if I might."

"I'm afraid I'm on my way out at the moment."

"I'll make it quick." I followed her down the driveway to the garage. "It's about the compost bin. Can you tell me about your arrangement with Wes Harding?"

"It wasn't an arrangement, really. We just let him use it."

"On a daily basis?"

"Heavens no. My husband and I, we dispose of most all our organic waste by composting, but lawn clippings and leaves were about all Wes ever brought over. And not that often." She paused and glanced toward his place. "He didn't care much for yard work, as you can probably tell."

I glanced next door. The grass was mowed—probably Jake's doing—but the weeds were abundant, the shrubs overgrown and the flower beds empty. It looked a lot like my own yard had when I'd first moved in after my father's death.

"Was this a recent arrangement?" I asked.

She shook her head. "No, Wes has been using it almost as long as he's lived here. The couple before Wes kind of kept to themselves, so we were happy to have a neighborly sort move in. He was handy too. Helped Herman install a new vanity in the bathroom."

I was surprised. I hadn't imagined Wes as the neighborly sort. But I was coming to realize that I'd been wrong about a lot of things where Wes was concerned.

"Did he check with you each time?" I asked.

"Before he brought stuff over?"

I nodded.

"It wasn't anything formal like that. He was welcome to use it anytime he wanted."

Willis must have loved learning that. Wes could easily have walked next door, disposed of the evidence—and no one would have noticed anything unusual.

"How come you didn't tell me about the compost bin when I talked with you before?"

Mrs. Lincoln opened the garage door, then dusted her hands on her slacks. "I didn't think about it," she said.

"You told the DA, though."

She looked me in the eye. "He asked." Then she scowled. "If I'd known I was going to end up with a bunch of heavy-hoofed cops poking around my yard, I wouldn't have told him either."

"Do you mind if I look as well? I'll be careful."

She hesitated. "I guess it's okay. Just watch out for my tomato plants."

When Mrs. Lincoln had driven off I walked around the garage and into the rear yard. There was a small patio close to the house, rimmed with roses and well-tended flower beds. Farther to the back was a large vegetable garden, and behind that, partially screened by raspberry vines, were several wooden frames for composting. Nearby I noticed a matted area where the police had apparently raked through the compost mounds, spreading them thin. I could see how their efforts to restore order had fallen short of Mrs. Lincoln's expectations.

Turning, I followed what I thought was the most likely route between the two yards. There was no fence separating the Lincolns' property from Wes's, but a row of pines ran along what I assumed was the property line. Along the street in front a dense hedge obscured the yards from public view.

Wes could no doubt have hidden evidence in the compost bin without raising suspicion. But it would have been almost as easy for anyone approaching from the street, particularly at night. For that matter, with Wes in jail and his house empty, anyone could have followed the same path between the houses I had.

From my position near the corner of the house I surveyed Wes's rear yard. It was largely scrub brush and dry, wild grass. There's a fine line between neglect and natural, and I thought Wes had probably crossed it. On the other hand, Jake had said he was focusing his efforts on the interior remodeling. He could hardly be expected to tackle a major landscaping job at the same time.

Out of curiosity I approached Wes's house and peeked through the rear windows. I could see a laundry room and an enclosed back porch that served as a storage area, and next to that the breakfast nook where Wes had begun stripping off layers of wallpaper. I knew from experience what a chore that was, especially when you reached those early papers that had been applied with hard-drying paste. It looked like Wes's efforts had become stalled there, at an era when kitchen chic meant walls of watering cans and stenciled geraniums in pots.

When I got back to my car I checked my watch again and decided it was late enough to call Sam. Someday, when I was no longer scraping by, I was going to get myself a car phone. My perpetual search for pay phones had gotten old, fast. At the Chevron station I found a phone booth, but no phone. My luck was better at the convenience store next door.

I reached Sam and told him about the underwear discovered in the Lincolns' compost bin.

"Have they made a positive link to Wes or either of the victims?" he asked when I'd finished.

"Not so far. Benson thinks it's unlikely the forensics tests will turn up much."

Sam sighed. "We'd better keep our fingers crossed all the same."

"I'm not sure how much it matters. Willis is going to play this for everything he can. And the press is going to have a field day."

"You're full of good news," Sam humphed.

"Actually, I may have some." I told him about my meeting the previous night with Jerry, Lisa's ex-husband. "I'm going to see if I can get another look at her drawings. Jerry said she didn't keep a diary the way Dr. Markley asked, but used her art for the same purpose."

"What's a drawing going to tell you?"

"I don't know; maybe nothing. But I'd like to see for myself."

When I hung up I fished out another quarter and dialed Ed Cole's office, hoping to get Lisa's key. Unfortunately, he wasn't in.

Knowing that people sometimes hid spares outside, I drove to Lisa's house anyway. I was a little uneasy about the ethics of entering without Cole's consent, but I tried to push my qualms aside. The police had finished with the house, Lisa's parents had taken what they wanted and I was only going to borrow the sketchbooks, not take them permanently. In any case, I was reasonably sure Cole would have given me the go ahead and I'd tell him what I'd done as soon as I could reach him.

I parked at the end of the long drive and walked around to the back of the house, where I looked under the doormat and nearby flowerpots and loose rocks. I climbed under the porch to inspect the posts and then moved farther afield to the area near Amy's tire swing. Nothing.

I was growing hot and sticky and cranky. I decided to give up, and was headed around front when I saw a large white Cadillac pull into the driveway. The car looked familiar, but it wasn't until Sheri Pearl opened the driver's side door and stepped out that I realized why.

As I stepped forward, she put a hand over her heart and let out a little shriek.

"Good heavens, Kali, you scared me to death. What are you doing here?"

"I might ask you the same thing."

"I came to look at the house." Sheri closed the car door and locked it. The alarm gave a little chirp. "I'm working hard on getting this listing. The place is going to go for a bundle, and I want to be in on it, one way or another. If I'm both listing and selling agent, so much the better."

"Have you talked to Cole?"

She tossed her head. "Of course I've talked to Cole. How do you think I got the key?"

"You have the key?" I tried to stifle my excitement.

She held it aloft with one finger. The key dangled from a loop of twine. "You think I'd drive out here on a weekend just to walk the property and size up the exterior?"

"Can I tag along for a bit? Cole let me in earlier, so I don't think he'd mind."

"You interested in buying it?"

I shook my head. "I want to take a look at Lisa's sketchbooks."

"Whatever for?"

"I'm probably chasing rabbits, but I thought her drawings might tell me something about her murder."

Sheri dropped her car keys into her bag. "I suppose it's all right. Truth is, I'm not any too happy going in there alone. It seems kind of spooky, if you know what I mean."

While Sheri toured the main floor of the house with clipboard and tape measure, I headed for the upstairs bedrooms. In the back of my mind I remembered seeing some spiral-bound sketchbooks in Lisa's bedroom. I found them, plus a pad of drawing paper, in a desk drawer. I picked up the sketchbook from Amy's room as well, then headed back downstairs to find Sheri.

"I'm taking these books," I told her, holding them out for inspection. "You want to make an inventory or something?"

Sheri wasn't interested. "Just be sure to tell Cole."

I nodded and stuck the sketchbooks in my canvas tote.

"Will you hold the end of this tape for me?" Sheri asked. "I'm trying to get a rough estimate of square footage."

I held the end of the tape measure with my foot while she walked down the hallway, trailing the tape after her.

"The house isn't much," she said, eyeing the narrow hallway with disdain. "I mean, it's nice enough, but compared to the value of the property, the house is likely to be a secondary consideration. Whoever buys the place will certainly want to remodel and add on, maybe even tear it down and start over. That would be the wisest move."

She reeled in the tape and we went through the exercise again across the back of the house.

"Anne Drummond loved this place," I said. "She left it to Lisa precisely because she didn't want it sold or torn down."

"Yeah, but they're both gone now."

"It seems sad somehow."

"It's not my decision, Kali. I'm simply doing my job." Sheri jotted something on her clipboard. "I guess I've seen enough for now. I want to take a look at the barn. Will you come with me?"

As we headed out back, Sheri continued to scrutinize the property in terms of sales potential. At the barn door she hesitated.

"It's okay," I said. "It's just an empty barn."

"It seems morbid."

"You're the one who wanted to see it."

"I'm going to suggest they tear the barn down before

listing the property. No buyer's going to have use for the thing anyway. And it will just remind people of the murders."

I led the way into the dim interior. Since my last visit there'd been a proliferation of cigarette butts and gum wrappers. A small pyramid of empty beer cans had appeared under the loft. The boys had apparently returned. I wondered if Bongo was among them, or if finding the bodies had scared him off forever.

Sheri sneezed. "It's dusty in here. And smelly." She looked around. "The structure is rickety; useless, really. I can't imagine why Anne Drummond didn't tear the thing down herself, years ago."

"I think she used it for storage."

Sheri's eyes surveyed the interior. She nodded in the direction of the storage shelves at one end of the barn. "Looks like she tried to make something useful of the place at one time. Seems a waste, though, to put shelving that sturdy out here where you couldn't store anything that might be harmed by the elements. It's got to be damp in the winter and infested with bugs the rest of the year."

We turned and started for the door, then stopped short when we heard a scratching sound from behind the barn. Sheri turned white.

"What was that?" she whispered.

"Probably an animal. A squirrel or rat—"

She grabbed my arm and pulled herself up on her toes. "Rat?"

There was another thump and then a cough. Sheri dug her nails into my flesh. "Animals don't cough."

I unwound her fingers from my arm and darted for the door. I got there just in time to see a hunched figure scurrying for the woods.

"It was only Granger," I told her.

"Who?"

I explained.

"I hope to goodness he stays away once the property is listed." She dusted off her skirt. "That's another reason to tear the barn down. Rats and bums don't do a lot for sales potential."

Probably not. But Sheri's single-minded focus on marketing and financial gain left a sour taste in my mouth. It also reminded me, however, that I'd yet to connect with Robert "Bud" Simmons. As we headed back to the front of the house, I asked Sheri if she knew him.

"Doesn't ring a bell," she said. "Why?"

"He has a client who's interested in the property."

"There are going to be a number of people interested. That's why I'm doing everything I can to be part of it."

Sheri unlocked her car. "I've got to run some stuff over to Mother and then get on to an appointment. I'm dreading it because I know she'll expect me to stay and visit. When I tell her I can't she'll fall into a funk. Assuming it's one of the days she even remembers who I am."

I nodded. It was hard to know what to expect with Irma Pearl. That's what made it so hard. Some days her mind was clear and lucid; others, she lived in a world of her own making.

Sheri tossed her clipboard into the backseat. "I hate to disappoint her, but I simply don't have time to sit there making small talk. It's taking a lot of my energy just getting her house ready to put on the market. I had to sort through everything before I brought in the movers and—"

"Why don't you let me take her whatever it is she needs."

Sheri lifted her head. "You wouldn't mind?"

"Not at all." On some level I owed Sheri a favor for letting me into Lisa's house. But I found that visits with Irma Pearl eased my conscience as well. Although it was the judge, and not me, who'd ultimately decided she needed a conservator, I couldn't help feeling rotten about my role in bringing it about.

I stuck the bundle Sheri had given me into my canvas tote, along with Lisa's sketches, and headed for the Twin Pines Rest Home.

28

Irma Pearl was having one of her better days; she was not only lucid but cheerful. Her hair was clean and combed, and she was dressed in a cotton shirtwaist rather than a robe. A smile of recognition crossed her face the moment she saw me.

"Kali. What a pleasant surprise."

"I brought you a package from Sheri. She wanted to come herself, but she had an unexpected business appointment."

"That poor girl works herself too hard," Mrs. Pearl said. "Always has. I don't think she knows the meaning of rest. And now, of course, she's got me to worry about as well. I hate being a burden on her."

"I'm sure Sheri doesn't see it that way." I figure white lies don't count.

Her face clouded. "It's no fun growing old, I'll tell you that."

We were sitting at one end of a large lounge—a pleasant, airy space that opened onto a patio and a garden. The walls were painted a soft yellow and adorned with framed landscapes. The floor was carpeted, the furniture comfortable and homey. Although the ambience was hardly nursing-home institutional, it reminded me a little of my college dormitory.

"And don't tell me growing old is better than the alternative," Irma Pearl added, "because somedays I'm not so sure that's true." Her expression was troubled, as though she'd bitten into a lemon when expecting chocolate. "I never thought I'd end up in an old-folks home."

I nodded in sympathy. "This is one of the nicer places, though."

"I suppose so, for what it is. It's just that it isn't home." Leaning closer, she gestured to the other end of the room, where a small group was gathered in front of the television. "The worst part," she whispered, "is that you have to put up with other people and their annoying habits."

She straightened, played with the fabric of her skirt for a moment, then sighed. "I forget things, though. Sheri's right; I can't care for myself anymore. And I sometimes make the stupidest decisions. It's like I've got some other person's brain inside my head some days. A very stupid person."

I pulled my totebag into my lap and retrieved the package. "Sheri sent this," I told her. "She said you were expecting it."

Tearing at the wrapped package as gleefully as a child, Irma let out a squeal of delight. "She got me three of them."

"Three of what?"

"Books on tape. My eyes are so bad, I had to give up reading. Then one of the women here introduced me to audio books. They make a tape of someone reading the book aloud, and then you listen to it. My friend likes to knit while she listens, but me, I just like to close my eyes and concentrate on the story. It's a wonderful invention."

I made a mental note to bring her a couple of tapes next time I came for a visit. "I brought you something too," I said, reaching into my tote for the box I'd picked up at The Sugar Plum on my way over.

Her eyes sparkled. She opened the box and offered me a cookie. "Why don't I get us some tea too?" she suggested. "There's a service set out in the dining room. We can have our own little party."

"That's a lovely idea. But I'll get the tea. You sit right here."

"I take mine with sugar," she said. "Two spoonsful."

I found the room on the other side of the hallway. Tea, coffee and juice were set out on the long buffet near the door. I had to give Sheri credit for choosing a decent place. I was sure the homelike amenities did not come cheaply.

When I returned, balancing the cups one in each hand, Irma was leafing through one of Lisa's sketchbooks. "You're quite an artist," she said with admiration.

I set the cups down on the coffee table in front of us. "Those aren't mine. They belong to a friend."

"Your friend is quite good. I always wanted to have artistic talent, though I suppose at my age it no longer matters. One of the classes they offer here in the evenings is a drawing class. Maybe I'll give it a try." She laughed. "Grandma Moses herself."

She nibbled on a cookie as she flipped through Lisa Cornell's drawings. Then she stopped abruptly and pointed to the page in her lap.

"Goodness, that's Barry Drummond."

"Barry Drummond?"

"I haven't seen him in years. He was married to a woman I used to work with."

"Anne Drummond?"

Irma Pearl looked up. "You knew her?"

"Are you saying that's a sketch of Anne Drummond's husband?"

"Wasn't much of a husband, if the truth be told. How did you know Anne?"

"I only knew her by reputation." I scooted closer. "Are you sure that's him?"

"It certainly looks like him. Like he looked twenty years ago, anyway. Cleft chin, broad forehead, wavy hair. And that killer smile."

I wondered if her choice of words was prophetic. "Tell me about him."

"There's not much to tell. Anne and I both worked at the library. Barry worked for some company back East, was sort of their western sales representative. I never did understand exactly what it was he did, but it involved a fair amount of travel. Then, all of a sudden, a couple of years after they married, he just up and left her. I recall that she got a card or two from him, then nothing."

Irma sipped her tea. "He had a reputation as a womanizer, and most of us figured he'd just moved on to greener pastures. Of course I always suspected Anne had herself a beau on the side too. Not that I fault her. Barry was one of those fellows who could pour on the sweetness and charm but didn't give a hoot, really, about anyone but himself."

"Why'd she marry him then?"

"Well, he was good-looking. And like I said, he could be a real charmer. Then too, Anne was kind of impulsive. She wasn't what you'd call a weighty thinker."

"But she never divorced him?"

"Not as far as I know. She never remarried, anyway. Barry's leaving seemed to sober her up quite a bit. She kind of kept to herself after that."

"Do you remember when it was he left?"

"Let's see, it must have been in the mid-seventies." Irma frowned. "It was the summer Sheri got engaged. She didn't do a whole lot better than Anne in choosing the right man, but at least she didn't give up trying."

As I recalled, Sheri had tried to find the right man on at least three separate occasions. And I knew for a fact that she was still trying.

"Your friend who drew these pictures, how did she know Barry?"

I shook my head, perplexed. Although the question in my mind was not only how Lisa knew Barry, but why she would be sketching his face some twenty years later.

When I got home I called Sam first thing. He wasn't in, but I left a message relaying the key points of my conversation with Irma Pearl. I was anxious to hear his reaction.

I tried Tom next, but he too was out. I'd barely hung up when the phone rang.

It was Curt Willis. He tried his best to be cordial, but he couldn't keep the gloating tone from coming through. "You've heard about the panties the police discovered? They were hidden in the yard of one of Harding's neighbors."

I hate the way men say *panties*. I don't know one woman

who refers to her underwear that way. "I heard," I told him.

His voice smoothed out. "Just wanted to make sure you knew. I wouldn't want anyone accusing me of not playing fair and square with the defense."

"That's awfully kind of you, Curt."

"I mean it. I'm not one of those attorneys who maps out a dramatic surprise to spring at the eleventh hour of trial."

If he thought he could get away with it, I was willing to bet he'd try. "Only because the law won't allow it," I said.

"In this case it doesn't matter. The evidence is lining up nicely for the prosecution."

"You really think the underwear belonged to Lisa and Amy?" I asked.

"It's too much of a coincidence to be otherwise. Of course, we'll know more when the lab results are in."

"Benson wasn't so sure they'd show much."

"He's overly cautious. I imagine he was also trying to soft-pedal the bad news. He seems to have a thing for you, you know." Curt's tone sounded vaguely petulant.

"It's not the sort of thing you imagine," I explained. "Daryl Benson is a family friend from way back."

A chuckle. "So that's it. I didn't figure him to be your type, although I could see how you might be his."

"In this case you figured wrong."

He laughed appreciatively. "I got to tell you, Kali, I'm looking forward to this trial. I hope it doesn't sour what's between us."

"I don't think that will be a problem." I didn't know there was anything between us but professional cama-raderie. Besides, butting heads at trial was the way attorneys bonded. Kind of like dogs sniffing at each other's hindquarters.

"Most of the lawyers in this hick town are a bunch of yo-yos," Curt said. "But you and I are different. We've got the smarts and the drive to play with the big guys."

"Maybe."

"Of course, you've been on the front line before. For me this is a new experience. This is the most prominent case I've worked on." Curt paused. "I feel like I'm stepping into the spotlight, playing on Broadway. And it's just the beginning."

"I hate to burst your bubble, Curt, but you haven't won yet."

His laugh was good-natured. "But I will."

"In case you've missed them, there are a whole slew of holes in your case."

"Like what?"

It was my turn to laugh. "Wait and find out."

I'd thought I might spend the afternoon putting the first coat of paint on the dining room walls. But Curt's call left me feeling unsettled, as though an elusive gnat were buzzing near my head. I got out the drop cloth and brush and then decided to bag it.

What bothered me in large part was trial strategy. The possibilities were numerous and seemed to fly off in a new direction at every juncture. Sam and I had to pin down an approach, and soon.

I was also bugged by Curt's attitude, although I understood where he was coming from. Curt's legal career had never quite come up to his expectations. It had stalled at an early stage, and he'd spent the intervening years jock-

eying for a second chance at the brass ring. It remained
to be seen whether this trial would help him, but to his
mind it was his best shot. He was going to give it everything
he had.

In some respects my own situation wasn't all that different. My career had stalled at a later stage, and I wasn't
so sure I wanted the brass ring. But the trial was important
to me too. And I wanted to win as much as Curt did.

I poured myself a glass of iced tea, then sat down at the
kitchen table with my case notes and files. Curt's attitude
and my own professional ambitions aside, this newest development with Barry Drummond raised enough questions that my head was beginning to spin. I couldn't wait
to talk it over with Sam.

I took out paper and pen, then spent several minutes
staring at the blank page. There were two starting
premises—either Wes did not commit the crimes in question or he did. I decided to set the second aside for a moment and concentrate on the first.

I believed Wes's account of having picked up Lisa at
the Last Chance. Ricky, the bartender, had pretty much
corroborated that. Also plausible were Wes's explanations for the rabbit's foot in Amy's pocket, the dirt on his
motorcycle, and the bloodstains on his clothing. Of
course, to get all that into evidence at trial we'd have to
put Wes on the stand—and that proposition didn't thrill
me at all.

Left unanswered, though, was the question of why Lisa
had left so abruptly the night she'd gone home with Wes.
Had she simply changed her mind about him, or was she
playing the tease all along? It was equally possible, of
course, that Wes's own behavior had caused the cooling

of Lisa's ardor. He might not be a killer, but that didn't mean he was a saint, either. I was willing to bet his version of events had been sanitized at least a little.

There was also the matter of the Friday night phone call. Had Lisa actually received a call? If so, was it related to her death?

I wrote down questions and jotted a few stray thoughts. Then I started with a clean sheet of paper and Dr. Markley's death. She'd called me Wednesday afternoon, presumably because she'd remembered something she thought might have bearing on Lisa's death. Had the doctor been killed because of what she knew? Or was I reading too much into a simple accident?

I pulled out the sketch of Barry Drummond—or the man who looked like Barry Drummond. Had Lisa found a picture of him among her aunt's things? But why, of all the faces she could practice sketching, would she choose his? I wondered if perhaps the man had returned to Silver Creek.

I flipped through the sketchbook. I recognized the barn at the back of her property, but that was all. Many of the drawings resembled doodles. Flowers, trees, birds. Even a geranium in a flowerpot that looked as though it might have been inspired by the old wallpaper in Wes's kitchen. Maybe it had been.

Drummond's picture was roughly halfway through the sketchbook. I examined the other pages on which she'd worked on her rendering of chins and eyes and mouths. Except for one exaggerated drawing of a cleft chin, I couldn't see that the features bore any resemblance to the drawing of Barry Drummond.

A thought came to me. I checked the file notes from my

conversation with Ron Swanson, Lisa's stepfather. Her childhood stay with Anne Drummond was likely to have coincided with Barry's departure, but Lisa would have been only four or five at the time. Would she remember a face from that far back?

It was possible, I supposed. Maybe, through hypnosis, Lisa had remembered something damaging about the man. It seemed pretty far-fetched, and I couldn't imagine who would care at this point except for Barry Drummond himself.

Of course Irma Pearl could have been mistaken. In light of her deteriorating mind, it was more than possible. Surely there had to be someone in town who could tell me whether the sketch was truly of Barry Drummond. I was wading through a mental list of people who might be able to help when I heard a knock at the door. Tom's knock.

"It's open," I yelled.

Loretta jumped to her feet and went to greet him.

"I thought I'd take a walk," Tom said. Barney shot past, headed for Loretta's food dish. "You want to come along?"

"Sure. My brain could use the exercise." I changed shoes and grabbed a hat to block what was left of the sun. I'd spent so many summers baking myself to a golden brown that my skin was probably beyond help. But encroaching age lines and graying hair made me anxious to hold on to whatever youth I had left.

"Did you see Benson this morning?" Tom asked as we headed down toward the main road. The day was hot and I could feel my cotton T-shirt sticking to my back.

"Yes, but I didn't learn much more than I did over the telephone."

"Rumor has it there are bloodstains."

"Where'd you hear that?"

"The guy covering the story was gabbing with one of the lab people."

"That doesn't mean it's her blood," I said bleakly.

"No, it doesn't."

"And it certainly doesn't prove that Wes Harding was involved. Anyone could have gotten back to that compost bin."

"Anyone willing to risk being caught."

We turned off the main road and onto a fire break. "If you were going to get rid of evidence, would you dump it in a compost bin? Seems like you're almost asking for it to be found."

"I guess it would depend on what my other options were." Tom bent down to unleash the dogs. They trotted off to sniff the trees.

"There's something else that's been troubling me," I said, brushing aside a gossamer strand of spider's web. "The underpants the police found were black lace, very skimpy. Yet Lisa was dressed in comfortable clothes—old jeans and a jersey. Her bra was white cotton."

"So?"

I shrugged. "It just seems like an odd combination."

"Not all women have the same pedestrian tastes you do."

I nudged him with my elbow. "Thanks a heap. You really know how to lay on the compliments."

"It's a statement, Kali, nothing more."

"Those G-string things are uncomfortable," I grumbled. "And lace scratches."

He grinned, held up his hands. "Okay, you win. It's an odd combination."

"You want to hear something else odd?" I told him about

the sketch of the man who might be Barry Drummond. "Do you think he could be here in town and no one would recognize him?"

"Sure, especially if he didn't want to be recognized."

"That's spooky."

"You think Barry Drummond might be connected to the murders?"

Tom's train of thought had followed my own, but the theory sounded pretty outlandish when I heard it aloud. Why would a man who'd disappeared from Silver Creek twenty years earlier return to kill a woman he'd barely known?

"I don't know," I said. "Maybe the sketch isn't Drummond. Or maybe Lisa ran across a picture of him and simply drew the face for artistic exercise."

"Maybe Drummond wanted his old home back."

"Enough to kill for? Not likely. Especially not after twenty years."

"It's worth quite a bit. And Lisa was inquiring about property records, remember."

I nodded. "The property angle was one of the first I thought of. There's apparently a fair amount of interest in the place. Some guy from San Francisco even called Cole because he has a client who's interested."

"How did he even learn of the property?"

"I have no idea. The guy's name is Simmons. I've been trying to reach him for days."

I stopped to pick a handful of wild blackberries. "Enough of this," I said, plopping a couple into my mouth. "It's giving me a headache. It's what one of my law professors called *flee-flow.*"

"Is that some fancy legal term?"

I laughed. "No, it refers to thoughts that flee as fast as they flow. You can't hold on to any of them."

I awoke Sunday morning with a kicker of a headache. Tom and I had taken in a movie, then come back and settled outside with a pitcher of margaritas. Tom mixes them strong, but they slide down so smoothly, I tend to forget.

It was after nine when I finally pulled myself out of bed. Tom had left early to spend the day with his children. I swallowed two Motrin, took a shower and fixed myself a cup of coffee. *The Mountain Journal* doesn't publish a Sunday paper so I was stuck with *The Hadley Times*, which ran the underwear discovery as front-page news.

There wasn't much in the way of hard facts, but the reporter used the opportunity to review the murders and the case against Wes Harding. He'd obviously talked to Curt Willis, though he hadn't called me or, to my knowledge, Sam. Curt was quoted as saying that the prosecution had a strong case, which had been made even stronger by yesterday's discovery. He felt confident tests would show the bloodstains to be the victims'. It wasn't a long quote, but it contained enough words like *justice* and *morality* that Curt came across like a white knight. I had no doubt the article pleased him immensely.

Sabrina called while I was still lingering over the paper. "Do you think there's a battered-mother defense to murder?" she asked.

"Who hit you?"

"No one, I just feel battered. I can't believe I'm raising such selfish ingrates. I asked Joey to take out the garbage this morning and you'd think I'd sent him off to work in the coal mines. Then, because he was mad, he didn't pay attention to what he was doing and dropped the bag right on the new family room carpet. Coffee grounds, salad dressing, jam—I'm so infuriated, I might just strangle him."

I suppressed a smile. "Aren't you the one who's always telling me how much I'm missing by remaining childless?"

"Well, forget everything I ever said about it." She took a breath. "Anyway, how are things with you?"

"So, so." I told her about the latest developments. "I don't know how we'll do in a court of law, but the tide of popular opinion is certainly against us."

"You wouldn't have to deal with this stuff if you worked for the bank, you know."

"I told you, I—"

"Lighten up, Kali. That was a joke." There was a pause. "Why would a killer steal his victim's underwear?"

I told her my theories. "Sex, power, humiliation."

"I don't know. If you ask me, it sounds more like a childish prank." Her voice rose to a sing-song pitch. *"I see Paris, I see France, I see Sabrina's underpants.* Remember?"

"What I remember is the way you clobbered the Jones boy with your lunch pail when he tried that at the bus stop."

"God, if I'd remembered how obnoxious boys could be I'd never have had any myself. Well, I'd better go clean up the carpet before the stains set in for good. I told Joey to pick up the garbage, but I'm going to have to work on the stains myself."

I was heating water for a second cup of coffee when Sabrina's words triggered something in my mind.

Have you ever been to Paris, France?

Oooh, la.

Boys will be boys.

Granger's words echoed in my head. Was he referring

to cigarettes and beer and girlie magazines? Or was there maybe something more?

It was a long shot, but one worth exploring.

I turned off the kettle and went to pay another visit to Bongo.

29

"Tell me again about the afternoon you discovered the bodies of Mrs. Cornell and her daughter."

Bongo was slouched on his living room couch, bare feet resting on the table in front of it. A bowl of popcorn was cradled in his lap, a can of Pepsi nearby. He'd yelled at his younger brother, Kevin, for letting me in while their mother was at the grocery, but he hadn't thrown me out. I was hoping we could finish up before Mrs. Langley returned.

"I told you about it last time you were here," Bongo grumbled.

"I know, but sometimes it helps for me to hear things a second time."

"What part do you want to hear again?"

"All of it. It was a Sunday, I believe."

Bongo nodded, took a swig of soda, then wiped his mouth with the back of his hand.

"In the afternoon," I coached.

"Yeah."

"Were you supposed to meet someone in the barn?"

"No, I just thought . . . I thought my brother might be over there." He looked quickly at Kevin and then away.

Kevin straddled a straight-backed chair as though he were riding a horse. "Why were you looking for me?"

"I just was, all right."

"So you checked inside the barn," I prodded.

"Yeah. I just sort of poked my head in. The place stunk something awful. When I saw those bodies all bloody and swollen I took outta there. Just about lost my lunch."

"And that was it?"

"I told my mom and she called the police."

"And now he's afraid to go back," Kevin said smugly. "I bet him my whole month's allowance he couldn't spend ten minutes alone inside the barn."

"I don't want your stupid money."

"Oh, yeah?"

I tried again. "So you weren't there long. Probably less than a minute?"

"A lot less."

"Thirty seconds?"

"Not even that long. I told you, it was gross."

"What strikes me as peculiar," I said off-handedly, "is the way you saw the two bodies straight off. Not only noticed them, but knew right away the condition they were in. All in less than thirty seconds."

He shrugged.

"I've been inside the barn. It's dark in there. Coming in from the bright afternoon sun, it took my eyes awhile to adjust. Until they did, I couldn't see a thing."

Bongo popped the metal on his soda can. "Maybe it was

longer than I thought. A scare like that makes it hard to remember straight."

"Still, it seems funny that the first thing you'd focus on would be inert shapes at ground level, clear on the other side of the building."

Bongo shrugged, but his face had paled considerably.

"I think you're not being completely straight with me," I said.

"What'ya mean?"

"I think maybe you spent more time inside the barn than you're admitting to."

He shook his head vehemently. "No way. It was a minute max. They were disgusting. They hardly looked like people at all. I wouldn't even have recognized them if I hadn't—"

"Hadn't what?"

"Nothing." Bongo's breathing was rapid and shallow. A fine film of perspiration covered his forehead. He tossed Kevin his pocket knife. "Go see if you can find a piece of wood for that boat you been talking about making."

"I don't know what to look for."

"Yes, you do. About this size." Bongo cupped his hands into a shape the size of a football. "You can start by peeling off the bark."

"Mom don't like me using a knife when no one's around."

"I'll be there in a minute. You go wait for me, okay?"

Kevin hesitated, then swung his leg over the chair and shuffled out. I waited for Bongo to continue, but instead he finished off his can of soda.

"You were telling me about finding Mrs. Cornell and her daughter," I reminded him. "You wouldn't have recognized them if you hadn't what?"

He looked up and then away quickly. "I don't know. I guess I knew it had to be them 'cause it was their property and all."

"You keep stalling like this and we're going to get to the dicey part about the time your mother gets home. You want to have this conversation in front of her?"

Bongo crushed the can in his hands. "I don't know what you're talking about."

"They found the underwear, you know."

His head jerked up. "They couldn't have." Then he realized what he'd said and his eyes took on a glint of panic.

"Both pairs. They were in a trash bin. The police are going to be able to trace them back to you," I said, lying through my teeth. "Modern forensics is truly amazing."

Bongo swallowed hard.

"It wasn't me," he protested. "It was Tim. And they were already dead. We didn't have nothing to do with that. All we did was take some of their clothes."

"Who's Tim? I thought you were alone that afternoon."

There was a moment's hesitation. "I was. But Tim and me were there Friday night too."

"That's when you found them, Friday night?"

He nodded, his eyes averted.

"And you undressed them?"

"It was Tim's idea, I swear. I just took a quick peek."

"Sure." I made no effort to hide my disgust.

"They were dead; they weren't going to care." His voice held a touch of insolence.

"Was it Tim who took the underwear?"

Bongo nodded, pulled himself up straighter. "He said it was kind of like a souvenir."

"So why'd he toss them into the trash?"

"Beats me. It was only yesterday he brought them out so we could take another look. I think he'd had plenty of looks himself in between. He kept them hidden under a loose floorboard in his closet."

"Yesterday?"

He nodded.

If Bongo was right, then the garments found in the compost bin weren't Lisa's and Amy's. I leaned forward. "You're sure it was yesterday?"

"Yeah, I'm sure. Tim didn't say nothing about getting rid of them either."

I sat back a bit. "Why didn't you report the deaths on Friday when you first discovered them?"

He shrugged.

"We're going to get to the bottom of this one way or another," I told him. "If not here, then down at the police station." When he didn't say anything I stood. "Okay, if that's the way you want it."

"Wait." The word squeaked out.

I eased back into my chair.

"We were staying at Tim's Friday night. We were supposed to be watching his little sisters, but after they were asleep we snuck out with a six-pack of beer. Tim's dad woulda beat the shit out of both of us if he'd known."

"But why wait until Sunday?"

"Tim said we should just keep quiet about the whole thing, that someone else would discover them eventually. But I waited all weekend and never heard a word about it. Not in the newspaper, not on the radio or TV. Finally I couldn't stand it anymore so I went back to see if they were still there." He stopped and put his head in his hands. "They were. And they were so much worse this time.

Swollen and ugly and crawling with bugs." His voice faltered. "It was disgusting. I couldn't even look."

I had no doubt Bongo's distress was real, but I had trouble working up much sympathy. "I want Tim's full name and address. And you'd better not say a word to him about this conversation, you understand? You mess up this investigation any more than you already have and you'll be in trouble big time."

Bongo's forehead glistened with perspiration. "I won't say a word, I promise. Tim'd kill me if he knew that I'd told. He's already mad cuz I told my mom they were in the barn."

On my way out I passed Kevin sitting on the front steps. The pocket knife was closed and he had no stick.

"Is he going to get in trouble?" Kevin asked.

"You were out here eavesdropping the whole time?"

Kevin glanced at the door, then back at me. His mouth stretched in a wide, gap-toothed grin.

"You'd better not say a word either."

He nodded, but the grin never left his face.

The car was hot when I climbed in. I started the engine, turned the air-conditioning on high, then rolled down the windows until it kicked in. My skin was damp and my head felt light, but it wasn't simply the heat of the afternoon. My whole body burned with the sense of discovery.

If Bongo was telling the truth, then the underwear in the compost bin had been planted there to make Wes look guilty.

What I couldn't decide was how to proceed. Part of me was eager to confront Tim, to find out for sure that he still had the underwear he'd stolen from Lisa and Amy. But I knew that wasn't the best approach, not if I wanted to make sure the evidence would be introduced at trial. The safest strategy would be to convince Benson to get a search warrant, although I knew he wouldn't like the idea. And the longer it took, the more likely it was Tim would dispose of the evidence.

There was also the issue of locating the killer. As long as he thought his ruse with the planted underwear had worked, he was likely to let down his guard, thereby increasing the likelihood of his being found out. But I knew that it would be difficult to keep the search of a young boy's room from hitting the papers.

Sam hadn't returned my call from yesterday. I was still anxious to hear his thoughts on Barry Drummond. But now, in addition, we needed to discuss the planted evidence. And I knew we'd make more headway in person than by phone. With luck, I'd be able to catch Sam at home.

His car was parked in the driveway, but when I knocked on the door it was his sister, Pat, who answered. She lived in Chicago and usually came to visit during the winter. I was surprised Sam hadn't mentioned that she was coming.

"Sam's not here," she said wearily. "He's in the hospital. Something with his heart. They called me yesterday and I flew in late last night."

I was stunned. "Is he going to be all right?"

"I don't know. No one does." Pat's makeup was streaked, her gray hair flattened on one side and jutting out at odd angles on the other. "I just came from the hospital. Maybe by later today they'll know more."

"Is there anything I can do?"

She shook her head, fighting tears. "There's nothing any of us can do."

I drove to the hospital in a blur. It felt as though my throat had closed down and my lungs filled with dust. My mind could focus on nothing but Sam's kindness and generosity, and the fact that I'd never really told him how much I valued his friendship.

The parking places near the hospital entrance were taken, so I pulled into a spot around to the side. The volunteer in the lobby directed me to ICU on the third floor.

"They may not let you see him," she warned, "but they can tell you how he's doing."

The elevator was slow in arriving and even slower making its way to the third floor. As I was getting ready to push the intercom button outside the double doors of ICU, Jake Harding approached from the other direction. His white medical coat was wrinkled. There were dark circles under his eyes, and you could see the tension in his face.

"You heard about Sam?" he asked.

"His sister told me. How is he?"

Jake took a breath. "Not good, frankly."

"Can I see him?"

Jake hesitated, then nodded. "For a minute. I'll come with you so you won't have to hassle with hospital procedure."

With Jake leading, we headed through the double doors to a room with about a dozen beds, at least as many nurses and an array of medical equipment that looked as if it were straight out of a science fiction movie.

Sam lay in a bed near the nurses' station amid a tangle of wires and plastic tubes. His eyes were shut, his mouth contorted by the accordion tubing of a ventilator. He looked ancient, as though his frame had shrunk overnight, leaving his pale skin slack and loose.

Gently, I touched the hand with the plastic shunt. He

raised his lids and looked at me, blankly at first and then with a flicker of recognition.

"Hi, Sam," I whispered. There was a lump in my throat that made it impossible to talk further. But it didn't matter; I couldn't think of another thing to say. I gave his fingers a gentle squeeze and felt the slightest pressure of acknowledgment.

Sam's soft, liquid-gray eyes were filled with sadness—a pleading sort of anguish that almost broke my heart.

I squeezed the hand again. "You take care of yourself, Sam. Listen to the doctors and nurses. We're all rooting for you."

He struggled for a moment, as though he was trying to raise his head. His mouth twisted around the ventilator tube. Jake touched Sam's shoulder in sympathy, then adjusted a valve on the IV. In a moment Sam slid back into sleep. I waited while Jake conferred with the nurse and made a notation on Sam's chart; then we left.

"I'm going to get some coffee. You want to join me?" Jake sounded exhausted.

"I think he recognized me," I said as we started for the cafeteria. "That's a good sign, isn't it?"

"I'm afraid it doesn't count for as much as it appears."

"Is he in pain?"

Jake shook his head. "He's probably confused, though. And being attached to all that machinery isn't exactly fun. That's why we try to keep patients sedated."

We got our coffee and found an empty table.

"When was he admitted?" I asked.

"Yesterday. We'd planned to go fishing, but by the time we got to our favorite spot Sam was complaining of indigestion and dizziness. I tried to convince him to go to the hospital right then, but you know how stubborn he is. He did agree to let me take him home. He apparently called 911 later in the afternoon."

"What are his chances of pulling through?"

Jake stared into his coffee. "I honestly can't say. Sam's not in great shape. He won't exercise, eats all the wrong things and won't give up his after-dinner cigar. But even if that weren't the case, I'd be hard pressed to give you odds. It's simply too early to tell."

I bit my lip and stared into my coffee. "He's not going to be in any shape to take on a trial, is he?"

"No," Jake said glumly, "I'm afraid not."

Which left Wes Harding squarely on my shoulders.

As though he'd been reading my mind, Jake asked, "You think you can handle it?"

"Yes, I do. But if you and Wes decide you want someone else, I can understand."

Jake gave a noncommittal nod. "How are things shaping up?"

I knew Sam gave Jake daily progress reports, so I figured he wasn't so much interested in an answer as he was in filling a conversational void. Still, there were some recent developments he might not have known about.

Jake seemed preoccupied as I told him about Lisa's drawing of Barry Drummond. "It may be interesting, but I fail to see how it's going to help Wes. Shouldn't you be focusing more on getting ready for trial?"

There was a quality of ridicule in his tone that I found irksome. "I'm doing that too. But if we can point to someone else, someone with a clear motive for murder, that's got to raise reasonable doubt in the minds of the jurors."

His expression remained skeptical.

I'd started to tell him about my conversation with Bongo when his beeper went off. My breath caught. I looked at Jake.

"Is it Sam?"

He shook his head. "They'd have paged me," he said. "This is my service."

My lungs started working again.

Jake rose. "Try not to worry. I'll keep you posted on any changes in Sam's condition."

"Thanks." I finished my coffee, then used a pay phone in the hospital lobby to call Daryl Benson.

"You got my message, then," he said.

"What message?"

"I called you about half an hour ago. The initial lab reports for the underwear found in that dumpster came back. The woman's pair tested positive for blood. Type B, same as Lisa Cornell's."

"And millions of other people."

"It's an odd coincidence, Kali."

I took a breath. "That's actually the reason I was calling." I repeated what Bongo had told me. "Tim apparently has the underwear hidden beneath a loose floorboard in his bedroom closet. Bongo saw it there yesterday."

"Or so Bongo says."

"Will you check on it?"

"Kali—"

"Please?"

He made a whistling sound. "Willis isn't going to like this."

"He doesn't have to like it." I shifted the receiver to my other ear. "Will you do it?"

"I'll try. I may need to reach you. Are you at home?"

"I'm heading there. At the moment I'm at the hospital."

I told him about Sam, and in the telling found my voice breaking repeatedly. When I hung up I pressed my forehead against the smooth plastic of the telephone and took long, slow breaths to compose myself.

30

Whether or not Jake kept me on the case, the work Sam and I had done to date needed to be catalogued. Besides, work was the one thing that might take my mind off Sam's illness.

I decided to go by his office, pick up the case files and notes and try to put things in some semblance of order. Later I would call Sam's sister, Pat, and see if there were any relevant papers at the house. If I had to turn the case over to another attorney, the materials would be ready. If I ended up staying on, I'd be prepared.

Sam's office was in a two-story building of fairly recent vintage—an all-purpose structure housing a travel agency, an insurance company and various small companies with uninformative names like KK Associates and VRA Inc. What the place lacked in charm, it more than made up for in amenities of the sort my own office lacked.

Sam had a library, a conference room, a kitchenette, a decent-sized reception area and a private work space with adequate light and ventilation. He'd given me the key because I often came at odd hours to use his reference materials and, when I was first starting out, his fax machine and laser printer.

I let myself in and began gathering case-related documents. There wasn't much. Sam was notoriously disorganized, so it shouldn't have surprised me, but it did. I knew for a fact that he'd talked to Wes's co-worker, Harlan Bailey, yet I couldn't find any record of the conversation. And I couldn't find any notes from his interviews with Wes Harding or from our own strategy sessions. Knowing Sam, though, they could be anywhere.

On the off-chance he might have actually listened to my nagging and transcribed his notes on disc, I flipped on his computer. As I expected, the only documents pertaining to the Harding case were official pleadings, motions and correspondence—no doubt typed by his secretary. Sam is of the generation that can't think without a pencil in hand. And he believes his case notes ought to look like notes—the kind of yellow-tablet scrawlings that saw him through college and law school.

From memory I started a list of the particulars Sam was to have covered, filling in the results when I could. On a separate sheet of paper I kept a running list of open questions. When I'd covered everything that came readily to mind I grabbed a soda out of Sam's little refrigerator and settled back to take stock.

The big question in my mind, aside from the issue of the underwear, was Lisa's sketch. Was it really Barry Drummond?

I tried to think who would have been in town twenty years ago who might be able to tell me. Tom might be able to unearth a picture from the newspaper files, but it would be a long, tedious search with no guarantee of results.

Then it hit me: Ron and Reena Swanson. As I'd hoped, I reached Ron and not Reena.

"Would you happen to have a picture of Barry Drummond?" I asked.

"Reena might have one somewhere. I'm not sure. Why?"

I explained. "I'd like to know whether the sketch is really him before I invest much time in this line of thinking."

"Why don't you fax us a copy of Lisa's sketch?" Ron said.

The joys of modern technology. I complain about it sometimes, but it's mighty useful when you need it. "I think her sketchbook is still in my car. I'll run down and get it."

Ron gave me his fax number. I hurried to grab the picture and slid it through the machine. Then I sipped my soda and waited. Five minutes later the phone rang.

"Reena says it looks like him. She thinks she has a picture somewhere, but it will take time to find it."

"Would Lisa have known Drummond when she was a child?"

"Yes. In fact, Lisa was staying with Anne and Barry at the time he took off. I think she'd been there for several months by then. It was right after Barry left that Anne insisted Reena come get Lisa and take her home. I think the shock of losing her husband probably upset her more than she let on."

The pieces fit. If only I could decipher the picture they made. I thanked Ron Swanson for his help.

"No problem. Let me know if there's anything else."

"Actually, there is one other thing."

"What's that?"

"I was trying to remember what you said the other evening. Didn't you tell me that you and Reena hadn't talked to Lisa in months?"

I could sense the caution even before he spoke. "That's right."

"I wanted to check because a woman who worked with Lisa said you came by the diner to see her about a month ago."

There was a moment's hesitation. "We hardly talked."

"But you did come to see her?"

"Yes." He sighed. "I did. I was in the area. I wanted to see if I could mend the rift, for Reena's sake. She always hoped Lisa would get over whatever it was that turned her against us. And then, when we learned we had a grandchild . . . well, it made losing Lisa even harder."

"What was Lisa's reaction?"

"She said she was working on it. That maybe things would be different soon. I didn't want to tell Reena because I didn't want to give her false hope."

The truth or an easy explanation? I wasn't entirely sure, but I leaned toward the former.

When I got off the phone I stared at the picture of the man I now knew to be Barry Drummond. Barry Drummond as he looked twenty years ago. Why had Lisa drawn him? And more importantly, what role, if any, had he played in her death?

I called the hospital to check on Sam. No change. I tried to convince myself the news was encouraging. I called Tom, but he wasn't at home. Tried my own number to see if Benson had left a message. He hadn't. Finally I gathered my papers and called Sam's sister, Pat.

"I don't think there's much in the way of Sam's work here at the house," she said, "but you're welcome to look. If you don't mind prefab microwave, you're welcome to stay for dinner, as well. I could use some company about now."

That made two of us.

* * *

Pat had showered and changed since I'd seen her that morning, and probably found a couple of hours' sleep too, since she looked a bit less ragged.

"I hate feeling helpless like this," she said, leading the way inside. "Sam's in the hospital fighting for his life, and there's nothing I can do to help."

I nodded agreement.

Her short legs set a brisk stride. "I was just going to fix myself a vodka tonic. Would you like one?"

"That sounds wonderful."

While Pat made the drinks, I went into the spare room that Sam used as an office. It had been his wife's sewing room before her death and he'd changed very little. A four-drawer file cabinet occupied the corner alcove where the dressmaker's mannequin had stood, a wall of books had replaced the cubicles of yarns and threads and the desktop was strewn with papers rather than pieces of pattern and fabric. But the walls were still yellow, the curtains edged in eyelet and the narrow wicker chaise with its floral covering still occupied a major portion of the room.

I checked the desk first, then the file drawers. Nothing relating to the Harding case. On a pad beside the phone he'd scratched Barry Drummond's name and doodled a border of concentric circles around it, the way he often did when he was thinking. I imagined Sam sitting there in his chair, listening to the message I'd left yesterday after my visit with Irma Pearl. It seemed ages ago now.

When I'd satisfied myself that Sam had no case files at home I went to find Pat. She handed me my drink and suggested we sit on the front porch where it was cool. We sipped our drinks, shared anecdotes about Sam, speculated about what his future might hold. Pat stuck a couple of frozen meals into the microwave and made us a second drink. Our conversation moved on to other topics, but neither of us focused much on what was said. We were simply filling the empty spaces, going through the motions of social discourse, so that we didn't have to think about what might happen to the man we both cared for.

By the time I headed home the rich, varied hues of sunset had faded to a flat ash-gray. I pulled into the driveway, retrieved the box of papers I'd taken from Sam's office and headed for the house.

The front porch light had burned out since I'd last noticed and I had trouble seeing. I stepped carefully to avoid tripping on the loose stones in the path. When I got closer I saw a sprinkling of fragmented glass under the light socket. The thing had not only burned out but exploded. Which meant I was going to have to somehow get the remains of the bulb out of the socket without electrocuting myself.

Cursing, I brushed the glass aside with my foot. Then, with the box of files against my hip, I reached into my purse for the key. Suddenly there was a movement behind me. Before I could turn I felt a hand slap roughly over my mouth. An arm grabbed me, knocking the box to the ground and pinning my own arms to my sides. My assailant pressed against me from behind, shoving me against the wall. He was strong, though not especially big, and smelled of stale cigarette smoke and beer.

Panic flooded my body. All at once I understood that the porch light had not exploded but had been knocked out. The man had been waiting there in the shadows. Waiting for me.

I couldn't scream. I couldn't move. I couldn't see anything but the paint-peeled siding of the house. I wondered if Lisa had felt the same rush of terror, the same bleak certainty.

The man's breath was hot on my neck, his weight crushing. I tried squirming loose, but he tightened his hold and pressed closer. "You move like that again, I get maybe my own ideas about fun, eh?"

His voice was soft, with a faint accent I couldn't trace. Maybe Spanish or Italian. When he spoke his hand on my mouth relaxed. I opened my mouth just enough and bit hard into the flesh of his fingers. He pulled back with a yelp and slammed me harder against the house.

"Bitch!" His voice was a coarse whisper. He pulled out a knife and held it at my throat. I felt the sharp edge press against my skin. "You listen and listen good. I got a message for you."

The scuffle had set Loretta to barking. Too bad there were no neighbors close enough to hear. I tried to swallow my fear, to concentrate instead on his movements.

The man brought his mouth close to my ear. I could feel the puffs of air against my skin as he spoke. "You've got some friends in town think it would be wise for you to take a vacation. A long one. Too much work isn't good for pretty ladies. They think you should leave real soon. Better that way for everyone."

"Are you one of these friends?" I mumbled against his palm, mindful of the knife against my neck.

He laughed without humor. "Me, I'm just the delivery man."

Out of the corner of my eye I caught a glimpse of the hand with the knife. It was a stubby hand, covered with dark hairs. The arm was hidden by a shirt.

"So, you got the message?"

I nodded as best I could.

"Good."

Suddenly there was a flash of pain at the back of my skull. I fell, and then there was nothing.

Darkness had settled in by the time I came to. I noticed that first, the darkness. And then the pain. It came slowly, the way you wake from a heavy slumber. An almost undetectable sensation at first, then building until it took charge.

Slowly easing myself to my knees, I felt for the key and crawled inside. Loretta sniffed, unusually subdued. Maybe it was the fact that I was on all fours, or maybe it was that sixth sense animals have about the wounded. Whatever, I was thankful she didn't leap and bound as she usually did.

Gripping a chair for support, I dragged myself to my feet and shuffled into the bathroom. Surprisingly, the movement helped.

I stared at my reflection in the mirror. My face was scratched. I could tell that my shoulder and hip would be bruised by morning. But I certainly looked better than I felt. It was an encouraging discovery. I took a double dose of Motrin and washed the grime from my face and hands.

When I felt strong enough to move again I called Tom and told him what had happened.

"Do you want me to call the doctor?"

"I don't think there's anything a doctor can do."

"How about the police?"

"I'll make a report in the morning. There's nothing they can do either. Not tonight anyway. What I need is to not be alone."

"I'll be right over. Don't open the door until you know it's me."

He was there almost as soon as we hung up.

31

I awoke the next morning stiff and sore. And tired, since Tom had insisted on waking me every couple of hours to check for signs of a concussion. I did manage to get some sleep, however, which is more than could be said for Tom. He'd stayed awake the entire night, watching over me like a mother hen.

He left at seven. I stayed in bed until almost nine, then downed another double dose of Motrin and a cup of strong coffee before calling the hospital to check on Sam.

"He's resting comfortably," the nurse told me.

"Does that mean his condition has improved?"

"I'm not in a position to say."

"Is he off the ventilator?"

"I'm sorry; you'll have to talk to the doctor for specifics."

I thanked her, although it wasn't clear why, and called Daryl Benson. "Were you able to get the search warrant?" I asked.

"Yeah, finally. Last night."

"And?"

He sighed. "The underwear was there, just where you said it would be."

"Did the boy cooperate?"

"You bet. After the detective threatened to haul his ass in for tampering with a crime scene the kid wouldn't shut up."

"What did he say?"

"Pretty much what your friend Bongo told you. I don't think the boys were involved with the actual murder, but their behavior is certainly disgusting. Here we have two dead bodies, a woman they both knew and her little girl, and all those kids can think about is undressing them and running off with their underwear like it's some fraternity prank."

Loretta came to rest her head in my lap. I began scratching her ears. "I don't suppose you've any idea how the underwear in the compost bin got there."

"Nope. It could be happenstance." Benson didn't sound convinced.

"You know it isn't. The person who killed Lisa and Amy Cornell is still out there running around, hoping like hell Wes gets put away for the crime."

"There are other explanations, Kali, but I'm not going to argue the point. You could be right."

"Are you going to rethink Wes's arrest?"

"At this stage it's not up to me. The ball's in the DA's court."

"Does Curt Willis know the latest?"

"Yeah. Took it like the death of his favorite grandmother. Poor guy made the mistake of counting his chickens way too soon."

Unfortunately, he still had a good case. I wasn't about to point that out, though. "I've got another reason for calling," I said, and proceeded to tell him about the assault the night before.

"My God, were you hurt?"

"Not badly."

"Did you see the man? Recognize the voice?" Benson's tone was a mixture of concern and police efficiency.

"No. He had a faint accent. I'm sure I would remember it if I'd heard it before."

"You think it's related to the Harding case?"

"What else could it be? I don't know who these 'friends' he mentioned are, but I'd guess they're not happy about some of the things I've been looking into."

Benson's tone softened. "It might be worth listening to them, Kali. Next time it won't be a warning."

"I can't just drop the case. Not unless Wes decides he wants a different attorney."

There was a sigh. "You want to make a formal police report about the attack?"

"Later. For now, just make note of it. Okay?"

"I could send one of my men out to keep an eye on you."

"Thanks, but I intend to be careful. And Tom's going to move in for a couple of days."

Benson responded with a humph. "You tell Tom he ought to make it more than a couple of days."

"He'll stay here as long as there's danger," I said. But I knew that wasn't what Benson was talking about. As a man who'd never been successful with love himself, he sought to even the slate by seeing that others were.

With my two pressing phone calls out of the way I turned my attention to the remainder of the day. Tom had walked Loretta before leaving for work and had set out a bowl of corn flakes for me. All I had to do was add milk.

The first I appreciated, but I couldn't stomach the idea of food just yet. I poured the cereal back into the box, spread makeup over the scrapes on my face, slipped into comfortable slacks and headed for the office.

There's nothing like an aching body to make you appreciate the fully functioning one you usually take for granted. I was keenly aware of every movement. I drove slowly, knowing my reflexes were as bruised as my body. I parked the car at an odd forty-five-degree angle because the turning and twisting required to park it correctly was beyond me.

I thought my stride into the office was smooth, but Myra picked up on it right away.

"What happened to you?" she gasped. "You're moving the way I did after giving birth."

Encouraging thought. Whatever interest I may have had in motherhood dropped considerably. "I had a run-in with a delivery man," I told her.

"What was he delivering? A six-hundred-pound gorilla?"

"Close." I explained the events of the previous evening.

"My God, Kali, you could have been hurt." She jumped up from her desk to take my elbow.

I ignored her offer of assistance. "I *was* hurt," I said.

She made a face. "You know what I mean." She followed me into my office and held the chair as I sat. "You want some coffee? Maybe a pillow for your back?"

I shook my head, slowly so that it didn't pull the muscles in my neck.

"Let me know if there's anything I can do. Just say the word."

I undertook an expression of gratitude, then said, "Well,

I'd planned on washing the office windows today and waxing the floor. They both need it badly. Now I don't know whether I'm up to it."

Myra hesitated. Her hands worked nervously, as though picking dust out of the air. "Yeah, sure. If that's what you want. There are some letters I need to finish, but—"

I grinned. "Joke, Myra. Take it easy; no floors or windows." I could see her relax. "You could bring me my messages, though."

"Sure." She fairly bounced from the room and returned with a couple of pink message slips. "Anything else?"

"Not at the moment."

She beat a hasty retreat.

I returned Jake's call first. He'd phoned not long before I'd gotten into work and I worried that something had happened to Sam. His receptionist put me on hold while she went to find him.

"No, nothing new on Sam," he said. "I called to see if you were free to discuss Wes's defense. I talked with him last evening. He feels you're okay, but to be perfectly frank I have some doubts myself. There's nothing personal about it, you understand; it's just that I think we might be better off with someone more experienced in criminal defense work."

I told him I understood, but also that I felt confident I could do a good job. Under normal circumstances it would have been Wes's call entirely, but since Jake was footing the bill he clearly had to be comfortable as well.

"Perhaps we can get together this evening," he said. "After I've finished seeing patients. Let me give you a call later in the day, when I know my schedule."

"I'll be free whenever you are."

The second message Myra had handed me was from

Simmons. He'd finally gotten around to returning my call from last week.

"Simmons here," he said, picking up on the first ring. No secretary, no company name or department.

I introduced myself. He apologized for taking so long to get back to me, explaining that he'd been out of town.

"I understand you have a client interested in the Cornell property," I said.

"Yes . . ." He drew the word out, so that it was a measured pause as much as an answer. "May I inquire, are you a member of the family?"

"I'm an attorney."

"Ah, with Ed Cole."

It wasn't a question, so I let it be. "Can you tell me a little something about the party you represent?"

"Unfortunately, I've been asked not to."

"By your client?"

"Yes. That's why I'm acting as spokesman in this matter. Is the estate ready to be settled? My client is eager to take care of the matter as quickly as possible. My client is willing to meet, and better, any other offer."

An eager client. It was a unique piece of property, but that unique? I wondered what the real story was.

"We'd reached a tentative agreement with the previous owner," Simmons continued, "and then, unfortunately, she was killed."

Lisa's death was indeed unfortunate. But not for the reason Simmons was suggesting. "Lisa Cornell had agreed to sell the property?" I asked.

"Tentatively. No papers had been signed, of course, or we wouldn't have a problem now."

Except for the problem of a double murder. "I'm afraid the current owners will want to know who the buyer is," I explained. "And what use he, or it, intends. The property has been in the family for years. They wouldn't want to see it spoiled by crass commercialism."

Simmons ho-hoed for a moment. "I assure you, my client has no interest in developing the property."

"I'm afraid that won't be sufficient."

He paused. "Let me check and see how much I can divulge. Maybe we can offer some assurance that will satisfy the present owners. I'll get back to you when I've had a chance to confer with my client."

I thanked him and hung up, then mentally ran through the conversation again. I'm not opposed to lying when necessary, but I try not to make claims that will put me in hot water with the ethics committee. It wasn't my most sterling moment, but I hadn't actually misrepresented myself either.

Before I returned the other calls I took full advantage of Myra's kind offer and had her bring me a blueberry muffin and a cup of coffee from The Sugar Plum. When she returned I pulled out Sam's files and my own and got to work. It surprised me to realize how much I wanted to stay on the case. If I could show Jake Harding I was on top of things, maybe I'd make enough of an impression that he'd keep me on.

When lunch time came I sent Myra out again. She didn't balk at the role of personal servant, and in fact brought me my food much more efficiently than she did anything else.

By early afternoon I'd blocked out a plan for Wes's defense, made a list of possible witnesses and another list of points that would most likely be raised by the prosecution. Sam's files still seemed on the thin side, but I had found the police reports and the notes on blood and trace evidence. I started tying up loose ends.

My first call was to Wes's neighbor, Mrs. Lincoln, to ask whether she'd recently noticed any strangers on Wes's property or in the vicinity of the compost bin. She hadn't.

Next I went through the list of Lisa's neighbors. I'd talked with most of them earlier, in person, but I was following up on the off chance they'd remembered something in the intervening week. I also reached several of the neighbors who hadn't been at home the day I'd canvassed the neighborhood. Sally Baund, I remembered, had gone to visit her daughter in Boston. I got the number from my notes and called her there.

"Yes," she said when I told her who I was. "I spoke to the gentleman the other day."

"What gentleman?"

"The lawyer, what was his name, Sam—"

"Sam Morrison?"

"Yes, that's it."

Why hadn't Sam made a note of the call? "Sorry to bother you again," I said, stumbling a bit as I tried to regain my train of thought. "We like to be sure we've covered all the bases."

"I understand. I couldn't tell him much anyway. He asked about the vehicle I'd seen the night Lisa Cornell was killed. It was a van. A white van with a band of some darker color along the side, and some lettering. I couldn't read the lettering. Couldn't tell him what kind of van it was either. I'm not very good when it comes to identifying automobiles. It wasn't really at Lisa's place anyway, but on the road at the back of her property. I happened to be driving that way because I was coming home from bridge night at my friend Maybel's."

"What time did you see it there?"

"A little after nine."

"And it was parked?"

"Yes, back off from the road a bit. I didn't think much about it at the time. You know how cars run out of gas or break down. You often see them alongside the road."

Except that most of them don't pull in and park. "Anything else you can tell me about the van?"

"It looked like it might have been one of those vans that transport the handicapped. I can't say what specifically gave me that impression, but I remember thinking it was a terrible place for someone with limited mobility to get stuck."

"You told this to the police?"

"Oh, yes. They weren't particularly interested, though. But that other man, Mr. Morrison, he was."

"Did he say why?"

"No. He didn't say very much at all, but I could tell."

It was likely Mrs. Baund had lived in the neighborhood for years. I tried on her the second question I'd been asking the others I called. "Did you by chance know Barry Drummond?"

"Of course."

"You haven't seen him lately, have you?"

"Goodness no. He ran off years ago; just up and left his wife one day. Or so they say." Mrs. Baund paused. "There was a rumor going around back then that Anne did him in and got rid of the body in pickle jars. She did a lot of canning that summer."

32

Of course she hadn't really believed the rumor herself, Mrs. Baund assured me. But Anne Drummond had changed that summer; there was no getting around that. She was sure that's what prompted people's tongues to wag, the way Anne Drummond had changed from a fun-loving sprite into a somber-faced recluse.

I gave her my number in case she remembered anything more about the van she'd seen near the Cornell property. When I'd carefully noted the conversation in the file I called Philip Stockman.

"I don't believe we have anything to discuss," he said curtly.

"Just two quick questions."

"Your client's guilty and you know it. You're wasting my time."

"Did Lisa say anything to you about selling her property?"

"You don't give up, do you?"

"No, I don't." I tried to keep the tone light. "So you

might as well answer my questions and be done with me."

Stockman grumbled, but he answered. "We talked about it some. Lisa's aunt left her the place because she wanted Lisa to live there. Lisa suggested that we make that our home and let Helene have the family house. But that was out of the question, and I told her so."

"Why was it out of the question?"

"Ours is a much nicer house. And it belonged to my parents. I wouldn't think of moving."

I couldn't understand how Lisa had ever agreed to marry the man. "So Lisa decided to sell?"

"I know that she'd been approached by someone who was interested, but I don't know the details."

"Or the name?"

"Afraid not."

"Did she ever mention the name Barry Drummond?"

"He was her aunt's husband. I knew him myself, though only to say hello to."

"What was he like?"

"Rude, impatient. The kind who's over-impressed with himself. Lisa asked me the same thing not too long ago."

"Did she say why?"

"No, she didn't. And you've more than used up your two questions." Stockman punctuated this last remark by hanging up on me.

By late afternoon my back and neck were stiff from work. But I had the case files in order and was feeling pretty confident about convincing Jake Harding that I was the woman for the job. I was also feeling optimistic about our chances at trial.

At five o'clock Jake Harding called. "Sorry I couldn't get back to you sooner. It's been one of those days. Are you free about eight? I've got to admit a patient for surgery, and then I've got to make rounds, so I'm afraid I won't be free any earlier."

"Eight is fine."

"Why don't you meet me here at the office. Hopefully I'll be through for the night and we can go out for a drink somewhere. Maybe get a bite to eat."

Softening me up before he fired me, no doubt. But I'd made a decision: I wasn't going to roll over and give up. And I wasn't going to remove myself from the case unless I heard directly from Wes.

I worked for another hour, then went home, took a shower and put on clean clothes. I chose a professional-looking mid-calf skirt and jacket of navy gaberdine. I carried my leather briefcase and hoped I remembered to hold it so that the impressive brass monogram was readily visible.

On the way to Jake's office, I stopped by to see Sam. He was heavily sedated. There was no sign of the recognition I'd seen on my first visit. No fluttering of the eyes, no response when I squeezed his hand. I had trouble recognizing anything of the man I remembered.

The nurse I'd talked to that morning was right—Sam was resting comfortably. But only because he was no longer able to experience discomfort.

I leaned over and kissed his forehead lightly. In a storybook tale he might have woken. But this was life, and Sam remained as motionless as a waxwork.

Jake's office was across from the hospital. I walked there and found the main door to the building locked. I pressed the intercom button, identified myself to Jake and was buzzed in.

On the main floor I passed a janitor sweeping the hallway. He didn't look up. Most of the offices were dark, but occasional lights shone from inside. Jake Harding was not the only doctor working late.

The waiting room to his office was empty, as was the reception desk. I knocked on the glass partition.

"Is that you, Kali?" he called out.

"It's me."

"I'll be with you in a minute."

Before I could take a seat he poked his head around the corner. "Come on back while I finish up."

I followed him past the examination rooms to his office at the back. The desk was wide and highly polished. To the side was an array of family pictures. One of Grace and the three girls, another of Wes and himself with fishing poles. Jake's various diplomas were arranged on the wall straight ahead, along with certificates for service on the hospital board and recognition within the community.

He smiled when he saw me looking. "Myself, I think it's a bit pretentious. But if you don't have them prominently displayed, patients wonder what you're hiding."

The phone rang. Jake picked it up. "Charles. Good of you to get back to me."

The conversation progressed to gallstones and bilirubin levels. I tuned out and mentally ran through the major arguments in favor of my remaining Wes's attorney.

In the process of reaching for a pen Jake knocked some loose message slips off the desk. I bent over and picked them up for him. As I handed them back, I caught a quick peek at a phone number that looked familiar. I tried to place it and couldn't.

When Jake was off the phone he looked my way and smiled wearily. "Let's get out of here. You up for a drink?"

"Sure."

"Good; so am I." He gathered some papers from his desk. "Is it okay if we take your car? Mine's low on gas."

"Sure." As we headed down on the elevator, it hit me why the phone number on Jake's message slip looked familiar.

"How do you know Bud Simmons?" I asked.

Jake gave me a curious look.

"I saw his number on one of the message slips I handed you."

The scrunched brows eased. "He does real estate work for me. I have some investments in small commercial centers, medical office buildings, that sort of thing. He puts deals together. Why?"

"Probably nothing. It's just that the man's name has come up before. He apparently has a client interested in the Cornell place." We left the elevator and walked through the lobby. "You haven't heard anything about development of that property, have you?"

Jake shook his head. "Zoning restrictions would make that difficult, I should think."

The parking lot had emptied out. Visiting hours at the hospital must have been over. "It's the blue Subaru," I said, nodding in the direction of the car. It hardly looked like something a successful attorney would choose. I started to apologize.

Jake smiled. "I don't pick my attorneys by the car they drive."

I smiled back. "Good thing."

I opened the door and set my briefcase in the backseat, monogram side out. I'm sure he didn't pick his attorneys by the briefcases they carried either, but I'd learned early on that success breeds success. And it never hurt to look the part.

"I have a good grasp on the facts of Wes's case," I told

him. "I've laid out some ideas for his defense and I think we can win. I've interviewed most of the people involved in the case. It would take anyone else weeks to get up to speed."

He mumbled noncommittally.

"There've been a couple of recent developments you might not know about." As I started the car and backed out of the parking space, I told him about the planted evidence in the compost bin, about Lisa's drawing of Barry Drummond, even about Sally Baund. I was trying my darnedest to be impressive.

Jake listened and nodded. Polite, but clearly not enthusiastic.

As I talked, I made a sweeping turn around the back of the lot to head out the east exit. We passed the doctors' parking lot and then a row of white vans. They all had wheelchair racks affixed to the rear, and a wide dark stripe down the side with printing above.

Just like the van Mrs. Baund had seen at the back of Lisa Cornell's property the night she was killed.

There was a tickle in my brain. Suddenly I didn't like what I was thinking. Jake Harding had a message from Bud Simmons, a man who was representing a mystery client interested in the Cornell property. Jake Harding no doubt had access to a white handicap van with a stripe on the side.

I turned to ask him about the vans and saw a gun in his hand.

"You *are* a smart attorney, Kali. Too smart for your own good."

33

I tried swallowing but my mouth was dry. My pulse was pounding at my temples, my chest tight. My stomach felt as if it were playing hopscotch.

Fleetingly, I considered jumping out of the car and attempting to escape on foot. I knew I'd never make it, though. The surrounding area was wide open and empty. If I could just stay calm, maybe I'd be able to attract attention later when we weren't so isolated.

But Jake had me turn right at the exit instead of left.

We weren't going out for drinks, after all. We weren't even going in the direction of town.

"Where are we headed?" The words came unevenly, as though I were speaking an unfamiliar foreign language.

"You'll see. Just do what I say and don't try anything funny."

I nodded, gripped the wheel tighter and took a breath. "It was you who killed Lisa Cornell and Amy, wasn't it?"

His jaw twitched. After a moment he said, "I didn't want to."

"Why did you, then?"

"It's a long story."

Jake kept the gun pointed at my head. His eyes were cool, but his voice was slightly frayed. "I didn't want to kill them. I really didn't. Just like I didn't want to kill Donna Markley." He paused. "Or you either."

Good. That made two of us.

"And I *doubly* didn't want to kill Sam. Hopefully I won't have to."

The words took a moment to register. "You caused Sam's heart problem?" My voice rose till it scratched in my throat. "You did that to him on *purpose?*"

I remembered the pleading look in Sam's eyes the first day I'd visited. How he'd pulled at the ventilator tube, struggling to speak. A prisoner in his own body. "How *could* you do that to him? He's your friend."

"He's alive," Jake said.

"But why any of this? Merely so you can get your hands on the Cornell property?"

Jake shook his head. "It's not that simple."

"You're Simmons' mystery client, aren't you?"

He sighed. "I wanted the Cornell property, but only to keep it from falling into other hands. That wasn't the reason why I had to kill Lisa."

"You didn't *have* to kill anyone."

"But I did, you see. I'm not happy about it."

"Why?"

"Why doesn't matter. You won't be around long enough to care."

"Then it wouldn't hurt to tell me."

Jake licked his lips. "Turn here," he said. We climbed

higher into the hills. The road was narrow and winding. I could think of no plan for escape.

"I never wanted any of this to happen," Jake remarked with only a trace of emotion in his voice. "If I could only go back and change things, change that one moment . . ."

"What moment?"

"It's been more than twenty years, and I remember it like it was yesterday. When Annie said she wished she'd never laid eyes on him—"

"Annie?"

"Anne Drummond."

"You knew Anne Drummond?"

"I was in love with her." Jake paused. "Years ago, before I married Grace. I was just out of medical school, just setting up practice here in Silver Creek. I thought the feeling was mutual."

"It wasn't?"

"Oh, it was. For a while. That's the irony of the whole thing. She was married to a first-class jerk. He knocked her around, treated her like dirt. Always so full of himself. She complained about him constantly."

"Why didn't she leave?"

"At the time I thought she was afraid to."

"And now?"

"I guess on some level she also loved him." Jake shook his head in bewilderment. "I only wanted to help. I was trying to protect her. Trying to protect the woman I loved."

"Protect her how?"

Jake's voice was growing softer. I had to listen hard in order to make out the words.

"He must have been following us," Jake said. "He found us together at my place and dragged Annie home. I was afraid of what he might do to her. I went over later to have it out with him. We got into a fight. He was big and strong, and drunk. I pulled a gun, thinking that would make him back off. It didn't."

I held my breath. "You killed him?"

Jake nodded.

I'd been driving slowly, trying to buy time. Now I almost came to a complete stop. "Barry Drummond didn't run off, then?"

"No. We buried him in the barn. Later Annie poured concrete over the spot and built some shelves there. She told people he'd run off and left her. Even fabricated stories about some postcards she'd received from him. All the while he's been right there, under the barn."

I glanced at the gun in Jake's hand. He still had a firm grip, still had it pointed in my direction. "Couldn't you have claimed self-defense?"

"It wouldn't have worked. I came looking for a fight. I brought a gun with me."

"What about you and Anne?"

A bitter, sardonic laugh. "I thought that once she was free of him everything would be okay, but it wasn't. Maybe it was the horror of what we'd done, or maybe she was never serious about me to begin with. Whatever the reason, it didn't work out."

Jake had killed Barry Drummond years ago. I couldn't understand why he was so worried. "All that happened so long ago," I said. "Even if the body was discovered now, who would suspect you had anything to do with it?"

"My watch. It was engraved with my name. Annie buried it with the body, along with a sealed account of what had happened. She'd agreed to keep quiet and to bury the body on her property, but she wanted some assurance that she wasn't going to be charged with his murder if everything came undone."

We came to a fork in the road and Jake motioned for me to take the left branch. It was a dirt and gravel road, heavily rutted.

"Just a little farther," he said. "There, up ahead; pull off onto the shoulder. My car's behind that row of trees."

The moon was full, the route almost as well lit as if it were day. The gun glimmered with reflected light. I took my time inching to that spot ahead. I was now certain Jake Harding intended to kill me.

"I don't understand how Lisa Cornell and Amy fit into this."

"Lisa was living with Annie that summer," Jake explained. "She saw me shoot Barry Drummond. Annie sent her back to bed, told her it was an accident and that we were going to take Barry to the doctor. But later, when we were burying him in the barn, we found Lisa standing at the door, watching.

"Annie made up some story about burying a dead cow and sent Lisa home to her mother a few days later. We were worried about what Lisa might say, but she was only four and we hoped no one would believe her. In fact, she seemed to forget all about it. Even later, when she was fourteen and came to spend a week with Annie following her mother's remarriage, she seemed to have no memory of the event at all."

No conscious memory, maybe. But I remembered what Ron Swanson had told me about Lisa's abrupt change in behavior following his and Reena's marriage. Maybe something about the visit with her aunt *had* triggered a memory. Maybe even some of the fear and confusion she'd felt about Jake had been transferred to Ron. They were both doctors, both about the same age and build. It was understandable that Lisa's feelings about her new stepfather were mixed.

"If she had no memory of the event, why kill her?" I asked, bringing my thoughts back to the present.

"The return to Silver Creek, living in her aunt's house— she was beginning to remember. I ran into her one day when she was on her way to see Dr. Dobbs about her headaches. Apparently our encounter caused a violent reaction."

I remembered Dr. Dobbs mentioning the sudden, blinding headache that had come on in his office.

"Lisa called me one day." Jake sighed. "Said she was trying to piece together parts of her past, and hadn't I been a friend of her aunt's? She'd checked the property records for the house where Wes lives. After she went home with him one evening she remembered she'd been there as a child. I knew it wouldn't take long before she worked out the whole thing, especially with Donna Markley's help."

"So you killed her," I said, pulling off the road where Jake had indicated.

"I had to."

"And Amy?"

He sighed again, deeply. "That tore at me. It was like déjà vu. When I'd finished with Lisa I turned to see another little girl standing at the door, watching. I couldn't take the chance again. If I'd let Amy go, it would be the same as before, never knowing when the truth might come out."

I parked the car where Jake indicated and turned off the engine. "And Dr. Markley? Had she figured it out?"

"She was close. Donna Markley was very good at what

she did, intuitive as well as smart. She'd figured out that the house, my old place, had triggered Lisa's anxiety about being with Wes. It brought back some of her earlier memories. And under hypnosis Lisa had apparently remembered bits and pieces of the evening Drummond was killed."

"And now it's me and Sam. You're making it worse the more people you kill."

"I never wanted any of it. It kept sucking me in like a whirlpool, pulling me under."

I shook my head. "There were other choices. Even after you'd killed Barry Drummond. You didn't have to keep on killing."

Jake's face was tight, his body rigid. He held the gun steady, pointing it directly at me. "I did. I couldn't let that one reckless deed bring down everything I'd built for myself."

"So you decided to let Wes take the blame."

"I never wanted that either. It was a fluke that he was arrested. I didn't know he'd been out there that night. When they arrested Wes I felt as if the weight of the world had been dropped on my shoulders."

"But you still didn't come forward with the truth."

"I hired Sam, and then you. I gave you carte blanche with expenses."

"You planted the underclothes in the dumpster," I said. "Seems to me you wanted to make sure the jury found Wes guilty."

Jake shook his head. "I had nothing to do with that. I did everything in my power to see to it that Wes would go free."

Everything short of taking responsibility.

"I'm sorry, Kali. I tried to warn you, tried to get you to leave town."

"That gorilla who attacked me was a friend of yours?"

"I didn't want it to come to this."

Jake was breathing hard now. His forehead glistened with sweat and I could see damp spots on his shirt. "I want you to get out of the car now, slowly and with your hands in the air where I can see them."

I opened the car door, raised my hands.

"I promise, you won't suffer. I'll make it quick. I wanted to make Lisa's death quick and painless too, but she kept fighting me." Jake got out of the car. "Let's go into the woods a bit. You first."

Even with the moonlight it was difficult to make my way across the uneven ground. I went slowly, eyes darting in all directions, waiting for the right moment. I could outrun Jake; I couldn't outrun a bullet. My hope was that, at night, his aim would be off enough that I'd have a fighting chance.

Maybe twenty yards from the road we came to a slight drop-off. There appeared to be a spot of dense vegetation toward the bottom of the grade. It wasn't perfect, but time was running out.

When I was even with the steepest part of the embankment I dropped quickly, crouched behind a tree, then jumped to my feet and took off for the shrubbery.

There was a gun blast. Then another.

I felt something tug at my shoulder. When I tried to shake free the tugging grew heavier. I could feel dampness begin to soak into my shirt. One of Jake's bullets had found its mark.

I pulled to the left, around a stand of small firs, then

dove into the mound of vegetation, discovering too late that I'd landed in the midst of poison oak. But there near the center, close to the ground, was a hollow space large enough to hide me. I pulled my knees to my chest and held my breath.

The tugging sensation in my shoulder had given way to shooting pain. I bit my lip and tried to ignore it.

"I can outwait you," Jake called. "You might as well come out now."

I could hear his footsteps. The snap of a twig, the barest vibration of the earth's surface as he stepped.

Another shot, and then another. There was a ping near the far edge of the poison oak.

The pain from my shoulder screamed inside my head as well. My throat tickled. I needed to pee.

I was afraid to do anything. Afraid even to breathe.

Another shot.

I closed my eyes, picked the word *yellow* at random and repeated it over and over, trying to override all other thoughts.

After awhile I became aware of the quiet. Nothing around me stirred. I opened my eyes and waited.

The moon moved slowly across the sky. The evening passed to night and then to early morning. Far off I could hear the howl of coyotes.

Another shot rang out.

I pulled my cramped muscles tighter, willing myself to be transformed to a statue.

Dawn came slowly. A fading of black, a sweep of gray and finally the muted colors born of the rising sun. Around me, life began to stir.

Was Jake gone?

Or was he waiting?

I felt along the ground for a hard clump of dirt and tossed it.

Nothing.

Jake had to be waiting for me to make a move. He'd told me too much. There was no going back for him now.

I held off until the sun was high in the sky and the day hot. My mouth was parched and my head felt as though it were filled with cotton. My shoulder throbbed. I tossed another dirt clump. And then another.

A blue jay squawked overhead.

But there were no gunshots. No footsteps or cracking twigs.

Finally I inched myself forward. Looked to the right and the left. In the distance I could see my Subaru parked alongside the road where we'd left it. Jake's car was still off to the right.

Where was he hiding?

I couldn't outrun him now. I knew that. But if I could make it to the car before he saw me . . . and if the key was in the ignition . . .

My options were limited. I decided to go for it.

I tried springing to my feet and found that my muscles had frozen. My mind had made it to the car while my body was still extracting itself from the brambles.

No shots, though.

I hobbled as quickly as I could, staying low to the ground, seeking the shelter of rocks and bushes when I could. I reached the road and opened the car door.

Jake was in the passenger seat. A gun in his hand.

And a bullet through his head.

34

Tom's hands worked the muscles of my neck and shoulders. I could feel the relaxation spread throughout my body, like liquid sunshine filling my veins. Of course, the margarita helped. It was icy cold, not too sweet and very strong. I sipped it slowly.

"It's still hard to imagine Jake Harding as a killer," he said.

I murmured agreement. Barry Drummond's death I could maybe understand, but not the subsequent ones. Not Lisa, and Amy, and Donna Markley. And maybe me and Sam, if things had gone differently.

"The way Jake saw it, he had no choice. Each murder dug him in deeper."

"Do you think Lisa would really have been able to remember what happened?"

I leaned forward so Tom could reach my lower back. "Apparently she was remembering more and more all the time. After she went home with Wes that night she suffered a terrible anxiety attack. Wes was renovating the kitchen and he'd stripped the walls down to the old paper from Lisa's childhood. I don't know whether it was that or something else, but being back in the house where she'd gone with her aunt, the house of a man she knew as a killer—it seemed to trigger a flood of memories."

"It's kind of spooky to think your mind knows things it hides from you. We might all have terrible secrets in our pasts."

"Except that in Lisa's case there were some fairly strong outward indications of trouble."

Tom's fingers worked a knot near my left shoulder. "Does that hurt?"

"No, it feels nice."

He worked carefully, taking care not to disturb the bandaged wound on my right arm. I'd been lucky; the bullet had only grazed the surface. Six inches to the left and I might be dead.

Sam had been lucky too. He was still hospitalized but improving. I had my doubts that he'd ever regain his full strength, however, or his zest for life. He'd saved a client but lost a friend—and, I imagined, a good bit of faith in his fellow man.

"Wes called while you were asleep," Tom said. "He wanted to see how you were doing."

"Probably better than he is."

"He walked out of jail a free man. He ought to be happy."

As with Sam, I was sure there were shadows cast on Wes's inventory of things to be grateful for. "It must be hard knowing that the man you think of as a father, one of the few people in your life who's treated you decently, was not only a killer but willing to let you take the blame for it."

I reached for my drink and took another swallow. The

icy cold liquid soothed my throat, loosened the stiffness in my muscles. "You know those porno films Wes was keeping for a friend? They were Jake's. Wes was willing to damage his own credibility to protect his stepfather. And look what he got in return."

"Do you think Jake would have let Wes be convicted without admitting his guilt?"

"I don't know. Neither does Wes."

Tom sighed. "Between his father and Willis, Wes really got shafted." The undergarments in the compost bin had been Willis's doing. Complete with his own type B blood.

I pressed the cool glass against my forehead. "I never thought Curt would stoop to something like that."

"The guy's got no morals, just unbridled ambition."

"And arrogance," I added. "Rather than trust the system to mete out justice, he wanted to tip the scales in his favor."

"It's frightening to think that he might have succeeded."

How close he came to succeeding, I amended silently.

Tom lifted my hair and kissed the back of my neck. "Be back in a minute. I've got to check on the steaks."

I leaned back and closed my eyes. If Jake hadn't been so anxious to get me off the case, if he hadn't panicked and shown his hand, if he'd sent Sally Baund to Europe instead of Boston, the chances were good that he'd have gotten away with it. And what about Wes? Would Sam and I have been able to persuade the jury to find reasonable doubt? I didn't like thinking about the way things might have gone.

Tom returned smelling of hickory smoke and teriyaki sauce.

"The upside of all this," he said, sitting next to me, "is that you've earned yourself a reputation as one hell of a lawyer."

I laughed. "That's all I've earned, though. Jake never got around to paying us a single cent."

Tom draped an arm across my shoulder and gently pulled me closer. "I suppose there are worse things in life than a skimpy bank account."

There certainly were. I sank back against the solid comfort of Tom's body. Fortunately, in my life, there were better things as well.

Please turn the page for
an exciting sneak preview of
Jonnie Jacobs's
newest Kate Austen mystery
MURDER AMONG US
now on sale wherever
hardcover mysteries are sold!

1

I could have said no. In fact, I should have said no. I knew that the moment I found myself agreeing to her visit. But it's not easy to refuse your mother-in-law, especially when she plays the grandchild card.

"I haven't seen Anna since last Christmas," she'd wailed, bellowing into the phone as though to propel her voice, by volume alone, all the way from Florida to California. "I tried to get you to come here over the summer, remember. Only you couldn't find the time, so now I'm coming to you. You're not going to deny your daughter a chance to know her own grandmother, are you?"

I assured her that wasn't my intention, but I did point out she might be more comfortable in a hotel than with us.

"Nonsense," Faye said. "I'll be perfectly fine staying with you. No need to go to any trouble, I can make myself at home almost anywhere."

That was partially what worried me.

It wasn't that Faye Austen was particularly difficult, as mothers-in-law go. And she doted on Anna. But the house was tight and cramped, even for the four of us who regularly inhabited it—a population, I reminded her, that currently included a man other than her son Andy. This was a detail that seemed to elude her. Or maybe she simply chose to ignore it.

Now, as I pulled the comforter up close under my chin, warding off the brisk October morning, I kicked myself once again for not having stood firm. I'd managed to get through the first night of her visit with the help of several glasses of zinfindel. An occurrence that Faye had noted with raised brows and starchy silence. Would I make it through the remaining nine? Certainly not without help, I decided. I made a mental note to stop by the store and pick up more wine. Maybe even a bottle of good champagne to share with Michael when Faye departed.

Michael. That was the hardest part. My right foot drifted to the empty space in the bed beside me. The space occupied for the last five months by Michael's lovely, warm body.

His moving out for the week made no sense to me at all, but Michael had been adamant. "I'd be uncomfortable," he said.

"But this is your home now."

"The last thing I want is to be stumbling around the kitchen in my pajamas making small talk to Andy's mother."

Since Michael doesn't wear pajamas, his argument was flawed from the start, but he had made up his mind. Nothing I said (and I said plenty) persuaded him to change it.

I rolled onto my side and punched the pillow in frustration. If only I'd stood my ground with Faye, insisted that she stay in a hotel. It seemed so easy in retrospect.

The story of my life.

At the other end of the house, the water pipes thunked, signaling the end of Libby's shower. That was another situation that seemed clearer with the benefit of hindsight.

It had started as a temporary arrangement early last spring, a favor to a friend. But temporary is a relative concept, and it now looked as though Libby would be with me until she finished high school. Although I was genuinely fond of Libby and had come to think of her as family, I hadn't, at the time, given due regard to the repercussions of living with a teenager. Particularly as they affected an impressionable six-year-old.

Finally, the bathroom door creaked open and Libby padded down the hall to Anna's room, which the two of them were sharing during Faye's visit. I hugged the comforter for a moment longer, then forced myself out of bed. No time this morning to wait for the steam to clear and the hot water tank to refill. Friday was one of my teaching days.

Not that much teaching went on in beginning high school art, dubbed by the students *Art for the Artistically Challenged*. The class was required for those who chose not to take the more rigorous course in drawing and design, but it was offered on a pass/fail basis with the understanding that attendance in a wakeful state practically guaranteed a pass.

From my perspective, this was a win/win arrangement. The students got class credit and I got a regular, though paltry, paycheck. My soon to be ex-husband, Andy, had certain virtues, but fiscal dependability was not one of them.

My shower was quick, my attempt at makeup even quicker. Fifteen minutes later I was pouring milk on Anna's cereal, trying to decide whether it would be wise to point out to her that orange and green pinstripe leggings were not usually paired with a purple print top.

"Where's Grandma?" she asked, kicking the table with her foot.

"In bed." Where I hoped she would remain until I was out of the house for the day.

"She promised me pancakes this morning."

"Grandma's tired after her long trip," I explained. "And she's still on East Coast time." As soon as I'd said it, I realized that I had things backwards. But Anna nodded wisely. She found the idea of time zones fascinating. I think she confused them with time travel.

"Tomorrow," I told her. "We'll all have breakfast together and we'll have pancakes."

"Even Daddy."

"I don't think Daddy will be here for breakfast."

Anna raised her chin. "Grandma said so."

"She did?"

My daughter nodded with authority.

"She gets things mixed up sometimes," I explained.

I was sure Faye saw Michael's absence as a promising sign, even though I'd taken care to point out that it was only temporary, and had been occasioned by nothing other than our concern for her comfort. Faye still clung to the hope that Andy and I were simply going through "a rough phase" that would eventually pass.

As I was pouring my own bowl of cereal, Libby made a pass through the kitchen, picking up a Coke and a handful of pretzels on the way. "I'm going in early. There's a newspaper staff meeting before school. And don't count on me for dinner. I'll get something to eat at the football game."

"You'll be careful?"

"It's a football game, Kate. There'll be hundreds of people around."

"Just make sure you don't wander off anywhere alone. Remember, they haven't caught that guy yet."

Libby flashed me an exasperated smile, swung her backpack over her shoulder, then nodded at Anna's attire. "Rad-looking outfit," she said, giving Anna's nose an affectionate tweak.

In between mouthfuls of corn flakes, I put the milk back in the fridge and started on Anna's lunch.

"Can I have pretzels and a Coke?" she asked.

"For breakfast? No way."

"Lunch then."

"Sorry kiddo. That's hardly nutritious."

"But Libby—"

"Libby's sixteen and you're six. There's a big difference." Though not as big as I would have liked. Under Libby's tutelage, Anna was whittling away at those ten years with unsettling zeal.

By the time I turned around again, Anna had fed her cereal to Max, who was lapping the remaining drops of milk from the floor. Doggy heaven. I was glad Faye was still in bed.

"Anna Austen," my mother-in-law called sharply from the doorway. "We do not let animals eat from our dishes."

I turned abruptly. "I thought you were still asleep."

"I'm afraid not." Faye's thinning gray curls had flattened considerably since her arrival yesterday afternoon, giving her a somewhat moth-eaten appearance. "In fact, I hardly slept at all. I'm accustomed to a firmer mattress."

Her tone was matter-of-act, but I felt a reprimand all the same. "Why don't you try my bed tonight, see if that's better."

Faye brushed the air with her plump hand. "Don't be silly. I can manage." Emphasis on the last word. She planted a kiss on Anna's head. "How's my grandbaby?"

"I'm not a baby."

"No, of course you're not. But a grandbaby's something different."

I handed her a cup of coffee. "Anna and I are going to have to run off. Help yourself to anything you want. Cereal's in the cupboard and there's bread for toast on the counter. Jam's in the fridge."

"Don't worry about me. I never eat much anyway."

This from a woman who'd eaten as much of last night's meatloaf as the rest of us combined.

When I arrived at my classroom, my star pupil, Julie Harmon, was leaning against the wall, waiting for me to open the door.

"Good morning," I said, sounding to my own ears so teacherly it brought me up short. I'd never been fond of school in my youth, but now that I was on the other side of the desk I found I was enjoying it.

Julie raised her eyes and gave me a smile that barely touched the corners of her mouth. She was a tall girl with cornflower-blue eyes and straight blond hair that brushed her shoulders. She had a kind of regal bearing and grace that most of us never achieve, even in maturity. Her classmates found her standoffish. A number of the teachers agreed. For myself, I was inclined to see Julie's reserve as a sign of uneasiness rather than disdain.

"I thought there was a meeting of the newspaper staff this morning," I said.

"There was." Her voice was soft and without inflection.

"It's over?"

She shrugged. "I didn't go."

I unlocked the door and we moved inside.

Julie stood for a moment near the front of the room looking uncertain. Finally, she turned my direction. "Can I work more on that charcoal drawing we did the other day?"

"Sure. You know where the unfinished pieces are, in the right-hand closet at the back."

Julie was the only one of my students with any real talent. She actually belonged in the advanced course, but since she'd enrolled in school after the deadline, her class schedule had been determined as much by available space as suitable placement.

She glanced toward the back of the room but showed no inclination of retrieving the sketch. Instead, she hovered around my desk, fingering the strap of her backpack. Twice, she cleared her throat as if to speak.

"You have a question?" I asked.

She tugged harder at the strap, clamped her lips together, and studied her feet.

From the look on her face, I thought it might be more than a question. "You want to talk?"

Julie's shoulders rose and then fell in an almost imperceptible shrug. I took a seat at one of the desks and motioned for her to join me. "What's on your mind? You seem bothered by something."

"You won't tell anyone, will you?"

"It depends. If you're in trouble—"

Just then Mario Sanchez appeared at the door, slouching against the frame as if he owned the place. "Mornin', Mizz Austen," he said, then crinked his neck in Julie's direction, beckoning her.

She chewed on her lower lip for a moment before heading for the door. "Guess I'll work on that drawing some other time," she told me. "Thanks, though."

"Anytime."

I'd have to ask Libby if Mario and Julie were an item. I hadn't seen them together before, but I'd learned that romantic pairings among teens were as ever-changing as the ocean. Still, it would be an odd match.

Five minutes later, on my way to the office, I passed Julie and Mario in the breezeway. Mario leaned against the gray stucco exterior, bracing his wiry frame with his elbow. His voice was low and intent, his jaw tight. Julie, who was several inches taller, stood facing him, arms crossed, face determined. If they saw me, they didn't acknowledge it.

I picked up my mail and the daily stack of announcements, grabbed a cup of coffee from the faculty lounge, and was headed back to my classroom when Yvonne Burton, who teaches biology, beckoned me into the science lab.

"You haven't forgotten the ten dollars, have you?"

"Ten . . ."

"For Sarah's baby gift."

I offered an apologetic smile, set my coffee on the table, and reached into my purse for the money. "Sorry."

Sarah's unexpected maternity leave was the reason I was now employed at the high school. Two days into the fall semester, she'd received a phone call from the adoption agency. Twenty-four hours later, she was a mother—and her art students were without a teacher for the semester.

Yvonne stuck the two fives I gave her into an envelope and added my name to the list of contributors on the front. Like the rest of her, Yvonne's hands were small and delicate. With her olive complexion and cap of jet-black hair, she looked like an exotic, handcrafted doll.

"Any luck finding a painting for our front hallway?" she asked, sticking the envelope in her bottom desk drawer.

Art consultant was a career I'd stumbled into a year earlier when the gallery where I was working closed. Yvonne and her husband, Steve, were clients of mine, and well enough off that they could afford to select artwork based on what they liked rather than what fit their budget—a situation that was nice for both of us.

"The more I think about it," Yvonne continued, "the more I like your idea of something abstract. But subtle. We want our friends to know that it's *art*, not some class project Skye brought home." She smiled. "That's no reflection on your teaching, Kate. It's just that squares of black and red aren't what I have in mind for the hallway."

They weren't what I'd had in mind when I asked the class to sketch an everyday object, either. But when I told Skye I didn't want to see another horse, she'd settled on a checkerboard.

"I've got my eye on a couple of things," I told Yvonne, "but I'm not sure any of them are right."

"No rush. I don't want to settle for something that's a compromise."

I picked up my coffee and turned to leave, then stopped

in my tracks. A shiver worked its way down my spine. Harvey, the lab skeleton, was grinning at me from under a hooded black cape. A scythe had been wired to his right hand, a knife to his left.

"I see you've decked Harvey out for Halloween," I told her, stepping back.

"This wasn't my doing. If I had to guess, I'd bet it was someone from my senior physiology class. There are a couple of real pranksters in there."

"They've got a macabre sense of humor."

"That's what I thought, too. But then I figured maybe I was overreacting, letting what happened in the park get to me."

This was common shorthand for the murder of a twenty-year-old Berkeley coed whose body had been found two weeks earlier near the duck pond in Walnut Hills' Reservoir Park. With unspoken accord, we'd somehow adopted the manner of speaking obliquely, as if by avoiding the word "murder," we could avoid the fact itself.

Not that we'd talked of much else since it happened. Walnut Hills is a quiet, comfortable suburb whose residents are more at home talking golf handicaps and bond yields than crime. And while this wasn't the first homicide in the town's history, it was one of the most unsettling because it had the earmarks of big-city depravity. A young woman had been strangled to death, her body discarded with indifference, like the used tissues and bottle caps that littered the shore. Her blond hair had been shorn on one side, her Toe nails painted with blood-red polish.

"I think it's gotten to all of us," I told Yvonne.

"Except certain high school seniors." She gestured toward Harvey.

The notion of a madman loose on our streets had shaken the town in ways too numerous to name. It wasn't just that we looked over our shoulders as we left the grocery and jogged only with a friend, even in daylight. There was a subtler, more unnerving change as well, a sense of undefined menace that hovered continually somewhere in the back of our minds.

The killer shadowed us all.

I took another look at Harvey and met his ghoulish grin with one of my own. "Maybe the kids have the right approach, after all. Thumb your nose at the dark forces and ward off evil with a little humor."

"I'm not sure," Yvonne said, "that I consider this humor."

The warning bell rang and I headed back to my classroom. Julie was once again waiting by the door, along with half a dozen of her classmates. As the others settled into their seats, I took Julie aside.

"I have some time after class if you want to talk."

She shrugged. "It's nothing important."

"It doesn't have to be important."

Julie's hair fell across her face, obscuring her expression. But she nodded. "Thanks. I'd like that."

After I'd taken roll and read the morning's announcements, I started the class on their self-portraits. With back-to-school night approaching, I thought it would be fun for parents to pick out their own child. I'd stolen the idea from Anna's kindergarten teacher, I admit, but I thought it would work just as well for older students. It also tied in nicely with last week's exercise on facial drawing and representational portraits.

I saw a number of eyes glaze over while I gave instructions. Julie stared out the window, motionless as a statue.

Once I let them get to work, however, the energy level picked up. I'd learned, early on, that with teenagers, artistic expression is stymied unless accompanied by a certain level of verbal expression. As long as the conversations were good-natured and not too loud, I didn't mind.

While they worked, I walked around the room answering questions and offering help when needed. A couple of the female students took the assignment quite literally. They pulled out mirrors to study the planes of their faces, the width of their eyes and, I imagine, the state of their makeup. Others decided to have fun with the assignment. Grant depicted himself on a surfboard atop a giant wave, Michelle behind the wheel of her dream car, and Skye, predictably, shared the page with her horse.

Julie was back to staring out the window by the time I made it to her seat. Her sketch occupied only a small part of the page. She'd drawn the top half of her body, positioning it in the lower-right-hand corner so that her lower torso disappeared into space. Her front-button blouse, hoop earrings, and wispy, shoulder-length hair were drawn with close attention to detail. She'd begun the nose, but the face was otherwise featureless.

"Why don't you finish it," I suggested. "You've done a wonderful job so far."

Julie studied the picture a moment. "It is finished," she said, meeting my eyes with a look of defiance.

Just then Mr. Combs, the principal, stuck his head into the room.

"Mrs. Austen," he said without preamble. "I'd like a word with you after class."

"Sure."

"My office." He nodded, without looking at me, and was gone.

Skye made a face—pantomimed shock—but it was veiled in smugness. "Not to worry you or anything, but Mr. Combs must be pretty upset. He wouldn't come barging into class like that if he weren't."

"He didn't exactly come barging in," I replied, irked by her tone. Skye often used her mother's position on the faculty to intimate inside knowledge. In much the same way, she liked to flaunt her stepfather's status as judge. Usually, I ignored it. What bothered me this time was that I had the sinking feeling she just might be right.

About the Author

Jonnie Jacobs lives in Northern California with her husband and two sons. Jonnie loves hearing from readers and you may write to her c/o Zebra Books. Please include a self-addressed stamped envelope if you wish a response. Jonnie can also be reached via e-mail at Jonnie@net-com.com

AMANDA HAZARD MYSTERIES
BY CONNIE FEDDERSEN

DEAD IN THE CELLAR   (0-8217-5245-6, $4.99)

DEAD IN THE DIRT   (1-57566-046-6, $4.99)

DEAD IN THE MELON PATCH   (0-8217-4872-6, $4.99)

DEAD IN THE WATER   (0-8217-5244-8, $4.99)

Available wherever paperbacks are sold, or order direct from the Publisher. Send cover price plus 50¢ per copy for mailing and handling to Kensington Publishing Corp., Consumer Orders, or call (toll free) 888-345-BOOK, to place your order using Mastercard or Visa. Residents of New York and Tennessee must include sales tax. DO NOT SEND CASH.

THE MYSTERIES OF MARY ROBERTS RINEHART